PFUMP

The Partnership Funding Upper Midwest Pipelines

Bill Nemmers

authorHOUSE®

AuthorHouse™
1663 Liberty Drive
Bloomington, IN 47403
www.authorhouse.com
Phone: 833-262-8899

Published by AuthorHouse 05/06/2024

ISBN: 979-8-8230-2462-4 (sc)
ISBN: 979-8-8230-2461-7 (e)

Library of Congress Control Number: 2024907199

Print information available on the last page.

This book is printed on acid-free paper.

CONTENTS

CHAPTER 1

REMEMBER THE ALAMO

TUESDAY, NOVEMBER 8, 2016

THE DOORMAN, COSTUMED TO SUGGEST he's Davy Crockett, tugs open the heavy door, to allow Will Basehardt, costumed to suggest he's a Texas oil guy, to assertively stride himself through it, and thus to enter the Alamo. The pneumatics hiss softly as the door closes behind him. The electricity arcing about inside this private club on this most spectacular afternoon, smashes him in the face.

Will sucks the testosterone-enhanced vapor into his nostrils. "Boom!" It's like he's stepped inside some science experiment. He brushes off the coat-check guy and the host guy at his pedestal, and not unlike a cruise missile, he hurries through the West Texas Oil Field Lounge and enters a second room labeled North Dakota Fracking Lounge. He quickly scans the room. He spots Brian Bast in his usual booth along the west wall.

Will's halfway across this North Dakota Fracking Lounge before he's confident Brian Bast recognizes him. Bast waves to him, springs to his feet, stumbles toward him, and like the little monkey he is, jumps onto Basehardt, attempting a monster hug. Will hadn't expected he'd jump him like that! Will staggers back from the impact while swatting the little creep away.

Bast regains his composure, retreats a bit, and smooths his suit jacket. "Wahoo, Will! The greatest day of our lives, right? Waa ... freakin' ...

hoo?" He pumps the air with one fist, then the other, then tries again for the executive hug.

"For Christ's sake, Brian." Basehardt brushes him away, like he does his bulldog, Yankee, several times a day. "Down! Get the hell down!"

These two political hacks, and the third one—the unemotional one hiding deep in the green leatherette booth—have all flown into DC today, one day after what Brian Bast claims is "the greatest election victory in the history of elections." Bast, of course, must say that 'cause he is a verifiable hack. And what that means is that no one, not even a wannabe hack like Will, should take anything leaving Bast's mouth as suggesting any reality, especially today. Though all these Texans are aware that today is a different kind of animal, everyone in this room, especially Will Basehardt, knows that today, his normally creepy friend Bast is actually speaking the truth. They all celebrated last night's greatest election victory in the history of elections and are still feeling their bones tingle. They are, all of them, different animals today: palominos, tigers, and maybe even sharks.

These three confident sharks are meeting in this swanky Washington, DC, bar a few blocks from the Capitol and are three of probably a hundred political hacks swimming in the electric atmosphere in this rather dark Alamo, made somewhat darker than it should be by the sad, melancholy music of fellow Texan, Jimmie Dale Gilmore, being pumped in at high volume. Basehardt is not into melancholy today. He's thinking maybe Guns N' Roses type noise would be more appropriate—something using monster amps and appropriate pyrotechnics.

The Alamo is the favorite watering hole for Texas's very thirsty oil lobbyists. The story, printed on the back of the menu, claims its front door is exactly 1,836 steps from the front door of the Capitol. Texans know this number well. It's a mystical symbolic number—the year of the Alamo. They understand that step count is a meaningful tie to the essence of being Texan.

That 1,836-step story, like many other things in this town, is nowhere near bein' the truth. Perhaps it's true for Will Basehardt's bulldog, Yankee, because he does take little bitty steps, but it's not true based on adult steps, especially adult, male, Texan strides. And Will, along with every Texas oil guy now pumping down booze in here, knows the story's garbage. And they also know the corollary to this lie—that there are few words, read or spoken by hacks inside this Alamo, that should be considered as true. That 1,836-step story is both a warning and a stimulus. It's both a joke and a threat.

Though most Texans speaking and reading words in this room know most of those words are not true, they compensate by speaking those words louder than necessary and by embellishing them with plenty of spicy Texas language and emphatic hand-pumping motions. The din in the room overpowers any attempt to eavesdrop. And despite the excited motions and raised voices, most of the political hacks in this room believe they're invisible, or at least well concealed from most non-Texans hiding among the mahogany woodwork, the brass-potted ferns, and the high-topped, forest green, leatherette booths. Plus, their moods are bein' smothered by Jimmie Dale's sad guitar, blasting on high volume from the numerous cheap speakers.

Technically, only two of the three guys sitting in this booth are political hacks. Will Basehardt is but a wannabe hack; a hack-in-training. He's not yet served in any elected or appointed political situation. But he was, last night, elected to the North Dakota state senate, representing the oil-drilling and fracking area around Williston. And Will is responsible for arranging this-here meeting at this-here venue. He sees blood, or more likely, economic opportunity, and certainly crude oil, being spilled or maybe pumped into North Dakota's political waters. And so, powered by the surprising and stupefying result of yesterday's election, he immediately flew himself out to DC to meet with the new president-elect's wannabe energy advisors. He sees a roomful of Texas oil guys getting drunk and doin' business. He's gonna take advantage of this situation—maybe to take some candy from some baby today.

One of the gentlemen listening to Will spew out his extensive résumé's highlights is a seasoned political hack named Brian Bast, who, though a Texan by birth, moved up to North Dakota a dozen years ago at the same time Will migrated up to that tundra. And so they know each other quite well. They also share a few business connections. Hell, all Texas oil guys have business connections. Oil pipelines are a bit like spiderwebs, huh? Lots of connections.

"Hey, partner," Bast says. "Good to see you again. Warmer in DC than up in the tundra, right? Glad you took the time to come out here to see us. Shows dedication, right? Shows some drive and self-assurance, right? Our new president-elect's looking for guys like you. Guys with drive." He pumps his arm like the drive rod on a steam locomotive. "Drive!"

Will thinks he maybe should have donned his cowboy boots for this meeting. He knows Bast pretty well, and so he knows it's possible he might need his Texas shoes, especially meeting here in the Alamo, smack in the center of the BS capital of the world. The third man at this table is Clifton (Bing) Cherry, the former governor of Texas and current oil interest lobbyist who's rumored to be the pick as secretary of energy in the new administration. Will and Bing also share a history, and it goes back to their college days in Texas. They were both put on probation by different schools—SMU and Texas Tech—on the same football weekend as a result of an altercation at the same sorority party.

"Hey, partner," Cherry says. "Haven't seen you since you migrated up to the tundra. How ya doin' Buddy?"

Will Basehardt is the guy responsible for allowing both Brian and Bing to become fellow partners in the Partnership Funding Upper Midwest Pipelines—PFUMP—a rather convoluted organization now surreptitiously trying to slip a forty-two-inch stainless steel pipe under Basehardt's North Dakota prairie.

"Partnering up is the modern way to compensate one's lawmakers," Brian Bast says. "Right?" He executes one more overly aggressive arm pump and watches several dollars of expensive scotch slosh onto the tablecloth as a result.

Will most surely believes—though he cannot possibly know for certain since these things are all blind partnerships—that the new president-elect is a master partner, and the probable new secretary of energy could not have spent two terms as governor in Texas without making master partner. Everyone who's anyone in Texas has already partnered up, even though their damned pipeline ain't even in Texas. It goes from North Dakota over to Illinois.

Will Basehardt's working a three-pronged agenda today. First, since he's spent his entire life in the oil bid-ness in Texas—and more recently in North Dakota—he's lobbying for a higher position than a piddling state senator from the mostly uninhabited state of North Dakota. He's thinking of himself as the assistant secretary of energy in that new world

4

order promised by his new president-elect. Or, since he's got a background in resources, he can easily handle the director of the national resources commission. He can picture himself in that role and thinks he'd do a great job. Will considers this trip to this particular bar in DC a "necessary bid-ness trip."

His second prong is his fallback position. If he must remain a state senator from one of the leading oil-producing states in this great country, he's volunteering himself for the position of the new administration's official point man for energy affairs in his now home state of North Dakota. It's a position he's just now made up, but he knows he could—if provided with the correct credentials by the new administration—ensure that his own investments in Dakota's Bakken Oil Fields will return the maximum rewards he was expecting them to produce when he first got involved in North Dakota.

Will's third prong concerns the fact that the Saudis are now selling their crude at bargain-basement prices. As a result, he and his various partners are hemorrhaging—losing unbelievable sums of money.

"This bleeding has got to stop, gentlemen," he says. "And the president-elect has promised me he's going to immediately fix the situation. He says he's gonna ramp up the war on Islamic terrorism. He's gonna bomb ISIS's oil fields, take 'em offline. Boom! Smash their revenue stream. Give my Dakota oil a chance to slip into the world market without no Arab interference."

"Sure, we all heard him say that," says Bast. "But I can't believe that's gonna happen. He'd be inviting ISIS to retaliate."

"Right! That's what I'm told," Will says. "It's possible we'll soon see suicide bombers blowing Williston's oil facilities sky high."

"I don't think that'll ever happen, Will," says Cherry. "He appears pretty much risk averse in his present condition."

"Sure it could," says Basehardt. "Stranger things than that have happened. ISIS guys blew that gay bar in Florida to smithereens, right? And there weren't even no oil involved! But we all know ISIS is coming for our oil. I'm thinking something strange might happen up in my Dakota oil fields, right?"

Basehardt notices his guest's glasses are empty and signals the waiter for another round.

"Once we hit their oil fields, we gotta assume they'll retaliate. And ISIS ain't stupid. They won't hit Texas. We're armed to the teeth in Texas. But there ain't no army bases in Dakota. Hell, hardly any people up there. That's where I'd attack if-in I were gonna attack. We can't let ISIS get into North Dakota to bomb my fracking wells. The president-elect told me he's got a plan to protect my oil fields. And I'm just the guy to administer his plan up in North Dakota."

After two hours, and an $1,150-bar tab, Will's unsure of just what it is he's accomplishing here. He knows it's not nothing though because he's been discussing oil bid-ness with his PFUMP partners. He's feeling positive vibrations. But then, his brain always vibrates, and his ears always ring much like they are now, especially when he ingests such large quantities of such high-quality booze at such a long business meeting with such influential partners.

CHAPTER 2

FORGET ABOUT NORTH DAKOTA

A S THE THREE POLITICAL HACKS gather in DC to formulate plans to protect North Dakota's oil fields from imaginary attack by ISIS, three more sober and serious men meet in the North Dakota governor's office to discuss real political problems regarding the real oil business now hemorrhaging in their state.

Governor Leon Rolfes and his unofficial advisors, Larry Oosterhaus and Russell Cordoba, discuss two recent news stories, which, if true, could crash the state's economy, especially considering last night's astonishing election results. These three men are not oil guys, nor are they beholden to oil interests. They're only reacting to these oily stories from positions set outside the oil culture.

Larry owns a cattle ranch near the Canadian border. He, Leon, and a third friend, Nathan Goodbrother, have been buddies since grade school. The three of them, playing for their rural consolidated high school, beat Bismarck Central in the state championship basketball tournament back in 1970, and they've been a tight trio ever since. Then, two years ago, the dynamic changed. Nathan, their power forward and leading scorer, died from a monster heart attack, and when Leon, the point guard who ran the team, gained the governorship a few years ago, Larry stayed close as an advisor. Governor Leon's current pressing task is managing the pounding problem between Dakota's native Standing Rock people and the PFUMP Pipeline being funded by Texas oil interests who are shoving their monster pipeline under land very close to the Standing Rock people's land, flows under the Lake Oahu Reservoir, which holds most all their water, and under a lot of other land all the way to Illinois.

Russell Cordoba, Leon's other advisor, is twenty years younger and a gazillion times richer than Leon. He sold his share of a Silicon Valley tech start-up two years ago, and with the proceeds bought the ranch he grew up on in southwestern North Dakota. Then he added fifty thousand acres to it and now operates it as a nature preserve. Russell is keeping an eye on the extremely volatile world oil market for Leon, ensuring that rational decisions and policies regarding North Dakota's position in the global oil economy can come floating out of his office with some degree of accuracy. Russell begins today's discussion with the most devastating piece of bad news.

"I've got some spectacularly awful news, Leon. Multiple reports of exorbitant puddles of oil have been newly confirmed down in Texas. It means we've got to take serious measures to protect North Dakota's stake in this crazy market. It's possible our entire state economy—not just Williston's—could be in the toilet before next summer. That's your state's economy, Leon. This is seriously destructive news."

"You guys've made my day. I need you to tell me some good news, or ..."

"Or what? You're gonna quit? There ain't any good news, Leon. It's a matter of what degree of bad you're gonna take before you do quit and head yourself to Mexico."

"All right, all right. What's the damage?"

"Well, first ..." Larry leans his tall lean frame back, pushes his Stetson an inch toward his quickly receding hairline, and winks at his friend. "Before we get to the bad real news, I'm required to briefly mention the bad science-fiction news."

"Cut it out, Larry."

"I'm talking about yesterday's surprise election results. I can report that one of the first official things our new president-elect said this morning is that by next summer he expects to eliminate so many regulations, increase so many subsidies, build so many pipelines, and lower so many taxes that North Dakota's gonna start looking like Saudi Arabia. Except, maybe, for snow and cold," Larry points out the window, where many million tons of that early snow spread out to that cold horizon. "He didn't say he'd do anything about that."

8

"Yeah, I know. Kathleen called me last night. She's gonna keep track of the story for me."

"I don't think 'keeping track' is enough," says Russell. "We may have to blow up some Texas oil fields. The new president-elect says he's gonna bomb oil fields in Iraq to cut off ISIS's funding. And then, our own little demigod, Will Basehardt—who also won election last night—this morning suggested that after we bomb Iraq, Islamic terrorists might then target our Dakota oil fields to retaliate. Said we in Dakota must prepare for the certain explosions. He suggested you, as governor, must jump to defend his oil fields. He wants you to deploy National Guard troops to counter, what he believes will be, the certain ISIS attacks."

"I take it back, Larry, that is news from the science-fiction press."

"Okay, let's get back to the bad, though real, news." Russell shifts to his official government voice. "This first piece of bad news was broken a few days ago by *Bloomberg News*. An article explained geologists have recently found three, and perhaps four, different oil deposits in Texas, out in their Wolfcamp Formation. And their report used language like," Russell refers to his notes, "'the single largest US unconventional crude accumulation ever assessed,' 'bigger gushers than the geologists forecast,' and one even says it's 'second only to Saudi Arabia's Ghawar field,' and on, and on, and on."

"Seems *Bloomberg's* having trouble controlling their enthusiasm?"

"And it gets worse," says Larry. "We, in North Dakota, can only harvest 3–8 percent of the oil trapped in our Bakken shale. Geologists claim Wolfcamp's yields may be as high as 50–80 percent."

"If that's true, everyone's gonna start running south tomorrow morning. Williston'll be a ghost town in a month."

"You could be right, Leon. This story has the potential to move very fast. What oilman in his right mind would stay in North Dakota pumping at 3 percent when he can pull 80 percent out of the same rig in Texas?"

"And remember, it's not zero degrees of cold and two feet of snow down there."

"But the good news might be that all the Texas oil guys who moved up to Dakota for the oil might be moving back to Texas now, so to be closer to their families, their head offices in Houston, and cheap slave labor from Mexico. Closer to their bank vaults. Poor North Dakota can't come anywhere near matching up with that."

Leon gets up, walks over to the bookcase, removes the team-signed basketball from the state championship back in '70, and starts to dribble it on the polished wood floor.

"You can't do that, Leon," Larry says. "We both know you can't call Nathan down here to help us out anymore."

"You're right, Larry. I was thinking about Nathan. I desperately need his advice here. I gotta worry about Williston's crazy oilmen pulling their equipment out of North Dakota—and one crazy oilwoman, Nathan's daughter, Kathleen. She's gonna be creating many ghosts around here all by herself. What the hell would Nathan want me to do with Kathleen, Larry? How we gonna figure all this out without Nathan's help?"

Leon dribbles the ball a few times and then shoots a no-look pass over the desk to Larry.

Larry's expecting the thing, and it presents him no problem. "No, you don't, Leon. This is no longer a team sport. Kathleen may have been Nathan's daughter, but you're her godfather, and the only one who can reason with her. For some reason, she respects you, thinks of you as a fellow human."

"I know, I know," says Leon. "And Williston's just the start, huh? She's big into the Canadian fields too. Their oil's even more expensive than ours to extract, pump, and refine. Their stuff'll be even more worthless, right?"

"Yup, and specifically worthless as an export. And that brings me to the second economy-busting bit of horrible news we bring you this fine afternoon."

"Oh, God. There's more?"

"Yes, there is," Larry says. "And this next story has to do with that nifty PFUMP pipeline you've asked me to keep my eyes on. According to information put out by an investors consortium and quoted in *Motley Fool*'s latest oil report, PFUMP and its partners have already stuffed over $3.8 billion into the project, and they claim they've now got the thing nearly completely constructed—and they've customers signed up and locked into long-term contracts for most all of its 470,000-barrel-a-day of capacity. That thing's almost completely constructed and completely subscribed—and with long-term contracts. You know what those words mean now. Leon? After this Texas news?"

"Means I should've bought shares in PFUMP, right?"

"Yeah, shouldn't we all have? But no. What it means is, that as soon as this new PFUMP super-pipe goes online, and that's scheduled for next April—four, maybe five months away—every one of the existing oil carriers—our local existing pipeline companies, local railroads, and several thousand locally owned trucks—are all, boom, immediately dead. Our own North Dakota operations lose big-time, Leon. We lose mega-jobs as soon as that pipeline opens. North Dakota loses. Texas wins."

"I thought the argument was thirty thousand new jobs?" Leon says. "That's what PFUMP promised me."

"Promises are cheap. Most all those jobs are for guys in China, Texas, and Louisiana, and they're mostly past tense, Leon. Didn't you hear me? The thing is, as we are speaking, mostly built, so starting now, we in Dakota will actually be losing those full-time construction jobs. The math's simple."

"Listen up, Leon, those investors have, as of right now, already dumped huge amounts of their money into paying for the new line. *Motley Fool* says the line is already completely paid for. PFUMP's pipe is completely paid for! Do you know what that means? Means they'll carry it on their books as having 'no value.' Means they're going to win, no matter who loses. Hell, it means they've already won. Big money begets more big money."

"Oh, God," says Leon. "I see the future coming in here on a fast break. It's hard to miss, huh? Once these new Texas fields suck up the entire domestic oil market with sixty-dollar oil, who's gonna buy the expensive stuff we and the Canadians want to sell. Dakota and Alberta will shut down, and then that brand new, state-of-the-art PFUMP pipeline will have no crude to pump."

"That's about it. That's the whole deal. By the middle of next summer, certainly next winter, all you're gonna see in Dakota are dead oil wells and empty oil pipelines."

"Well, I don't think that's quite right, Russell," says Larry. "If I'm not mistaken, you're gonna see one other thing in Williston next summer."

"And what might that be, Larry? It's another nasty surprise, right?"

"You betcha. I've heard reports of a Texas-style barbecue scheduled for Williston. Will Basehardt said the president-elect's gonna come out and cut the ribbon on PFUMP's silver pipe. It's the Big Oil-Independence Party. And, I swear to God, Leon, only Texan oil billionaires do stuff like this—they set the party date for, ta-da, July Fourth. They're gonna call it 'Energy Independence Day.'"

"God," says Leon. "What a train wreck. They stop pumping oil, throw a big party, and then blow up their wells, hop into their jets, and zoom back to Texas. And they leave me holding their damn empty pipeline. I really appreciate you telling me this stuff. What the hell do I do with that all that expensive empty pipe?"

"Maybe you get Basehardt's new Washington buddies to help us out?" says Larry. "They're bringing coal back to West Virginia. They'll bring oil back to North Dakota, right? Piece of cake, right?"

"That's not gonna happen, guys," says Leon. "After what you just told me, there's a good chance we'll never, ever, hear from any of those Texas clowns again. They'll be hanging down in Texas with their cheap oil."

"Texans runnin' back to Texas. That might be construed as good news, Leon. What ya think?"

"Yeah, could be you're right. But the bad part is that their money's going with 'em. Absolutely no money's gonna stay up here in the cold and the snow. Absolutely none."

CHAPTER 3

EXPECTING INSURANCE
FROM GOD

A T ABOUT THE SAME TIME, three sloshed equity partners are discussing possible oil field terrorism in DC, three sober politicians are discussing the end of prosperity in Bismarck, and three bar owners in Williston, North Dakota, are discussing their insurance policy. It's only midafternoon, but already it's dark inside the Drilling Platform because no lights, except those glitzy beer-ad things, are burning. And there's no help from outside. The heavy cloud cover sucks up the daylight before it can smash through the big windows. Inside that glass, Gary Gralapp leans against his copper-covered bar and watches the heavy slushy rain assault his huge front windows.

"Ya know the good thing, Hank?" Gary points toward the windows. "I don't have to wash 'em now. But there's a bad thing. We got no customers noticing they're clean."

"Ya shouldn't be worrying about washing 'em." Hank der Ord arranges the five shots of Johnny Walker Black in front of him in a precise geometric pattern. "Nobody's gonna be lookin' through 'em anyway. Hell, nobody's gonna be drinkin' our beer. Face the truth, guys. We're not gonna make it through this month."

"Our customers've all left for Texas," says Paul Burtress. "S'pose we should follow our customers? Hey, Gary, how about we chainsaw this bar into truck-sized pieces, put 'em on trailers, and have your Peterbilts haul the damn stuff to Texas? We reassemble them down there?"

These three partners—Gary, Hank, and Paul—are, for all practical purposes, alone in this big Drilling Platform on this cold, rainy Wednesday afternoon in November. The three of them have positioned their stools at the sharp curve the bar top makes as it winds itself around a steel roof support built to look like an oil derrick.

"I'm seeing no way out, guys." Hank's basically a truck driver. He drives one of Gary's Peterbilts from seven to seven—when it's not raining ice pellets like it is now—for his day job, and he's not equipped for this entrepreneurial life he now finds himself slogging through. He's in way over his head. He's terrified. He is lost. He's busy micro-adjusting his shot glasses. He pushes #3 about a quarter inch east and then #4 a tad north. He surveys his precision work—a very nice arch. Next, with a reasonable amount of flourish, he reaches down, pulls a pearl-handled replica of a Colt .45 pistol from somewhere around his waist, waves the thing to make an appropriate point, and then centers the shiny weapon with some precision under the gentle arc of the five shot glasses he's arranged on the bar top. "'Ceptin' maybe with this .45. I'm thinking it's my only way out. It's my private insurance plan."

"Jesus Christ, der Ord," Gary says. "You're freaking me out. Put that revolver in your pocket. For God's sake, ease up. I'll get us out. I'll think of something."

Hank reaches over the handgun, grasps glass #1, quickly gulps down the first shot, and slams the glass back onto the bar top, not much concerned now with its proper symmetrical placement. "I'm going down, guys."

"All of frickin' Dakota's goin' down, Hank," Paul says. "But not like that. Give me the gun." He holds out his hand. "Please, Hank. We're entrepreneurs. We gotta think positive. We go down in style. We throw a party. We make noise all the way down."

"Good God, guys!" says Gary. "Will you two idiots settle down?" Gary's the CEO of the limited liability corporation (LLC) that owns and operates the Drilling Platform. And he's allowed Hank and Paul, his two grade school buddies, to take relatively minor stakes in it as a humanitarian gesture. He's also a partner in the limited master partnership (LMP) that technically owns this building that contains this here presently non-populated Drilling Platform. Paul Burtress, the second partner in that LLC, provided the notorious motto arcing over the front entry: "The Best

Fracking Bar in All of Williston." Hank der Ord, the third partner and a bit of a chainsaw artist, carved Paul's nifty logo into that huge slice of cottonwood now polyethylened to death and hanging above the bar.

The Drilling Platform is, or at least used to be, a gold mine (or maybe a gold pipeline). It used to be party central for fracking contractors, pumping mechanics, pipe layers, and truck drivers. On a few occasions, things got testy when a chair or two or a punch or two were thrown. But nothing, or hardly anything, really got seriously unstable.

"We had our run, guys," Gary says, "but those old days are gone. They ain't never coming back. If, one Saturday night, I drive one of my Peterbilts through that front window and onto the dance floor," he motions with his empty beer glass to the empty space behind him, "I wouldn't cause as much excitement as what used to happen on one of those normal Saturday nights."

"Hey, Eric!" Paul yells at his bartender. "I'm thirsty!"

Eric's down at the other end, next to another oil derrick structure, talking to a couple nurses. They're regulars, and normally they both, or at least Wendy, would be right here talking with them. Though that hasn't happened lately. Not since Hank started showing up with his revolver.

"You've nothing to fear, guys," Gary says. "Ya don't have to worry. We've got insurance. My big boss has a plan. He'll get us out of this financial sinkhole, save us from diving off that cliff. He says we, being real estate moguls, have access to his golden parachute. Says we should think it's a para-*sail* rather than a parachute. Para-sail sounds positive, don't it? Least compared to *shoot*? We still gotta jump off that cliff, but we can float away into the sunset and leave the piles of flaming debris, broken bodies, and other miscellaneous devastation in a smelly heap at the base of that cliff."

"Ya got me intrigued," Paul says. "Sailing sounds like it may be fun. Whereas shooting, well, shooting seems not so much fun."

"It ain't fun, Paul. And worse, it ain't fun for, like, permanently. The word sailing, on the other hand, infers a heavy degree of continuity. I can see myself sailing off Saint Kitts, but I can't see shooting as having any continuity at all—not even on the beach in Saint Kitts."

"You escape your way, Gary." Hank caresses his Colt 45. "I like my way."

That parachute, or para-sail, Gary's talking about is the arrangement he thinks he's engineered to insure the various slapstick buildings he, with help from his big boss, quickly erected several years ago to take advantage of the huge influx of Texas money flooding Williston. All Gary and his buddies now need to do is to wait till those buildings, including, unfortunately, this one housing the Drilling Platform, burn themselves to the ground. After that bit of bad—or perhaps good—luck strikes, they grab the insurance money and hightail it to Saint Kitts.

"Problem is," says Hank, "don't we need to find some expert in that kind of work? You're not gonna find us three guys running around with no torches."

"Relax, Hank," Gary says. "This kind of specialized work can be subcontracted to a higher-level operative." He rolls his eyes up toward the top of the backbar where they keep the higher-priced booze. "The big boss tells me we can get an 'act of God' to answer our technical need for a flamethrower or two."

"An act of God!" The idea of subcontracting the conflagration of his bar to that high a power stuns Hank. He quickly downs the second of his five glasses.

"Sure!" Gary says. "I've talked this over with LD's big boss. Our insurance covers acts of God. The collapse of international oil prices is an act of God, right? Texas finding easy oil to bubble from their wells is an act of God. Fire and brimstone raining down on Williston could certainly be construed as being an act of God, right?"

"You are nuts, Gary. What kind of idiot thinks like that?"

"That's what the big boss tells me. He's arcing down, just like us, and we all know he ain't never gonna crash. Get singed a bit, maybe, but he's from Texas, and those guys ain't never gonna crash. He's got great 'insurance.' And, since we're his partners, his insurance is our insurance."

"Tell me you're not talking about Roseborough? That bastard's stiffed me so often, I'm ready to shoot him." Hank grabs his pistol and waves it for emphasis.

"Put that pistol away, Hank. Jeez, you're scaring me. Roseborough knows guys. Guys from Baton Rouge who know about Louisiana lightning."

"Roseborough's an idiot. You've got signed papers, right, and legal insurance forms, don't you? From your big boss?"

"Will you guys ease up?" Gary says. "There are no legal forms for insurance like ours. It's all built on trust. Trust me. I've got stuff under control. Roseborough's big boss figured this out, and that guy's one smart dude."

"Doesn't sound like 'figured out' to me," says Hank. "He's praying God is gonna cause lightning and brimstone to jump from the clouds and burn Williston to the ground. Then our insurance kicks in and dumps money into our bank accounts?"

"It's something like that," says Gary. "We can be far away on the beach with a girl on each arm, and we won't even have to stay here and watch our investments burn to a crisp."

"A bit of a reality check here, Gary." Hank der Ord, even considering the chugged shots, seems closer to reality than his two buddies. Maybe it's the pistol, still staring at him, that's sending him reality signals. "You suppose the insurance guys'll be suspicious if all our buildings burn at the same time? Wouldn't we have to be extremely sneaky in order to slip such massive arson past their reality sensors?"

"The big boss assures me his God has figured that out," says Gary. "Says we can legally claim the destruction of our former assets will be a work of God."

Paul Burtress gags on his beer and sprays some on the bar top. "Can't imagine my God doing arson like that!"

"I don't mean our God, Paul. I can't think He'd do anything like that either. Least not since Sodom and Gomorrah. You remember that? Wow. That was some fire. Somebody collected an insurance bundle on that baby."

"That's before my time, Gary, but I'll bite. What other God you know does firebombing?"

"I think my big boss's talking about Allah," says Gary. "We all know Allah's an expert in firebombing stuff."

"What? You thinking Allah's gonna hire ISIS to come to Williston and throw firebombs at our underwater bar?"

"Sure," Gary says. "I think that might happen. Stranger things than that have happened, right?"

"No, Gary. I don't think so."

"Sure they have," says der Ord. "What about ISIS shooting up that gay bar in Florida? And then ISIS shoots up that grade school in Connecticut? Those are strange things too, right?"

17

"ISIS didn't do that Connecticut shooting, Hank."

"Sure, sure. Thought I heard some gal on my TV say that just this morning. Why wouldn't ISIS throw firebombs around in Williston? In a big, complicated fire like that, the entire town might burn, so everybody gotta lose something, and nobody ends up the only winner. It seems like a magical solution to me."

"Well, yeah," Hank says. "Yeah, I see it now. That does make some sense." He downs the third of his five glasses. "Maybe that just might work. Maybe not as effective as my Colt though … at least for me!"

CHAPTER 4

INGESTING MOM'S MEAT LOAF THERAPY

LEON ROLFES UNDERSTANDS ONE ADVANTAGE of being the governor of North Dakota is that his mother is required to baby him. She'll provide food therapy whenever his tired mind and body require it. And, after yesterday's election, and today's aftermath, he's certainly in need of therapy. He's expecting meat loaf therapy—with mashed potatoes and scalloped corn casserole. And, as a bonus for today, he's hoping the doctor will throw in pecan pie. Now that is therapy.

The other thing about having his mom's place so close is he can use it for secure, introspective, perhaps even angry meetings with his friends and not worry about producing official reports of things talked about or having to carefully consider every word he says. He can relax, make mistakes, and be as snarky or as grumpy as he needs to be. And, stacked atop these benefits, he gets the meat loaf.

His mom called midafternoon, informed him of the menu, and required he show up before six—or she'd lock the door. She seemed unusually serious about the schedule, so that must be important. She also said he shouldn't keep the others waiting, yet she wouldn't tell him what "others" meant. His mom's not the only one who plays this game—keep the governor in the dark—but she is the only one he lets get away with it.

* * *

Leon's reasonably proud of himself. He opens his mom's kitchen door at 5:42, thinking he's got time for a brandy before the meat loaf summons him to table.

"Hey, buddy!" Larry Oosterhaus yells at him. "About time you showed."

"Jeez, Mom," Leon says. "You didn't tell me he'd be here tonight. I had enough of him this afternoon."

"Take your boots off, dear," says his mother. "No tramping mud into my house. You'd best thank Larry. He's the one called me, sayin' you're grumpy and are needing my meat loaf fix."

"He's thinking only of himself, Mom. Won't you ever learn?"

The front doorbell rings.

"Oh," says his mom. "She's right on time."

"You invited Steffie? Why? She doesn't share the scalloped corn."

"Just lookin' out for my flock, dear. She's alone tonight. Ross is down in Vermilion watching their Davie play basketball. So I invited her over too."

* * *

"Okay, guys," says Leon's mother, "here're the ground rules. First, nobody gets more than a quarter of the scalloped corn casserole. See, I've marked cut lines on top. Second, we're not saying a word about 'Washington politics' tonight." She wiggles her fingers to suggest the necessary quotation marks. "I've been listening to that crap all day, and I'm sick of it. I'll penalize anyone doing so by extracting two forkfuls of scalloped corn for each offense, and third—"

"If you don't stop talking right now," says Steffie, "Larry and I'll grab your portion of casserole."

"Quiet, children. Behave yourselves. Larry, tell us what's happening at Standing Rock. How're those poor Sioux folks doing?"

"I was down talking with Chief Two Deer this morning. Those pipeline bullies've brought in angry police-type dogs to growl at the protesters. You imagine that?"

"I stopped there this afternoon," says Steffie. "Interviewed that Bowstringer guy for a Sunday feature the *Plainsman*'s running. I see no one compromising. People are soon gonna freeze. It's gonna be terrible."

"You sure this is happening in my North Dakota?"

"Those guys aren't Dakota guys, Mom. They're Texas guys. And they're oil guys. They think they've special rights. Told 'em if they didn't put those dogs away, I'd shoot either them or their dogs. I was mad." He excavates a forkful of mashed potatoes. "That's why I called Mom. I've had a rotten day. I'm the one needs her meat loaf therapy."

"Both sides are dug in and determined," says Steffie. "And the air's too cold for compromise. And neither side sees the opposition as being fellow human beings."

"I've got the Army Corps of Engineers working on a fix," says Leon. "Somebody's gotta do something fast to protect those protestors. I might have to bring in the National Guard. Maybe jail folks just to keep 'em from freezing to death."

"Texans aren't thinking you should be protecting protesters," his mom says. "They'd rather your Guard boys start shooting them. I don't think anybody now chewing on my meat loaf would ever order such shooting. Am I right, son?"

"You're right, Mom. Your meat loaf's got magical powers. Maybe we ship big platters of the stuff down to Standing Rock. Distribute it to both sides. Suppose that might help ease tensions?"

"I, for one," says Steffie, "think that'll make a great story for my newspaper."

CHAPTER 5

PFUMP VERSUS THE STANDING ROCK PEOPLE

THURSDAY, NOVEMBER 10, 2016

Leon Rolfes, the governor of North Dakota, is multitasking at his Sunday breakfast. He's leaning over his plate so he can make out the small print of the *Bismarck Plainsman*, which he's folded in quarters and rested against the quart milk carton he's placed precisely one inch above the top of his plate to hold his paper. His left hand's dabbing a wedge of rye toast into the yolk of his over-easy egg, and he's intending to pull every last drop of yellow from its carcass. His right hand is arcing toward his mouth with his Sunday-only, ceramic coffee mug. He's just started on both the food and Steffie's article in the paper, but he already feels the signs. He knows heartburn's gonna visit him soon after he swallows these eggs.

"You okay there—or do you need another hand?" His eighty-five-year-old mother's pretty snippy for a Sunday morning. "If you want, I'll operate on your egg so you can manipulate your paper?"

Leon knows better than to throw a sassy rebuke with his mouth full. He pays no attention to his mother. She's been up for hours, has memorized every pithy quote from the *Plainsman*, and has multiple topics to discuss with him. His job is to quickly catch up. He knows the drill. Right now, he's into Steffie's front-page article on the status of the PFUMP pipeline protest.

Leon wants the Standing Rock people Versus the PFUMP pipeline story to disappear. Instead, it keeps growing. It's been building for months now, and with the onset of the December cold, snow, and wind, it'll quickly turn from a philosophical "treatment of the land" story to a hard, physical-confrontation, "treatment of the protestors" story. And there's great potential for mass human suffering out there in the cold and snow. It's the kind of theater that makes exciting TV news, but it is horrid publicity for his state. Plus, it's gonna be aggravating his heartburn something awful.

Leon is a cynic. He's sure the story's flamboyant publicity has pushed Robert Bowstringer and Hank Ford—the two leaders of this Standing Rock protest operation—into thinking they can milk the suffering out here for all it's worth. Ford's a thin, geeky, underfed guy, a doctoral agronomy student at UND studying exotic prairie grasses or something. Bowstringer, a rather chunky, linebackeresque type guy, considers himself an environmental musician, and he has made himself a quite comfortable life by selling his oversweet soprano saxophone music, a sound he superciliously calls the "music of 'our' land."

Bowstringer's recruited, invited, or enticed a relatively large assortment of both Sioux and non-Sioux from within and without the state to come out to this barren site and add some heft to his protest urging a stop to the construction of the pipeline as it passes under the Oahe Reservoir. Leon knows most of these protesters are well-intentioned, serious environmental warriors. Some are here to support their brothers and sisters against the weather and the injustice. But there are a few guys, mixed in, who are basically thugs, looking for a fight.

The pro-pipeline forces are also a diverse lot. The pipeline is owned and being installed by PFUMP (Partnership Funding Upper Midwest Pipelines), an elegantly fabricated—though hard to pronounce—Houston-based entity that believes it's been given a right by some universal authority to bury steel tubes in the earth wherever it wants to hide them. The subcontractors they hire to do the actual easement acquisition and construction work are forced to sometimes obtain local permits and easements to effect that construction, even though PFUMP itself does not accept the authority of any local or state permitting agency.

This bit of touchy situation is made all the more ethereal because many of the subcontractors employed by PFUMP, including its enforcement contractors, are stand-alone limited liability corporations—LLCs—many of which are owned by the same Texas-based partners who are stakeholders in the Partnership Funding Upper Midwest Pipelines. Leon's found it hard to know which entity the guy sitting across the table from him in a meeting represents. Who must he address a "stop order" to? Who will drop off his bribe money? Which one of these guys might tinker with the brakes on his red GMC pickup? And there are other pro-pipeline guys who are basically thugs, just looking for a fight.

Leon knows neither the state nor the protesters have any argument with the environmental, technical, or legal aspects of the pipeline installation. PFUMP's subcontractors have acquired all the proper permits, their construction methods have been monitored, and the installation's been inspected. There has, so far, been not a single question with the quality of the installation. The explosive issues here are moral, philosophical, and even theological. It could also be just an irritating issue designed to throw a little mud on the glorious image of PFUMP's benevolent work. The argument now being argued at the barricade concerns whether the PFUMP pipeline construction, or its eventual operation, violate one or two universal ethical principles.

The Sioux insist all people have the right to set limits to theoretical contaminations of the drinking water. They also insist that any agent, in this case either Standing Rock or PFUMP, must respect any soil where a culture has lived for thousands of years and buried its dead, its refuse, and even its steel pipe. Specifically, all the soil from North Dakota to Illinois through which this pipeline is to be built is—in this sense or some similar sense—someone's sacred soil.

PFUMP counters with the argument that there are no such things as universal ethical principles regarding dirt. They maintain dirt is not sacred and that the indolent Sioux are only trying to gain some economic remuneration for a perceived discomfort from a superrich entity such as PFUMP certainly is. PFUMP has tons of unused money hidden in offshore accounts. Seems realistic to expect they'd be able to donate a few bucks to the poor Sioux so they don't have to stomp around in the cold and snow begging for it.

PFUMP's argument, when exposed to the masses, grew legs in a hurry, and within a few days, young ladies wearing moccasins were throwing themselves in front of yellow diesel bulldozers. Then, this last week, history, protest, and construction interests were attacked by Mother Nature. On Tuesday, the temperature dropped to ten degrees, and on Thursday, they got hit with three inches of snow. And Leon got hit with some monstrous heartburn.

None of the protesters, freezing out on the prairie, have a relationship with Mother Nature anywhere near similar to that their grandparents had. Historical Sioux were used to living in cold and snow, and they prepared all year for the scourges of Mother Nature's winter nature. The fools freezing out there now had prepared for about fifteen minutes before they ran out the door in their flip-flops. This means that, if someone doesn't react quickly, these modern natives are going to start getting hurt—or perhaps even dying. The situation's tending toward the explosive. And if it explodes, it will be seen as the governor's fault. Thus, Leon's bubbling heartburn.

CHAPTER 6

SOME OTHER GOD BLOWS STUFF UP

M ADELINE SCORRIE, THE OVERNIGHT 9-1-1 operator for the Williston Police Department, has been answering this same phone for the past nine years, and she has heard many odd things come pouring out of that tinny speaker mounted in the console on her desk. She's stuffed her overstuffed body into an overstuffed chair set to "full-recline" mode, and she's reading a novel about a New York hedge fund pulling money from North Dakota's oil fields. She's halfway through the book, her shift's almost over, and she's feeling pretty mellow. At 8:48 on this deathly quiet Sunday morning, the 9-1-1 call explodes from the tinny speaker.

"Williston 9-1-1 here, this is Maddie," she speaks into a microphone cantilevered off the console by an adjustable chromed snake. "What's your problem?"

"Allah Akbar! Allah Akbar!"

A jagged muffled explosion sounds in the background. Then comes shouting—or maybe it's cheering.

Maddie opens her mouth, but she cannot find the energy to force any words through her lips.

"You hear that explosion, American dog? That is the Islamic State in Syria destroying your oil wells."

A second explosion booms within the background noise.

"All oil belongs to Allah. You have no right to remove Allah's oil. Only ISIS has the right to remove the sacred liquid from our sacred mother."

26

Sporadic gunfire, and then a rough voice—Madeline recognizes it's a second, deeper voice—shouts from the background: "Allah Akbar! Allah Akbar!"

Madeline immediately loses her professional composure. "Oh my God!" She aims that scream toward some generic god, the one most screams are aimed at. Then, again, and more specifically, certainly to the one God she hopes is the real one, "Oh ... my ... God!"

As those words leave her lips, Sheriff Jessie Faber charges into her office from his location at the front desk just outside her door.

"Oh! My! God!" Maddie repeats. "Listen to this." She pushes a few buttons, and the tape, or whatever it is, rolls. Those terrifying words, "Allah Akbar," now blast into Faber's brain.

Maddie quickly works her keyboard and brings an area map up on her screen, which includes a red ring circling the cell tower that initiated the 9-1-1 call.

"It's tower 459, off County Road 342, east of Williston," the sheriff says. "Get every officer and every emergency piece you can find headed out there. Denny and I will leave now. If things are really blowing up, we'll just aim for the smoke."

Maddie's 9-1-1 phone rings again.

"Williston 9-1-1." She immediately recovers her professional voice. "This is Maddie. What's your problem?"

"Did you hear those explosions?" a panicked woman's voice shouts. "They rattled the dishes in my cupboard. Oh, my God. There's another one."

"Please calm down, ma'am. Tell me, where are you located?"

"I'm in my kitchen. D'ya hear my dishes rattling?"

It takes a while, but eventually Maddie gets the caller's address. Then assorted lawmen run for their cruisers, and Maddie sends the address to every fire and ambulance barn within ten miles.

And then Maddie's excitement appears over. Or, it could be, it's only starting. Maddie won't be sure for some time.

*　　*　　*

When Sheriff Faber and Deputy Denny Black get within four miles of tower 459, the landscape opens up—and they see the smoke plumes jumping angrily into the sky. Two miles later, they hear another explosion and see another plume of black erupt.

Faber zeroes in on the smoke and screams down CR 342—and then onto a half-mile gravel drive. It dead-ends at a ten-foot chain-link fence enclosing a field of a dozen drilling and pumping rigs, equipment trailers, and clusters of storage tanks. He and Denny sit in his cruiser and watch the pyrotechnic show. Faber notes the time—9:05—and then calls the office and reports his position.

Faber gets out and leans against his cruiser. Then, he reflexively dives to the ground in reaction to another explosion inside the fence. He's practiced ground-diving before, but he's never before done it for real. He looks under his car and sees Deputy Black, also eating gravel, on the passenger side of the car.

"Hi, boss," whispers Denny. He meekly waves a couple fingers.

Though they see no activity except the rampant smoke, they both feel vulnerable. They've been trained to be wary, to stay down until the danger level is understandable. Another cruiser skids to a stop next to Faber's. It's window quietly slips into the door.

Faber, prone on the ground, yells up to the open window. "We'll wait till Dugger and Carlyle get here, guys. Then maybe we take some chances lookin' around."

Kerr-blamm! Another rig explodes on the far side of the field.

"I see nothing moving inside the fence," says Deputy Black. "The explosions must be ignited by timers or remote controllers. Nobody's wandering around with matches. Seems quite sophisticated for your typical North Dakota arson."

"Agreed," says Sheriff Faber.

*   *   *

Faber arranges the three cruisers so their three onboard cameras will be able to monitor most of the facility from the drive outside the fence. The fence gate's locked, but a short distance away, a small section of the fence has been cut and then, not very carefully, pulled back into place.

The lawmen pull back the loose piece of fencing and enter the compound. They begin a careful walk around the perimeter. They separate themselves about thirty feet apart so if anything close to one of them explodes, it won't cause multiple casualties. A trio of attached office-module type trailers huddled near the center of the field suddenly jumps off the ground and bursts into orange and black flames.

"Holy shit!" yells Faber.

The lawmen instantly reacquaint themselves with the ground.

"Those dirty beige trailers may look like pieces of junk," says Deputy Black, "but they're filled with exotic, high-tech electronics. I'm guessing a million bucks just jumped itself into the sky."

They stay motionless on the ground for a while, but nothing else explodes. Additional fire and emergency crews arrive and start poking around inside the fence. They see no additional bombs—or bomb-looking devices—but Deputy Black finds the body. It's dressed in obvious, Middle Eastern, terrorist garb, propped limp against a pump, concealed behind a couple steel pipeline-expansion loops. A beat-up assault rifle rests horizontally across the guy's lap.

"Hold it, guys," says Faber. "We're all gonna step back slowly. I smell something fishy. Seems this body's been arranged, don't it? I don't trust such careful positioning."

"And look, Sheriff!" says Black. "From here, that guy seems just a kid, sixteen? Maybe even fourteen?"

"And thin, and haggard," says Carlyle. "Like he's not eaten for months. And he's a Somali kid, right, Sheriff?"

"This is quite a crude message. Peaceful-looking dead guy, his rifle on his stomach, and oil rigs blowing up all around him? It's damn spooky. What's the hell's a Somali doin' out here?"

"I've not seen an ISIS soldier before, but this guy's not like I imagined. He's thin! Looks almost malnourished. And he's been planted here, special, just waiting for us."

"It's a strange message," says Faber. "The terrorist callin' 9-1-1 said the Islamic State. That means ISIS. But Somali terrorists aren't ISIS, are they?"

"I took anti-terrorist training," says deputy Black. "Somali terrorists call themselves 'al-Shabab.'"

"I don't like the feel of this," says the sheriff. "I want all of us to very, very, carefully get ourselves back outside that fence. Retrace our exact steps so we don't trigger a mine. I gotta think 'bout this a bit. Before we do anything else, I'd best talk with the governor. It's Governor Rolfes's new terrorist protocol. It requires me, if I even find even a hint of terrorism, first thing you do is call him. He set up a hotline for us. I'd best use it."

CHAPTER 7

THE GOVERNOR'S BREAKFAST IS BLOWN APART

Leon Rolfes, the governor of North Dakota, doesn't think many of his constituents understand how difficult it is to defuse the PFUMP Pipeline confrontation exploding in Standing Rock, a settlement half an hour south of his office. He is, however, aware that his eighty-five-year-old mother is not one of those constituents. She sees nothing difficult here at all. "It's simple dear," she's said several times. "Just stop the construction and jail any Texas contractor who stays on the site." She'd be down there herself except she can't find a ride, and both she and her son know she wants to be on that frigid protest line being part of his problem. She'd rather be down there than up here in her cozy, warm kitchen serving that stubborn son eggs and toast.

"Are you listening to me, son? Somebody's gotta step up and protect those good people."

"I suppose you think that shining knight who's gonna step up and save everyone is gonna be me, huh?"

"I don't know about no shining knight guy around here, but there's that governor guy who stops in to grab breakfast once in a while."

Luckily, he hears his cell phone yelling at him from somewhere deep in his bathrobe pocket, interrupting his mother's diatribe.

"You want me to hold your toast so you can excavate in your jammies for that phone?"

"It's okay, Mom. I've got stuff under control." And he's right. He's able

31

to put both the paper and the jellied toast down without incident, wiggle the phone out from his bathrobe pocket, and look hard at the screen.

"Oh, damn it, Mom. This can't be good. This call's on my terrorist hotline. Damn, what I don't need on this particular Sunday morning is anything to do with terrorists!"

"It's nine thirty on Sunday morning, sweetheart. No terrorists would be so irreverent as to work on Sunday morning, would they?"

Leon resists the urge to throw a toast wedge at her. "This is the governor."

"Morning, Governor. Sheriff Jessie Faber out here in Williston. Sorry I gotta interrupt your Sunday, but you said to call if terrorist stuff happened. So I'm doin' what you said. I'm standing here watching a bizarre incident. Apparently, some ISIS group just attacked an oil-drilling station out here on my prairie."

"ISIS? That's absurd, Sheriff. ISIS is in Iraq or someplace, right?"

"The 9-1-1 caller identified himself as ISIS first thing—before they told Maddie they're blowin' stuff up."

"Well, I'll be damned. What did they hit?"

"So far, I got several drilling rigs, a few equipment trailers, and some oil storage tanks."

"Hell, Sheriff," says Leon. "I don't know what my next question should be. What about casualties? Anyone hurt?"

"That's an even weirder part, Governor. We found one lonely body, lookin' for all the world like an ISIS guy, fitted out in full terrorist gear. And the body was arranged nice and orderly, like ISIS or somebody's sending us some message. I didn't touch 'em. Thought it could be booby-trapped. It frightened me. I'll you that, Governor. I'm not goin' back inside that fence till the federal guys show up. I called them just before I called you."

"Good, Sheriff. I'm thinking it's best if the ISIS part isn't broadcast yet. Least till you can confirm it is really ISIS and not just some drunk making a sick joke. We'll see what the fed's think, but whatever they said on the 9-1-1, seems to me, ISIS involvement's far-fetched."

"That it does, Governor. I'm keeping the lid tight here, until I know exactly what's goin' on."

"Sounds good, Sheriff. Keep me in the loop."

Leon slowly puts his phone down on the table next to the small plate with the toast and then looks up at his mom. "Did you hear that?"

"Enough to know you're not gonna be finishing either the paper or your breakfast, huh?"

"Some fool's blowing oil rigs up near Williston. Makes an impressive picture, I'd expect." Leon shakes his head in disbelief. "Billowing black smoke and orange flames, ruining my nice blue sky."

"What about casualties? And did I hear you right? ISIS?"

"You heard right, Mom. Guys callin' 9-1-1 said they were ISIS. That doesn't make sense yet, and I'm guessing it's not true. Though the sheriff found one body, dressed all in black. Guy was dead at the scene."

"That's plain weird, son. Don't ya think? Especially for North Dakota?"

"Who'd attack oil wells in oil country? Oil's sacred out there."

"Williston's a fairly rough town. I'd guess they've had a saloon or two shot up. Blowin' up oil rigs though? How does that make sense?"

"It absolutely doesn't, Mom. And you're right … I'm not finishing breakfast. I better get into my office. ISIS terrorists bombing Williston? Jeez, Mom, ain't that the absolute weirdest thing?" He drains his orange juice. "That shouldn't happen in North Dakota—not in my North Dakota. I'm running upstairs and getting dressed."

"You want me to call Margie, dear?

"Sure, Mom. Thanks. I'm gonna need her today. And I'd best give Steffie a heads-up too."

CHAPTER 8

THE UNFORTUNATE DOMESTIC BLOWUP

S TEFFIE COBB SHUTS OFF HER phone, puts it on the end table, and her eyes tear up. She turns and faces her husband and fights back the tears. "Damn it, Ross. I'm really sorry." She puts her hands to her face. "I really wanted to go—"

"You're making me go to church by myself again, aren't you?"

"I'm sorry, Ross."

"You promised me." He pulls his suit coat off the hanger and grabs his Bible from the dresser.

"I know. I know. But I can't schedule bad news, honey. It happens whenever it wants to. And Susan agreed ... I must—"

"It's not right, goin' by myself. This is three weeks in a row, Steffie."

"I did better than last week, Ross. See, I even have my dress laid out. Doesn't that count for something?" She retrieves it from the bed, looks at it longingly, returns it to the closet, and removes a pair of jeans.

"I'm sorry, Ross. I really wanted to go. It's just that stuff happens. Somebody's blowing up oil wells in Williston. Susan fixed it with Channel 5, and I'm flying out on their plane."

"So something's blowin' up. You can't do nothing 'bout that. What you should do is go to church. Prayin' will do more good than reporting will. That's what's important." Ross stomps out the bedroom door and down the stairs.

Steffie hears the door into the garage slam. His diesel pickup coughs and then come to life. She hears the thing scream out the drive, and head toward the road.

Only a few minutes before this domestic explosion, her friend, Governor Rolfes, had called and told her of Sheriff Faber's report of the strange ISIS attack near Williston. And that call instantly ruined her day. She then called Susan Busker, her boss at the *Bismarck Plainsman*, and they agreed it was necessary for her she get out to Williston. Susan would arrange a seat for Steffie on the plane co-leased by the *Plainsman* and Channel 5.

As a reporter, Steffie knows stuff about explosions. And she's certain things more important than oil wells are blowin' up in the Cobb household today. But she hasn't time to care much about that domestic explosion just now. "Damn," she says. "Damn, damn, damn."

CHAPTER 9

THE BLOWUP OVER THE PFUMP PIPELINE

As if Leon doesn't have enough crises on his Sunday plate, as soon as he's seated at his office desk, Larry Oosterhaus calls.

"I'm headed down to Standing Rock, Leon. Got breakfast with Two Deer, then gonna take another hack at that PFUMP confrontation. Supposed to meet with Bowstringer and Ford later. You got any words of wisdom?"

"If those PFUMP guys show up, tell 'em that if they don't behave, their governor will personally sic his mom on them. They'll back off then, right?"

"I'd love to do that, buddy, but that ain't gonna happen. I've never seen a PFUMP guy down there to talk to. Only guys on site are subcontractors— truck and bulldozer drivers, security guards, and dog handlers. All of them moving dirt or laying pipe—or harassing protesters. I've never seen a single official PFUMP guy standing around supervising. Just worker bees doin' their job in the cold."

"Can't we call Houston? Talk directly with PFUMP?"

"Don't think that's possible, Leon. PFUMP's but five letters on a folder in a file drawer someplace. PFUMP's a paper company. It doesn't have employees with mouths and ears. One thought though. I've have heard our friend Kathleen's got her tentacles around this pipeline."

"Yeah, I wouldn't be surprised."

"I'd like to talk with her. You know where I can reach her?"

"Not exactly. But there is a way. I'm her dad's trustee, so there are legal pathways to find her—or at least find her lawyers."

"I wouldn't bet on it, Leon. Seems Kathleen's made herself a ghost. She's damn hard to find."

"I'll find her for you ... though it might take some time."

"We don't have time, Leon. It's already the middle of November. It's been fairly mild and little snow, but we know that ain't gonna hold. Weather guys are forecasting minus ten and major snow by next weekend."

"We got one week—seven days—to make those PFUMP subcontractors disappear."

"I've got a fantasy ray machine in my briefcase, Leon. It's either that or, old buddy, we get Mom to pray for a miracle. I'll talk with Bowstringer. You find Kathleen. Then you keep pressure on the damn Army Corps of Engineers."

"Can do, Larry. And thanks for setting me up for meat loaf the other night. It was a pleasant evening."

"Not a problem, buddy. Just looking out for myself."

CHAPTER 10

WATCHING SMOKE
FILL THE SKY

S HERIFF FABER IS BATTERED BY some exotic visual stimulation. Huge black smoke plumes billow off the burning oil rigs into the otherwise clear blue sky. A slight west wind pushes that cloud east, stretching it toward the horizon. It's 9:22, about an hour after that first explosion, and everything's stone quiet on the Dakota prairie. Not a single bird. No rustle from any waving of any grain. Quiet as that ISIS guy, scrunched up over by that pump.

A dozen vehicles, mostly volunteer firefighters, are parked on the north side of County Road 342. Police roadblocks, set several miles out from the explosion site, keep nonessential vehicles at a distance. Curiosity seekers at that distance can do nothing but watch the growing black cloud crawl east across the sky. That sky, excepting for that amazing cigar of black smoke, is still blue and cloudless. The temperature's about fifteen, the wind at ground level seems nonexistent, and there's absolutely no sound.

At 9:51, Sheriff Faber hears the sound. He can't see its source yet 'cause there's a slight rise blocking his view, but he hears it. And soon it's obvious to the waiting volunteer firefighters parked on the north side of CR342. They also hear the sirens screaming, still a couple miles out to the west, and many open their car doors and step out into the cold to wait.

Soon two black vehicles with flashing lights break into view. A few minutes later, those two GMCs stop behind Sheriff Faber's cruiser and extinguish the sirens. The watchers watch Faber speak to the driver of the first SUV, return to his cruiser, and then lead the small parade of fire trucks and ambulances east on CR342 toward the burning oil rigs.

After the parade heads down the drive toward the fires, a deputy pulls his cruiser up to re-block the gravel drive. He exits his car to address the small group of reporters and vetted watchers. "As you've seen, FBI agents from the Minot suboffice have just arrived. Additional FBI and Terrorism Task Force help are flying in from Minneapolis and will be here shortly. That's all I'm authorized to tell you. The sheriff will hold a briefing later, probably in town, though he's not set anything up yet. We know you're anxious, but you'll be more comfortable if you go home and watch this play out on your TV."

The crowd slowly disburses, and the several vehicles turn themselves around and head west, toward Williston. The wind freshens. The few local reporters remaining notice some angry clouds slipping in from the southwest. They feel the cold start to bite. They turn up the collars on their coats and the heaters in their cars.

CHAPTER 11

THAT OTHER GOD BLOWS MORE STUFF UP

B Y ELEVEN O'CLOCK, THINGS HAVE settled down. And though the temperature's dived and the wind gusts have spiked, nothing additional has exploded. Most of Williston's fire equipment is back in its barns. The dead man is in the morgue. The explosion site is static. Fire crews can do little to combat oil rig fires. They can only watch them burn until the oil fire experts arrive from Texas. Sheriff Faber's back at city hall, prepping for a news conference he's scheduled for twelve o'clock. On the surface, things seem under control, but below the surface, echoes of the explosions continue to reverberate. Faber sees nothing making sense.

*　*　*

The small plane carrying reporter Steffie Cobb touches down at 11:12 on runway N/S 1 at the Williston Regional Airport, located a couple miles northwest of the city center. The plane taxis to a stop adjacent to the brand-new general aviation building with two rental cars—a Chevy Cruze for Steffie and a Jeep van for Channel 5's camera crew. Steffie opens the passenger door, stows her stuff on the seat, and circles around to the driver's side door.

As she opens that door, a tremendous concussive blast reverberates off the general aviation building behind her and shakes the ground beneath. She grabs the cold doorframe for support. Then, almost immediately, there's a second blast. Boom! And then again. Boom! She jerks around and sees two sets of black, angry smoke bubbles exploding into the sky over the city. Even at that distance—perhaps two miles—the sound panics the folks out at the airport. Steffie hears alarms sounding inside the terminal building and then in the open parking garage to her left. There's another explosion. Steffie jerks her head again toward the city and sees a third pile of bubbling smoke. She looks up, thinking perhaps a plane should be up there dropping these bombs. A dozen people deplane from a small commercial flight, and in haphazard panic, run across the tarmac toward the terminal building.

The Channel 5 crew quickly has their camera up and running. Their Jeep wheels away with the camera guy poking his machine through the roof window, trained on the black smoke billowing into the sky over Williston.

Steffie uses her phone to do a ten-second movie of Channel 5's van with the camera through the roof and the black smoke in the background. She allows a flash of Iraq or Afghanistan to jump into her consciousness, and then she jumps into her car and follows Channel 5 into town. Both vehicles run toward the smoke.

"I've never been in Iraq, Afghanistan, or Syria, but I've seen several documentaries and news reports and have seen footage of frenzied news crews driving SUVs similar to Channel 5's, crashing through debris-strewn fields. I remember those scenes. They come with billowing smoke, running, screaming people, sirens, and automatic rifles firing from car windows. Except for the automatic rifle part, that's what I'm seeing here, at 11:22 on this Sunday morning in Williston." Steffie speaks these words into the audio recorder on her phone, which she's wedged into the travel mug holder. She's recording real-time impressions that will find their way into the news story she'll write later this evening.

Since the serious fracking started in Northwest Dakota's Bakken Oil Fields, Williston has grown itself a lot faster than its city planning office can plan for. Solutions to most traffic problems are built straight from planning department sketches, and road construction is a constant and piecemeal thing. However, last year the city did complete a major infrastructure project; the main north-south highway through the valley was removed from the downtown and relocated to the west of the built-up area. But the new road only benefits through traffic. All local and business traffic still must crawl down Second Street through Williston's Highway Business District. It takes little pressure to cause tremendous traffic tie-ups. And it's made worse because Williston's traffic contains a great percentage of eighteen-wheelers carrying unstable-looking stacks of sixty-foot pipe, high-piled overflowing fracking sand, and massive extra-wide drilling rigs.

Williston's railroad yards and oil pipeline terminals are south of Williston. However, 85 percent of the oil field operations are north of the city. Therefore, most everything headed from the railhead into the oil fields, or from the oil fields to the terminals, must be trucked through that Highway Business District on East Second Street, a partially divided four-lane road lined with restaurants, motels, and other highway and oil field-related service businesses. East Second Street's been under continuous construction for several years, and continuous commotion exists even at noon, on a Sunday, in the dead of winter, during football season—and even with oil fields running at diminished capacity.

Steffie finds it's much worse on this particular Sunday afternoon. She exits Second onto a side street and pulls into a closed chiropractor's office parking lot. She knows it's closed because of the crossed two-by-fours nailed across the entry doors carrying the words "Office Is Closed" in red crayon. She does a quick 360-degree scan to put this place in both her and her phone's memory, runs the half block to the main road, and turns south, heading toward the smoke.

The place is absolute chaos. Sirens from fire equipment, police, and emergency vehicles compete for attention with billowing black clouds laced with bright orange flames that bubble into the sky. A brutal wind, kicked into a higher gear by the raging fires, shoves thick tendrils of black smoke darting through the chaos not twenty feet above the ground. Steffie realizes the smoke is now laced with snow. Not fluffy New England Christmas movie flakes, but icy pellets, and driven by a wind—which now has swung around to the south—right into Steffie's face.

Another explosion reverberates though this maze of smoke and snow. Echoes rumble around like thunderclaps. She cannot place its direction, but it generates its own storm of excited screaming through both the crowd in the street around her and the emergency crews working in haze beyond her ability to see. With the sirens, constant honking, numerous obscene noises from the fire, and screaming people, Steffie feels like being a print reporter is a worthless thing. This is a video reporter's story.

On another level, Steffie understands it's necessary that a print reporter is embedded into this story. There's no way any details of what's actually happening can be known for some time. Until order is realized, this mess will be an impossible thing to understand. Plus, everything and everyone out here is in the process of being frozen solid. Steffie knows she's wasting her time, shivering on the sidewalk, getting pelted by the snow, exhaust fumes, and the overpowering constant noise. The temperature's still diving, the wind is accelerating, and the police won't let anyone cross to the west side of Second Street where the big fires are. It's time to rethink her role.

She decides any news must come to her. She walks south, pushing her way through gawking crowds overflowing the sidewalk on the east (northbound) side of Second Street, and notices a reasonably gaudy sign for Hurley's Irish Pub. She studies it for a few seconds, turns left, crosses a parking area, and enters the building. It's not as crowded as she thinks it should be. There's even a two-top table vacant by the big front window.

"May I sit over there?" she asks a guy with an apron, looking like he should know the answer.

"Sure, lady, wherever. Ya want something ta drink?"

"You bet. Since it's an Irish pub, I'll have a Guinness."

"I'll bring it over." He spins away and addresses four bundled customers entering the bar.

Steffie throws her coat and scarf over one chair, sits on the other, and puts her phone on the table in front of her. She pushes the button to get the time, 12:15, which surprises her. She would've guessed it to be around eleven forty-five. Boom! Just like that, she's lost half of the first hour she's been in Williston.

"Damn," she says, "I forgot about the mayor's news conference at noon." She looks up to the large flat-screen TV, which normally would be doing Vikings football on a Sunday afternoon in November, but which now shows a frozen reporter standing next to a truck carrying three huge culvert-sized tubes of galvanized steel pipe. She looks out the window and actually sees that truck with that pipe stopped three vehicles south of her window. Snow's swirling about, illuminated by flashing emergency equipment lights. She realizes no news conference is happening. She knows from experience that such things never follow the announced timelines.

The young man brings over her beer and puts a menu in front of her. "Thought you might want this. You look hungry."

"Thanks. I missed breakfast." She points to the TV. "Could you turn up the sound. The mayor's news conference should be happening any time now."

"Oh, sure," he says. "That's a great idea. I'll hike it up when I get back to the bar. Crazy out there. Huh?"

"Crazy? Huh?" Steffie mimics the server after he leaves. She looks out the window at the mayhem. Not much real news will limp out of those swirling black clouds for a while. She removes her notepad, picks up her phone, and makes the first of three necessary calls. The first is to Susan, her boss at the *Bismarck Plainsman*. Steffie informs her she's on top of this new story—operationally and physically—and will be sending her story late tonight, possibly after deadline. She requests they save her front-page space in tomorrow's edition and promises to email her a great photograph for the front page. Next, she calls home and leaves a message for Ross that she will not be home tonight as planned because she's run headlong into a career-busting story with explosions, fires, and extreme panic. She then readies herself for her third call—to her favorite governor.

CHAPTER 12

STEFFIE NARRATES THE SECOND ACT OF GOD

TWO YEARS AGO, A NEW York hedge fund attempted to sneak an oil refinery project past the planning staff of the North Dakota Office of Environmental Protection. Worse still, they'd planned to erect this refinery near Leon Rolfes's hometown of Rugby. At that time, Steffie Cobb, the *Bismarck Plainsman*'s investigative reporter, worked very closely with Rolfes—the Senate president at the time—to expose that scam. Then, she acted as his press corps liaison during Rolfes's run for governor. Since then, she's kept Governor Rolfes and his office informed about political and other problems in his state. She's apt to call him several times a week with questions or responses or to make him aware of spicy tidbits of political information she's dug up.

"Steffie's on the phone," Margie yells this through the open door to Leon. "Claims to have hot, hot, hot news. Three hots! She's on video, Leon, so FaceTime it on your computer. Sounds like she's in a bar. I'm not sure what hot news is happening in a bar—and on a Sunday afternoon? Ya sure ya wanna talk with her?"

"I'll take the chance, Margie."

"Hi, Steffie," Leon says. "Margie tells me you've got yourself in trouble again. It's Sunday afternoon. Shouldn't you be home watching football? What's got your priorities screwed up?"

"I'm working today, Leon. Just like you. And you better pull on your working boots quickly. I've got a flash for you from Williston, which is where I happen to be. Look and listen." She holds the phone up to the window and scans it so Leon can see the flashing lights and billowing smoke and hear the sirens and horns of the fire truck working itself through the mess of metal tangled together on the street out front. "Look at this, Leon! All along Second Street here, Williston's blowing itself up. I see a dozen buildings ablaze. Maybe more. Who the hell knows!"

"I talked with Mayor Allison around eleven," says Leon, "regarding his exploding oil rigs. He didn't mention explosions in his downtown. What the hell's happening out there, Steffie?"

"This place is a war zone."

"What you know about war zones?"

"Trust me, Leon. I know. For several blocks of Second Street and First Street, Williston, or some major parts of it, are on fire. And how this story fits in with the story I rushed out here to cover—the oil rig explosions you smashed me with this morning—I haven't a clue. I've not thought about connecting things yet, but you can bet your farm that those oil rig explosions are connected to these downtown explosions. It's just that nobody knows how that connection is structured yet. Nobody knows anything yet. Makes my job damned impossible."

"You've put an extraordinary rotten punctuation on my already rotten day. Thanks a lot."

"And stuff's still exploding out here, Leon. It's hot, hot stuff. There were many explosions—five, six, eight—who the hell knows. They hit along Second Street. Some over on First too. Place is filled with big trucks and flying debris. Second Street's a war zone. Smoke's all over! Wind's swirling fierce!"

Margie rushes in and turns Leon's TV to Channel 5.

"My advice, Leon, is go home and get some rest. I'm betting you'll have to fly out here tomorrow or certainly the next day. Though maybe, by that time, there won't be any town left. You're gonna be on somebody's prime time news tomorrow, so you'd better get a haircut."

"You gonna be safe there tonight?"

"Haven't had time to think about that yet. I've got bigger problems. Your call kept me from getting to church this morning. That made

Ross livid. Now I'm wet, smoky, and extremely irritable. This is all your fault, Leon. You started it. And you're going to pay. Nevertheless, thanks for the heads-up call. If you hadn't called me, I'd have gone to church and missed this whole thing. I do owe you for that. I gotta go. I'll check in later."

CHAPTER 13

MAYOR CLEM ALLISON'S FIRST PRESS CONFERENCE

THE MAYOR'S 12:00 PRESS CONFERENCE is continuously postponed. He shoved it back to 3:00, and then 4:00. Finally, at 5:07, the TV cameras planted in the northbound lanes of Second Street near the burning Bakken Extended Stay Hotel, and just down from Hurley's Irish Pub, reveal two forms advancing toward the camera. It's black out there, with no streetlights activated, though red, blue, orange, and white emergency vehicle strobes bounce around like a video game. The sun disappeared several hours ago, so fire crews brought in arc lights to illuminate portions of wreckage. Snow is falling at a moderate rate, and black smoke is swirling about, blurring Mayor Allison and Sheriff Faber as they stand in front of the camera.

Steffie, watching the TV in Hurley's Pub, sees the fuzzy images approach the podium through a black-and-white, rather medieval-looking scene. Immediately, the pub crowd quiets. A piece of falling roof or caving wall suddenly generates crashing noises and additional smoke around the podium. Things are delayed for another bit of unspecific time.

"Evening!" says the mayor. He unzips his parka, fumbles about, and then pulls out several papers. "For the record, my name's Clem Allison. I'm the mayor. Standing beside me is Sheriff Jessie Faber. Other law enforcement and emergency folks are on the scene, but for the time being, all the information will be coming from the two of us. Later, that'll change. Right now, we're busy sorting things out."

Allison picks up his papers, shakes the snow—or maybe it's soot—off them and then motions to a young man in the first row of the crowd to come up so he can hold his large black umbrella over him, and his notes, while he talks.

"Thank you, Jimmy. Damn snow is smearing my notes. Now, first, I'm gonna tell you what we've put together as happened east of town this morning, and then I'll tell you what's happening behind me, at least as far as we know. Much is preliminary or unconfirmed, so we're being very careful."

Allison makes a production of blowing his nose, a small proof that he's human, and thus vulnerable. He wants the press to take notice and pity him.

"Maddie Scorrie's a veteran 9-1-1 officer," he says. "She's been with us for nine years. She took the 9-1-1 call at 8:48 this morning. That's what my notes say, and Sheriff Faber can vouch for the time, but I don't accept that's only eight or nine hours ago. Seem it's been days by now. Normally, I wouldn't read the word-for-word transcript from a 9-1-1 call, but I'm gonna do so because somehow the gist of this thing's already bouncing around. Both the FBI and I think it's necessary the truth gets out. This call is so weird, that maybe, if I give you the real words, you'll get some idea of the problems we're having trying to figure stuff out. So, this is how everything started. I'm reading the actual 9-1-1 transcript."

> Voice 1: Allah Akbar! Allah Akbar!
> Explosion 1, men yelling in background.
> Voice 1: You hear that explosion, American dog? That's
>   the Islamic State in Syria destroying your oil wells.
> Explosion 2.
> Voice 1: All oil belongs to Allah. You have no right to
>   remove Allah's oil. Only ISIS has the right to remove
>   the sacred liquid from our sacred mother.
> Sporadic gunfire, then yelling.
> Voice 2: Allah Akbar! Allah Akbar!

"That's the entire call, folks. Poor Maddie Scorrie. Like I said, she's been doin' this for nine years, and this call really slammed her. Sheriff Faber and several of his deputies responded to the call and rushed to a site in East Williston. They found a fenced-in extracting facility containing eight pumping stations, oil storage facilities, and a typical set of control trailers. They found four pumping stations on fire, throwing black smoke into the sky. Shortly, they witnessed several additional explosions, apparently set by timers or triggered by phone calls, which blew up other pieces of equipment just so the sheriff could watch 'em explode, I guess. However, they saw no evidence of active human activity within the compound. Even so, Sheriff Faber waited until reinforcements arrived and it appeared no more explosions were imminent. Upon investigating the site, the inspection team found two important things. One, five explosions were set at drilling or pumping rigs, one at the control trailers, and one at the oil storage tanks, each was probably a simple pipe bomb device, equipped with a cell phone-triggered fuse. This isn't sophisticated stuff. Any teenager with computer access could've made and set off those bombs.

"Two, we found one body, a young man dressed in Middle East terrorist-type gear. We have, as of yet, absolutely no idea who he is, or where he came from, or if he's part of any group. The FBI is working on that. What I can tell you is that this man was dead even before the first explosions, so he played no part in them. That is, unfortunately, about all we know about this attack, or whatever this thing was. I think the entire episode—the 9-1-1 call, the explosions, the dead young man—seems less a terrorist episode than performance theater of some sort—the rationale for which we must unravel quickly. Somebody's trying to send a message to somebody, though right now, neither sender nor recipient is obvious. Neither to me—nor to the federal folks working this case either.

"This second incident," Allison motions with a finger pointed over his shoulder toward the mayhem raging behind him, "started blowing itself up a little after eleven o'clock this morning. Several explosions destroyed buildings in the Lancing Center Complex." He motions with another finger over his shoulder. "We don't expect to find ignition devices until we sift through the ruins. However, I'm confident we'll find completely different packages than the pipe bombs used this morning. In fact, it seems everything about these afternoon fires is very different from everything about this morning's explosions. I'm not sure any of us know what to think about any of this yet!

"There were six or seven separate explosions that destroyed three vacant hotel buildings, including the Bakken View Hotel just behind me. The adjacent Oilfields Management Complex had but one of its four suites occupied. Beyond that, a building housing a bar called the Drilling Platform and a warehouse/distribution firm, a mostly vacant office building currently being used by a Houston technical consultant, and a warehouse used by a firm servicing fracking contractors. The fires then jumped First Street to three additional properties. Two are currently vacant, and the other is a warehouse leased to Oilfield Maintenance and Construction, LLC. Because of the wind, I believe several neighboring properties will be damaged before we can get all these fires under control. Our primary job is to keep the fire from jumping across Franklin Street to a bank and office building. If that happens, I can't imagine the potential damage. Just pray the wind doesn't pick up. These fires feed off each other and are so hot and dangerous we cannot get near enough to investigate. Fire crews from other towns within a hundred-mile radius are helping us out.

"Also, I must tell you that even though we believe these fires were deliberately set, we haven't yet legally confirmed that, or where they started, or the type of explosives, or whether we've got casualties. We've not found any yet, but I wouldn't be surprised if there were some, especially in that bar. I think that was the only business open at the time of the explosions. I am not gonna comment on that until I have absolute proof, one way or the other. I just thank God this happened on a Sunday.

"There's one more thing before I let Sheriff Faber talk about the response to these events and the people helping us cope with them. Note I used the word 'vacant' often, and that brings up a troubling question. We're having a hard time finding several of the property owners to advise them of their losses—or to find out if a building contains flammable content. Several buildings have, or at one time had, something to do with oil. And oil, as we all know, is flammable. That makes the conditions extremely dangerous. If anyone knows, or has heard rumors about, who owns these buildings, or the land, or the leases, or does any management work for these properties, please immediately contact the sheriff's office. Thank you. Okay, Jessie. It's your turn."

* * *

Steffie feels like she's cheating, perhaps not doing a proper job of reporting. She's sitting in a warm room, sipping a Guinness, and listening to the TV. She's doing her job, though, watching the press conference as it happens in real life, maybe a hundred feet down Second Street, on the exterior of her window. Because of the blowing snow, the scene's barely visible from her vantage point. Her friends from Channel 5 News are braving the freezing wind and snow because they have to be out there. It's their job to capture the visual aspect of this press conference. Steffie's job is to capture the words, and the mood, and she feels she's able to do that from her window seat in the bar. She watches Sheriff Jessie Faber switch places with Mayor Allison at the microphones.

"Good evening," Jessie grabs his trooper-type hat and pulls it down snuggly on his head. "First, I want to thank the folks from the Terror Task Force and the FBI for getting here from Minneapolis so quickly. I know that's their job. It's what they are supposed to do. Nevertheless, I'm thankful they got here fast. This stuff's way over my head." Faber then goes down his list, telling reporters the specialists who've made the trip here to help, what each person's job is, and how they're connected via computer to certain databases and experts in many disciplines, so that any evidence can be processed almost instantaneously. He next explains the timeline of the explosions in East Williston, and several things their examination of the oil field attack have revealed.

"A hell of a lot of planning went into the setting of these fires. They were meticulously planned and executed. And I want to emphasize that no matter what things you're going to hear about this 'attack,' these fires are deliberate, unsophisticated, low-level arsons, and not even close to a terrorist event, even though the perpetrators made a weak attempt to suggest that. Also, we found one body in East Williston this morning, but we've not yet found any here in town. We may find bodies after things cool down and are able to look. But if we do, there's apt to be fire damage, and I doubt body remains will be easily identified."

The sheriff describes the limits of the damage, notes that several owners of both the land and the oil drilling equipment, neither of whom are local, have not yet been contacted. He explained attempts to connect the morning "episode" with the afternoon "episode" have failed, but that the coincidence of the two incidents occurring within hours of each other is powerful evidence of a coordinated effort.

"These fires are still much too hot to allow investigators to get anywhere near them. Fire crews are concentrating their efforts to contain the damage, to keep fire from spreading to other buildings. But the wind is fierce, and the ice is dangerous. And the intense fire is creating its own localized wind, which is pushing flimsy flaming materials airborne and making our job difficult. I saw a flaming four-by-eight sheet of plywood sailing across Lincoln Saint and crashing through a glass window on the other side. Our guys are trying to work their way over there, but I don't know how that's gonna end."

There are few questions from the news corps. There's really nothing to ask. There seems to be no information regarding damage potential, no ideas as to motives, and no promise any answers are imminent.

Steffie's convinced that staying inside where she can concentrate on the spoken words is the correct decision. When the conference ends, the crowd, in a cathartic exercise, votes to switch the TV back to football. Steffie walks over to the bar and retrieves her phone, which she'd had the bartender place up next to the TV, a move that allowed her to record the audio portion of the news conference without having the bar chatter mask the TV voices.

"Thanks, Vicki," she says to the bartender.

"Not a problem, Steffie. You need something to eat before you go?"

"That's a reasonable thought, but I think I better find a hotel first and work on my story. I'm on deadline."

"You don't want to chance finding a hotel room in this town tonight," Vickie says.

"Damn thing might burn down before you get your story done." This word of encouragement comes from, Alex, the guy on the next stool. She'd talked some football with him, during the Dallas-Giants game while waiting on the news conference. He's a sales rep for Caterpillar and one of the few jacket-and-tie guys in the pub. "I stay in a B&B on a ranch a few miles west of town." He opens his wallet and extracts a business card for "Our Prairie Home." "I know they're booked tonight, but if you want, I'll give Ginnie a call, and tell her you need a room. She's networked to other

B&Bs and can find you a safe room." He pulls out his phone. "She's done it for me before."

"I've got a better idea," says Vickie. "I'm house-sitting my folk's house in the suburbs while they're wintering in Arizona. Don't you worry about a room, Steffie. I got three bedrooms for you to choose from. I'm working till seven. You grab yourself a bite to eat, and then you can stay at my house. This town's gonna be a zoo tonight. You don't want any part of that."

"Vicky's right," says Alex. "You'd best jump at that deal."

"Wow, Vickie. Thanks! That's great! How can I turn that down? You're on." Steffie slides onto the adjacent bar stool. "And I'll have time to eat. Let me see that menu."

CHAPTER 14

GARY GRALLAP'S VAGUE INSURANCE EXPECTATIONS

GARY GRALAPP, HANK DER ORD, and Paul Burtress used to be partners in the Drilling Platform, a fairly rowdy bar that, until this afternoon, actually existed. They've spent the afternoon watching their investment reduce itself to a charcoal pile. It's still belching pungent black smoke into the black sky above Williston. They watched the thing burn, fizzle, and collapse for hours, and now, completely desensitized and quite drunk, they've pulled themselves away and walked the half a dozen blocks southwest to Gralapp Construction's shop and warehouse. The three of them stumble into the makeshift lunch/break room. Two secondhand overstuffed sofas, a microwave, a refrigerator full of beer, and a table—a four-by-eight piece of three-quarter-inch plywood casually bolted to two aluminum sawhorses and surrounded by half a dozen metal stools—are arrayed in the space that is used for meetings, breaks, and conferences.

Since there are no windows in this room, the miserable weather and the pyrotechnic display emanating from the flaming pyres several blocks away has little impact on these three partners. There are, however, other distractions. Some guy is leaning hard on a grinder in the metal shop in the next room. A yellow front-end loader maneuvers a wooden crate onto a flatbed trailer just outside the open overhead door.

With the door open, the kerosene heater kicks into high gear and blasts hot air, accompanied by much fan noise, into their conference area. All this extraneous clatter requires Gary to crank the volume of KOIL's classic rock. It's a busy place, even on Sunday, because oil pumping and extraction work operates continuously, 24/7, so Gralapp Construction's shops must also operate 24/7.

Gary Gralapp returns from the refrigerator with a six-pack of Bud and bangs it onto the makeshift plywood table. He removes three bottles, attacks them with his keychain opener, and passes them around.

"Thanks for the beer, Gary," says Hank der Ord. "Damn, it's quiet in here."

"What ya mean, quiet," says Gary. "I can't hear myself think. I got Beach Boys screaming from the radio, that stupid fan growling, and that damn grinder whining. Don't hear nothing exploding though."

"I don't hear sirens or bombs," says Paul Burtress. "That what you mean?"

"Yeah, that's what he means. Seems like a tomb in here compared to that war zone over on Second Street." Gary points out the open door toward the exotic vibrating red glow reflecting in the windows across the alley. "Damn, everything's making too much noise. It's hurtin' my head."

"It's 'cause we're operating under pressure," says Paul. "Like in science, remember? You increase pressure over here, and then other stuff, like sound, gets pressurized over there, right?"

"Yeah, maybe it's pressure." Hank finishes his beer in a couple gulps, returns the bottle to the six-pack, takes out a full one, and hands it to Gary to open. "Heard anything from the insurance guys yet, Gary?"

"Holy Christ, Hank, our damn restaurant only just exploded six hours ago." Gary looks at his watch. "Maybe seven. It's still burning. Hell, it'll be months 'fore we'll be cashing that insurance check."

"Really? Ya think it'll take that long?"

"You livin' in some fantasy zone? Jeez! You know how it works. Say some subcontractor sends you a bill. You ever pay the jerk the next day?"

"We gotta let that subcontractor wait three months. You taught us that, Gary. Don't never pay no bill for three months … till just before the collection guys kick in the door."

"I can't wait that long, guys," says Hank. "I need money now. I'm gonna get big guys with tire irons banging on my door—and pretty damn quick, too!"

"Everybody's in the same fix, Hank. All of Williston's one big cash flow problem." He stares a bead right at Hank. "I thought you were flush for a while? You didn't put money on the Vikings today, did you?"

Hank looks at the floor and concentrates on the stain patterns in the concrete.

"Jeez, Hank, you promised me. You're not to bet on football anymore. That's a thousand bucks could 'a gone for groceries."

"It was two this week, Gary. But ya notice the odds? Great odds. And with Peterson back from IR? And those huge holes in the Bears secondary?"

"No more, Hank. Not a single dime more. You're not a sports gambler. Ya got enough problems with real estate. If you don't quit, you're gonna lose the rest of your shirt. Just quit it, man."

"Can't you call your insurance guy? Your big boss man? Ask him, as kind of a favor for me, what a normal payout schedule might look like? I need guidelines."

Gary opens a second beer for Paul and another for himself.

Hank looks a question toward Gary like he's saying, "Where's mine?"

"What?" Gary laughs at Hank. "It's a six-pack, you goofball. You already had your two."

Hank hangs depressed, like someone just stole his candy bar or his bike.

"What a bunch of babies I got in here this evening," says Gary.

"This ain't funny, Gary," says Hank. "I need lots of help, and I need it, like, immediately. And, just for your information, it's way past evening. Seems close to midnight to me."

Gary's got the best insurance deal of the Drilling Platform's three owners because he knows the path through L. D. Roseborough to the big boss. It's but a dirt path; it's not no interstate highway. And Gary, to be honest, has never once even set foot on that dirt path. Hell, he's never even seen it. L. D.'s told him it exists, and L. D.—BX&F's main guy in Williston—told him he's put the Drilling Platform's insurance in the same package with his big boss's real estate.

Gary feels the snug warmth of that security blanket, even though it's snowing and the wind chill is in the single digits. Could be it's only the beer? He knows Hank and Paul will be a bit trickier to accommodate. His two partner-buddies are one level down the food chain than he is, so the possibility exists that any insurance money will run out before it reaches 'em. But he's their buddy, and they need his reassurance. "There's absolutely nothing to worry about as far as insurance, guys. It's fairly solid."

"I may be drunk, Gary, but your words 'absolutely' and 'fairly' mean two different things, right."

Gary's worked construction for BX&F for many years, and though he generally trusts L. D., the guy's still a Texas oil guy operating under Texas rules. So he pays invoices at the ninety-day limit. Everybody does that, so eventually he's paid most every invoice, except for certain fees, kickbacks, and business expenses like his insurance, which, of course, Gary would deduct as expenses to ease his own tax load. L. D. gave him a hell of a deal on that. And, of course, he can deduct those same fees from the subcontractors he is using, guys like Hank and Paul. Plus L. D. brought up all those Mexican construction workers who build stuff at half price. They built Gary's Missouri River mansion practically for cost. He paid almost nothin', thanks to L. D.

"The whole system works smooth as shit." Gary has explained this to Hank and Paul maybe a hundred times. "Seems you two lummoxes don't understand the great deals you're getting. But if you guys wanna be businessmen, ya gotta be super-tough, quick as a bunny, and mean as hell!"

Gary still feels positive. He's pretty sure L. D. will alert him if any problems materialize up or down this particular chain. It's conceivable that, by now, he's been in the system long enough so he's situated above any frickin' food chain. And he also believes his very good "insurance rate" is based on the fact that he's helped L. D. out from time to time with "special projects." Gary often thinks that his position, vis-a-vis protection in general, is, like, maybe, even better than real insurance.

"Don't worry, guys," he says to his two partners. "In addition to insurance, I've got this two-by-four I can swing at L. D.'s head any time it needs swinging. That's almost super-insurance." He says this quite loud, above the blasting ZZ Top and the grinding of that metal grinder. But his words, absorbed by the noise, fade quickly—and they leave no impact crater.

It was over a month ago, Gary remembers, when L. D. had asked him, kind of from left field, if he remembered that short African guy he talked with about bringing the brothel operation into his hotel. Gary remembered telling L. D. that he, personally, hadn't contacted anyone. That brothel wasn't his idea. It was that black guy, Joe, who contacted him. Anyway, after some discussion regarding insurance, Gary had given L. D. Joe's number. But he'd been cautious. He'd always kept Joe's number unmarked only in his paper files like, for, in case of emergency. And he'd stayed away from email. Like in the olden days, he wrote the number in his little black notebook in code, without a name or anything. He thinks nobody, not even L. D., could trace that.

Gary though, did ask L. D. why he needed "this Joe guy's" number?"

"I'm looking for better insurance."

"What's that pimp's number got to do with insurance?"

"Could be those new oil fields opening in Texas need brothels too."

"I'm just wondering here, L. D., but what connects insurance to brothels."

"Brothels are, pretty much, like insurance, right?" L. D. actually said those words, but his sneer said it wasn't close to true.

Now that he's thinking about this insurance angle in this new light— the light from his burning real estate—Gary has this other light go on, and it signals to him that maybe his own insurance is not as real a concept as L. D.'s comments once suggested it was. Perhaps he should start thinking more about liability than about insurance. He's suddenly feeling quite vulnerable. He's troubled weighing preservation against insurance. He's thinking these are slightly different concepts. He's thinking about his other real estate. *Jenny got herself out of town quickly. Maybe I also should be running out of my house on the Missouri too? I'm clear on my beach house in Saint Kitts, and ISIS ain't never gonna firebomb that place—huh?*

CHAPTER 15

THE MAYOR'S SECOND NEWS CONFERENCE

HAVING STEFFIE STAY AT HER house worked out well for Vickie because her car—that is, if indeed there was anything left of her car, being the fire crews wouldn't let her get close enough to it to find out—is now trapped in that parking lot just next door since it's inside the lockdown area around the still-flaming Bakken Extended Stay Inn.

"I'll gladly trade you a bed for a ride home," says Vickie. "What a deal."

So, by eight twenty, Steffie has settled herself in the basement apartment Vickie's folks originally built for her when she first came back after graduating UND six years ago.

"I'm sorry, Vickie. I'm afraid I gotta run back and play reporter. I forgot about the news conference. I must go back, poke around a bit, and see if I can sniff out some news. The mayor's scheduled the conference for nine thirty, and he'll be on time because the story must make the ten o'clock news."

"That's fine. I'll get you the back door key. Oh, and Steffie?"

"Yes?"

"Would it be okay if I went with you? I could make myself useful finding shortcuts, recognizing people you might want to talk to. Stuff like that."

"Not a bad idea. It's dark and confusing as sin out there. And you know the landscape."

*   *   *

They park in the same lot Steffie used earlier and walk south the few blocks till they intersect the police line. Steffie notices the press corps has grown since this afternoon—reporters from Minneapolis, Denver, Cheyenne, Omaha, and stringers representing several agencies. Five microphones are fixed to the podium, compared to one this afternoon. Fire crew activity seems about the same as earlier, though smoke and flame production seem reduced. The anxiety quotient is way down, meaning the threat of additional explosions is much diminished. The snow has stopped falling after throwing several inches around this afternoon, the temperature's jumped into the teens, and it is supposed to continue rising. It's obvious, to her trained eye, that the keen edge is off this situation.

Mayor Clem Allison's face, however, reveals no sense of relief. "Good evening. The good news is I believe we're getting a handle on this thing. I'm hoping that, by dawn, we should have all fires under control. We'll be here throughout the night protecting against flare-ups. Chief Trudeau and Sheriff Faber will brief you after I'm through, and they'll give you the technical details. What I can verify is that these fires are, 100 percent certain, arson. Several independent fires were all deliberately set. And several were punctuated by explosive blasts set separately from the fires. That's strange. It seems like a *Terminator*-type movie fire, set to get one's attention but set separate from the gasoline-fueled fires actually burning the structures. It's all very weird. And nothing we've found here matches anything about those explosions at this morning's oil well fires. Someone, thinking he's being clever, is burning our vacant buildings, while giving great attention to the visual effects.

"These two incidents are separately planned actions, but they're obviously coordinated. They were organized together, by the same perpetrator, and are part of a single message. I have no idea at this time what that message might be—or whom it might be aimed at.

"Though the fires and explosions were effective, they do not seem to have been disguised to look like anything but arson. There's a chance one vacant hotel might catch fire—say an electrical problem—but it's almost bizarre to think of a vacant hotel exploding from an accident. That thing went up—boom. Also, because there's no gas service to these buildings—everything's electric around here—so these coordinated explosions cannot be anything but arson. Some of the FBI guys think these fires were designed for the TV coverage. And I have no idea what that even means.

"Now, the big question comes to my mind is why would anybody deliberately make a common arson look like a *Terminator* movie set? A chief rationale for arson is to fraudulently grab an insurance payout. But if you do something this outlandish, you can guarantee no insurance payment is gonna come save you. Unless, that is, you can prove the damage your property received is but collateral damage of someone else's arson. But that's almost impossible to argue. So, why would someone blow up all these mostly vacant buildings if it wasn't for the insurance? I'm thinking this is looking more like a publicity stunt. But for who, or what, I don't have a clue. And certainly *stunt* is the wrong word.

"I'm scared to death these two events may be part of a wider attack on our community. We're working with the FBI, Homeland Security, and the Terrorism Watch people, and none of these groups see suggestions of additional attacks, but they have no evidence that the show's over either. There's no evidence either way. Makes me frustrated. So, people, keep your eyes open. Let us know if you see anything strange happening. Here's Chief Trudeau. Be easy on him—he has no more answers than I do."

"What about casualties, Chief?" Steffie asks Trudeau. "Ya find anyone hurt or dead?"

"Like I said this afternoon, we've found one casualty at the oil rig fire, but we've not combed through the ruins here yet. Things are still too hot, too dangerous, and too dark. I'm not guessing about what we may or may not find. Maybe tomorrow morning when we have more light, less smoke, and manageable ice, we can do some investigating and find some answers for you."

*   *   *

"There's nothing more to learn here, Vickie. You had enough? I could've written the same story in the bar this afternoon while waiting for that first news conference. Let's go home. Then I'll write my story. It's gotta be posted by 1:00 a.m. Maybe, then, I'll get some sleep."

At 12:30, she emails her story and goes to bed. She's just put down her head and closed her eyes when she hears another boom. It seems far away, and it could have been a car backfire, a transformer overload, or maybe thunder. She's not expecting it to be another pseudo-terror event. She closes her eyes and mumbles to herself, "If it's something requiring my attention, I'm sure someone will call me."

CHAPTER 16

―――――――∿――――――――

GARY'S ALONE, UNLOVED, AND PROBABLY UNINSURED

Aᶠᵀᴱᴿ Gᴀʀʏ Gʀᴀʟᴀᴘᴘ ɢʀᴀᴅᴜᴀᴛᴇᴅ ꜰʀᴏᴍ UND in 1990, he worked with his dad, a small contractor of steel service buildings and farm structures. When Texas oil guys started drilling in northwestern North Dakota, Gary realized he'd make more money working for drilling operations than erecting outbuildings for farmers. Then, around 2004, after fracking technology bloomed in the Bakken, Gary bought out his dad's stake in the business and grew it very quickly to satisfy the need for oil field development.

He self-financed his firm's growth internally, using several Texas oil contractors he worked for. He didn't need bank financing for his big yellow Caterpillar loaders and his fleet of Peterbilt tractors with their Smith side-dump trailers. He called what he did "self-financing," though he realized the "self" part of that was a sham. Gary soon found himself umbilically tied to, or enslaved by, a couple of those big fracking contractors, and he knew that position made him vulnerable. And yet, he kept getting himself dug in deeper. He—hell, all of Williston at that time—was consumed by the fantasy that the upside of the oil boom will be utterly monumental, and would never end!

By 2010, Gary had a couple hundred guys on his payroll, many millions of dollars of work under contract, and millions of dollars in casual business loans. He was making more money in a week than his mother and father together did in a year. Much of that work and large portions of the payment for the work were, of course, done without formal contracts or proper paper trails. He couldn't keep up with it all. He knew he was playing with real money though because he used it to buy stuff like his condo in Saint Kitts. He used it to buy a plane so he could fly down there whenever he wanted to. He bought a ranch in the hills along the Missouri and built himself a nice vacation getaway with a heated pool with a sliding plastic roof for winter use. That house, containing that pool, when dangled in front of his girlfriend's eyes, persuaded Jenny to move into the place with him. Well, the pool certainly, but also that diamond—and that powder blue Jaguar? Those things helped too!

Gary soon thought himself a legitimate business leader, and from that elevated position, he saw the massive need for local non-oil field development—residential hotels for migrant workers, services for trucks and oil field equipment, places for all these thousands of new workers to eat, sleep, play, and spend money. He, along with several equally delusional buddies, believed that they, with financing from his Texas fracking partners, could take on the responsibility to satisfy Williston's growth needs. Over the years, he brought in cheap materials and workers from Texas and Mexico, and his firm built hotels, warehouses, office buildings, bars, service areas, and distribution centers—most all mortgaged by the same Texas players financing the oil field construction work. And, of course, he brought in, or encouraged the bringing in, or subsidized the bringing in, even owning or franchising, the associated shady pseudo-business entities that follow any booming economy—the Jaguar dealership, the loan sharks, the pocket casinos, and a couple of rather high-class brothels.

Then, maybe six months ago, came "the Crash." As all too-good-to-be-true deals do, Gary's deals crashed. His flying days crashed-landed too. In a couple of months, the whole damn thing blew up. Since then, it's been getting worse. Oil prices dropped from eighty to sixty, to forty, and now to thirty bucks a barrel. And the Saudis promised to take them lower. Williston fast became a ghost town, at least with respect to its previous stature.

All Gary's angels quickly turned to ghosts—and he was not alone. Many of his high school buddies had also leveraged themselves into equally outrageous financial structures, cantilevered off the cliff of appropriate business behavior. And they watched as their highly leveraged bridge loans to Texas money sources, which supported their cantilevered lifestyles, were sawed off behind them. Gary has no doubt at all. He is going down. Everyone he knows is going down. And it's a long way down. He sees the carnivores gathered at the base of their cliff, smacking their lips and anticipating their lunch falling from the sky. The first thing Gary sells is his plane.

Tonight, Gary is all alone in that chick-magnet castle he built overlooking the Missouri, twenty miles southeast of Williston. He's so drunk he can't remember the drive down. He spent time looking for Jenny before realizing she's in Philadelphia, visiting her parents for Christmas. Damn! He forgot that! Granted, Christmas is over a month away, but, like before, he made the mistake of thinking Christmas was a single-day event set somewhere near the end of December. And so, as before, he'd squabbled with Jenny about the timespan of the Christmas holiday, the scheduling and quantity of Christmas money he'd be required to spend on gifts, and about the need to replace her out-of-date blue Jaguar with a seasonally appropriate red one. She also expects to spend Christmas—not just the day itself, but the entire damn season (whatever that means)—in Saint Kitts. "It's already Christmas in Saint Kitts," she'd argued. She then gave him her Christmas moue.

Unfortunately, he went a bit short with her. The entire bottom's falling out of his financial empire, yet all she's worried about is getting adequate beach time and a car matching her bikini. Gary had to put his foot down. He started it off well, launched his attack by giving in regarding the red Jag. She'd skipped across the room, jumped into his lap, and gave him a wonderful kiss.

What the hell, he thought, *Since it's Christmas in Saint Kitts—could be Christmas in Dakota too.* The Jag arrived the next day, and Gary thought he'd shove the remainder of her wish list down that time-tunnel a few weeks until his financial situation improved. Maybe that insurance stuff L. D. promised might kick in. But then, a couple days later, she's back to pouting. She restarted the Christmas discussion, and things went downhill quickly. And she's throwing this stuff at him after he sticks her red Jaguar into his garage!

The result being, within a couple days, Jenny's off for Philly in an exaggerated huff. Gary did notice that she didn't fly; she left driving her new Jag. He thinks that's significant. He gives her the benefit of the doubt, thinks it means she's accepted at least part of his deal. He's almost sure it means only a short-term "inconvenience." She needs "room to think," so she must "go home." Gary had been operating under the impression this mansion on this hilltop overlooking this beautiful Missouri was the accommodation what was "her home." Jenny, apparently, thought otherwise. "It doesn't seem like 'my home' around here anymore." Her words were accompanied by glittering tears. "At least not at this particular moment in time!" He thought those words seemed more positive than they were before.

"Women?" He throws a pillow. It just misses the lamp and hits the wall above the leather couch.

Gary understands business like a master, but he has no ideas about girls. It's been two weeks since Jenny left in that snit, and he's still mad. "Adequate beach time? Bah!" He gets another beer and wonders if the repo guys will be able to trace that thing all the way to Philadelphia. He throws another throw pillow at the big picture window. "Bah!" It's dark outside that window. He sees absolutely nothing out there. Not the hot tub set into the deck or the Missouri at the bottom of the bluff. The scene's nothing but a void. He's getting used to voids. As the pillow hits the window, his cell phone begins playing the theme song from *The Magnificent Seven*— not the new movie, but the old one. That new theme is so much crap. The music means it's Hank. He walks across to the table, grabs his phone, and pushes the button.

"Damn it, der Ord," Gary says. "Didn't I just leave you? What you doing callin' me already? It's the middle of the night. Jenny's waiting in the bedroom. Can't this wait?" Gary holds the phone down by his waist and yells softly into the other room: "Be right in there, sweetie. Won't take but a minute." Then he brings the phone back to his mouth and hisses, "You better make this quick, der Ord. I gotta take care of some biss-niss here."

"Ya see that news conference tonight, Gary? Mayor Allison says whoever set those fires today were idiots. Said any fool could tell the fires were intentional. My question is, if everyone now knows they're arson, what're the chances our insurance kicks in anytime soon?"

"I don't know, and to be perfectly honest, der Ord, right now, I don't care!" He jabs the off button and throws the phone onto the couch.

Oh God! This is it, huh? Is this the end? He walks deliberately into the kitchen, opens the fridge, and grabs another Bud Lite. He hears his phone playing *Magnificent Seven* from the other room—this is the new version.

"Damn, gotta be the other one. Why do those two clowns think I'm the one's gotta solve their problems?" He lets the call go to his machine.

He unlocks the patio door, opens it, and steps out into the cold night. He still can't see his damn Missouri, but he knows it's out there. He stares into the nothingness. *Damn! If L. D.'s insurance doesn't kick in, I'm toast. I gotta think about separating from L. D. and solving my own insurance problem. It's time for plan B.*

Gary's plan B isn't really a plan. It calls for him to skitter about haphazardly in the absolute absence of a plan, hoping somehow to slip himself out of the mess he finds himself in. He really can't see where he, himself, did anything criminal, but he knows guys who probably have—and those guys know he knows. Back in October, he gave L. D. that Somali pimp's phone number. L. D. told him he needed it for the "insurance." Said the big boss needed to talk God into firebombing stuff. But how's he gonna do that? He remembers it made sense back then—he was sober then. Anyway, he can't believe that number has anything to do with half of Williston blowing up. That number was about Texas brothels. And even if it wasn't, L. D. wouldn't try to put it back on him. Would he?

"I'm your buddy, L. D." he yells out to the black Missouri. But then he thinks about L. D. as one nervous Nellie and whispers so only the squirrels can hear, "Ya think you're smart enough to realize I can link you to that dead Islamic terrorist the FBI found in East Williston?"

L. D. definitely heard the mayor connecting ISIS to the explosions. So if L. D. is connected to that dead ISIS terrorist, and if I'm the guy gave L. D. that pimp's phone number ... Gary holds his hands wide and seeks wisdom from the black Missouri to flow up the bluff to his patio. Enlightenment does not come. Nothing comes. *My life isn't worth a single nickel, is it, Gary old buddy? Not a single stupid nickel!* He crushes the Bud Lite can and throws it out over the cliff edge toward the Missouri. *Just like that phone number, nobody's ever gonna find that can, huh?* Understanding that association makes him feel better.

But it won't help him in the long term. Thinking things out clearly, making the chain obvious, one link by stupid link, is not something Gary's good at, especially when he's as drunk as he is now. He goes back inside and climbs into his warm bed with the heated comforter. And, lying in his bed, all by himself, in his empty playhouse, on this high cliff, above that black Missouri, a few basic conditions start seeping into Gary's skull. And the first condition he pulls up is that he's all by himself—with no one else within miles. He's high on a cliff and overlooking the black Missouri. And there ain't nothin' else!

"And I'm all alone. All by myself, aren't I?" He speaks this with some force, daring some power to answer him. Under normal circumstances, that might mean he's in a vulnerable situation. But these aren't normal circumstances, what with things blowing up and guys getting killed. He's alone. He's all by himself. He's got the comforter cranked up as high as it goes. Still, he's shivering. That scares him some. He gets up, goes downstairs, and checks to see if he's turned the heat down too far by mistake. He checks, again, to see if the alarm's activated. He enters his den, removes the semiautomatic assault rifle from the gun cabinet, and notes the magazine is inserted. Then he returns upstairs and crawls back under the comforter.

There, that should solve it. He pats the weapon next to him beneath the comforter. "I'm no longer alone," he says. He's fairly sure the Missouri's not listening to him babbling under his comforter. "No way you take me out now, Roseborough!" He's talking to the rifle, or to God—his God, certainly not that other god, Allah. "No way, Roseborough!"

69

CHAPTER IV

THE SPANISH INQUISITION

Monday, November 14, 2016

THE MAJOR REASON L. D. Roseborough won't be taking out Gary on this dark night is that he's in Brusly, Louisiana, a small town on the west bank of the Mississippi near Baton Rouge. It's where he spent his youth. L. D.'s sitting at a picnic table on the back porch. He's drinking beer and talking with an old Special Forces teammate, Manny Sanchez. The two of them go way back to high school and through stints in Afghanistan and Iraq. Sanchez operates a firm—a consulting and operations group— that undertakes specialized security operations for L. D.'s big boss and selected other oil field development firms. L.D's just flown Sanchez and his four-man crew back from North Dakota where they completed a certain piece of demolition work for his big boss.

"Ya did a nice job up there, guys," says L. D. "Ya happen to catch the mayor's press conference? He has no idea what happened to his town. Said he thinks it could've been ISIS. Could've been a work of God, right? Stupid mayor doesn't have a clue."

"Why would he, L. D.?" says Sanchez. "Everything went down perfectly. That's how works of God are supposed to work. God doesn't make mistakes, ya know? Perfect every time."

"Of course, up in North Dakota, any work's easy. No one expects the Spanish Inquisition up there. Ain't that true, Manny?"

"Right, L. D." Manny looks at his watch. "It's almost sunrise, guys.

I've gotta check in with the big boss and then get some sleep." He takes a throwaway cell phone from his briefcase, pushes some buttons, and talks to a machine. "Allah's work is done," he says to some other machine, somewhere else in the world. It could be Iraq, though it's probably more likely in Dakota. "And, yes, the birds are back in the nest."

CHAPTER 18

STOP THE HEMORRHAGING

I T'S WAY EARLY ON MONDAY morning, yet even as his crippled city continues to pump smoke into the sky, Mayor Clem Allison flies himself east to Bismarck to confront his governor. He must get on his knees and beg his friend, Leon, to designate Williston an official state emergency area. He arrives at the governor's door at 7:40, just as Leon's assistant, Margie, finishes brewing the day's first pot of coffee. That ensures they both will be well caffeinated—and they'll have Clem's attack plan outlined when Clem's friend, the governor, walks through the office door at 8:00 sharp.

Leon stops abruptly, taps his watch a few times, and holds it to his ear.

"Watches don't tick anymore, Leon," Margie says. "Ya can't hear batteries. Ya think the thing stopped?"

"Either that—or I just entered a time warp. What the hell you doing, Clem? Getting into my office before I do?"

"I had to, Leon. I have more problems than you have."

"I don't know about that, but come into my office and make yourself comfortable. I'm guessing Margie's taken care of ya?"

"She's been a big help. And Williston needs your immediate high-powered help too. I'm here, on my knees, pleading for it."

"We talked about your fires yesterday. They hit private nonmunicipal property, right? I don't think I can help you with private damage."

"Those fires are just the tip of the iceberg, Leon. I'm talking major economic collapse. Half the buildings in Williston not on fire are in foreclosure. I'm losing taxable real estate by the ton. Everyone in town will be claiming refunds on their 2016 returns, not paying me taxes. Means I'll be giving them money! Estimates for city revenues for next year are under half of what they were for last year."

"Wow. Your revenue down by half?"

"Yes, and business taxpayers are asking for reimbursements for this year's losses. We're gonna be giving back as much money as we're taking in. The oil price collapse hit us hard. And now idiots are setting the remaining rubble pile on fire. I need help. I got nowhere else to go. On top of that, I'm one year into our billion-dollar infrastructure spending plan. Sales taxes were supposed to fund that, but everyone's leaving now. I get no sales—thus no taxes. I've got zippo funds coming in. And I've got four more years of now-unneeded infrastructure planned and contracted for. I need miracles, Leon. Big miracles."

Leon and Clem settle into a serious discussion of how to restructure several programs to help Williston cope with its huge cash flow problem. And much of the problem is based on the fact that since Williston's grown so fast, many items of emergency infrastructure—like that several-hundred-million-dollar airport expansion—were quickly planned, designed, and begun under state emergency programing. And now, with construction underway, the need for the once-pressing need for upgrades has suddenly collapsed.

"So many unfinished, and now unneeded projects—many will not be used even if completed—are cluttering up my city's budget, manpower, and attention. I'm wondering if there's a way to move state infrastructure money over to emergency funding for our pressing problems. It's a difficult situation, Leon. And if I cannot keep Williston solvent, then it's possible the whole state might follow us down into the hole. You understand what I'm saying?"

Margie bursts into the room and interrupts their deliberations. "Excuse me, Leon. I've got Will Basehardt on hold." She brandishes her clenched fist at Leon. "I'd like to put a permanent hold on that guy—maybe a sleeper hold."

"I could use a gal," says Clem, "who knows about sleeper holds."

Margie smiles at him. "He just told me he's appointed himself chairman of the Legislative Infrastructure Task Force. You're a consultant to that group, aren't you, Clem? Is that fat blowhard telling me the truth?"

"That committee neither has, nor needs, any chairman. It's an advisory committee, and though we invited him to several meetings, he's yet to attend any of 'em. If any guy needed to receive a sleeper hold …"

"Basehardt wants us to put more infrastructure improvements into next biennium's spending proposal."

"You'd better be careful with him," says Clem. "He claims he's tight with the new bunch gonna be running Washington. Says he'll bypass Bismarck and jam federal projects down our throats straight from DC."

"He's in some fantasy land, Clem, thinking he can build highways, airstrips, and pipelines and get Mexico to pay for them."

Margie says, "I'm gonna tell him you're not feeling well—or maybe you're in Jamaica?"

"That won't work, Margie. I spoke with a couple of his tribe walking through the lobby this morning." Leon takes a gulp from the orange juice, returns it to the desk, and winks at Margie. "Tell him, I'll give him fifteen minutes. That's his limit. I've got no appointments this morning so whenever it's convenient for him, he can pop in. But make sure he understands, once through that door, his fifteen-minute timer starts."

"Can I stay and watch the fireworks?" asks Clem. "I'm an expert on pyrotechnics now."

"I don't think that would be productive. Things could get violent, and since you're my friend, I wouldn't want you to get hurt."

"I gotta to give you a primer on Basehardt, Leon. He's a huge player in the Bakken. Next to your friend Kathleen, and K&F, he probably controls more oil rights than anyone else. He's pretending he's from North Dakota and that he represents Williston. Do not be fooled. That pompous bastard's representing himself first—and then maybe Houston second. Dakota, especially Williston, is way down his list. Now that those new Texas fields have been found, we all know he's gonna be moving south in a hurry. And the scuttlebutt is he's not all that concerned that his buildings are burning behind him. I haven't tied him to those fires yet, but I'd not be surprised if he's involved somehow. I've got my spies watching every move that weaselly SOB makes."

"I'll remember that, Clem. I need weapons. And, being a cultivated guy, I, unlike Margie, have never learned sleeper holds."

CHAPTER 19

GARY CONFIRMS HIS SHAKY INSURANCE SITUATION

GARY GRALAPP THINKS HE MUST do a bit of due diligence. He's gotta call L. D. and make sure things are moving smoothly with respect to the insurance on the Drilling Platform. He's not feeling comfortable, and he needs to assuage the paranoia his management team is wallowing in. Gary steels himself and calls the number.

He understands the protocol. He's been following it for six or seven years. Roseborough never answers his own phone—or at least the phone he has the number to. To reach L. D., Gary must call this number, and after his secretary, Mary C., answers, he gives her a message. If she thinks it's important enough, she'll have the very busy L. D. Roseborough call him back. It's a cumbersome pre-cell-phone drill, but that's just the way this business is.

However, as soon as he hears the words "This be Roseborough Drilling, whatcha need, honey?" he knows he's in trouble. When Roseborough is in the office, she'll curtly answer, "L. D.'s Office." Her relaxed telephone etiquette means L. D.'s unavailable, and Mary C.'s running the place. He's never met Mary C. Skenn, so he doesn't really know if she's in Williston, in Baton Rouge, or the north slope of Alaska. He doesn't even know if she's a human being. Mary C. controls the flow of information, and certainly the flow of money, through the several levels of the several entities Roseborough fronts for his big boss. Gary has often crossed swords with Mary C. Skenn.

"Hi, Mary. This is Gary Gralapp, and—"

"Afternoon, Gary darling. What ya got for me?"

"I had a brief conversation with L. D. yesterday about insurance payments on—"

"Oh, Gary, honey, you know better than to ask me about that now. You'll get your money when I get mine. Well, probably not precisely when I get mine. It will take time for all that cash to work its way through the system. So, if I were you, honey, I wouldn't go order that red Jaguar yet. Oops, gotta go, sugar. Got another call."

"Well," says Gary into his instantly dead phone, "I did learn one thing. She already knows about the red Jag, so its cost will probably be deducted from any insurance payout first. Damn!"

As it turns out, the call was not a waste of Gary's time because it got him thinking about the real-life definitions of the words *accounts payable* and *accounts receivable.* Gary, reacting to the danger compressed into that brief call, is forced to consider these definitions in a bit of a different context now.

And, as he does this additional considering, he can see clearly that he doesn't have as strong a handle on that insurance stuff as he previously thought he might. In fact, when he views everything from this different angle, he realizes it's quite possible he'll *never* collect anything on that insurance policy. Gary actually has a little black thought about this, but he's not ready to admit he should start thinking about food chains just yet. It might be prudent to make some fairly specific plans regarding the future of one of those food chains.

He knows he's gotta talk directly with the big boss about insurance, but he hasn't the foggiest idea how to do that. The big boss is a long walk down the dirt path through that oily jungle. It's dangerous in that jungle. It seems L. D.'s gone—perhaps he's run down that path to visit the big boss—and now Mary C.'s blocked all access to that path. Does that path even exist anymore since everything else in Williston's gone ker-boom?

CHAPTER 20

GOVERNOR ROLFES CONFRONTS THE DARK, OILY KNIGHT

Leon's desk phone buzzes, and then Margie's quite formal voice says, "Mr. Basehardt just came through my door, Governor. I'm winding up my timer, so we all understand he's on the clock?"

"Thanks—and bring a couple orange juices in with you please. I'm all out in here."

Leon watches Will Basehardt bounce over the threshold like a salesman in heat, but he refuses to let his excitement show. "Morning, Will. Ya want an orange juice?"

"Nice digs ya got here, Leon. Great view over the mall." He points out the window to make the point. "The sun's now shining out there, Leon. I've ordered nothing but sun for the next few months."

"You didn't answer my question regards the juice. And get a grip on reality, buddy. You and sunshine occur in two different worlds."

"I mean the president-elect and I, we inherited your mess. You and I, we're like partners now. And being partners means you gotta change the Transportation and Infrastructure Budget. It's a new day, Leon. We're gonna be changing lots of your silly rules."

"I'll take that as a no on the juice."

Basehardt glares at him. "First item's your preliminary budget." He lifts a paper and waves it in Leon's face. "Your budget doesn't include continuing funding for highway work already started in my district. I'm gonna need least $150 million for that. Create *mucho* jobs right there,

Leon, and I'm gonna accelerate my airport reconstruction. I got some great ideas. Bigger ideas than you ever thought possible."

Leon elevates his juice bottle, ceremoniously unscrews the cap, takes a swig, screws the cap back on, and then looks back to Basehardt. "Listen, Will. It's Will, right? Not, Wil-bur? Or Wil-lard? Or Wil-son? Or Wil-liam?"

"Yes, it's Will."

"Okay, so, listen up here, just plain Will! You read newspapers? Maybe watch a bit of TV? You realize western North Dakota's now in the process of either shutting down or blowing up, don't you?"

"That's the second thing we gotta talk about. Those ISIS attacks. You've gotta instantly post National Guard troops up there to prevent ISIS attacks. First thing our president-elect's gonna do is bomb ISIS's oil wells in Iraq—"

"Slow down. You know oil prices are close to record lows, right? Ya read that? Williston's drilling towers and office buildings are exploding, and pumping rigs are flying south like Canada geese. They're all headed back to Texas, Will. You familiar with Texas?"

"I'm not talking about Texas, Leon. I'm talking about North Dakota."

"I'm not so sure. In case you didn't notice stuff the last time you were home, Texas is where all the oil growth's gonna be happening, so that's where they'll be needing new roads and disposal facilities. You gonna be trotting down there too, right? Hardly anyone's staying up here in the tundra. Folks are pulling up rigs and leaving huge prairie dog holes in the ground. I'm the governor, remember, and I'm saying nobody out there's goin' to be needing any big, wide roads and shiny new infrastructure for a long, long time."

"You're the one not reading papers, Leon. You should read about what your president-elect will be doing. Bang!" He slaps the table. "Soon as he's on the clock, you and your liberal agenda's gonna be toast. No more sissy wind power. It's gonna be drill, baby, drill."

"We've been pouring state money into Williston for years, Will, but it's been at the expense of the rest of our state. We haven't paid enough attention to outlying areas for at least four years."

"We're sayin' it's the infrastructure out west in the oil fields that needs the most attention. Infrastructure's a magic word. I'm gonna insist we start building roads and bridges right away. Oil's the only moneymaking industry this state has."

"Ya ever heard the word *agriculture*, Will? That's the real machine that supports our state's economy. Being from Texas, you probably missed that. Oil's but frosting on the cake of agriculture. You guys down in Texas actually grow stuff other than dust down there?"

"You're nuts, Leon, absolutely nuts. We're gonna make oil flow like water, especially after that PFUMP pipeline is complete."

"You, of all folks, should know that Dakota oil ain't ever flowed like water. In fact, that's the big problem we have with our oil. If it flowed like water, we wouldn't have to frack the stupid stuff to get it out of the ground. We could do like the Saudis do—stick a straw into the sand then let the stuff bubble out the top. I believe that's how oil flows."

"You're on a new team now, Leon. You know Bing Cherry? He'll be calling you daily tellin' you which stupid regulations you gotta throw in the trash. Once the regulations are gone, our oil will bubble out just like the Saudi's does. They have no frickin' regulations, and we don't need them either."

"It's not regulations making our oil difficult to mine, Will. It's that our oil's hidden five miles deep in the shale formations, and it's not like the Arab stuff—sitting in big bathtubs on the surface."

"Oil's gonna flow like water. I guarantee it. And pumping's gonna be back to record levels. We're gonna need those new roads and airports. You'd best start listening to me—so you won't embarrass yourself when your new boss calls you on this."

"I'm the governor of North Dakota. I work for my people and not for the president of the United States, the head of Exxon-Mobil, and most certainly not you."

"You better drop that attitude, Leon."

"You must leave now, Will. And until you don your humble coat, I'll not let you back into this office. If you need to see me, tough bananas. I'm not talkin' to you."

"You're wrong there, Leon. I'm gonna be the highest-elected Republican official in this state. I plan on being elected leader of your state senate."

"Good luck with that, you pompous bastard."

"I've always said, 'If ya wanna be big, ya gotta plan big.' I'm planning big. And the new president-elect? He's planning big too. He's backing me 1,000 percent."

"Goodbye, Will."

"Once January 20 rolls around, the president and I will be givin' the orders. So, technically, that'll make me your new boss, right?"

"Well, no. It makes you one arrogant SOB. And also, just so you know, your guy's not president yet. Goodbye."

"You better get used to me standing here and blasting you, Leon. The president-elect doesn't recognize your homegrown, Dakota First Party piece of garbage as a legal political party, and so he'll pay no attention to you. That means I'm not paying attention to you either."

"That's the best news I've heard all day, Will. I'll look forward to you not paying me any attention. Now, get the hell out of here." Leon makes a big visual production of looking through files, organizing things on his desk, and taking a sip of orange juice. He looks up and sees Will still sitting there. "You still here? You said you weren't paying me any attention, so scram."

"You watch out—"

"I don't normally treat fellow North Dakotans like this, Will." Leon rises and walks to the window. "But, in your case, I'm going to make an exception. Don't you ever foul my office with your presence again. If, for some reason, you have a valid reason to talk to me, I'll meet you outside. Say, over there, under that elm tree. You are not welcome in my office. Out! And don't close my door. I'm gonna open this window. I need to fumigate! Get some fresh air flowing through here."

* * *

Margie's taken pity on him, and in an attempt to lighten his soggy mood, she enters Leon's office with a couple wedges of carrot cake from the cafeteria. She sets his filled coffee cup next to the cake and glances at the TV. "Gray smoke, fire tongues shooting out window openings, and icicles hanging from jagged beams? Wow!"

"CNN's showing us scenes from Syria again. Sure glad I'm not over there."

"We both know that's Williston, Leon. I don't think Syria gets that much snow."

"Last week it's the PFUMP Pipeline and the freezing protestors. This week it's Williston looking like Syria. I didn't sign up for this, Margie. It's a governor's PR nightmare."

"We're not a big enough state to have two national news stories poking us at once. Perhaps the Standing Rock people freezing at the barricade story will flitter away now."

"I certainly hope so. I might suggest a positive aspect to these stories. If the media's attention stays focused on the human tragedy surrounding the pipeline protest, and on Williston imitating Baghdad, no one might notice me sneaking my Subsurface Materials Ownership Act through a special session. Whatcha think, Margie?"

"That's possible, Leon. You might even slip it past your mama."

"And maybe, in the midst of that distraction—" Leon looks toward the memorabilia stashed on his bookshelf.

"I sense another basketball analogy's gonna come zipping in here."

"Could be. I think it's time for a quick outlet pass. Amid all the confusion, I think I see Nathan. He's screaming down court, lookin' for a pass."

"No, Leon. I don't think he is." Margie turns and walks back to her office.

"Maybe that's a signal telling me I should go home," Leon shouts after her. "Then I can take a nap. Mom's making pot roast tonight. After that, I'll grab me a beer, sit in front of the TV, and fall asleep watching *Monday Night Football*."

"You want me to come with you? I could help you reallocate Basehardt's infrastructure budget?"

"No! We're not doin' any work on that crap. Oh, I get it, Margie." He walks out to her desk. "You want in on the pot roast, don't you?"

She smiles up at him.

"Oh, all right. If you drive me home through this extremely intense snowstorm, you can stay for dinner."

"Thank you, Leon."

"We've done some wonderful work today," he says. "We've solved every problem on my list."

"No, you haven't. What about Will Basehardt? He's gonna come running through here with a meat cleaver tomorrow morning. You gonna be ready for that."

"You betcha, Margie." He goes over and looks out his window. It's almost dark out there, and the snow is falling heavier. Leon's pleased he's tricked Margie into giving him a ride home. "What can Basehardt do? He's got no power. Though he does jump up and down and scream like a banshee?"

"I don't want him screaming around here, Leon. Though I don't mind watching banshees jump."

"Oh, wait! You won't be able to watch that. I told Basehardt this morning that I won't have him in my office until he grows some manners. He's not welcome up here. Sadly, you're not going to have to take him on with your meat cleaver tomorrow."

"Thanks for fixing that, Leon. We'll see if your plan works. Somehow, I doubt it."

CHAPTER 21

OPENING OLD WOUNDS AND NEW LEADS

Tuesday, November 15, 2016

STEFFIE'S IN HER OFFICE AT the *Bismarck Plainsman*, ingesting wire service accounts of the still-smoldering Williston fires. Two days ago, from inside Hurley's Irish Pub, she'd watched Williston burning. Now, reading the news accounts, something odd pops into her head. She remembers, back at the pub, a snippet of conversation flitting over from an adjacent table—stuff about the building exploding across the street being the same hotel where that brothel scandal occurred last spring. She'd heard one voice saying, "Louisiana oil workers trashed that damn hotel last spring after they got fired and before they left town. They left it a real dump. It's been closed since. Maybe this fire's doin' us a favor, huh?"

That guy was right. She remembers last spring, watching with Minneapolis reporter Hasani Indaak as the FBI sex trafficking bust went down at that hotel. It's a strange thought connection, a somewhat raw coincidence. She understands coincidence is a reporter's best friend. And she knows another person walking through that hotel on that day last spring. Sheriff Jessie Faber organized the attack on those Somali sex traffickers. *Hmmm, maybe I should talk with Faber. Take a trip down memory lane. Open a few old wounds.*

* * *

So, two hours and 130 miles after this thought popped into her head, Steffie enters Faber's office armed with a fresh cup of coffee from Faber's gurgling machine. She sinks herself into his dirty beige couch. "Sheriff, I'm percolating this nagging little thought, so I must ask you some hypothetical questions, which you don't have to answer, but which I'm asking so you'll understand the kind of possibilities such a question might suggest to a certain reporter lady, like your old friend Steffie."

"I've no idea what your words mean, Steffie, though I'm fairly certain they don't make a question. But I know you, so I'll play along. I may even learn something."

"I don't want to pressure you into telling me things you want to keep secret, okay?"

"Like hell you don't. You want me to blab every secret thing I know. Things I won't tell my own mother."

"Enough of this. Here's question one. At your news conference Sunday, you described the 9-1-1 call and noted the caller used the words, 'Allah,' 'ISIS,' and 'Islamic State,' correct?"

"Yes, I did, Steffie. The caller actually used those words. I've got 'em recorded."

"Good! And then you stated the dead man was dressed in 'terrorist gear,' right?"

"Correct, the black full-body sheet and head-scarf-wrapped-around-the-face type thing. And I'll let you in on some breaking news. We found another body, wearing the same type terrorist gear, in the rubble of that Drilling Platform bar yesterday morning. Close to where we found the remains of the bartender and waitress."

"Thank you for that. But, again, you very carefully did not mention if that dead man was Arab, Iranian, or some other Middle Eastern kind of terrorist. Could he have been Japanese or Swedish?"

"What? I said they were dressed in terrorist gear. That's all I said. I made no reference to nationality. Why would I? How do I know where they're from? And where'd you get Sweden?"

"Aha! But we both know where that dead guy was 'not from,' don't we? And you had a good reason not to divulge that information to the common, run-of-the-mill reporters standing before you at that time, huh? But you might be thinking of confirming that information to this specific reporter who's already deduced the answer, huh?" She points to herself, shakes out her blonde curls, and smiles sweetly at him.

"Good grief, Steffie. Will you cut it out. Can't you ask me simple questions, put in simple sentences, that I can answer either yes or no?"

"Okay. I'm thinking you specifically didn't tell us the dead guy's nationality, even though at that time you knew he was not an Arabic terrorist. You knew he was a black African youth, specifically a Somali youth. And you did not want to tell us that because you were afraid we reporters would immediately assume he was from your local Williston Somali community. And you didn't want to rustle up those awful feathers again. Right?"

"I have no idea where you are going, Steffie. I did not have a hidden agenda. That's just the way it came out. I'm not going to release information on those boys until I know who they are. That's standard procedure, I think."

"Okay, let's say I accept that. So then, there comes question number two. You ready?"

"This is not a game show, Steffie. Turn down the drama dial a bit … please."

"Will do, Sheriff. Here's a straightforward question. If, for some reason, a guy needs a dead ISIS terrorist to participate in a fake terror tableau out in western North Dakota, where, it is well known, there's a shortage of real Arab terrorists to hire for the job, where do you suppose he might find one?"

"You didn't turn that dial down much, huh? Again, Steffie, I'm not making guesses. I can't do that."

"But you do have a reasonable Somali population in Williston, right?"

"Well, yes, it's a small population, but—"

"And you and I also both learned last spring that the members of the Somali community in Williston are not Muslims. They are Catholics who came up here from Des Moines to work the hotels. They escaped from their Muslim terrorist neighbors back in Mogadishu. These folks would never yell: 'Allah Akbar.' Your Williston-based Somalis are much more likely to be shouting, 'Hallelujah!' Right, Sheriff?"

"You are right there, Steffie."

"And most Williston folks know that, don't they? So there's zero possibility that the dead Somali-looking man you found was a local Catholic Somali, right?"

"I am quite sure you're gonna be correct."

"But both dead men you found were Somali, right?"

"That's one of those things I'm not telling my own mother."

Steffie pumps her fist, "Yes, I knew they were."

"Ya need a refill?" Sheriff Faber rises, walks into the alcove to his coffeemaker, and pushes a few buttons.

"No, Sheriff. I'm still good. Not only are Williston's young Somali men not Muslim—they hate being isolated out here. Upon graduating high school, they rush back to Des Moines to go to college or find a wife. Essentially, there are no young Somali males living in Williston, right?"

"Please, Steffie, that's not for publication. But, okay, the men were Somali, and, as you've deduced, I'm certain they're not local. But where are they from? I've got no idea."

"But, Sheriff, we both know some Muslim Somalis have been in town recently, don't we? Those from that sex trafficking group you busted? The Somalis who ran that were based in Minneapolis, and they were Muslim. Do you think any of those miscreants happened to be guys hanging around Williston and finding no work except to help blow up a few things for Allah?"

"Jeez! I'd forgotten about them, Steffie, but I don't think so. I think they're either in jail or someplace far, far away. I've not seen any of them around here."

"You remember my reporter friend, Hasani? From Minneapolis? I'm thinking maybe I should ask her a question or two about Muslim Somalis. I'm not yet sure I know what I can ask her, but at least she knows everything that is happening in the Somali community over there. She could maybe poke around and see if, like before, she's heard any stories or rumors fluttering around concerning missing Somalis. Maybe rumors of missing young men this time rather than the missing young women she was looking for last spring."

"I never want to think about that episode again."

"Does that mean you don't want me to talk with her?"

"No, it means I am going to hold all my information locked in my file drawer until I get a better handle on this thing. And I'm gonna insist that this investigation proceed at a measured pace so I can understand everything at one level before I move to the next level."

"Does that mean you don't want me to talk to Hasani? You know her. You can trust her. You wouldn't have broken your sex trafficking story without her, right?"

"That wasn't my story, Steffie. Just cool it. Have a little patience. We haven't even received autopsy reports back from the FBI on the two men yet."

"Oh! And that's some delicious tidbit of interesting news. Should a reporter lady like me be interested in why it's taking so long for an autopsy to pop into your hands?"

"First, it's not my case. It's the FBI's. You'll have to take that question to Agent Brock. He's running that case. And, second, there are complications. That's all I can tell you."

"When can I see the autopsies?"

"You can see them after I'm able to understand them."

"That sounds mysterious. You thinking maybe this is connected to your sex trafficking case after all?"

"It's not *my* sex trafficking case either. I'm not going back there, Steffie—and you should not go back there either."

But Steffie's already back there. So, since the sheriff doesn't want to help, she must face that question herself. She must make certain there is no possible connection between last year's sex trafficking thing and this year's fake-ISIS thing. She tries to bring up Sheriff Faber's exact answer to her question, and she cannot remember him forbidding her to talk to Hasani. She looks up Hasani's number and punches the button.

"Hi, Hasani, Steffie Cobb calling from North Dakota. I've a philosophical musing question."

"Oh, this might be interesting. Wait a sec. I gotta pull over." The phone goes mute for twenty seconds. "Okay, Steffie, I can talk now. Wow! It's been ages. It's good to hear from you?"

"Yeah, Hasani, I know. Except this here's about business, and that means you won't feel so good once you hear my question." Steffie explains she's in Williston, and the ashes of a building they both know are cackling and smoldering right in front of her.

"Is that good or bad, Steffie?"

"I haven't the foggiest idea, but I'm wondering if there's a factoid in common between these two outrageous occurrences at this same hotel. Except, right now, Sheriff Faber would prefer I don't tell you what that factoid is."

"I understand what you're hinting, Steffie. How can I help?"

"If you understand what I've said, you're doing better than I am. I have no idea what's happening. That's why I called you. Can we chat for a few minutes about the history and geography of that sex ring thing and see if it starts any lights flashing in my memory unit?"

*   *   *

In last Tuesday's election, Texas transplant, Will Basehardt, upset the longtime existing state senator from the Williston area. Basehardt immediately started acting like he was the gorilla in the room. Unlike most Texas oil guys, he'd moved himself up to the tundra years ago, and he thinks of himself as one with those Dakota natives who are personally feeling the pain and uncertainty of the crash in world oil prices. Many residents are hemorrhaging just like he is, and they believe him when he promises to personally bring back high oil prices and reopen the oil fields. This, of course, is not something Basehardt can possibly do by himself— even if he is from Texas. It's something only the Saudi sheiks can do.

He cannot, by himself, make the price of Dakota oil cheaper than Arabian or Texas oil. And so he is telling the people now standing and cheering in front of him a big, fat, absolute downright lie. And he knows it's a lie because he, himself, is, at the same time he's speaking these words, also in the act of moving as fast as he can, much of his own equipment and money out of Dakota and into Texas. And he's hoping, and perhaps even praying—which he understands is the only way to get gods to work on your side—for additional acts of God that might ignite several more of the vacant facilities still standing behind him, even as he's speaking these lies to this crowd. The oil people in the crowd are yelling and screaming. They don't know what he's doing, but they're so desperate for the hemorrhaging to stop that they'll believe any story leaving his lips.

"West Virginia's suffering the same problem as you folks." He's said this continuously during his campaign, even though it's a lie, or at least a gross exaggeration. He reinforces the concept once again. "Just as our new president's gonna bring coal back, he and I are gonna bring Williston's oil back."

* * *

Steffie Cobb and Mayor Clem Allison are leaning against the front wall of Hurley's Pub, listening to Basehardt spew drivel.

"The same story happened in Ohio," Steffie says to the mayor. "A fracking contractor won a seat using a similar lie to convince out-of-work manufacturing workers. Salvation ain't gonna be swooping in from the clouds for any of those folks either. Nevertheless, folks voted men into office who actually promised such salvation."

"Basehardt's appeal sounds good," says Clem. "But everyone knows—if they'll only stick their heads out of their windows and into the haze hanging in the air here—that fossil fuel is gonna be dying. Sooner or later. Either it dies—or we all will."

* * *

In order to keep the fire lit under his supporters, and to counter all the evil that's swirling about Williston today, Basehardt is, he says, holding this "Thank-You Rally" for the people in his district who voted him in. He thinks it will be symbolically spectacular if he holds this rally in a place with still-smoldering ruins of the several buildings ISIS blew up a couple days ago as a backdrop. He thinks it might give a symbolic boost to the occasion. He's thinking of a Phoenix rising from the ashes of the failed regime of his predecessor. He's also thinking that exploding buildings frighten people, and the more he frightens them, the stronger they will support him. As he plows through the garbage of his speech, there are quite a few in this crowd, even those who voted for him, who are having second thoughts already—folks thinking he's lost his marbles, is drunk, or maybe both.

And it's three of those specific listeners—Gary, Hank, and Paul—who are the quite drunk ones in this crowd. Their own bar, the Drilling Platform, is now a smoldering pit of cinders in the oily background behind

Basehardt. Nevertheless, these three have found enough beer elsewhere to do the job. They've stepped through the portal to a land where normal definitions of what is true and false are unknowable.

Gary's already convinced himself that Basehardt will put that plane back in his hangar—and perhaps bring Jenny back from Philadelphia.

The crowd chants, "Save Dakota, save our oil! Save Dakota, save our oil!"

Will Basehardt steps up to the microphone array, and chants with them—at least the "Save our oil" part.

Hank der Ord jumps off the rails and yells, "You son of a bitch. We helped you. We dumped thousands into your campaign. Now, you gotta help us stop our commie governor from stealing our oil!"

Will Basehardt replies, "I don't think the legislature's gonna pass the governor's evil proposal. I plan to be president of your state senate next January for the spring session. I'll guarantee it won't pass. But even if those idiots do pass the governor's 'Subsurface Materials Ownership Act,' our new president promised me he'll fly out here and personally tear it up. It's an unconstitutional money grab by the elite politicos, and neither the president nor I will let it stand."

The crowd cheers, even though there are very few voters in the crowd, other than Basehardt, who currently own the rights to any of that oil. Basehardt's fellow Texans own most all the rights, and those guys don't vote in North Dakota.

"We need secure jobs for the working folks of Dakota. Believe me!" Will has learned that if you tell people they gotta "believe" him, they tend to do it.

"You can't take my land, you Commie Pinko!" shouts an agreeing well-lubricated voice from the crowd.

"How can anyone believe a word that blowhard says?" Mayor Allison asks. "He knows the president's not gonna come out here and force the Saudis to raise their oil prices so we can keep our hotels full. That ain't gonna happen. And I'll wager almost everyone in this crowd knows that ain't gonna happen. Hell, everyone's pulling up their own pipe up as fast as they can. Most everyone in this crowd will have their equipment in Texas by the summer."

Steffie says, "Is there a way to tell who owns which wells so we can tell which drillers are running for Texas."

"Actual ownership is a bit tricky to determine, Steffie. All we can know is which site drilling contractor manages which rigs. And we all know that no one in the oil business actually owns anything himself. Except the profits, of course. I think there are people who actually do own those."

"Is there a way I can substantiate which North Dakota wells our friend Basehardt owns?"

"Substantiate will never happen. Basehardt acts like a player, but I can't be sure he technically owns stuff. Could be he only collects the money that bubbles up off the top of the various mythical Texas partnerships he's connected to. These guys bury ownership deeper than their wells. You might ask the other players, Kathleen Carter of NAFCO, if you can find her. Or Peter Burns at Kendell and Figg, if you can find him, or J. D. Roseborough for BX&F. He is easier to find, but he doesn't know anyone or anything, doesn't talk much, and doesn't tell the truth much when he does."

"Okay, Mayor, enough of this little game of 'Who's got the Monkey.' Let me change the topic to something real—something knowledgeable people really care about. Are you picking Denver to repeat as Super Bowl champs?"

"That's not fair, Steffie. I'm trying to help you here."

"Ya could have fooled me, Mayor. I'm feel I'm getting absolutely nothing." She pulls away from the wall and checks her backpack zippers. "I'm sorry, Mayor. I don't mean to be snotty, but I'm absolutely exhausted. I'd best drive home. I'll take a long bath and fall asleep with a novel."

CHAPTER 22

INTRODUCING KATHLEEN
AND HER BUSINESS

WEDNESDAY, NOVEMBER 16, 2016

FOR THE LAST TWO YEARS, Leon's "Subsurface Materials Ownership Act" has been much discussed, but the legislature has never coalesced enough to actually bring the measure to a vote. But, given the results of the national election last week, and reports of Will Basehardt's rant in the office on Monday, and his fire-breathing press conference yesterday, Governor Rolfes realizes he better wake up and slap the pompous Basehardt hard and quick if he wants to maintain control of his message going into the future. Leon fears that the results of the recent election have slashed his timeline for finding a solution, perhaps to a month. He cannot wait until the spring legislative session as he'd planned to do. He's got to form this snowball quickly and start it down the hill immediately.

Leon's Subsurface Materials Ownership Act reacts to the fact that most all the rights to pump the oil hidden beneath the state are currently owned by out-of-state interests—mostly by Texans or ethereal, nonhuman, financial entities—that now can extract, sell, and pump Dakota's oil on their own schedule, with little or no regard to the interests of North Dakota. To correct this bizarre situation, Leon is proposing that the state of North Dakota, by edict, nullify all existing simple claims of mineral rights and then have the state simply claim its right to harvest that oil. This action will give the people of Dakota the ability to manage, and thus profit from, oil hidden beneath their state. His proposal will provide conditions similar to those now existing in Alaska and Alberta, most BLM lands, and even in most offshore areas.

After being governor for two years, Leon's convinced that the state absolutely must have the control over its own resources if it's ever going to operate under its sovereign capacity and not simply exist as a toy for Texans to play with. Because of the recent crash in oil prices and the introduction of oceans of much cheaper Texas oil into the pool, North Dakota must take that action immediately or risk becoming one giant hedge pool for all the massive Texas oil field profits. If North Dakota doesn't act immediately, the state economy and the state value will plummet because the state's only role will be as a hedge against the outrageous profits of Texas oil billionaires. And now, Leon senses that if he doesn't act immediately, the state and federal governments taking office in January—both driven by Texas oil guys—will be even less favorable to Dakota's needs.

And then there is the second big obstacle to the passage of his Subsurface Materials Ownership Act, and that is the reaction of the one half-Texan, half-North Dakotan, half-New Yorker, and half-carnivore who probably owns more oil rights claims than anyone else: his goddaughter, Kathleen Carter. He must either persuade her to honor her North Dakota roots and help him throw out the Texans or ruin her credibility as an opposing voice. Leon doesn't like his odds of succeeding with either of those options.

To address this problem at the highest level, the governor is, this morning, convening an emergency meeting of a core group of his allies and lobbyists. They are not meeting at the Capitol, but in the nonpublic conference room of Charlie Neubauer's Agribus Corporation headquarters in downtown Bismarck.

"My dear Dakota neighbors," Leon says. "We must make this move immediately. This afternoon, right after this meeting, I'm going to announce that I'm ordering an emergency session of the legislature next month, for two days only. Then, after the legislature approves the Subsurface Materials Ownership Act, I'll sign the thing."

"I don't like emergency sessions, Leon." Jared Murphy is the Republican senate leader from Williston. Just a couple weeks ago, he lost his seat in a dirty fight to Will Basehardt, who is now calling himself the president-elect's self-appointed representative in North Dakota. "I absolutely hate the damn things. Always have. But I'm behind you 100 percent on this idea, Leon. We have to secure the oil rights out there before Basehardt and his oil-soaked Texas buddies get into Washington. Otherwise, he'll grab every loose barrel of our oil he can for his big-oil partnerships in Houston."

Charlie Neubauer chairs the agribusiness sector of the coalition for Leon. "I would agree, Leon. You have to move quickly. And if you don't, you know somebody's gonna blow up more stuff out in Williston. Those damn Texans are blowing up our state, and this proposal is the only way I can see that allows us to take back some control over them. Please, Leon, North Dakota agribusiness needs this legislation. And we need it immediately."

*   *   *

That evening, Leon's busy at his mom's kitchen table, laying out papers, organizing stuff, and trying to schedule himself over the next weeks so that he can lobby the many elements of his population. He must convince them that his radical Subsurface Materials Ownership Act is good for their interests.

His mother walks over with two glasses of brandy and gives one to Leon. "Come into the den, son, and take a break."

"You're right, Mom. I think I hit a wall. There is just so much to do."

"You'll be okay. You've got a stronger case than you think. All the girls in my bridge club are with you. What more do you need?" She retreats to her favorite place on the left-hand cushion of the blue couch. "However, I think you may have forgotten one important oil player who you need to be standing behind you when you sign that bill into law a couple weeks from now."

"Okay, Mom. I'll bite. Who is that?"

"We both know that there is one player out there sloshing through the oil fields, who doesn't play by normal folks' rules. A player who almost certainly has playmates who actually might think about things like blowing up buildings and killing various people. Ya know who I'm talking about, don't you?"

"Kathleen? You're wrong. I have not forgotten about her. But you're also right. I'm a chicken, and I have been putting off taking that step. That's gonna be a very painful thing to do—and I am not a masochist."

"I suggest you kidnap her, and we'll keep her tied up in my basement here for a couple weeks until the heat dies down."

"That's a brilliant move, Mom. I know a specialized contractor I can use to make that happen."

"You have to be careful, dear. I'm just saying. She's going to be involved in some way or another, so you'd best consider that—and plan for it."

"I'm not sure anyone can plan for what she's going to do."

"But you and I know a couple things about her."

"Yeah, she is unpredictable and vicious."

His mom pays him no attention. "The first is that she has—in some way I can't come close to understanding—a sort of bipolar condition, one node of which drives her to do absolutely brutal things to people who get in her way. However, the other node drives her to strive to be— oh, I don't know—almost a reasonable and somewhat borderline lovable human being. I think she has positive feelings toward North Dakota, and specifically for you, Leon. You're the only one she comes close to respecting. Depending on which node she's operating under, she can either be a very dark knight with a high-voltage light saber or a respectable young woman in a frilly sundress."

"I can picture her in full body armor, Mom, but I can't imagine her doing frilly. Anyway, it's winter now, and she won't be wearing sundresses for a while. You're being too kind to her, and I know that's because of Nathan."

"Understand that her father, and your dear friend Nathan—he was almost a brother to you—was almost a son to me. I often talked with him as a mother would, and later in his life, such talks often concerned his Kathleen. He knew she was like him, smart as a whip, sly as a fox, and hard as a rock."

"Yeah, like two years ago up in Rugby. We all suspected she was involved in the killings of those hedge fund guys at her father's funeral. The FBI grilled her fiercely, but no evidence surfaced, and she walked out of their clutches victorious. She's slippery as a ghost."

"We know she owns people who know what matches are used for. And though she's a vicious corporate predator, and fully capable of blowing

95

things up to make a point or make some money, I truly believe she'd never execute young Somali men so casually. It doesn't fit whatever weird moral code she operates under."

"Though I believe an overzealous underling, hoping to make a few points with his boss, might perform some nefarious deed on his own—with the specific goal of separating the deed from Kathleen."

"I'm not sure, Mom. I'd rather think that underling would not long be alive. So, how the hell am I gonna find out which Kathleen I'm dealing with."

"You want me to talk to her mano a mano?"

"Will you quit the fooling around, Mom? I need to make serious headway here. We know nothing in the Williston oil fields happens without Kathleen knowing it's going to happen and when it's going to happen, and most of the time, she has her own fingers either causing it to happen or preventing it from happening."

"And don't forget, son, that she probably has more to gain, or maybe lose, than anyone else in the state if your special session law is accepted. You have to prepare her. And, I think, there's another problem with Kathleen—a major problem."

"Oh God, Mom, and what's that?"

"We both agree that Kathleen had nothing to do with those Somali boys' deaths? Killing like that is the act of a psychopath."

"So, you're thinking we got someone, other than Kathleen—some psychopath—romping around Williston? Who might that be?"

"I might take a guess, son. But what I do know is that if anyone knows who that unknown psychopath is, it's Kathleen. I'm certain she keeps a dossier on every other Texas player involved in the Williston oil game. She's got leverage on everyone. I guarantee she knows exactly who killed those boys. Your job is to pull that information out of her. Talk with her, son. But make sure your defenses are up—and your sword is ready."

"You're my mother. What are you doin' talking to me like that?"

"I'm hoping to motivate you. You gotta handle Kathleen with caution, like you'd do with TNT for instance."

Leon's mother is right about Kathleen Carter. She is a formidable and, for the most part, uncontrollable force. The hard part is that she reminds

Leon so much of her dad. Nathan and Leon had been sandbox buddies in grade school, played basketball together, and counseled and promoted each other until Nathan's heart gave out two years ago. Nathan selected Leon as Kathleen's godfather and trust fund administrator, and when he lay dying, Nathan made Leon swear to watch her back and keep her out of trouble. The difficult part for Leon is that Nathan and his daughter are so much alike. They're smart, sneaky, ambitious, and willing and able to stomp on anyone who gets in their way. They both played basketball— power forward—for, and then earned their law and MBA degrees from, Harvard. Both made Wall Street partner in minimum time and then quit New York to build their own business empires. Nathan returned to North Dakota. The daughter stayed in New York with her mom until she died and then moved to Houston to play with oil. Father and daughter were never friends and seldom talked. For most of Kathleen's life, Leon acted as the tether connecting these two high-spirited loners.

Two years ago, Kathleen had given Uncle Leon, the incoming governor of North Dakota, a piece of advice as an inauguration gift: "You must understand who you're dealing with, Uncle Leon. Texas oil partners become billionaires by being either damn smart or damn lucky. The smart ones can often sustain their run for quite some time, until they get unlucky. The lucky ones are continuously at risk of losing it all. A prudent investor just has to stay clear of those lucky guys because, sooner rather than later, they'll flame out. And because the total pool of money is a fixed quantity, any partner who flames out essentially throws his money back into the pot for the other successful partners to fight over. Like other forms of high-stakes poker, eventually one guy goes home with the entire pot—and everybody else loses. I plan on being that one guy left holding all the chips. And, Uncle Leon, you know in your heart, that's gonna happen."

"Kathleen doesn't take stupid chances, son. And we know she'll not be among the Texas oil partners flaming out. Those losers are the ones who can't do it on their own. They're the ones requiring acts of God to keep them solvent."

CHAPTER 23

INTRODUCING SIMBA, KATHLEEN'S CARNIVORE

A BOUT FORTY MILES SOUTH OF Williston, deep in the woods near the border with the Theodore Roosevelt National Forest, is the rock-surfaced abode that is, not unlike an Anasazi dwelling, carved into the rock-strewn scree pile on the east side of a small unnamed mesa. It's a bit over five miles from the nearest paved road and expertly camouflaged so it's almost impossible to recognize as a potential living accommodation when viewed from a scant hundred-yard distance. Deer, coyotes, snakes, and hawks seem not to realize it's a foreign thing in the landscape. And there's an elderly mountain lion who often sunbathes atop the rock wall buttressing the front porch.

Today, the sun, though low in the sky, is strong, and warms the rock, so Simba's lolling atop it. That lion's not the only carnivore feeling secure enough to nap in the sun here. Not twenty feet away, on the inside of the reflection-proof glass wall, the strong sunlight also warms Kathleen Carter. All six foot three of her is spread out inert in a Navajo hammock hung in front of the blazing fireplace.

Teresa Cruz, who's been keeping her houses and cooking her meals for fifteen years, enters the central room and asks Kathleen if she'd like a glass of port. She knows Kathleen well, and so already knows her answer, and she quietly places the glass on a coaster on the tray cantilevered out from the wall next to Kathleen's hammock without Kathleen needing to answer her question. "Welcome home, Miss Carter. We all missed you."

"Thank you, Teresa," she whispers and then smiles.

Teresa moves to the other side of the hearth. "And here's your ouzo, Mr. T." Teresa puts two small glasses of the clear liquid on his coaster.

Trevor smiles. "Thank you, Teresa."

"So, Trevor," Kathleen says, "tell me, what's the story with the explosions and fires? I leave for a couple weeks, my country falls apart, and my Williston blows to smithereens."

"I've been poking around. We know of one contractor, works for L. D. Roseborough, one Gary Gralapp, who's been promoting the idea that the huge amounts of money folks have lost on North Dakota real estate investments could be leveraged by having ISIS firebomb said real estate, claiming such damage was caused by an act of God, claiming it was therefore a natural disaster, and covered by insurance."

"Although that idea does have a certain creative flair, no reasonable insurance company would buy it, right? It's a stupid, counterproductive idea."

"However, somebody appears to have bought into that screwball idea. We know of at least one Texas oil partner who is stupid enough to consider initiating such a scam, don't we? And look who is just up that food chain from Gralapp. L. D. Roseborough's there, then next link up, boom, there's the 'big boss,' Basehardt.

"So, my view is Basehardt planned it. He had L. D. execute it, and Gralapp spread the rumor around so when everything went boom, everybody thought they'd be reaping in the insurance. That's where my money is. I have Basehardt telling L. D. to do it and explaining how to do it. And I wouldn't be surprised to learn he held his hand while he did it."

Kathleen takes a sip of the port. "What are the odds that anyone's gonna find an insurance policy that's gonna payoff on that?"

"That'll never happen. I wonder which partnership string controls Basehardt's money stream? Those are the guys who are going to get hit hard."

"I don't know which partners control his management master partnership for the entities he runs. I have ideas—but nothing solid. Could be many guys."

"I understand blowing up the drilling platforms," says Trevor. "That kind of 'accident' happens all the time. What I don't understand is using ISIS suicide bombers, or whoever they were, as props. Why do that?"

"It's tied up with national politics, Trevor. The new president-elect says Islamic terrorists are gonna bomb our oil wells. Both Basehardt and his president-elect have been pushing hard for US energy independence. That means using our expensive local oil instead of buying the cheap Middle Eastern stuff. The US can make money exporting LNG and gasoline, but our coal and fracked oil, and Alberta's oil-sand stuff, are too expensive or too dirty to export. Plus, historically, it's been against the law to export it. If we start exporting high-priced crude, that's going to irritate the Arabs. Some folks think that might start an oil war. The president-elect says he's gonna bomb the ISIS wells. Then ISIS may blow up our Dakota oil so we can't export it in competition with them, understand that? That'll keep oil expensive."

"It's too convoluted for me, Kathleen. I doubt it will ever work. Most folks link ISIS with the Saudis, the dead guys are both Sunni, right? So, even if their ISIS buddies are terrorizing us, does anyone want to boycott cheap Saudi oil? I don't think so. Cheap oil is cheap. That's why people will buy it."

"That's an interesting question though. And the answer will depend on how the next couple weeks play out. Right now, everyone wants to move their drills to Texas and let their stuff up here rust in storage. I'm gonna play an asymmetrical game, Trevor. I'm in the process of buying out K&F and most of the little guys here at fire sale prices. That'll give them cash to transfer their operations to Texas. And by so doing, I isolate Basehardt. I'll force him to stay in Dakota, in a minority position, so he'll not be able to move back to Texas. I'll force him to hemorrhage. I'll break his back, and then, I will break his will."

"I don't understand, Kathleen."

"Okay. As of today, three Texas oil field firms—me, Kendell Figg, and Basehardt—control more than 70 percent of the Bakken. Given the new development of cheap oil in Texas, Brazil, and Africa, we all gotta move quickly. I understand next month my favorite governor's subsurface bill will kick in. By February 1, Kendell Figg will be totally gone. I'll be up to near 70 percent, and a few small independents will be at about 15 percent, which leaves Basehardt with 15 percent. He'll be in a vise, unable to jettison his unproductive wells, and he'll be forced to work with me. Then, if oil prices ever hit sixty dollars again—and if they do, it'll only be for a brief time—I'll be positioned to negotiate a monopoly with Uncle Leon for pumping and piping in North Dakota, while Basehardt will have to dangle and die. This here's a poker table strategy going to be playing out. The game's now called Texas hold 'em. Or maybe Texas drop 'em. Huh, Trevor?"

CHAPTER 24

LEON VISITS WHAT'S LEFT OF WILLISTON

Thursday, November 17, 2016

L EON'S FLOWN OUT TO WILLISTON early this morning, and he finds himself eating take-out sausage biscuits and orange juice from a folding tray in Clem Allison's office, while the mayor also feeds him an itemized proposal for emergency reconstruction funding.

"The Saudis cutting their oil prices and the Texans discovering puddles of cheap crude are two textbook examples of emergency situations happening beyond our capacity for local control. And, Governor, don't forget the damage caused by those strange 'ISIS' attacks. They certainly were not perpetrated by any force interior to North Dakota. It's a third textbook case of out-of-state interests causing unanticipated destruction to my city."

"That episode is so unreal, Clem. Any progress on the investigation?"

"I'm sad to report that we've got pretty much nothing. We've found a second Somali mock-ISIS soldier's carcass in a smoldering building. That's two young men, dressed like they're acting in a stage play, left behind for us to find. Also, we found two employees trapped in that bar—the FBI's keeping those bar deaths off the books for the time being. Beyond that, all the high-priced terror experts and FBI special agents have got absolutely nothing. At least nothing they're telling me—except that those pyromaniacs knew what they were doing. The torching of that Drilling Platform bar seems to prove that."

"How is that?"

"The Drilling Platform was the only occupied building targeted. The Vikings pregame started at eleven, and several customers were inside. So, whoever blew up that building was aware of that and specifically choreographed his inferno in stages such that the far end of the vacant warehouse next door went up first. The couple dozen people in the bar were blown off their barstools, causing some fairly ugly bumps and scratches but no major injuries. Of course, everybody in the bar ran for the doors. Only after the place clears out does the Drilling Platform explode. Somebody sequenced the explosions precisely to avoid human casualties—except the bartender on duty and a waitress got caught. They stayed to secure the place and got smashed by the second blast, which was set off inside the bar."

"And you said the dead ISIS guy was also found inside the bar, right?"

"Yes, Governor, and like the others, he was dead way before the fire started."

"You're telling me the dead ISIS terrorist was in the same bar with a bartender and waitress? I can't even begin to imagine how that could happen."

"I'm at the end of my rope. I can't run a city when folks are using it as staging for whatever ugly play they're putting on. And I've got no idea what's coming next. Everyone's worried about what's gonna blow, and nobody's working. Folks are visiting family out of town. The town's shut down. Except for the news media—they're still buzzing around.

"I could authorize National Guard troops to do overnight watch. It might prevent more dead ISIS fighters from sneaking around and planting bombs in other places."

"I know that's a worthless idea, Leon. It sounds stupid because there is no ISIS connection, but it might not be a bad idea. Maybe it'll give my people a secure feeling. Maybe they'll get some sleep—and maybe they'll come back to work."

"I'll declare Williston an official disaster area. That'll access federal grant programs and help you back to your feet. Get you funding for cleanup, utility reconstruction, and other things."

"Thank you, Leon. Now we gotta talk about the possibility of one other death."

"What's that mean?"

"It means if you don't do something pretty quick about shutting Will Basehardt's mouth, I'm gonna shoot that pompous jerk myself."

"I don't think any emergency authorization includes approvals for murder, Clem, but I suppose I could have Margie amend the standard wording in the federal guidelines."

* * *

After their quick breakfast meeting, Mayor Allison drives Leon past the various still-smoldering pieces of Williston. Several blocks of First and Second Street are closed for vehicles, and fire crews are mopping up and investigating the various sites. The podium used for other updates and messages, like the one Basehardt blasted out two days ago, still stands where it first stood, and a couple hundred people mill about in the street in front of it, anxious to hear the governor.

Right here, two days ago, while Williston's buildings smoked and crackled behind him, Will Basehardt ignited an additional firestorm speaking to supporters at a "thank-you rally." Mayor Allison pleaded with Leon to counter Basehardt's flame-throwing by coming to Williston, throwing retardant on that blaze, and perhaps igniting a backfire of his own. Though Leon resisted, Mayor Allison pressured him to fly into Williston and do the deed.

Leon hadn't seen it coming. He hadn't even admitted the possibility that his Subsurface Materials Ownership Act was in any political trouble out here. All the oil-savvy locals understood the situation. However, Leon had forgotten—or had not realized—that Williston is infused with an ocean of Texas oilmen throwing around their Texas money and their Texas ideas.

Leon understands he must use a different message to counter Basehardt. He's got to step up the defense of his Subsurface Materials Ownership Act immediately—while pushing hard on the offense. He'll turn Basehardt's aggressive behavior against him and make Basehardt the reason North Dakota needs his subsurface legislation. The state must rethink and restructure its attitude with respect to the control of its own resources—specifically its deep, expensive-to-retrieve oil reserves. The reason North Dakota needs to employ this fix is precisely because of the actions of Texas oil guys like Basehardt.

Leon stands behind the podium where previous news conferences have taken place. The still smoldering ashes of the Bakken View Hotel gurgle softly behind him. It smells awful. A crowd of several hundred—both townspeople and oil people—gather on Second Street in front of the podium.

"People of Williston," Leon says, "during the past few days, your city's witnessed three explosive attacks, each of which has been ignited by out-of-state interests, with the intent to benefit out-of-state agendas. These three incidents were set by perpetrators who have no North Dakota interests in mind. You folks living in Williston, and to be honest, every citizen of North Dakota, were attacked by what I'm considering to be a foreign power. And I'm strongly suggesting that foreign power is not ISIS—but Texas oil."

A truck driver standing in front wearing a BX&F cap yells, "There were two ISIS attacks, Governor, not three. You liberals can't even count."

"The problem is with you, sir!" Leon sticks a finger at him. "You are the one not counting an explosive attack. That third explosion, the one you didn't count, was the verbal bomb Mr. Basehardt flung at you two days ago, from this very location. In case you missed it, that bomber is himself, a member of several Texas oil interests, most likely representing the same entities that brought you explosions number one and two."

Instantaneous explosions, of two sorts, rise up from the crowd—a positive outpouring of cheering and yelling and a negative eruption of booing and hissing. Emotion swings in the crowd are fueled by much rage, a little beer—even at this early hour—and, of course, by oil.

"We in North Dakota must immediately unite behind our own principles and protect ourselves from these unprincipled Texas carnivores. And the one way to do this is to protect ourselves from future outrageous behavior. For the past two years, I've been proposing that the state of North Dakota take control of our own mineral rights, including oil, that we're fortunate to find hidden beneath our prairie. Folks, that oil is our oil—North Dakota oil. The Great Spirit who allocates such things did not give it to Texas. And we must take back the right to harvest it.

"It's necessary to pass such protective legislation quickly. I'm calling a special session of the legislature to meet, debate, and pass that legislation. I'll consider that to be a great Christmas present for the good people of North Dakota."

There's both cheering and jeering. Folks yell, scream, and smack strong language.

Leon detects threats of violence directed against both him and his plan. "And, in addition to all the arguments I have been making for the past two years, there's new stronger evidence that we must move forward immediately. We've got huge additional problems to worry about.

"Several oil industry sources have, in the past weeks, announced the discovery, down in Texas, of massive new oil fields, many times larger than our Bakken Formation. And their new deposits are easier to develop and more efficient to extract than our Bakken oil. That means our oil fields are no longer competitive; perhaps it even means they're worthless. In the short term, they can be used as hedges against big oil's Texas profits, but it surely means North Dakota and Williston are going to lose. Once those Texas fields are running strong, our Bakken fields will almost surely die. In two years, Williston could be a ghost town.

"The only way we in North Dakota can come out of this fast-approaching massive transition alive is for us to seize ownership control of the oil hidden beneath our state, so that Texans cannot use their losses from it as a hedge against their outrageous profits from their new Texas fields. It is the only way we can stay alive, folks. The only way we survive!

"If Texas wants to use North Dakota as a short-term hedge, that's fine, but they'll have to pay North Dakota for that right. That way, it'll be something we in Dakota can control.

"In one rather strange way, the fires of recent days have actually been a positive thing, or at least a wake-up call, and perhaps that's a positive thing. I've just informed your mayor that I'm declaring Williston and the Bakken area a federal disaster area, which qualifies it for federal funds for the cleanup and transition. That means that I, as governor, can make certain decisions responding to the negative forces and bring the state back to a healthy situation with respect to outside forces.

"With that as incentive, I'm calling a special legislative session to approve the Subsurface Materials Ownership Act and protect our resources and our economy by seizing ownership of the harvesting rights for materials resting under out state. We'll fight against Texas interests, and we'll increase our leverage. We'll become a stronger player in the oil wars we know are coming. Thank you!"

*   *   *

Four days after downtown Williston exploded, there are still hot coals hidden in the rubble. Mayor Clem Allison has been told nothing more is going to collapse and that he should expect no more burnt bodies to be found. A light freezing mist starts, making every step an adventure, and Allison is seriously thinking of sending everyone home and trying again when the weather's more accommodating and it's safe enough to tour the ruins. But he perseveres, and after the tour and its resulting commotion dies down, Mayor Allison drives Leon back to the airport. Throughout the drive, Mayor Allison remains in petition mode. He needs more police, a state probe on insurance fraud, a massive environmental cleanup effort, and a hundred other things to keep his small city from looking like an ISIS-style video game.

"Thank you for coming to Williston, Governor. We really need massive help."

"I know that, Clem, but as you can certainly understand, our state revenues are also down. We have a billion-dollar shortfall in state revenues projected for this fiscal year. And we have huge upgrade projects that are now stalled or left half-constructed. And we've money in accounts dedicated to those projects. I just can't stop in the middle of a project and switch the money over to Williston. State infrastructure construction financing doesn't work like that."

"But we are hemorrhaging out here, Leon. You gotta find me something."

"That's where the federal disaster relief determination can help. Once it is accepted by the feds, I believe that designation gives me power, as governor, to reschedule existing federal construction accounts, like your huge airport expansion project. Maybe we can shift some money to short-term disaster relief. We'll then push the airport project schedule out a couple years. Everyone in the state's in the same boat, Clem. Tax revenues are way down, and infrastructure spending is killing us. We all need some of that mythical cash."

"Damn it, Leon, do you suppose there's any way of getting money from Texas to help?"

"That's an interesting idea. Maybe we send those invisible oil guys in Houston a cleanup bill? I'll have to look into it. And you're right, Clem, most of the trucks causing such damage to our roads have Texas plates. They're Texas trucks, and Texas equipment's riding on those trucks. Texans are wrecking our roads and draining our aquifers. Maybe I'll ask my attorney general to send the state of Texas an invoice. Wouldn't that be something? Beats me standing on the street corner with a tin cup and a cardboard sign saying, 'Please donate to rebuild our infrastructure!'"

Leon is correct. There's no money left in North Dakota. North Dakota's lost one hundred thousand workers in a year and a half, and oil revenue is down by 40 percent—and it's most probably going lower.

"I can't tell how much further we have to fall," says Leon. "I know we're well outside our statistical ranges, but there's something else. Can you tell me if anyone on your list of Texas folks working in Williston might have the nerve to engineer those bits of—let's call it *terrorism* for the time being—that have been happening in your fair city?"

"Terrorism, my foot! My head of public works, a guy from Baton Rouge named Ruben, used the term 'Louisiana lightning,' and I think he's right. You mix desperate people, vacant buildings, and big mortgages, and you get fires."

"You're thinking there'll be more terrorism?"

"I guarantee there'll be more fires, perhaps more killing, but it's got nothing to do with terrorism—no matter what ISIS shows on their website. My explosive problem is not with Iraq or Yemen; it's with Houston. I'm gonna need massive investigating and squadrons of state and federal lawmen. I need help all over, Leon."

*   *   *

That afternoon, Leon and Steffie return to Bismarck. Leon is treating her and the crew in his office to coffee and popcorn.

Steffie says, "Like a good investigative reporter, I've been investigating things, Leon. I've found the owner of the ranch where the first oil rigs blew up. It's a longtime Williston farm couple who've retired to Arizona. They lease land to a neighbor for grazing. Another lease accommodates BX&F Exploration, which works for the anonymous LLC that claims the oil rights beneath their land. BX&F owns or controls the drilling rigs and other equipment they need to extract the oil. I see quite a few BX&F signs around —on oil rigs, trucks, even baseball caps.

"I stopped by the site and talked to an engineer, a friendly guy from Louisiana named Cletus. He was wearing a yellow and white safety flimsy with BX&F stamped on the back in big block letters. He told me most of the fires have burned themselves out, though two wells still are belching black smoke and orange flames. Cletus was analyzing the ruins and trying to ascertain if the pumping station he left Friday in pristine condition is salvageable."

"Pristine condition?"

"Those were Cletus's words, Leon. It's hard for me to believe this guy, though a polite and respectful chap, is aware of what the word *pristine* means. I doubt that word has ever been used to describe an oil drilling operation. He was polite, but he was firm. He wouldn't let me walk through the gate, but he did explain the workings of his formerly *pristine* equipment.

"He told me BX&F has—or when he left for last weekend, it had— eight active wells on that site working in a unified way to extract oil. All eight are drilled approximately five miles deep. Once his eight pipes are drilled to that depth, they're turned ninety degrees to the horizontal, then fanned out at forty-five-degree intervals and drilled horizontally into a circular field for distances varying from half a mile to two miles. He said all the drilling is—or until last Sunday, was—coordinated by a mobile laboratory consisting of four truck-trailer-sized modules filled with computers and periodically staffed by various engineers. Dozens of trucks visit the site every day, bringing sand, water, and chemicals to storage silos and removing the oil from the holding tanks.

"Though many drilling sites are not enclosed, BX&F surrounded this well cluster with a chain-link fence and a gate letting on to County Road 342. The fence protects the 'super-advanced proprietary equipment' that Cletus tells me BX&F has stuffed onto this site. What this fencing means to the sheriff—and I concur—is it suggests if some miscreant wants to set a bomb next to an oil drilling rig, he could find plenty of easier targets around without locked metal fences. The miscreant who blew these drilling rigs up must have had a hard-edged reason to blow up these specific rigs with the big orange BX&F signs."

"So, Steffie, you're telling us this was not a casual target," says Larry Oosterhaus. "You think someone specifically wanted to damage BX&F's 'advanced proprietary equipment' or send them some powerful message?"

"Except Cletus insisted the equipment is 'super-advanced.'"

"Whatever," says Leon. "So, knowing you, you must have talked to Cletus's boss at BX&F, right? What's his story?"

"Well, guys, here is where my serious investigation starts to go off the rails."

"What does that mean? I think I asked a straightforward question."

"I haven't been able to find BX&F yet. I've been told the B in the title probably stands for Basehardt, though I'm not sure there is a real company named BX&F. Turns out Cletus actually works for a subcontractor called Roseborough Drilling."

Leon says, "So … what does Roseborough Drilling have to say about having their oil equipment blown to smithereens?"

"I'm still working on that. I can't find a real person to talk to yet. Cletus told me if I needed information, I should talk to a guy named L. D. Roseborough. He gave me a phone number and said that would get me to Roseborough's secretary, Mary C., who would answer everything for me. Cletus has never met Mary C. They talk on the phone, but he doesn't know where she's physically located. He thinks maybe in Houston because most of the guys are from Houston. And Mary C. sure sounds like she's from Houston."

"This is getting ridiculous," says Leon. "So, okay, what does Mary C. say."

"Mary C. is central casting for a stone wall at the front desk. And, boy, is she good at it. Even a top-notch reporter gal like me gets stonewalled— and that doesn't happen often. Seems to me, Roseborough Drilling does not have any 'Office for Media Relations' anywhere in the vast virtual office spread out behind Mary C.'s desk."

Leon gets up. "Anybody else need an orange juice?" He goes over to the bar fridge and removes a bottle for himself. "Okay, then, Miss Reporter Lady, I'll take another tack. You didn't by any chance talk with the owner of the land, snug in his snowbird condo in Tucson, did you?"

"No. Turns out I couldn't do that either. And the reason is that those particular snowbirds are not currently in Arizona. They apparently booked a monthlong cruise through the Mediterranean. At least that's what their son's wife says."

"I believe they have phones in Europe," says Larry. "Just talked to my cattle broker in Latvia yesterday."

"Give me a break, Larry. I tried. Those folks in Arizona are not snowbirds. They are permanent residents, and their son is apparently living in his folks' farmhouse on the acreage now. Though I couldn't talk with that son either. He is rather conveniently incommunicado, ice fishing with friends in northern Alberta, and not yet aware his backyard has blown up. At least that's what his wife told me, and I did actually talk with her, or someone who said she's his wife, and someone, I'd wager, who learned about stone walls from Mary C. Oh, yeah, and it's this wife who made that second 9-1-1 call complaining about her rattling plates."

"Seems all their travel plans are timed perfectly," says Larry. "That's more than a bit convenient, isn't it?"

"Seems those Somali boys got awful lucky, huh?" says Steffie. "They pick a Sunday morning when the owners are in Greece, the son's in an ice fishing hut, and their tenant—who should be drilling oil—is hiding in a file drawer in Houston."

"Those boys are not that lucky," says Leon. "Somebody found them clomping about setting explosives, or perhaps doing something else, and killed them. Not many lucky guys end up in the morgue. I'm sorry, Steffie. I'm getting frustrated. Let's switch topics again. Have you found anything more about Williston's downtown fires?"

"That's also a strange story. Seems all the several separate businesses, including the four cruddy hotels and the diesel truck garage, each had different owners, and every separate building was owned by a different LLC. And they were all built on pieces of land that are owned by still different LLCs. Most all the building leases are handled by an agent called Pumpkinseed, LLC. Turns out Pumpkinseed is one of several LLCs whose property is managed by Ashton Minot/Property Management, that's AM/PM, LLC which also manages dozens of properties for other LLCs in the area."

"Hey, Larry," says Leon. "You remember the good old days when your dad owned his entire farm up in Rugby, all by himself?"

"Yeah. He owned the barn, the tractor, and the pickup that he made deliveries with. He owned everything himself. He, however, wasn't much of a global businessman. For better or worse, that's all changed now. Even I have a separate LLC, in effect a separate business, set up to ship my pregnant cows to each separate country. I've got a separate LLC to buy my cattle feed and another to take care of spreading manure. One has to spread the responsibility around now like, well, that manure, I guess, huh? It's the way you work now. A guy needs multiple limited partnerships and limited liability corporations to protect his investments and to limit liability—just in case his cows poop in the wrong place."

"And, I am thinking, to hide his revenue from the taxman?" says Leon.

"I don't think *hide* is the right word, Leon," says Larry. "Hiding's illegal. I think of it more like camouflage. Camouflaging stuff is perfectly legal."

"Enough semantics, boys," says Steffie. "Does your *Corporate Dictionary of Confusing Terms* say the fires set in these buildings are called arson, or maybe, I can call them *controlled burns intended to clear the place for urban renewal?*"

"Sheriff said separate fires were set in each building. Seems a stretch to think all these various buildings independently required a controlled burn in the same afternoon, huh? All these fires choreographed so precisely, aggressively push the thing toward very professional arson."

"That—and the explosive devices that were used. Fire is one thing. Many people have fires. Explosives are something else. Few folks use powerful explosives for remodeling."

"Good point, Larry."

"So ... whoever did the torching worked for the building owner?"

"That's *owners*—plural—and I'm positive *torching* is correct. The buildings I've been able to trace are all in receivership and have building and business LLCs hiding the ownership. One touch point to reality is the leasing agent over in Minot who represents about half the properties. They, for some reason, are a real business—with real people sitting behind real desks. I'm not sure how that happened."

"So … what is their tale? How are they reacting?"

"AM/PM's been around for a couple dozen years. It's a pre-oil-boom company. Talked to Amanda Maycomber, she's the AM part—and her husband, Paul, is the PM part. She seemed overwhelmed by the fire. She accepts it was arson, but she seems honestly devastated by the loss—even as she maintains it did come at the right, or at least the convenient, time. She's not expecting the owners to rebuild. She expects they'll take any insurance money and run south to Texas."

"Did she have any thoughts about why those specific buildings were targeted?"

"Though she cannot know financial details, she assumes were all underwater. There are still enough vacant and so-far un-torched buildings to keep arsonists busy for several weeks."

"So … she's expecting more fires?"

"Everybody I talked to expects more fires. I feel sorry for Mayor Allison. His town is burning to the ground around him, and he finds himself powerless to stop it. And since I'm the reporter, I gotta find out who benefits from all these fires?"

"Well, what are you doing sitting in my fuzzy, overstuffed chair? You gotta move, right?"

"I'm gonna move, Leon. You're right about that. I'm flying down to Houston tonight. That's where many of the LLCs and MLPs of the vacant underwater properties are registered. Maybe I'll find a real person to talk to. Maybe I'll find a partner who knows how to use a blowtorch."

CHAPTER 25

KATHLEEN EXPLAINS INSURANCE COVERAGE TO GARY

KATHLEEN'S DARK BLUE FORD PICKUP enters the gravel yard and parks adjacent to the overhead door. A bent rusted sign claims that particular stall is reserved for "official visitors." She thinks the small white letters stenciled on her truck door just under the windows, "The Great North American Fracking Corp.," qualify it to park here.

"We classify as visitors, right? Since we got our oil-soaked fracking outfits on." Both she and Trevor wear ancient, oil-stained Houston Oilers ball caps.

"Sure, Kathleen." Trevor points to a white Ram pickup with twin chrome pipes rising vertically behind the cab and a full rack of running lights strung between them. "That's Gary's beast."

"He's in a visitor's space."

"He's got no visitors, Kathleen. Nobody does. That word is past tense in Williston."

"Thing needs a wash, Trevor. Can't believe he's been so busy he can't run the thing through a wash."

"This ain't Houston, Kathleen. Dakota guys, unlike Texas guys, are proud of their mud."

They approach the gray unpainted steel door inset with an eye-level wire glass window. "Gralapp Construction" is painted carelessly in black block letters above the window.

Trevor turns the knob and swings the door open, and they walk into the space.

A long counter on the left is piled with UPS and FedEx boxes. Tools and equipment are strewn around. Another door, straight ahead, leads to a garage or shop. A man and a woman are bent over a desk, intent on some paperwork, and pay little attention to their visitors.

After about thirty seconds, Trevor drawls, "Mornin', folks."

The guy looks up. "Can I help? What ya guys need?"

"We need to talk, Gary. It's private."

"Right now?"

"Yup," says Trevor. "That the office?" He points at the door and heads right for it.

Kathleen waits for Gary and then follows him.

Trevor closes the door, and Gary walks over and leans against the desk. "Who are you guys? What ya want?"

"It's your lucky day, Gary," Kathleen says. "We're from your insurance company."

Gary goes limp. "I … I don't understand. Is that good or bad? You gonna kill me? Or what?"

"If you expect to be alive one month from now, you must listen very carefully," says Trevor. "You're on a narrow path. It's mined and booby-trapped. So, one misstep," he slaps his open palm on the desktop, "and boom!"

Gary, even seeing the hand come down and contact the desk, jumps at the noise.

"This dump is gonna follow your Drilling Platform into real estate hell."

"I don't follow—"

"It's your buddy L. D., Gary," says Trevor. "He set those fires for BX&F."

"I don't know about that."

"Sure you do. Says so in your notebook here." He holds up Gary's black business notebook. "And this also tells us who killed those Somalis—and who paid for it all. Pretty powerful stuff in here, Gary."

Gary lunges at it. "That book's my insurance policy. How'd you get that?"

"You got rotten security around here, Gary. But the upside? You do take good notes. And that means L. D. will soon be toast. But that also means L. D.'s boss will be coming after you once he finds out it was you who knew about his insurance scam. I'm certain you don't want to be anywhere near Williston when that happens."

"Take it easy." Kathleen plants herself in front of Gary—she's three inches taller and many times more fit. She grabs his shoulders and roughly massages them. "You are tense, Gary. You gotta loosen up. Gotta understand the new paradigm. Not only are we now your insurance company"—Trevor waves the little notebook in his face—"but now you are also my insurance. So ... we have a reason to keep you safe. I told you it's your lucky day, Gary. You're my get-out-of-jail-free card, Gary. We're gonna keep you safe ... and let's all of us hope we can keep you pretty much alive."

CHAPTER 26

SEEMS THERE'S A SNOW MACHINE IN THE LONE STAR STATE

FRIDAY, NOVEMBER 18, 2016

LEON AND LARRY EACH RECLINE in their own recliners, sipping coffee, as they watch *NFL Today*. They haven't said a word for several minutes.

Leon's mom comes into the room from the kitchen where she's finished her after-dinner chores. "You two goons sleeping already? Lazy SOBs."

"Have a heart, Mom," says Leon. "Larry and I've just completed perhaps the worst week any governor of any state has ever had. We're physically bushed and emotionally drained. We deserve peace and quiet."

"And also, Mom," says Larry. "That fine meal requires every bit of attention from my body to properly process it. I don't have energy left to dance and sing."

"Well, excuse me, you two prissy youngsters. Should I find you chores? Maybe keep your blood flowing?"

"Jeez, Mom. Sit down and behave yourself. Tell us fairy tales about life back when the world knew how to laugh."

Her phone—her landline on the end table—rings. She looks at the little screen, pushes the button, and puts the thing to her ear. "Evening, Steffie. It's good to hear you're still alive and kicking. We women have to keep alert so's the guys can relax from a hard day workin' in the fields."

"What the devil did I interrupt this time, Mom?"

"I got a couple old, worn-out men in this room who don't want to take me out dancing tonight. What good is Friday night if we girls can't go out and party?"

Leon walks over and puts his hand out. "The phone, please, Mom."

She smiles at him and gives him the phone.

"Hi, Steffie," says Leon. "I'm gonna put you on speaker so Larry and Mom can hear you too. There! So … how the boys down in Houston treating you?"

"I'm not a happy camper, guys. I just spent several hours fending off this unbearably hot Houston sun while trying to find BX&F Exploration—to find that those uppercase letters exist only on paper. And I really doubt they're even that substantial. They're probably only electronic blips on somebody's computer screen. Apparently, despite all those nifty yellow signs they've plastered all over Williston, there's no physical aspect to BX&F Exploration."

"No physical aspect? What the hell does that mean?"

"I found a fellow sleuth down here at the *Houston Chronicle*. He's been helping me trace several partnership strings through their expertly designed mazes. Since he's from Houston, he's developed a certain experience crawling around and lookin' for nonphysical aspects. And, it turns out, BX&F Exploration is one of the paper-only exploration outfits owned by a separate class-2 limited master partnership named BX&F Management Services, Inc."

"Glad you've got that figured out," says Leon.

"Take it easy on him, dear," says his mom. "Our boys have had a rough day, and they need their sleep. So, you talk to me. What does BX&F Management Services say about their equipment getting blown into the sky?"

"Well, to be honest, my new sleuth friend, Jimmy, could find no real BX&F Management Services either. They are also a paper firm, run by another class-2 partnership. But Jimmy did find me a guy who personally answers a physical phone and who assured me multiple times that he has a real desk in a real office, somewhere in the same space-time continuum."

"No science fiction, Steffie … physical stuff only … please."

"Okay. Jimmy directed me to a large fellow, Truman Potts, who led me to believe he actually works in a big room filled with other people working for the same firm, located on the fourth floor of a sprawling unmarked corporate castle, resting quietly in a generic office park north of Houston, out near the airport. That Jimmy, he's a magician."

"I know you sleuths get excited by this stuff," says Leon, "but I really don't care how you traced 'em. Did you find some guy sitting at some desk in Houston, who had some sort of control over a few oil wells in North Dakota?"

"Actually? No, I don't think I can be that specific, but ... technically ..."

"Come on, Steffie. Did you find anything out? I need facts. Did this guy, Potts, actually talk with you?"

"I've made progress. I've talked to a gentleman in a business suit, the aforementioned Mr. Potts, who told me that he did, indeed, do a lot of sitting at that specific desk where the phone, on which he talked to me, was firmly attached. Though he and I did most of our talking in a fairly swanky visitors' lounge with a flow of what I assume was either crude oil, or perhaps dark chocolate, bubbling over a stack of some faux-rock construction in the corner, and where he treated me to a liquid in a chilled glass with a very thin stem."

"You talkin' fine wine or that crude bubbling over that rock?"

"Though he treated the stuff like fine wine, it tasted like Lone Star to me. And right there in that lounge, drinking beer from a wine goblet, he activated his snow machine. Now, that's a device I wasn't expecting to encounter way down south, here in Texas."

"Steffie! Cut it out. Just tell me if you found out something—or hang up the phone and let me get back to ESPN, will ya?"

"So, Steffie," Leon says, "did you ask this guy, Mr. Potts, if he thought a couple teenage Somali boys could, all by themselves, walk the path you blazed through the bureaucratic quagmire and trace the ownership chain through three class-2 master partnerships to him at his desk in an office park in the suburbs of Houston? Seems a fairly impressive piece of detective work for a couple Somali teenagers."

"It's only two class-2 partnerships, Leon, but I get your point. I'll bet very few Somali boys can actually do that on their own. I'm also guessing the information flow goes from the top down to those Somali kids. Therefore, both Mr. Potts and yours truly know something else is going on."

"Had Potts heard the bad news yet … that his equipment's been blown to smithereens by ISIS terrorists?"

"He artfully dodged that question—and he got downright snooty when I asked him if he had activated the insurance claim yet."

"I'll bet he did."

"I'm guessing Potts is not used to talking to the press—or talking to anybody but other machines—because he does not have the armor or the skills to prevent a reporter's piercing questions to bounce off him without making an impact. He quickly turned red and started to sweat profusely. To me, that degree of wet redness means the answer to my questions are yes, he knew his equipment went boom, and yes, he's already filed the insurance forms."

"Ya think a jury's gonna decide his guilt based on your impression of face redness—even given you're a great reporter?"

"No, but that doesn't mean it's not true. The good news is that I now know there's a guy I'll call Mr. X, who's up in Williston and knows what happened, and that Mr. X certainly called or emailed Mr. Potts in Houston and informed him of the explosion, so this guy must know his phone number or his email. All I gotta do now, in order to solve this case, is find this mysterious Mr. X. My man, Jimmy, is working on that."

"I don't like your chances of finding that guy, Steffie. If I were that guy, I'd be in Mexico by now."

"That's probably true, Leon, but I am certain that, like all slimy dudes, he left a trail—and I am going to find it. Jimmy's talking to the local FBI, hoping for Potts's phone records."

"Have a good flight back, Steffie, and thanks for the info—or whatever it was."

"You're welcome, Larry. Oh, and Leon, just to let you know, I've got a five-hour layover in Minneapolis, and I've booked an appointment with my reporter friend, Hasani. She's my contact in the Minneapolis Somali community. She's helping me see if any young men—like the girls in that trafficking business last spring—are missing from their neighborhoods recently. I'll let ya know what we find out."

"Thank you, Steffie," says Ms. R. "You get some sleep now. Can't have you acting so ornery as the two bozos you're talkin' with up here are, can we?"

"You're right, Mom. Can't let that happen. I'm off to bed."

CHAPTER 27

MASTERING MASTER LIMITED PARTNERSHIPS

Saturday, November 19, 2016

STEFFIE HAS ENLISTED JIMMY BASSEAU from the Huston paper to continue the investigation into the paperwork entities that control the MLPs, which in turn control the PFUMP project that is causing all the consternation in North Dakota. He'll keep the pressure on in Texas, allowing her to return to sleuthing in the frozen north. She and Jimmy had a debriefing meeting over breakfast at one of Jimmy's standard hangouts, north of Houston, near the airport. Though Jimmy is excited to be hunting big game, Steffie's job is to keep him focused on her target. After the omelets are stowed and the attack plan confirmed, Jimmy drives her to the airport.

Jimmy will spend a couple days at the courthouse in Houston tracing the identities of the partners in the various partnerships, master partnerships, and equity master partnerships registered down in Houston and doing their business up in Williston. Steffie wants to learn which players are looking to make money with the PFUMP pipeline, and which are using it only for its hedge value. Steffie knows that only a select few of the many equity master partners call the shots and make the money. Everyone else is involved for the hedge. She's hoping Jimmy will find the partners who hold the future of Williston in their hands. What she can do with that information is unclear, but she'll figure that out later, depending upon what level of information Jimmy can unearth.

* * *

After clearing security at the Houston airport, Steffie finds she has enough time to do a bit of reporting. She calls Sheriff Faber in Williston.

"Good morning, Sheriff. I'm calling from Houston. I'm at the airport waiting for my flight back to the tundra, and like a good reporter, I have several things I must report to you, specifically about how oil tycoons act down here in Houston."

"Good morning, Steffie. I'm already feeling a bit uneasy about this call. What do you need from me now?"

"Ya have to learn to trust me, Sheriff. I need nothing from you. I've got interesting stuff going your direction."

"Okay, Steffie. Thank you ... I think."

"First, I know you know that I've a special information-based type relationship with our governor, and part of that special relationship is that I'll never divulge anything he and I discuss unless he gives me the authority to do so. It's exactly like the relationship I have with you, Sheriff. You know I'll never divulge any information you give me—not even to the governor—unless you authorize me to do so."

"I understand that, Steffie. I trust you, and I'm assuming that since you began with that elaborate preamble, you've some juicy news trailing along behind it."

"I do. First, I'm pretty sure I've found the owner of that exploding oil field ... or at least some guy who tells me he personally knows who the owners are ... or at least that he works for guys who know who the owners are."

"I beg your pardon, Miss Reporter Lady, but that doesn't sound to me like you've actually found the owner."

"You've got to listen closely, Sheriff. I think I said I was *pretty sure* I've found a guy."

"Yeah, I heard you. So ... why should I care about you being pretty sure?"

"Because this guy confirmed to me that he was aware of—and

understand 'aware of' are magic words meaning he's been told by an agent based in Williston—the fact that certain Williston properties, owned by the firm both he and the agent work for, were attacked by ISIS last Sunday."

"That's a start, Steffie. I'll admit that."

"This gentleman's name is Truman Potts, and I'll email you his address and phone number. By the way, I tested the numbers while sitting across the desk from him to confirm he was giving me truthful numbers, and I heard his computer beep and his phone ring."

"Nicely done, Steffie. Thank you."

"You're welcome, and I told him to expect a call from you. I'll bet he'll be sweating profusely while you discuss things with him. He's not used to operating in the daylight … if you know what I mean. The second tidbit is that the agent he corresponds with in Williston is fairly high up in the food chain because the topic discussed was about the insurance arrangements for several of those properties blasted into the sky by fake ISIS terrorists. I would think that anyone aware of those 'insurance arrangements' would be someone you would want to talk with."

"You are right, Steffie, but I can tell by your word choice that you don't know the name of that Williston agent, do you?"

"Not yet, but we now know he does exist, don't we? And we can probably isolate maybe a list of twenty folks, and that list will probably include our mystery guy, and—"

"I get your point, Steffie. We'll do the follow-up."

"Thank you … and there's a third thing. I'd like to tell the governor what I've told you."

"I understand. I trust him. He ain't gonna blab."

"And the fourth thing is that I am leaving this airport in thirty-five minutes or so and flying to Minneapolis, and then after a five-hour layover, I fly back to Bismarck. During my layover in Minneapolis, I'm meeting your friend Hasani Indaak. I would like to ask her to poke around and see if she can find any whispers or shadows that may contain evidence that a couple Somali boys may be missing. Do you think I can have her carefully look into that? Or maybe we could talk about the weather … about how much cold and snow she sees in Somalia this time of year or—"

"Enough, Steffie. Okay, okay, I know what you are doing. Sure, talk to your friend. That would be helpful. And I'll tell Agent Brock, the lead

FBI guy on the case, what you two are chasing. He'll probably want a debriefing with both of you also."

"No problem. Give me his phone and email. I'll check in—and you have Hasani's info also, right?"

"Yes, I do. I'm looking at it right now."

"Thanks, Sheriff. Oh, they just called my flight. I'll check in after I talk to Hasani. Bye."

"Bye, Steffie. Thanks. Have a nice flight."

CHAPTER 28

LOOKING FOR ANOTHER CASE OF HUMAN TRAFFICKING

THE TWIN CITIES HAS A large Somali population, and so it's inevitable that young men from that community get into trouble from time to time. Hasani Indaak, a forty-year-old, second generation American-Somali woman, and an investigative reporter for the *Minneapolis Star Tribune*, knows many things about the lives of young men living in that Somali community. And she's arranged to meet her fellow reporter, Steffie Cobb from the *Bismarck Plainsman*, to discuss certain of these young men of Somali descent. She has secured a booth at the Kafe Korol, a small café on the corner of Riverside Avenue and Cedar Street, across the street from the several rather spectacular towers of the Cedar-Riverside Housing Project, a combination HUD and UM student housing project built in the 1960s that now almost entirely houses a Somali immigrant community. According to both members of the Somali community and their detractors, this cluster of high-rise apartments is casually known as Mogadishu in the Sky.

It's taken Steffie only twenty-five minutes to exit the airport terminal, hop on the Blue-Line Light Rail to the Cedar/Riverside stop, and then walk the three blocks through the shadows cast by Mogadishu in the Sky, to the front door of Kafe Korol. Steffie's time is limited, meaning she and Hasani must complete the heavy lifting of the Williston problem first and catch up on their personal lives only if they have time remaining.

"I know this sounds bizarre, Hasani, but consider this for a premise."

"Everything you've told me on the phone's bizarre, Steffie. However, I'm prepared."

The two reporters order coffees and pastries from the waitress, a teenage Somali girl.

"Last week, out in Williston, two Somali boys, costumed as Middle Eastern terrorists, were found dead after two explosion events occurred, several hours apart, in Williston. The events were presented with lots of smoke and awe—but without the usual signature of normal ISIS or jihadi-based destruction. These dead Somali boys seem strangely unconnected to the mayhem that exploded around them. And certainly their deaths were unconnected to international Islamic terrorism, whatever that may be. One way these deaths might be explained is that these two boys were lured into some jihadist activities, found themselves in way over their heads, threatened to get themselves out, and got themselves killed trying."

"But," says Hasani, "there's no history here of Somali boys connected to ISIS. Are you sure?"

"I'm positive there's no ISIS goin' on here. However, two Somali boys have died. And their deaths connect somehow to both explosion events. Though the police have not released much information on the nature of the bomb devices used, everyone thinks that activities on the two sites are connected. Until both sites have been fully studied, the police are not going to make any statement about possible terrorists—or of any possible Somali involvement at either venue. That's going to take time. I'm thinking maybe we can look into the Somali aspect of the problem and maybe construct a different premise that accepts these strange jihadi-or-not-jihadi facts."

"I agree the two explosion sites must be connected," Hasani says. "You said they occurred only a few hours apart. That's not enough time for any ISIS copycat to do his copycatting."

"ISIS is nowhere near this, Hasani. My sneaky little mind is suggesting that these naive boys were recruited under false pretenses, let's say for doing some yard work, moving some equipment for a neighbor, or some such innocent thing, and then compromised somehow, kidnapped or killed, then brought to Williston specifically to be used as red herrings—to throw attention on Islamic terrorists and away from the normal suspect pool for such destructive actions. One of my Houston newspaper's wise guys labeled this 'Louisiana lightning.' I'm thinking these boys' deaths are but collateral damage in this extravagant arson plot."

"That's sounds like a bad movie, Steffie. Things may have happened that absurdly in Mogadishu, but here in the US? I cannot believe that."

"Stick with me here a bit. Business and the economy are really bad in Williston now. All that easy-money, boomtown stuff is in the mirror. Let's consider a lowlife who's borrowed much more than he should have borrowed to build some oil-service company, several residential motels, or a fleet of dump trucks. You know, boomtown type infrastructure stuff. You start raking in the big bucks while leveraged to the hilt, and then the price of oil suddenly plummets. Boom!" Steffie slaps the table for emphasis.

Hasani recoils from the sharp slap. "Take it easy, Steffie! Settle down." She takes a sip of coffee. "I understand the chance of an accidental fire or explosion occurring. A devious sort might think he can convince an insurance company he's the mistaken victim of somebody else's arson. That can't possibly work, can it?"

"No, I don't think so," Steffie says. "Especially not with the two of us on the case, huh?"

"Okay, so what should I do?"

"We start by investigating stuff. I investigate North Dakota. You take the Minneapolis end. See if any rumors of missing young men are flitting through Mogadishu in the Sky. Maybe some kids embarrassed their family. They flunked a geometry test or strangled a neighbor's cat and were shamed into hightailing it out of town. Perhaps you can find the point where these boys crossed paths with some clever but nefarious men who came down here from Dakota or somewhere to kidnap them. This guy should have left a trail, right? He must've stood out like a fairy godmother in this Somali community."

"Somebody must have seen him, Steffie. Unless, as with those girls last year, that bad man was a bad Somali man. Remember how we weren't able to find everyone connected to that human trafficking ring? I always thought several of the smugglers slipped through or slithered away. They've gotta be slippery guys. If this guy operated in our community here, I'll find him. I'll shoot the bastard myself."

"Good! And I'll go back to Williston, Hasani. I'll try chasing the money. Money usually leads back to the evil deed."

CHAPTER 29

WATCHING FOLKS WATCHING THE SIOUX

Sunday, November 20, 2016

L EON ROLFES—THE GOVERNOR OF THE state hosting this oil pipeline ruckus—finds himself straddling several white-line barriers hastily erected through the several chambers of the state capitol to separate those supporting PFUMP from those despising PFUMP. But Leon's situation is not as stressful as it might be because he's officially neither a Republican nor a Democrat. He won election from his own party—his independent North Dakota First Party. And the situation is that both his NDFP and the Republicans each hold approximately 40 percent of the votes—of both the people in the state as a whole and of the legislature—while the Democrats hover around 20 percent. That means Leon can usually design legislation to win the support of either Democrats or Republicans, and will, when added to his own 40 percent, have enough votes to pass almost any rational legislation he thinks needs passing.

But this pipeline thing is not divided into three choices. There are only two—start up the bulldozer or stop the bulldozer—which puts Leon in a difficult philosophical and moral position.

"It's like juggling Jell-O balls, Margie." He's told her this silly story many times. "Everything looks beautiful as long as the balls are in the air, glittering in the sunlight, committed to their arcs. Eventually, the balls must hit the juggler's hands. Splat! And, poof, the entire concept of juggling vaporizes. I visualize the demonstrators—both pro-PFUMP and anti-PFUMP—are now up floating in the high air of their elaborate philosophical constructions, unaware of the mess it's going to cause when the Jell-O hits the hand."

"I'll get you a mop and a bucket—so you can clean up your mess."

Leon's left envisioning that mess alone. Of course it will be a short-term mess, and like Jell-O, it will be messy. But there should be little long-term harm. And, sadly, it does make for horrible PR. Eventually the stuff will mostly evaporate, though the stain of political damage might linger, his legacy as governor might crumble, and his mother might take away his meat loaf.

The further truth is that this whole PFUMP demonstration, including the pushback against it, is a bit of kabuki theater. It's Jell-O for nothing. This pipeline construction is only a means of generating financial losses, which can be used as a tax deduction to offset the outrageous profits that have been generated by several Houston-based master partnerships. The project is also, by now, almost completed. And that means the construction and material supply jobs have mostly been completed, and most workers have already gone back to Texas or wherever. And since little construction remains, little disruption of any additional land, native or otherwise, is going to occur—no matter who wins the standoff. And, most importantly, little of its value as a "hedge" remains.

And here's the crowning joke—in a few years, Williston's oil fields will be dead, little or no oil will be pumping through the tube, and the lease payments, based on oil flow, will dry up. All the commotion at those barricades will be forgotten. The only purpose Leon can see in this entire bit of absurdist theater is as a means of making generalized philosophical statements about general metaphysical issues. It's a headache, and it's also a humongous waste of his precious time.

These profoundly absurd thoughts are swirling about Governor Rolfes's head along with the snow this morning while he walks the twenty minutes to his office, which puts him in a sour mood by the time he stomps his boots on the mats in the lobby. And then, as he rides the elevator up into the sky, the other pounding problem he has concerning the PFUMP pipeline attacks him again—it's his own sweet mother, who, apparently, is much taken with this kabuki theater. After he'd explained the stupidity of a grandmother going to Standing Rock to stand behind the barricades with college-age protesters in the snow, and after he told her he would not drive her down there even for the promise of meat loaf, she went around him, called Steffie, and hitched a ride down with her and her son. Leon was too mad to remind her to take boots and mittens.

Leon knows the problems dividing the two sides are much more significant and much more dangerous than this surface confrontation suggests. The two sides here are far separate entities divided by issues of religion, morality, politics, greed, environmental protection, and several others. There appears no common ground, no points accepted by both as perhaps a starting point for negotiations. And to make things more dangerous, or more confusing, the major arguments advanced by both sides are equally flawed—both morally and factually.

This great divide between the attitudes and the moralities of the two positions manning their appropriate sides of the physical barrier now erected between them permeates the community of North Dakota and the country as a whole. The extent of this very personal divide may be best demonstrated by the fact that Steffie and her son Jake are standing, with his own mother, in the light blowing snow, singing songs once sung by Dr. King, Pete Seeger, and Joan Baez about overcoming things and using moral power. And while Steffie and her son will be out in the cold, her husband, Ross, and her eldest son, David, will not. They'll be back in their warm house, watching the Vikings game with their buddies. They don't have time for stupid people dancing in the snow. They see no need for encouraging hoodlums to stomp around on the prairie. They want their governor to bring in the damn National Guard and use whatever force is necessary so they can concentrate on the Vikings.

"Just push those Sioux and their sympathizers back onto their goddamned reservation," Ross told Steffie as she left the house. "Then jail the trespassers. Let PFUMP finish building their pipeline. Create some jobs. Transport our sweet North Dakota crude to Illinois. Make some serious money. Build us the best damn pipeline we can get. Start making our US great again."

Steffie understands the power of these arguments. She and Ross have almost drawn a white line through their home, and they both recognize this imaginary line as a reasonable barrier that prevents any unreasonable conversation from crossing that thin invisible line they've mentally etched into the pine board flooring and the gypsum wallboard of their farmhouse. Leon also is under extreme pressure to start drawing more serious lines, pushing people around, and arresting them because today he's afraid the first person arrested will be his own mother.

It didn't help Leon much that he's in his office on a Sunday morning. He cannot show up at the demonstration and risk exploding the working relationship with both sides he's spent so much time and energy constructing. Also, he cannot even go down to Scotties Bar to watch the game for many of the same reasons. He'll be expected to choose a side. But he believes he must remain neutral if he's to remain his state's peacekeeper. He finds he's even too tense to enjoy watching the Vikings inept offense diddle and fumble their way to another tight loss.

"Bah! What I really need is a dog," he addresses this outburst to his four walls. "Maybe another Lab, like good old Bernie." Bernie used to snuggle up next to him on the couch, and back then, the Vikings were playing much better ball. Life used to be good.

Just after the Vikings receiver bobbled a perfectly thrown ball, resulting in a fourth down and long, Leon's cell phone jingles and dances a bit on his desk. He looks at the displayed message: "Call from Steffie." His first thought is to wonder what trouble his mom's gotten herself into now. His second thought is political panic. *Uh-oh! This must be very bad news. Steffie wouldn't dare interrupt my busy day for something trivial.* "Hi, Steffie. Am I gonna need an antiacid pill before we talk?"

"Hold on, Leon. Your mother just took a picture of me, and since it's such a great shot, we think you should see it too. She just texted it to you. Should be popping up on your screen now. Put me on speaker so you can both look at the picture and talk to me."

"Do you realize the Vikings need my attention more than you do?"

"Not today they don't. Concentrate, Leon, and look at that photo."

He brings up the photo on his computer. "You look silly, and Jake looks bored, and you're both pointing over your shoulders behind you."

"Good, Leon. That's very good. You catch on quick."

"I do? What am I looking at? Some rock star guy I don't know—"

"Concentrate, Leon. Think closer to home. I'm going to zoom in so you can—"

"Well, I'll be damned! That woman holding one end of that big sign behind you? Is that who I think it is?"

"We also think that person is who you think she is, Leon. Thus, this phone call. That's your goddaughter, Kathleen, isn't it? It's been two years since I saw her at her father's funeral."

"What the devil's she doing out there? She can't stand the cold. She lives in Houston, for God's sake. And now she's hanging in snowy fifteen-degree weather, dancing with the Sioux? Wouldn't you think she'd be on the other side, frantically digging that tunnel under the river all by herself?"

"One would think so, huh, Leon? Maybe even throwing stones or swinging clubs."

"Or worse! She's the one who owns that pipeline!"

"Right you are, Leon. And also, you recognize the hunk she's talking to? We've been watching them for a while. Your mother tells me she's positive that guy is doin' more to her body than just guarding it. You know what she means, don't you?"

"How Mom knows all that kind of stuff, I'll never know. I knew I shouldn't have let either one of you get anywhere near that pipeline."

"This is great, Leon. Since I'm an investigator, Mom and I are gonna do a bit of investigating."

"Please chain my mother to a post or a police cruiser so she won't get you in trouble."

"We're gonna follow our two suspects and see if they meet up with any bad guys. I'm gonna see if I can find their car and trace the license plate. We're off lookin' for clues. I'll let you know what we find."

"Tell Mom I'm not coming down or bailing her out of jail. She's on her own."

"Don't worry, Leon. She's been aware of that for several years. Hang on just a second. I gotta talk to Mom quick. Something just clicked in my head."

Steffie takes Mrs. R's phone back and enlarges the photo. "Look at this, Mom. I was so taken with taking Kathleen's picture that I didn't notice who's holding the other end of her banner. But I see her now; it's that Vander Meer girl who follows Miss Ecological Demonstration around like a lovesick puppy. And, sure enough, behind her, I see her buddy, Jane Blackburn. Well, well, well. The whole crowd is here."

"What's going on, Steffie?"

"I am studying that photo, Leon. I see other players from two years ago in the photo."

"Who?"

"Jane Blackburn and her Save the Prairie organization are helping Kathleen hold up her banner. I have no idea why those three girls would be standing in close proximity to each other on this freezing afternoon. Something is seriously wrong with this picture. Something is very strange."

"I'll email that photo to you, Steffie," says Mrs. R. "You can study it when you're back at your office."

"That's great, Mom. I have no idea what's goin' on. Kathleen the oil goddess shouldn't be singing folk songs in the snow with those tree-huggers. It doesn't make sense."

"Nothing's making any sense, Steffie," says Leon. His phone sings to him, and a text from Margie pops up on the screen. "Margie just texted me from the other room, Steffie. She says I gotta stop lollygagging with you and Mom and take care of some crucial business that just popped up. What do ya suppose she means, Steffie? What the hell is crucial business? On a Sunday afternoon? During a Vikings game?"

"Whatever it is, I'll bet it doesn't concern the Vikings."

CHAPTER 30

WATCHING GARY BECOMING AN EXILE

IT'S A QUARTER PAST NOON, and Gary Gralapp decides he's ready. He's packed everything he needs and piled it into his truck. Yesterday, Trevor supplied him with license plates, insurance, and registration packets he switched with one of L. D.'s Louisiana tagged trucks, a trick he believes effectively removes him from the sight of a potential tracker. His plan, as Trevor outlined it, is to drive to Miami, ditch the truck, and have a freighter take him and all his stuff to Nevis. For years, he's told people he owns a place in Saint Kitts, but his property actually is on the tiny nearby island of Nevis. Gary's proud of that little bit of deception, and he's convinced it'll add a couple days to the timeline of anyone with a sharp knife looking for him. *Stupid Jenny, she's spent four Christmas vacations there, and she still thinks she winters in Saint Kitts.* The beach is there. And the travel brochures he gave her said Saint Kitts on the cover. What more proof did she need?

"What a stupid twit." He locks the door, hops into his pickup, and drives away. "What a stupid twit."

As he drives, he wonders whether it's strange that neither Hank nor Paul has called him yet. He feels sad about that. He drank too much last night, and he gave them a rougher time than he should have. He thinks he should at least tell them goodbye 'cause he's probably gonna be gone for, like, the rest of their lives. But both calls go directly to their mailboxes.

Can those idiots possibly still be mad at me? Those two goofballs never held grudges. They're old buddies. They're partners.

*   *   *

He thought they'd call—they should have called—but it has been two hours. He's at a truck stop, just off I-94 near the Bismarck airport, and they still haven't called. Gary allows a bit of panic to sneak in. He tries calling both of them again, but still nothing. *Why the hell don't those idiots answer their damn phones?* Trevor guaranteed that the two of them were in no danger from L. D.'s big boss because they were too far down the food chain. They should be able to take care of themselves.

He raises his orange juice carton in a sort of commemorative toast. "Oh well, guys. Here's goodbye to you." He drains his juice, switches off his phone, and removes the SIM card so no cell tower can trace it. Finally, he checks the oil and tops off the gas. He's paying cash. He's headed first to Miami and then—eventually, he is confident—into some other dimension.

CHAPTER 31

THE ARMY CORPS OF ENGINEERS COMES THROUGH

MARGIE STOMPS INTO HIS OFFICE with an armload of stuff. She plops herself on the couch, and her laptop somehow lands on her lap. "Sorry to interrupt that conversation with your mom, Governor, but you've just got an official governor's-desk email you gotta see. Sit right here." She pats the cushion next to her. You gotta read stuff from my computer."

"Doesn't sound like I'm gonna like this, am I, Margie?"

"Actually, I'm betting you will. It's from the Army Corps of Engineers." Leon reads out loud. "A Notice: Declaration of Rule Making."

"Understand, Governor, it's addressed to you personally. And, as far as I can tell, nobody's copied. It's only you. That why I summoned you. Seems it's for your eyes only."

Leon reads the notice:

> As of 12:00, noon, Sunday, December 4, 2016, all work on the entire length of the PFUMP pipeline from Williston, North Dakota, to the east side of the Mississippi River in Illinois is hereby ordered to cease. Work will not be restarted without an approval order originating from this office. The Corps of Engineers finds serious questions regarding the legitimacy of information provided to the Corps of Engineers from the applicant, specifically on the environment safeguards to be utilized for installing the

pipeline on federal lands, under both the Oahe Reservoir
and the Mississippi River.

"It goes on for another couple pages," Margie says. "But I think the
important stuff's right there."

"That's fantastic! Send a copy to Larry—and also to Robert Bowstringer,
Hank Ford, and Carl Two Deer."

"I'll send a copy to Steffie too, huh? Give her a heads-up?"

"No, no, no!" says Leon. "Stop! We can't do any of that. Let's think
this through. You said they copied nobody. Right? So this is secret, huh?
No one else in the state knows about this?"

"Right. Seems nobody has this except you … and me, of course."

"Hmmm? So, this is my personal notice of action that's not happening
for two weeks? And the Corps of Engineers sent it only to me? Why just
me? I think I'll keep this notice off the street for a while. I must understand
the dynamics first. I'll call Steffie later. Give this time to settle in.

"So, it's not such a bad day, huh, Leon?"

"No, it could be it's a pretty good day. I want to talk with Larry
though. I'll do that right now, and after that, I'm going to keep it secret—
at least till I'm sure why they sent this only to me. We've gotta manage this
carefully. I don't want to screw up the dynamics."

CHAPTER 32

ORDERING THE NEW WORLD'S ORDER

MONDAY, NOVEMBER 21, 2016

WILL BASEHARDT, THOUGH HE'S IN line to be a future Republican state senator, is currently nothing but a standard-issue citizen of Williston. Nevertheless, he believes his election victory—especially as tied to the president-elect's victory—imbues him with superpowers. He crashes through the door to the outer office, strides across the carpet, and confronts Governor Rolfes's gatekeeper, Margie Drommer.

"Leon in?" Basehardt doesn't wait for an answer before he turns—or as guys with superpowers sometime do—kind of rotates in place, points his light saber toward Leon's office, then starts across the carpet toward that door.

"You stop right there, Mr. Basehardt!" Margie yells. "Or I'll shoot you right between the shoulder blades."

This does make Basehardt stop. He spins around, scabbards the saber, and stares at her. His look is strange: maybe anger, maybe awe, perhaps derision.

"You open the governor's door, and you're a dead man," Margie says. "Also, I'll bill your estate for scraping your body parts off the walls."

"How you gonna stop me, Little Miss Commando?" He regains his composure quickly.

"Is your memory shot? The governor told you that you are not allowed in his office, remember?"

"Sure, he said that, but I'm thinking—"

"You certainly are not thinking. I warn you, sir, there are three assault rifles trained on your head. It's gonna make an awful mess. You're not a married man right now, are you? So's I won't have to notify your wife to come over here and identify the bits and pieces remaining as being parts of your former body? And to answer your first question, Leon is not here." She jabs her forefinger twice on the desktop next to her jiggling coffee mug.

"Where is he?"

"Why do you care? The governor's not here." Another strong finger jab. "If you really need to meet, he's got fifteen minutes, starting at three this afternoon. He'll meet you on the mall, under that first elm tree, across the driveway from the base of the capitol steps."

"You're nuts!"

"The governor doesn't mind. Unlike you, he's used to cold. He's from North Dakota, ya know? Not Texas. But, whatever, he's not letting you inside his office."

Basehardt remains standing in place, looking at her, unsure of a proper emotion to project or a proper answer to make.

"You gonna take my offer ... or not."

He finally nods. "Sure, okay."

"Anything else, Mr. Basehardt? If not ..." She points at the door, turns to her computer screen, and starts to work the keyboard while paying him no attention at all. Eventually, she hears the outer door open and then close. At that sound, she gets up, walks across the carpet, and opens Leon's door.

"Nice work, Margie," the governor says. "I owe you one."

"I owe ya back, Leon. I enjoyed that. I think three o'clock fits into your schedule, right?"

"That'll be fine, Margie."

CHAPTER 33

STEFFIE REPORTS: RE: HUMAN TRAFFICKING AND ISIS

SINCE MOTHER NATURE IS NO longer required to pamper the demonstrators at the PFUMP pipeline, she is smashing Bismarck with a fairly typical November blizzard. It started snowing midmorning and should continue through midnight, so many businesses and government operations are quite deserted by two thirty. The few people remaining are coasting.

Steffie, on her way from her office to her farm, drops in to update Leon.

"Ya want some tea, Steffie. Take the chill off?"

"Sure, that would hit the spot. I've got a strange fairy-tale story to relate, involving several, technical, and reporter-type potholes I've been hitting as I try to make ISIS fit into the Williston oil fields."

"Don't think I'm ready for fairy tales, Steffie. Governors should be well grounded in reality, but I might mention some fantasy did come swooping into the office this morning—a self-appointed representative of a fairly extensive fantasy kingdom who disputes I am actually the governor of this fair state. I'm hoping your story will be more entertaining than his fairy tale."

"I've just stepped into something, haven't I? And, unfortunately, I left my boots at the door like I am supposed to."

"Enough, Steffie. First, tell me your messy story, and then, if you behave yourself, I'll tell you *my* messy story."

"I was in Minneapolis Saturday, and I talked to a reporter friend of mine, a fearless Somali girl who writes for the *Star Tribune*. We talked about jihad, human trafficking, and other despicable things. We're considering the possibility that, similar to last year, an enterprising entrepreneur from Williston may have gone shopping in the Somali community in Minneapolis for some fantasy jihadist actors to install in the explosive play he may have been staging in Williston."

"I don't like where your story's going, Steffie. You lied. It's not about flitting fairies, is it?"

"Nope, I'm talking kidnapping and murder. Remember, last winter, the story of the Williston brothel staffed by a Minneapolis sex trafficking ring."

"Thought you said this fairy tale was about jihad? Why are you bringing in sex trafficking?"

"Be patient, Leon. Jihadists and sex traffickers both fish from the same pool—or swamp. There is a history of teenage Somali girls being kidnapped, shipped, and used in cities around the country. Some were shipped to boomtown Williston to be used for certain nefarious purposes. My reporter friend, Hasani, broke that sex trafficking ring story. I've been talking with her, and we are wondering if your two dead Somali youths may have been taken from the Minneapolis Somali community and used as theatrical props in a certain act of God that recently took place in Williston, the same city where last spring's brothel story took place."

"First, they are not *my* dead Somali kids. And, second, you think some sleazeball non-jihadist kidnapped two Somali boys, brought them to Williston, ritualistically killed them, and placed their bodies next to the exploding things so we stupid folks out here on the prairie would think that big, bad ISIS was involved and so not look to homegrown, cowboy-hatted arsonists? That's the tale you're trying to sell me?"

"Yep, though it's not yet a tale—only a theory. So, is your story better than that?"

"Not so much better as different. Certainly more fairy-tale-ish than your black tale. My fairy tale concerns politics—or what used to be called politics."

"You mean 'used to be,' like before a few weeks ago?"

"Right. It seems one ambitious, newly elected state senator is affixing himself to the new president-elect and his cadre. And in his capacity as the self-appointed representative of this New Order in North Dakota, he believes he has the power to tell me how to run my state."

"Sounds to me that Mr. Basehardt is the one who just crossed that line into the fairy kingdom."

"I think so too, but I doubt he sees it that way. He thinks he's the representative of America's greatness, riding on his great gray tank and clanking onto my not-so-great mall outside my not-so-great window." Leon looks out that window toward that mall. "I haven't seen his great American tank parked out there for a while. I'm thinking the whole episode this morning was a mirage, or maybe a metaphor, just part of his fairy tale. I'm thinking it was a bad dream. I drank some orange juice, and both the fairy-tale senator-to-be and his dreamland tank went away."

"That's some powerful juice you've got, Leon. I might need some of that because I also have to tell you what I found out about in Houston."

"You're moving around a bit for a local girl, aren't you?"

"Aren't you the one who's been preaching oil as a global business? We may live right here ... and beyond the cold ... beyond the Mason-Dixon Line."

"And speaking of cold and snow ..." Leon walks over to the window and points across the driveway, down to the mall, which looks lonely and forlorn this afternoon. It's snowing lightly, and the sun, hidden on the far side of the clouds, has lost much of its power. "I'm holding an important meeting in," he makes an exaggerated point of looking at his watch, "about ten minutes at my Southern Office. Ya want a front-row seat?"

Steffie walks over and looks out. "Your Southern Office?"

"Sure, by that elm tree, right there. That's actually south of here. I'm thinking about 130 feet south of right here." He stomps his foot at where the measurement supposedly starts.

"You're nuts, buddy. Back in your fairy-tale kingdom, huh? I'm going to talk to Margie about what's really happening here."

"Be careful. I have it on fairly good authority that she's nuts too."

CHAPTER 34

MEETING WITH BASEHARDT AT THE SOUTHERN OFFICE

I
T'S A FEW MINUTES TO three, and Leon's standing beneath the same American elm tree Margie told Basehardt he'd be standing under. It's a month before the winter solstice, and what little daylight's left is obscured by the thick gray clouds. Leon's on his cell to Margie, who's standing by the window in his office, on the thirteenth floor of the state capitol tower.

"I see him starting down the steps now," Leon says. "This must be something really important for him to show up and stand out here with me in the snow. Do you know, Margie, that they don't have snow in Houston?"

"I think that's a fairly well-known fact."

"Tell you what I'm gonna do. I'll put my phone on voice recorder and then keep this call to you open—so I can record his words and send them to you guys in real time. You and Steffie can listen to the lecture he's gonna be giving me."

"Good! And I'll watch him on my phone from here in your office. You have a nice meeting, Leon."

Basehardt stomps across the snow. He's huddled beneath an umbrella, like folks in Texas do for rain.

Leon ridicules him. "Expecting showers, Mr. Basehardt? Welcome to my Southern Office."

"What ya mean, southern? This is North Dakota, as you must realize."

"It's exactly 130 feet south of my Northern Office way up there." Leon points dramatically toward his office window on the thirteenth floor. He wants to make sure Margie's video records him pointing, so if something exotic happens, Margie and Steffie can later coordinate the video with the audio. "So … what's so important I gotta come all the way down here to listen to?"

"Things are reaching a crisis, Leon. I need the National Guard stationed in Williston to protect against further ISIS attacks. My subcontractors are afraid to go to work out there."

"Please, be respectful and call me 'Governor.' You've hired yourself a bunch of sissies, huh? Tell you what. You play Texas Ranger yourself. Camp out near your wells and watch. When you see ISIS come bounding over the horizon on their camels, give me a call. I'll see what I can do." Leon turns and takes a step back toward the capitol stairs.

"I'm not finished yet, Leon. I also demand you send the National Guard out to Standing Rock immediately and arrest those protestors before they freeze themselves to death. It's the humanitarian thing to do. They're breaking the law."

"If I arrest all the protesters, then who is going stand in front of the bulldozers? You gonna do that? And please, be respectful. Call me *governor.*"

"Don't be a wise guy, Leon. In a few days, the high is forecast to be zero—and more snow too. People are gonna be dying out there."

"What the hell do you know about cold and snow? You're from Texas, and armed with an umbrella, for god's sake? And you … must … call … me … *governor.*" Leon fiddles in his pocket and pulls out a copy of the Corps of Engineers email he received yesterday. "What would you say if I told you I've already solved your problem?"

"I'd say you're delusional."

"Hmm, so look at this." Leon gives him the paper. "The federal government's doing the work it's supposed to do. We can all go home and watch TV now and not be disturbed by seeing our brethren freezing in their tents. Good news, huh?"

"This thing's not real, Leon! Is it?"

"Yup. And please, be respectful … call me *governor.* Why must I keep repeating that? Don't you have ears? Of course the letter is real. I got my advance notice yesterday, and the order will take effect in two weeks. The

Corps of Engineers tells me they're gonna publish this notice on their official website tomorrow morning."

"This ain't over like you think it is. Once the president-elect looks at this, this order will be reversed within hours. Just you watch." He shakes the paper violently, like he thinks that alone will reverse it. "You are one sneaky bastard, Leon."

"Please, be respectful. Though I am one sneaky bastard, you still gotta call me governor. Your president-elect has no power yet. He can do nothing until the middle of January."

"We'll see about that." Basehardt turns and stomps through the snow toward the capitol.

Leon takes the phone out of his pocket. "Ya get all that, Margie?"

"Sure did, Leon. Suppose we're gonna see some more explosions goin' off out here on the prairie?"

"Wouldn't be surprised. However, it's possible, since we had this discussion in my Southern Office, he'll have time to cool down a bit before he gets back to his own desk, wherever that might be. He'll put away his stupid umbrella, have his coffee, and maybe be able to see the value in the Corps of Engineers' decision before he talks to his big boss."

"I don't see that happening, Leon. You're gonna be getting a call from his special guy in New York."

"More explosions and smoke, huh? I'm ready for it, but I do need a hot cup of coffee. And since my work out here's finished, I'll be coming right up to my Northern Office for that."

CHAPTER 35

WHO IS SIOUX? WHO IS NOT SIOUX?

Jane Blackburn and Nancy Vander Meer have, over the past several years, built the once-ragtag Save Our Prairie Foundation into a Midwestern pro-environmental force to be reckoned with. Although neither half of this couple are Standing Rock people, or even native Midwesterners—and neither knew what a "prairie" was until each matriculated at a college located on one—Jane, at least, thinks she has a perfect understanding of the Sioux's history, attitudes, and motives regarding this specific war of resistance. Several days ago, she told Robert Bowstringer that she is "truly is a Sioux" in her heart. She remembers Bowstringer's reaction: "That's nice." He then spat on the ground and walked away.

Though that confrontation may not have been a confirmation of her claim to being a Sioux warrior, in her mind, she believes he did not, technically, reject her claim. To be fair, Jane's Save Our Prairie Foundation is responsible for delivering a good quarter of the protesters to this event, of which Bowstringer is the chief organizer. And even more of her troops show up on weekends when classes at the various colleges they attend are not in session. Though one must consider that a good number of the weekend college kids are here on assignment from their courses whose grades reflect their degree of passion and participation in such field work as this.

Jane's convinced that—or perhaps she only assumes that—given her credentials as an environmentalist, it's natural, and therefore a given, that Hank Ford will allow her to take over the ceremonial role of lead protester once the Army Corps of Engineers' order is implemented, once the pipeline workers are back in Houston, once Ford and Bowstringer go back to their science and their music, and once the confrontation essentially closes down for the below-zero forecast over the Christmas holiday. Nancy wants to stay on the site in the freezing weather and keep the protest alive since everyone here certainly is afraid the president-elect will open the spigot again as soon as he formally steps over the golden threshold in January. She hopes to plan some newsworthy rituals capable of grabbing holiday space on CNN. She thinks, or maybe only assumes, that Ford and Bowstringer will, in effect, deputize her as an honorary Sioux and then allow the Save Our Prairie Foundation to stay on-site and represent the Sioux by producing well-choreographed stomping and screaming rituals—even as the pipeline installers are back in Houston, and the real Standing Rock people have returned to their houses.

Jane walks over to Hank Ford's tent to offer her services to lead the opposition while he and Bowstringer—betraying, she certainly thinks, the Standing Rock people—leave for Christmas break. Even though Bowstringer has shrugged her off, maybe his partner, Ford, if he hears her plea from her own lips, might be moved to acquiesce.

"Mr. Ford," she says with a practiced authority, "I'm a professional. I know what I'm doing." She dramatically removes her sunglasses to allow the lasers to do their work. "And I have the Sioux's ability to withstand hardship." She decides to try the same argument Bowstringer earlier rejected. She's analyzed Mr. Ford, and he seems a bit more tolerant than his co-protester. "And I truly believe I understand your position because, in my heart, I'm also a Sioux."

Ford laughs at her. "Go home, woman. You're not Sioux."

Those few words sure hurt. Jane stops listening to Ford blast her motives and immediately switches to rebuttal mode. She ceases to hear Ford's voice continue to scold her.

"This is a Sioux issue. We're standing on Sioux land, and we're discussing Sioux rights. You can't pretend you're Sioux."

It eventually hits her that Hank's not on her side either. She understands she may have made a miscalculation. It's possible she's in big trouble.

So … she does what she always has done in circumstances like this—she attacks. "We may not be Sioux, Mr. Ford, but we are environmentalists, and we have a long track record of successful confrontations. We know the dynamics of the various social organisms—"

"Please …"

Jane is also an experienced crowd leader, and she can shout louder than Ford can. She will show Ford that she's the more experienced shouter. And, so, she shouts, "We love the land as much as, and probably a good deal more than, the average Sioux does. Why, my father—"

"Please, Ms. Blackburn. We've already won this skirmish. The Corps of Engineers has spoken, and the pipeline people have abandoned their equipment and gone home. The war's over, for God's sake. At least for now. Please go home."

"Don't you understand this lull is but temporary. PFUMP will be back as soon as the earth thaws out, and they'll pick up right where they left off. And you know the new president will never let the stop order stand. I'll bet one of the first things he does is—"

"Please, Ms. Blackburn, go home. This is not your fight."

"This land is my land too, Mr. Ford. I'm going to stay here until God himself pushes me off it."

Ford can only throw up his hands. He turns away and walks off toward his tent.

Jane, just because she can't let Ford be the winner here, immediately turns and stomps off toward her tent too. Or, rather, she stomps toward her VW camper van. Any third party watching will now certainly think that since she's stomping harder and with more passion than that prissy Ford is able to muster, she'll have to be declared the winner of this skirmish.

Unfortunately for Jane, the only person watching this confrontation is her partner, Nancy Vander Meer, and unfortunately for Jane, Nancy's mind is on another planet. Nancy is cautious by nature and certainly does not want to commit any act of disrespect either to the Sioux, her partner, or even to God. However, she has her feminist bonnet fixed firmly on her head today, and she feels it's up to her to make the necessary correction.

Nancy runs after Jane and yells as loud as she's capable of doing in her squeaky high-pitched voice, "Jane! Jane! How could you say that? I know you don't mean it."

Jane stops stomping and turns to Nancy. "What? What's your problem now?"

"You should have said, 'Herself,' Jane. 'Until God, Herself, pushes me off.' As feminists, we cannot—"

"Oh, for Christ's sake, Nancy." Jane turns back and continues her fervent stomping. "Grow the hell up!"

CHAPTER 36

PFUMP REACTS TO
THE STOP ORDER

TUESDAY, NOVEMBER 22, 2016

TODAY IS ONE BEAUTIFUL DAY—BUT only for those observers standing on the west side of the barricade. Bowstringer and his band are set up over there, and they're loudly celebrating all that beauty. The weather gods say it's probably the last kinda warmish sunny day before the deep freeze shows up, although in the past weeks, that predicted freeze has petered out before getting to North Dakota. The beauty so evident today has nothing to do with the sky or the temperature. The Corps of Engineers' decision to decertify PFUMP's stainless steel pipeline brings a larger than average group of protesters out for celebration duty.

There's no beauty evident to the east of the barrier. Or, at least, there's no joy. As soon as PFUMP received the Corps of Engineers' advanced notice yesterday, all their subcontractors—the truck and tractor drivers, the armed enforcement thug unit, and the dogs and their handlers—took off for Texas. That left this torn-up dump of a landscape free for Bowstringer, Ford, the Standing Rock people, and their friends to dance on. That allows the great number of college kids brought in by Jane Blackburn and her Save the Prairie Foundation to festively mill around, act like they're saving their prairie, and do that saving in a festive mood with no tension or opposition.

Over on the far side of the area, which is set off for car parking, two dark blue Ford pickups are parked next to each other, side by side and front to back. The owners of these trucks are leaning against their respective driver's side doors, and are having a quiet cowboy-to-cowboy conversation—or maybe it's a cowgirl.

"Trevor," Kathleen says, "I'm convinced that explosive excitement in Williston is Basehardt's work. He's a traditionalist. He still thinks about insurance the old way. He doesn't understand real insurance like a real partner has to understand it. Partners don't need insurance. They have *business operations losses,* which are cheaper than insurance because they don't require premiums. L. D. left his friggin' fingerprints all over those explosions. All he needed to use was a bottle of gasoline and a couple matches. But no, Mr. Hollywood Director had to go put the whole thing on the nightly news."

"I doubt that flamboyant ruse was L. D.'s idea," says Trevor. "Somebody else was driving his bus. He's a nuts-and-bolts guy, a local thinker with no creative streak, and his perspective's no wider than Williston. But that act of God stuff? That's a creative concept designed for a nationwide audience by a guy with a nationwide perspective."

"Creative concepts don't include shooting wannabe ISIS guys, Trevor. That's just weird. And it's stupid, bizarre, demented, and immoral. It's lots of stuff, but it's not creative. Though you *are* right about the nationwide part."

"You gotta admit it's confusing. Things are so confusing that it's going to take months to straighten out. And by the time everything's sorted out, say April or May, every tunnel will be drilled, the pipe will be inserted, and we'll be ready to tighten a few bolts and start pumping."

"If it takes that long to sort out, somebody's gonna trace the money line back—and, sure as hell, somebody's gonna suggest a connective link to Texas. We've got to excise a couple of those links immediately, Trevor. I'm sorry. I know Roseborough was with you in Iraq, but we gotta get rid of the weak links."

"Who else has to go?"

"Like you said, whoever L. D. brought in to help him with the creative aspects is part of the loop of responsibility. That loop must be broken, and the cancer excised so this ISIS stuff cannot ever be traced. You hear me, Trevor?"

"Yes, Kathleen. I'll figure it out. I'll take care of it."

"We don't have to talk about this ever again, do we, Trevor?"

"No, Kathleen, I'll take care of it."

Kathleen opens the door and hops into her pickup. "Oh … and, Trevor, you have to do one more thing for me."

The hair on his neck jumps up, but when Kathleen turns back and looks at him, she seems composed, thoughtful, and nowhere near angry.

"What's that?"

"I need you to drive out to our drill head insertion point, twenty miles east of the river. Make sure that site's shut down, vacated, secured, and sealed. Our crews should be halfway to Texas. Confirm that. Just make sure everything's secure, and then text me confirmation. Thanks." Kathleen's truck pulls away and crawls over the rough surface to the level roadway about two hundred feet away.

Trevor quickly returns his heart rate to normal. His Special Forces training taught him how to do that. Unfortunately, that Black Ops training didn't teach him much about Kathleen. He still has no idea what she's apt to do next.

The operation Trevor is confirming as shut down this afternoon is Kathleen's secret weapon. And since he has a special connection to that weapon, it is only proper that he be the one to confirm it's been put to bed for the holidays. She's leased this high-tech drilling rig from a Swiss firm that used it to tunnel pipelines under the Alps. Last spring, Trevor met the freighter when it docked in New Orleans, and then he rode shotgun with the truck driver as he drove the extra-wide load up I-29 to Fargo, and then I-94 west, almost as far as Bismarck. In a reasonable sense, that drill is his responsibility, and so it's fitting that he's the one to confirm it's safely stowed for the winter. The marvelous piece of equipment has already drilled a portion of the tunnel under the reservoir—that was finished two months ago before anyone was watching every truck on every highway in central North Dakota as they are now—and she's already inserted the fifty-foot lengths of forty-two-inch-diameter stainless steel pipe into it. But instead of this tunnel being, like normal, installed a dozen feet or so below the surface, this beautiful high-tech pipeline tunnel has been drilled very deep—a minimum of three hundred feet beneath the bottom of the reservoir—and it remains buried that deep for twenty miles on both the reservoir's east and west limits. It doesn't make any difference to Kathleen's wonder machine whether it drills its tunnel five feet deep or five hundred feet deep.

What her magic machine has been able to do has been to drill that entire piece of line from a safe insertion position twenty miles to the east of the river. That position, far out of sight of the protesters, is also the site where PFUMP is constructing the subterranean factory that will extract anhydrous ammonia from the raw crude oil being pumped through the line. Kathleen has a separate LLC that will collect and process that ammonia for use as fertilizer. Her drilling machine drilled its tunnel through the sandy clay above the shale deposits where its sophisticated GPS told it to drill—yet neither Bowstringer nor Ford physically felt the vibration of her tunneling machine as it worked under their feet.

Sometime next spring, when the full pipeline approval will surely be reauthorized, all PFUMP-MLP has to do is activate its pumps. Kathleen's super Swiss machine has already won that divisive philosophical argument that the aboveground protesters have been contending while standing out there in the cold and snow. Kathleen designed that whole confrontation for show—a bit of ultimate kabuki theater to distract observers from the fact that, as they were demonstrating, her pipe was being installed three hundred feet below them.

CHAPTER 37

COMPUTER DRAWINGS VERSUS DISTORTED PHOTOGRAPHS

WEDNESDAY, NOVEMBER 23, 2016

STEFFIE IS DRIVING TO WILLISTON this morning under dangerous conditions. The temperature is in the high twenties, the intermittent drizzle has installed a slick surface on the road, and the haphazard nature of the ice coverage makes the act of driving a bit surreal—more like a computer game. Sanding trucks are on the job, and that eases her tension some. But, after the third, and then the fourth vehicle she sees spun off into a ditch or field, she begins to lose confidence in her own ability to stay on the road. The concentration she spent and the chances she had to take, especially during the last fifty miles, have taken a toll. And as a result, she is numb and tentative as she enters Sheriff Faber's office. She understands her situation will give Sheriff Faber the upper hand, but she tries hard to put up a facade. She knows immediately that she's failed.

"Wow, Steffie! I'll better get some coffee in you quickly." Faber's quite proud of the product his high-tech coffee machine pumps out. "I've got a strong Peruvian blend that's designed to relax the stress from your drive."

Steffie laughs. "Sounds wonderful, Sheriff. Every muscle in my body is tight. I could use a couple swallows of good peach brandy."

"This Peruvian stuff is as close to that as I'm allowed to serve in here. It should work. But why'd you ice-skate all the way out here just to see me? You've heard of smartphones, right? Next time, just give me a call.

"It's because I'm an old-fashioned reporter, Sheriff. I need a face-to-face with you. I'm worried about those dead ISIS guys. I want to find out who they are. Then we can help solve your explosion story."

"The FBI's working on that too, Steffie. Trust them—they'll find out stuff."

"But we don't think they're working in the right places yet."

"Okay, I'll bite. What places got you so interested that you skated all the way out here? And, second, who do you mean by *we*?"

"Hasani Indaak and I are looking, and we know by the way you and the feds are acting as if there is a big piece of something out there you're not allowing us to see. I really like secrets, Sheriff, don't get me wrong, but, in this case, Hasani and I cannot make reasonable use of our time if we're missing key evidence. We must know everything the FBI knows to design the parameters of our search. Doesn't that make sense?"

"We don't know squat about those men, Steffie. That's precisely the problem."

"Hasani and I need the official autopsy and photos of the dead men before she can look for them. You think you can at least give us that?"

"Don't know that you knew this, but the FBI opened a suboffice here in Williston just a couple months ago—out on Forty-Second, across from the airport. You should check in with Special Agent Brock. I'll give him an introductory call and tell him he can trust you." Sheriff Faber reaches to the far corner of his desk, picks up a manila envelope, and removes two documents. He reviews each briefly and then hands them to Steffie. "Agent Brock emailed these over last night—computer-drawn images of the two men's faces. He'd just received them from Quantico."

Steffie looks at them. "I know this is a dumb question, but why drawings? Why not just use photographs? You wouldn't have to have gone all the way to the East Coast and take a week to get a computer-generated drawing. What am I not getting?"

"These computer-drawn faces represent how the men would have looked when they were alive. The actual corpses were quite distorted, and such distortion would've been obvious to anyone who knew them. It's much easier on friends and relatives to identify a drawing of true features of their loved one rather than a distorted photo."

"Distorted? I don't understand, Sheriff. I don't know what that means."

"The local medical examiner had the FBI ship the bodies to their crime lab in Virginia because he was unable to determine either the time of death or the exact manner in which they died."

"How can the FBI, for god's sake, not be able to tell us how they died? Aren't they, like, the best in the business of studying dead guys? What's the problem? At your news conference, you told us one was shot. You're telling me that didn't kill him? That's hard to believe."

"Pay attention, Steffie. That's not what I am saying. That boy was shot after he died."

"Oh! Sorry. I ... I ... didn't think of that. Who would do that? And why?"

"That's why we are being so careful with this information, Steffie. And the body we found in the hotel debris was burned awful bad so there wasn't much left to photograph. A sketch, based on bone structure, was necessary."

"Okay, Sheriff. At least I can understand that."

"One thesis they're working is that whoever did this were rank amateurs who didn't know exactly how murdering works."

"What? That's bizarre," says Steffie. "Or they could have been psychopaths and didn't seem to realize the men they killed were fellow human beings."

"Yeah," says Faber. "That's also possible."

"Thanks for these drawings, Sheriff. Since you have them as emails, could you email them direct to Hasani in Minneapolis? She can get cranking as soon as she receives them."

"Consider it done, Steffie. You must promise me you'll talk with Agent Brock and tell him what you're up to."

CHAPTER 38

LOOKING FOR THE
THIRD SOMALI

FRIDAY, NOVEMBER 25, 2016

THOUGH THE DRAWINGS AND DESCRIPTIONS of the two dead Somali youths looked to Steffie to be maybe high school freshmen, Hasani immediately saw them as considerably older. Her guess is closer to twenty, which gives her additional options. College attendance among Somali men is quite high, and local colleges seriously recruit them. So Hasani heads toward the U of M's Somali Student Affairs Office for a discussion with its director, Marsha J.

"Good Morning, Marsha," says Hasani.

"I know by now that when you show up at my desk, it means I'll not be having any good morning."

"I know, Marsha, and I'm sorry, but you're correct. My sad question today is this: Would your office know if two male Somali students left school, without notice, over the past month or so? Would a teacher be apt to contact your office if a student didn't show up for several weeks?"

"I might get a note from such a teacher, but it would be unusual. However, I believe there's a better way. Most all Somali students have jobs arranged by a desk in the university's Work/Study Office, one specifically established for the Somali community. If one of those students doesn't show up for work, the employer's obligated to report it. Let's walk down the hall and see what we can find."

They talk with the clerk manning that desk today, a pleasant young grad student named Said Amir, as he does a quick computer search. "I don't have two boys, but I do have one boy, N. R., a sophomore chemistry major. He stopped coming to work in the middle of October." He riffles through a file cabinet, retrieves a folder, and opens it up. "This report indicates this office checked the boy's home. The mother apparently said N. R. left Minnesota to visit an older brother and might return in February." He turns the form over, looks on the reverse, and notes that it's vacant of any marks. "That's odd. Absences occur periodically, but usually they're scheduled to extend a holiday break—or the transition's discussed with this desk before it happens. That way, we can put a proper note on the form so that when he returns, we're ready for him to continue his classes and his work. No such note is on N. R.'s form."

"Do you recognize either of these two drawings as being N. R.?"

"I've never met N. R. I don't know what he looks like."

"Seems strange he'd suddenly quit," says Hasani. "I'll visit his family."

"As you know, Somalis have strong family and tribal ties. Family duties often take precedence over class attendance."

"Do you have an address?"

"His family's apartment is at Mogadishu in the Sky, apartment #F1217. That's in the F Tower, twelfth floor."

*   *   *

The Cedar Riverside Housing Project—referred to as Mogadishu in the Sky by its Somali residents—is a huge construction of raw exposed concrete, housing more than eight thousand people. Another 1,500 live in two newer five-story structures. Hasani has two aunts and several cousins who live here and has visited this building many times. She knows the protocol, the pedestrian shortcuts through the concrete mazes, and the correct clothing to make the correct impression on the residents. As she leaves the elevator on the twelfth floor of the F building, she's smashed by the smells produced by Somali kitchens. Though Hasani has never been to Mogadishu, she can simply close her eyes, breathe in the aromas, and imagine life in the neighborhoods before her parents' country imploded with religious and tribal terror.

Many apartment entryways have been customized by decorations of flowers, cloth, and metal sculptures. Hasani finds apartment F1217 and knocks on the door. That elicits no response from inside the apartment. However, other doors along the hall open slowly. She expects that. Several Somali women peek their covered heads into the hallway.

Hasani moves over to the woman from the adjacent apartment. "*Subax wanaagsan ma'am*" [Good morning, ma'am.]

"*Maalin wacan?*" [Good day.]

"*Magacaygu waa, Hasani. Waxaan u shaqeeyaan wargeyska* Minneapolis Star Tribune." [I'm a reporter for the *Minneapolis Star Tribune*.]

"*Maxaad rabats?*" [What do you want?]

"*Waa inaan la N. R. hadasho.*" [I must talk with N. R.] Hasani points to the adjacent door and shows the two drawings. "*Ma mid ka mid ah wiilasha kuwaas N. R.?*" [Are either of these boys N. R.?]

The woman shakes her head, immediately tears up, and retreats into her apartment.

Hasani feels the pressure of other eyes on her back and turns around more abruptly than she intended. Several heads retreat, and a few doors close. Hasani senses they all, like the first woman, are quite upset, perhaps even frightened, by the simple question she said loud enough for their hearing.

Across the way, a teenage girl steps into the hall.

Hasani walks over and shows her the photos. "*Ma mid ka mid ah wiilasha kuwaas N. R.?*"

The girl starts to cry, shakes her head, and covers her mouth with a hand wrapped in her garment. She quickly retreats into her apartment and closes her door.

Through the closed door, Hasani hears the girl sobbing.

These women are all afraid. Hasani assumes such fear means her question has been positively answered. She's certain she's found N. R.'s apartment, but she also knows she's not going to get verbal confirmation without some additional work. Her phone vibrates to announce a text. She returns to the first floor, leaves the building, walks across the plaza, goes down some stairs, and walks toward the rental office.

FBI Special Agent Carol Parker is sitting on the concrete bench outside the office. She rises, steps toward Hasani, and gives her a quick hug. "Sorry, Hasani. I got here as soon as I could."

"Morning, Agent Parker. Thanks for coming."

"What ya got for me?"

"I think I'm on the right path, Carol. I talked to a woman and a girl, neighbors of the missing N. R., and I am sure they—and several others who watched me—were afraid. More than afraid, I'd say they were terrified."

"Let's go in and talk with the business office," says Parker. "Perhaps they have an explanation or some background."

* * *

The woman on duty scans a computer. "Yes, N. R.'s family rents unit F1217. And the November rent's been paid. And—this is odd—the December rent's prepaid as well. Probably means they're traveling. We have more than two thousand apartments in the complex, and they're all occupied. We even have a waiting list. If an apartment's been vacated, everyone knows about it—and it won't stay vacant long."

"I'd like to look inside the apartment," says Agent Parker. "Just a quick check to see if everything's all right? Might that be possible?"

"I cannot leave my desk," she says. "But I will send maintenance up with you. He will be able to let you in."

* * *

The apartment is in perfect order, with everything in its place, and nothing to suggest that it has been abandoned.

"Seems there is nothing here," says Hasani. "I do, however, want another chance with the girl across the hall." She knocks on the door, and the girl opens it a crack. "Miss, please," she says softly so no neighbor can hear. "I have Ms. Parker of the FBI with me."

Parker offers her identification.

Hasani says, "We really must ask you some questions about N. R. We won't talk here. Please meet us downstairs on the plaza, in that little garden with the crab apple trees. Please come down there and talk with us."

The girl nods.

"We'll expect you in ten minutes," Hasani says.

The girl closes the door.

Hasani makes a show of exasperation for the several other heads poking into the hallway to suggest no information was exchanged in the short interview. Then she and Agent Parker head for the elevator.

Hasani and Carol exit Tower F, cross the walkway and plaza, and enter a small garden. A wooden bench is located among several flowering crab apple trees—naked at this time of year—set in a huge concrete tub. It's a pleasant day for November, sunny and—she checks her phone—forty-three degrees.

"Agent Parker, I can tell from her reaction that the young girl across the hall from 1217 knows N. R. and fears he's in trouble. She's home today, and not in school, though I noticed she had her coat and boots on. She was ready to leave the apartment. I'm convinced she'll come down and talk with us."

Hasani is correct. The girl comes through the door and walks toward them.

Hasani says, "Miss, thank you for talking with us. This is Agent Carol Parker of the FBI. We are looking for N. R. Please ... can you help us find him?"

The girl immediately tears up and nods a weak consent.

Hasani points. "Over there ... on that bench."

They walk to a wood-slat bench and sit down.

The girl begins to softly cry. She wipes her eyes with the back of her hand and looks up. "Okay ... I will help you ... if I can."

"Thank you. What is your name?"

The frightened girl shakes her head and starts to sob again.

"That's all right, *gabar gacaliyo* [dear girl]. I talked with the Work/Study Office at the university, and they told me N. R. stopped working without notice. They gave me his address as unit F1217. He lives across the hall. So ... you do know him, don't you?"

"Yes, I do. And you are right. N. R. is missing. Though neither of the drawings you've shown me is of him." She takes the drawings from Hasani's hand and concentrates on them. She points to the letters "FBI" at the top. It's obvious she understands the insinuation of an FBI drawing. "Does … does that mean?" She lowers her head and begins to cry again.

Hasani holds the young girl close as she softly weeps.

Suddenly, the girl pulls herself up, wipes her eyes on her clothing, and installs a strong, defiant face. "I'm sorry. I'm ready now." She wipes a few stubborn tears from her face. "But I do know these two boys. This one is N. R.'s best friend, A. H. They often study together. A. H. attends Saint Thomas in Saint Paul. And this one's named T.N., a friend of A. H.'s and also a chemistry student at Saint Thomas. All three study together sometimes at the Wilson Library." She points in the general direction of a building a couple blocks east, down Riverside Street.

"Do you know where A. H. and T.N live?"

"I don't know T.N., but I know A. H. lives in Saint Paul on the Green Line, in those new apartments across the street from Target. N. R. pointed his building out to me once."

"Does anyone know what happened to N. R.? Where he might be?"

"Not that I know. N. R. is a special boy, Miss Indaak. He works very hard. He studies chemistry at the university. He's a brilliant student. Then, all of a sudden, one day, he does not come home—and then, four or five days later, his family also leaves. Nobody knows where they went."

"I want you to help me find N. R., *gabar gacaliyo*." She gives the girl a business card and a pen. "And I will need your name and phone. Will you do that?"

"Yes. But you think he's dead, don't you? You think soon you will have an FBI death mask drawing of him too, don't you?"

"That's the most likely case, but it is not yet known. I can always hope that is not true for N. R."

Agent Parker and Hasani discuss the sad situation with the young Somali girl and persuade her to help them. They cross the street to Agent Parker's car and travel to Saint Paul. They must bring the certain sad news of their children's death to the parents of A.R. and T.N. Such work is a horrible burden to place on a young immigrant girl, and it is late in the darkening afternoon when Hasani and Agent Parker return the totally spent Somali girl to her apartment at Mogadishu in the Sky. Agent Parker gives her a parting hug along with one additional odious task: to ask around and try to find out where N. R.'s family has gone so that Agent

Parker can contact them, confirm that their son is missing, and—based on the history of his two friends—inform them of his almost certain fate.

Hasani exits the complex concrete megastructure that is Mogadishu in the Sky into a light snow. She hugs Agent Parker goodbye, watches her drive away, and then walks two blocks to Kafe Korol. She sits at the bar, orders a cup of tea, and takes a deep breath. When the tea comes, she takes a sip. Only then does she feel she can summon the strength to call Steffie.

"Good evening, Steffie. I have awful news for you. I'm close to tears myself because it's extremely sad news, and it's all very confusing."

"I'm sorry, Hasani. The whole world's confusing. Why should your story be different?"

"I know, I know. It's just that once in a while, the answer should be clear and cleanly cut so the problem is solved. Bing, just like that."

"I don't like it when a conversation starts out like this, Hasani. What have you found?"

"I've just had the worst afternoon of my entire life, Steffie. I've had to tell two mothers their sons have died." She takes a deep breath and regains her composure. "It's something I'm afraid I will never get over. And, to another girl, that her friend—and I think perhaps a future husband prospect—is, most likely, also dead.

"Oh, Hasani, that is terrible. You poor girl!"

"But, on the positive side, Steffie, I now can tell you the names of all three dead Somali men."

"What do you mean? Three? I only sent you two drawings. The sheriff told me only two—"

"But three men are missing, Steffie. That I can confirm. And the two pictures I received from you are two of those three sophomore chemistry students. The three close friends all went missing from their classes and their apartments at the same time … in early October."

"What do I do now, Hasani? Must I tell Sheriff Faber he's to expect a third dead Somali to show up? Do you suppose his body's buried in the smoldering rubble I waded through this morning?"

"I don't know. Either that or the police are keeping some evidence secret. I've talked to FBI Agent Carol Parker, here in Minneapolis, and she thanks us for finding the boys identities. She wants us to keep this third boy's death quiet—until they can match it to a body. She's headed back to the university to get a copy of N. R.'s student ID photo and will email it to me and Agent Brock in the Williston office. Agent Parker and I will go back to our girl and confirm the ID photo as a picture of her friend N. R."

"Oh, Hasani, I'm so sorry. I want to give you a hug."

"This is awful, Steffie. So far, only this one teenage girl in the entire Somali community knows about this story. Agent Parker told her not to say anything, but Carol and I realize there's no way a seventeen-year-old girl can hold a story like this for very long. It's all going to explode unexpectedly. I know it, and Carol knows it. Once it explodes, I fear no one will be able to stuff this thing—whatever it is—back into a box."

"I know you're right, Hasani, but it's the FBI's case now. If it explodes, it will be on their watch."

"Technically, you're right, Steffie, but you and I are parked in the middle here. We both must be careful and keep looking over our shoulders. I don't want to be standing near this story when it explodes. I'm frightened, Steffie—I don't like explosions."

CHAPTER 39

REGARDING THE BURLINGTON-NORTHERN OIL TRAIN

THE TRAIN IN QUESTION IS 152 cars long, and each car is a tank car carrying at least 30,100 gallons—approximately seven hundred barrels—of crude oil. This oil train uses four locomotives in the front for pulling and one in the rear for pushing. Thus propelled, it averages thirty-seven miles per hour between the Williston terminal and its destination: a western Illinois refinery, across the Mississippi, near Saint Louis.

The railroad tank car in question is dull, grimy, black, and sprinkled with a set of originally white letters and numbers that probably mean something to some computer in San Francisco or Houston. One of the numbers—ELP44356—identifies the car. Another number—30,100 gal. max.—indicates the amount of oil it can carry. These and other white numbers are painted on this black tank just above the left wheel truck on each side of the car. The rationale for the other numbers is hidden in arcane regulations, and nowhere—unless it is in the coded numbers—is it indicated who owns, leases, or is using this tank car. As mandated by federal regulation, six white, vertical, two-foot-long stripes are painted on each side of the tank to allow it to be seen by the driver of a car approaching an unmarked railroad crossing at night. Finally, this car numbered ELP44356 is, counting from the front, the fifty-seventh of the 152 cars making up this train.

The black metal box in question is formed from a sheet of galvanized steel, painted oil-car black and bolted to the black steel angle supporting the metal stairs at the west end of tank car ELP44356. Though this box has been attached to this tank car for less than two weeks, it carries a patina of grime that masks this short history. A metal tag, embossed with an eight-digit number and some technical language, indicates this box carries a monitoring device of some sort belonging to a testing company with an address in Provo, Utah.

Mason Bracket saw the whole thing go down. Mason's doing this morning like he's done many Sundays for the past six years. He's walking the two and a half miles north from his house—a three-room cabin heated only with a wood stove—into the town of Mandan to the First Pentecostal Church of God. This Sunday, it's cold—around fifteen degrees—but there's no wind. The sun is bright behind him. He's been aware of the low rumbling sound for a while, but it still surprises him a bit when the four dirty, orange diesel engines emerge from behind a windbreak of evergreen trees and cross the farm lane a half mile ahead of where he's walking. The engines pull a long line of black oil tank cars across the dirt farm road that serves as his sidewalk this morning. Mason is not concerned. He doesn't think the train will keep him from making the service on time. He estimates that by the time he walks half a mile, the entire train will be out on the bridge over the Missouri River. He's not concerned about time. He has never, in his entire life, been concerned about time.

The Missouri River, a quarter of a mile to the east, is sparkling under the bright sun. To be honest, it's not the river he sees sparkling; it is the huge ice chunks almost filling the river's surface and slowly meandering south. Those massive ice floes, unlike the train, emit no noise as they move—at least none that he can hear from this distance. Except for the train noise, the land sits quiet as eternity is said to sit. Mason thinks maybe he should say a prayer. He believes some words must be uttered to celebrate this glorious Sunday.

Mason stops a couple hundred feet before the crossing. He'll stay an appropriate distance back from anything that black and noisy. It seems like the right thing to do, especially on a Sunday morning. He sees the orange diesel engines are out over the Missouri now, crossing that long steel trestle-bridge, and the low winter sun is bouncing sparkles off the angled glass of the engine's cabin, which flashes bits of glare right back at him. Mason blinks and is immediately and unexpectedly aware of a black and orange plume springing up from the line of black tank cars, probably three-quarters of a mile east, out over the river. A second or two later comes the expected sound of the explosion.

That sound physically shakes him. He drops to his knees—just in case this has anything to do with God. The whole thing plays in slow motion. A second car explodes, and both tank cars break into in several pieces, which jump off the trestle and dive onto the ice floes. A veil of flame flows off the bridge after the cars. More black smoke than he's seen in his entire life billows into the air. The momentum of the following tank cars carries them into the pile of exploding metal out there on the trestle. Boom. And then again. Boom. And then again.

Mason stays on his knees on the frozen snow-covered farm road. The unbearable noise continues as the pusher engine, unaware of the trouble at the front of the train, and unable to stop even if necessary, keeps pushing more tank cars into the growing heap of twisted, coal-black, liquorish-stick like cars. He hears much grinding and gnashing as the cars crumble into each other. When the grinding and shrieking of metal finally stops, he summons the courage to look. The length of black oil tank cars in front of him is no longer moving, but it is still blocking his path. Several cars are off the track in front of him. He sees two buckled, broken cars pouring black syrup over his farm road, and he realizes he is not going to be getting himself into church this morning—but he's confident God will understand he did sincerely intend to do so.

Though it's over half a mile away, he can see burning oil pouring from the ruptured cars over the side of the trestle and onto the ice floes on the river. Floating pads of burning black ice are inching slowly south, downriver, and will soon bang into the ice-covered reservoir. The echoes of the last several blasts subside, and it's eerily quiet. Mason thinks he should be doing something, but what can he possibly do? Is there someone he should call? He has a cell phone, but the thousands of citizens of Mandan living north of the tracks are much closer and have surely seen and heard the same thing he's seen and heard. Those who must be told have probably felt the blast, seen the smoke, and already been called into action.

He realizes he can do nothing—except perhaps pray. But for what?

He understands it's black, but it's only oil. Nevertheless, he remains on his knees in the white snow. Two more cars explode. This apparently is the religion he'll be getting this morning. He'll take it, but he has no idea what this strange ritual is meant to symbolize. Another car explodes, this one almost in front of him, and the concussion knocks him off his knees. Prostrated before this sacrifice, Mason senses a message sent straight from the back of God's hand. And since he's the only one here, this message must be aimed at him.

"Oh my God," he prays. "Forgive me for my sins." He watches the smoke ascend to the heavens. Mason is not totally sure, but he believes that is what smoke is designed to do, especially on a Sunday morning during the Advent season. "Oh my God," he prays once more. "Forgive me for my sins."

CHAPTER 40

SMOKE IN THE SKY

ROBERT BOWSTRINGER AND HANK FORD stand near the entrance to Bowstringer's tent and discuss how they should react to the impending Corps of Engineers' stop construction order regarding the PFUMP pipeline they've been protesting for several months. These two have hastily arranged a giant celebration in response to the stop order. They've won the fight—though, to be honest, everyone on both sides knows this fight's not won, but only paused for a month or two. For now, everyone can go home. Bowstringer's eye notices a smoke plume jumping into the sky in the northeast.

"What the hell, Robert?" Ford says. His hand, in a reflex action, zips up and points at the plume as a second one explodes high in the sky.

A low sharp-edged sound, a distant thunder crack, smashes and then rumbles over and around the low hills and loess dunes adjacent to the Missouri. Just as it dies out, another rumble of sound bounces around the clear blue sky.

"I can't imagine what's over there that's capable of exploding like that." Bowstringer points. "You suppose we should run over and find out?"

"That's miles away, probably near Mandan. There are plenty of people over there, Robert, and they have access to fire equipment. We've only got an hour and a half before our news conference starts. Where'd you put that copy of the stop order?"

"I'm worried, Hank. Maybe people are hurt."

"If you want to go, Robert, then please go. I've got things to do, stuff to organize, and comments to prepare. Go. Go. I'll be fine."

CHAPTER 41

MORE SMOKE IN THE SKY

Larry Oosterhaus and Carl Two Deer are finishing a late breakfast at the huge wooden table in Two Deer's congregation room. The room is semicircular, like a meeting room should be, and facing generally east, so the morning sun pours through the entire great window. Two Deer and Oosterhaus both sit on the table's south side so the sun's not in their eyes so much; at least they don't have to squint to appreciate the vista over the Oahe Reservoir.

Larry's been visiting Two Deer every Sunday since Leon gave him the job of solving this standoff over the pipeline installation. Both men realize they can do little to ease tensions or frame arguments that will get their people out of the freezing cold, but the talks are satisfying to both gentlemen. They are the same age—sixty-four—which Two Deer thinks is past the age for stirring up crowds, but they have not yet reached the age to be classified elder statesmen.

"I'm just an old man." Larry points out the window to the north-northeast. "What the hell is that? Looks like a fire, and there's another one." Just as his pointing arm reaches full extension, they hear the concussion. Even at this distance, it shakes the huge table. However, some of the shaking may have been caused by Larry's knee hitting the table leg as the noise startles him. "That's no normal fire, Carl. That's an oil fire. Look at that black smoke and those flashes of orange in the billowing black. That's oil—I'd bet my farm on it."

The two men stare in silence as more and more smoke piles high into the windless sky.

"I don't remember an oil tank farm or refinery over on that section of the river. Do you, Carl?"

"No, I don't think so. Seems to me those plumes are farther east than Mandan."

"But there's nothing east of Mandan. Nothing but the river. The Missouri's almost a mile wide there."

The two men look hard at each other.

"That smoke doesn't look right, Carl. Something's very wrong. It makes me nervous." Larry pushes his chair back and stands up. "Something's not right. I'm gonna drive up and find out what the hell's happening. Wanna come along?"

CHAPTER 42

EVEN MORE SMOKE IN THE SKY

L EON AND HIS MOTHER ARE attending an annual Advent event at Saint Olaf's Lutheran Church in Bismarck. His mother holds some position on the Grandmother's Christmas Clothing Drive, which collects, repairs, and then packages and sends clothes, blankets, and other goods to various native reservations in the state. The collection and repair phases are year-round efforts, but the packaging and distribution functions occur over a two-week period in the middle of Advent. His mom's been at the church almost nonstop for these last weeks, and that's cut way down the number of lunches Leon's been able to sponge off her.

This morning, Leon's red GMC pickup, like several dozen other pickups, is parked along the east side of the church parking lot, back end to the curb adjacent to the walkway, so other volunteers can walk the armfuls of clothing out the door of the church hall and down that sidewalk to the appropriate truck. The procedure's been tested for about thirty years, and most all the kinks are now worked out. Of course, everything is right on schedule—as it always is—and everyone is having a glorious time doing the distribution work in the warm sunshine.

Leon's pickup is halfway full of paper bags and boxes the local grocery store has been saving for this effort for a couple of weeks. He moves briskly from the tailgate back to the growing pile and places new boxes and bags there. He's actually working up a sweat. His phone sounds from his front shirt pocket.

He unzips the pocket, removes his phone, sees it's Margie, and sits down on the side rail of the pickup box. "Good morning, Margie. Since it is ten thirty on Sunday morning, I'll bet you don't have any good news for me, do ya?"

"You're right, Leon. It's not good. It's fairly damn bad news. I'm afraid I must inform you there's been an accident of some sort on the Burlington-Northern trestle crossing the Missouri just south of Mandan."

"What kind of accident, Margie? Anybody get hurt?"

"Don't know the details yet. The only thing I've been told is that it's an oil car train and several of the cars have jumped off the bridge and into the river, and several others are on fire. You're over at Saint Olaf's, right? You can probably see that black smoke from there. It's only about twenty miles, and it's profusely bubbling up into the sky. I can see it from my house, which means that every damn house in the city of Bismarck can see that damn smoke too."

"You're throwin' me an awful lot of 'damns' for a Sunday morning, Margie. This may sound like a terrible thing to ask, but what the hell does anybody expect I can do to help lessen the damage over there? Shouldn't I just stay away and let the cleanup crews do what they're supposed to do?"

"That's absolutely right, Leon. If I were you, I'd go back to boxing up clothes or whatever. Just thought you'd like to know."

"Margie?"

"Yes, Leon."

"With all those sudden fires happening in my state recently, what are the odds this event's not, as you just insinuated, an accident?"

"Neither I nor the Mandan fire chief, who called me, are going to make any estimation as to the non-degree of non-accident status of this event."

"Those are fairly well-chosen words, Margie."

"Yup! That they are, Leon. However, keep in mind that the chief informed me of this event on the governor's terrorism hotline, which means—"

"Yeah, Margie, I know what that means. And now we both know that even though the word *terrorism* will probably never be mentioned, at least for the next few days, we all know that whatever the hell happened down there is not any accident."

"That's about it, Governor."

"Thank you, Margie. It sure is interesting being governor. Let me know if anything else blows up."

"Yes, Governor. I most certainly will."

CHAPTER 43

OIL BURNING OUT ON THE TRESTLE

LARRY AND CARL DRIVE NORTH on County Road 101, and four miles after they leave the reservation boundary, they approach the point where the Burlington Northern railroad track crosses County Road 101. They run into a knot of congestion—a dozen cars crawling toward the intersection—monitored by police from several jurisdictions. The queue slowly edges north.

An officer standing on the railroad track at the point where it crosses the highway waves his arms to force the traffic to move faster.

As Larry moves his truck over the tracks, Carl looks to the east, down the tracks toward the black clouds bursting into the sky. "Jesus Christ, Larry. Seems like dozens of oil cars are on fire. How can that possibly happen?"

"The train's been bombed, Carl. Most likely in several places. That can only happen if humans did it. Oil cars don't burst into flames on their own, especially those out over the middle of the river. This is not an accident; it's a deliberate act of sabotage. Hell, Carl, it's a terrorist act!"

"I cannot believe anyone would do such a thing on purpose, Larry. What's to gain by blowing up oil tank cars? Especially in North Dakota?"

"I can think of one possibility. People on one side or the other of this PFUMP controversy are trying to make a point about how dangerous it is to transport oil across a river."

"But that stop order defused that issue, right?"

"Could be a protest against that stop order, Carl. That could happen. It's a weird world out there."

At the first intersection north of the tracks, Larry turns east onto County Road 73. He talks with the police officer preventing access to that road, informs him of his and Carl's credentials, and receives approval to continue east.

After another quarter mile and another discussion with another officer, Larry is allowed to park his truck. He and Two Deer walk the short distance to the riverbank where the entire scene is revealed. Approximately half of the 152-car train is dead still on the bridge out over the water. The remainder is bungled up west of the water on solid ground. The orange engines that are supposed to be pulling this train have almost made it to the east end of the bridge, and the cars on fire are a third of the way between the last pier on shore and the diesels at the front end. All of a sudden, another car explodes, spraying fire, oil, and metal into the air.

The power of the concussive boom almost knocks Carl Two Deer off his feet. "Damn, that's powerful, Larry. And we're probably half a mile away."

"And that explosion means that whoever's responsible for this is watching this thing burn and is still blowing up cars with phone-activated detonators. Somebody around here is evil." He swings around, thinking he might just catch a guy with his finger on a button and stars in his eyes.

Larry takes out his phone, takes a quick video sweep of the fire on the bridge and the small crowd watching it, and emails the video to Leon. Then he calls him.

"Leon, I'm standing here with Carl Two Deer. Carl and I are enjoying another day in the neighborhood. We're on the banks of the Missouri, just south of Mandan, and we're watching oil tank cars exploding and throwing burning oil into your river."

"It's not my river, Larry. It belongs to Uncle Sam. I just talked to Margie. She received a heads-up from the Mandan fire chief. He'll be keeping me up to date. I'm with Mom now, doing Christmas baskets at Saint Olaf's. I'm maybe twenty miles away, and I can see the smoke from here."

"This is very odd, Leon. I'm positive this fire's the result of a deliberate action by some idiot. Hell, though I very much doubt it, let's for now call him a terrorist. And this thing ain't over. Cars are continuing to blow up. Whoever is doing this is smart, Leon. One has to be a pro to be able to blow up a train on a trestle half a mile out over the river."

"Thanks for stopping by and checking it out, old buddy."

"No problem. And I'll bet we'll find it's connected with those other explosions in Williston last week."

"I'm not sure I agree with that, Larry. Remember, in just one week, that stop order takes hold. This could be someone making a point about the need for a safe, tamperproof silver pipeline for shipping our oil."

"I suppose you could be right. The thing that bothers me though is the surreal nature of all this mayhem. I'm having difficulty actually believing somebody's doing this. It just not like the way real people act, especially in North Dakota."

"I know, Larry. It's got me baffled too. Would you do me a favor, old buddy? Would you stick around there for a while? Keep your eyes and ears open. Maybe some clue will fall into your lap. Oh, and if you see him, let the Mandan fire chief know you're there representing the governor, will you?"

Larry puts his phone in his pocket and then takes it right back out. "Carl, that last explosion means this guy's still pushing buttons. He'd have to be standing somewhere where he can see the train on that trestle, and that means he could be standing around here, among this crowd of folks, and watching his handiwork."

Carl immediately looks left and right, hoping to see an obvious terrorist. "That means he's not a terrorist but a vetted, perhaps trusted, citizen who could talk his way past the roadblock up there. Look at the trouble we two distinguished gentlemen had getting past security."

"So, Carl, you and I must casually photo-document this entire crowd—everyone who's standing around here—from multiple positions. As we walk around, we'll keep our phone cameras operating and try to get every mug and every license plate. We'll give our videos to the FBI and let them do their magic with all this information. Maybe we'll get lucky. Maybe, just maybe, the bastard makes a mistake."

"What do you mean by mistake, Larry?"

"I'm thinking our terrorist must be hanging around to watch his handiwork. Maybe he's got a different look on his face. He'd be satisfied, right? Looking pleased with his efforts, as opposed to being horrified by this mess as any normal human being would be. The FBI has video analysis programs that can analyze faces for that stuff."

"Really? They can do that?" Carl takes out his phone and turns on his camera. "Two eyes are better than one, right?"

CHAPTER 44

WHO OWNS DAKOTA'S OIL?

N ORTH DAKOTA AGRIBUS IS THE local subsidiary of an international conglomerate based in Zurich. NDA owns, partly owns, or controls the operation of thirteen ethanol refineries across North Dakota. They also have a majority interest in the several dozen corporate farms that produce most of the corn and other custom-designed grasses used to fuel those refineries. Charlie Neubauer, NDA's CEO, cochairs Governor Rolfes's business roundtable group with Russell Cordoba, one of the larger private landowners in the state.

These two native North Dakotans are successful businessmen with keen political skills, and they are dedicated to ensuring North Dakota remains a strong and independent state. Their several businesses—even Charlie's mother company, headquartered in Zurich—are structured to ensure that money earned in North Dakota is taxed and invested in North Dakota and not shipped to Houston, New York, Zurich or, even worse, Saudi Arabia. These two businessmen and their business roundtable strongly back the governor's Subsurface Materials Ownership Act.

Charlie and Russell are also Minnesota Vikings fans, and since it's Sunday afternoon, Russell's huge TV is running the Vikings game. Russell's turned the sound down almost to mute. Even with little sound, viewing live action at that scale is impressive. Even more impressive is the view through the floor-to-ceiling glass that allows Russell and Charlie to comprehend the thousands of acres of Cordoba's Dakota prairie land stretching toward the western horizon. A few dozen buffalo—a feature

Russell inserted to add scale to his tableau—are grazing, in a clump, in the distance.

Russell points out toward his buffalo. "The Sioux aren't the only residents of this great state who think that land out there is sacred. If we take care of it and work it properly, that prairie will sustain us all. But if we let those Texans ..."

Making sure Texans cannot suck the value out of the riches buried beneath the North Dakota prairie is the reason these two men are meeting today. Governor Rolfes has given them the job of building a consensus for his plan to have the state seize ownership of all subsurface mineral rights. The governor understands it's a radical idea—one many think is too liberal or even a bit socialistic—for a stodgy state like North Dakota, but it's an idea the governor, Charlie, and Russell are all committed to. They believe they can design an argument that can be sold to their conservative citizens as basically a conservative idea. They propose operating North Dakota as a conservative businessman might run his own corporation.

Under Leon's plan, the state of North Dakota will not legally own the oil hidden five to ten miles below the surface. Like now, nobody will own that treasure. It remains as a natural resource. However, it will be the residents of the state who, acting in common and through the state government, will reclaim the right to harvest the oil hidden down there. The current legal condition—the case since the state was first chartered— is that the deed holder of the surface land does not own the oil buried beneath his land. That oil, as a legal entity, does not even exist. However, as is the case with other natural resources in most places around the country, any entity—either a single live person or a five-lettered entity on a paper in a file drawer in Houston—can legally claim the right to harvest that resource, and once the commodity is harvested, that entity can sell it— even though the ownership of the oil itself has never been technically, or even legally, established. And the present situation adds another degree of ambiguity because, when the state charter was established in 1848, even the concept that any material could be removed from a mine located five to ten miles beneath the prairie surface was like a fairy tale.

Though Russell owns the prairie grass, weeds, scrub bushes, and buffaloes, some faceless limited partnership with a legal mailbox in Houston has claimed the right to harvest any piece of interesting solid or liquid sleeping below the surface of his prairie, even—there are no vertical limits associated with this undefined right—down thousands of miles to the center of the earth. And that five-lettered Texas partnership can renew its claim in perpetuity, without any cost—except, in some cases, a filing fee—and even considering that to the best of anybody's knowledge, there is no oil hiding beneath his land. Much of subsurface western North Dakota has been claimed by out-of-state—mostly Texas-based—partnerships and hedge funds rather than by citizens of North Dakota. Many "owners" are unknown entities, partners in blind partnerships of several forms, and most of these entities are registered in Texas.

And there's a second problem making ownership of that deeply hidden oil a rather amorphous thing. The horizontal drilling techniques currently in use can pull oil horizontally from more than a mile away from the surface location of the wellhead. The buried oil puddles pay no attention to the property lines laid out on the surface, which set only the surface boundaries and not any limit on the subsurface boundaries. That pumping rig you see working in your neighbor's pasture is, most likely, sucking oil out from under your land!

And an even sadder thing is the surface owner, by law, must allow access to those hidden assets to the claimant of the hidden materials. It turns out, he also becomes responsible for much environmental and economic damage occurring as a result of the drilling and sucking that the Texas entity is doing five miles deep under his land. Leon argues that the state of North Dakota must hold the harvesting rights for that deep oil—without respect to any human-drawn property lines on the surface. He argues that the only way to fix ownership problems is to return the value of oil reserves to the citizens of North Dakota. Then, if North Dakota owns the harvesting rights, North Dakota has the authority to market and sell the oil. North Dakota can then decide how to transport the oil and determine the parameters of the pipeline designed to send any oil they pump up to the surface—to some faraway place like Illinois.

The people of North Dakota can keep their own collective interest paramount, above the interests of hard-to-pin-down, politically connected, well-leveraged, and fairly amorphous limited master partnerships registered in Houston. As of now, however, it is those strange, irresponsible, and shrouded entities that do not even own the oil that are now fracking, sucking, pumping, and eventually selling the stuff to entities outside of North Dakota. And if the experts are correct, and that new cheap Texas oil comes online, all the debris, the rusting wells, the oil spills, and the highway damage remaining in North Dakota will, by default, be assumed by the residents of North Dakota.

Leon has scheduled an open meeting next Tuesday evening at the Standing Rock Community Center to outline the parameters of this subsurface rights issue to the representatives of North Dakota's various tribes. Russell Cordoba and Charlie Neubauer will represent Leon's initiative at that meeting, arguing the case for his Subsurface Materials Ownership Act before the assembled Native American communities. After all, it's also their oil rights that are being ignored by those sneaky Texan partnerships.

Opposition to Leon's plan will come from the out-of-state oil development companies that benefit from the current conditions. Those carnivores will automatically oppose any rule or regulation they haven't written themselves and that might give oversight authority to anyone but themselves. Some opposition may come from the conservative business community, which believes that any restriction on any business is the first step taken on the eventual path to socialism. And that purposely misunderstood word—*socialism*—is a powerful weapon the oil companies often use, though few folks on either side actually understand that word's definition or meaning. The word still carries an immense *memory baggage quotient,* which recalls other twentieth-century incendiary isms like Marxism, Bolshevism, and Communism.

"Our job, Charlie, is to find the correct descriptive words and then package this action properly. We have to make people realize the state will be protecting Native American subsurface heritage and securing natural resources for the people, doing high moral things normally associated with angels or Abe Lincoln—"

"You know, Russell, that sounds like something Two Deer would say: 'We two are doing our work while respecting the Great Father Spirit who gave us this land.'"

"Yeah, that sounds promising, but how you think we're gonna pull that off?"

"I'm not sure yet, but we've got till Tuesday night to do it."

"You may be onto something, Russell. We could get Carl Two Deer to put his name on this thing too and have him do some talking. Leon and Two Deer dancing on the same stage. How can that go wrong?"

Russell's phone interrupts their creative musings.

"Hey, Governor. How ya doin'?"

"I need some help, buddy. Where the hell are you?"

"I'm way out west, Leon, at my place. I'm with Charlie. We're watching the Vikings and doin' some planning for your special session."

"Damn. I wanted you to be here in Bismarck."

"Why? What's the problem?"

"What's not a problem? ISIS, or some other idiot, is blowing up oil cars on the bridge over the Missouri!"

"What?"

"Yeah, things are goin' to hell quickly, and I'm stuck helping my mom with Christmas stuff at Saint Olaf's! And that megalomaniac Basehardt just announced he's holding an impromptu rally near the site on the Missouri where the oil cars are exploding! Larry and Two Deer are poking around and monitoring the damage. I thought if you were around … you know … I'd have another pair of eyes and ears to monitor that bastard's three o'clock rally. Or maybe I need some guy who knows how to use a bludgeon."

"Sorry, Leon. That's not possible. Charlie and I are …"

"You're doin' good work out there, Russell. You guys get back to work. Say hi to Charlie. I'll find some other guy to push Basehardt off the bridge. Maybe I can sic Mom on him!"

CHAPTER 45

SMOKE IN THE SKY, FIRE ON THE ICE

AFTER BASEHARDT'S SHORT ADDRESS WHIPS up his crowd, the sun vanishes, and the temperature dives toward zero, many of Basehardt's followers—and numerous incidental folks interested in spectacular visual displays—are still in the area to watch the almost-frozen Missouri slowly slogging its way toward South Dakota. Normally, watching an almost frozen-over river slog southward on a dark, overcast night in the middle of winter is not a whole lot of fun. Tonight, a crowd of perhaps two hundred gawkers stand at the Standing Rock Overlook, fighting for viewing space to do just that. Tonight, watching the river flow is bizarrely spectacular entertainment. The river's not completely frozen, and it's too dark to make out the crowded field of block ice—some pieces as large as football fields—which slowly bungle down the river, rub against and bounce off each other, form larger pieces, break into smaller pieces, and all the while making a reasonable amount of low rumbling noises.

That is the audible part of the excitement and normal behavior for the almost-frozen-over river in the last days of November, but that is not what is bringing the crowd out here this evening. Tonight's excitement is a visual performance by the river. Tonight, at this overlook, located four miles downstream from the Burlington Northern railroad trestle, the wide, almost fully frozen Missouri is on fire.

Actually, it's not the river itself since water and ice do not burn. It's the oil that's burning. It's pouring fire and dripping sludge from the wrecked tank cars on the Burlington Northern trestle. Since the river's mostly covered in ice chunks, most of that burning oil splatting itself out of the cars fell, sprinkled, or oozed down onto the ice chunks. And there was a lot of oil, and those oil puddles are, like candles, still burning since the morning's explosion. Periodically, a car, adjacent to one already aflame, attains a critical temperature, explodes, and throws even more burning oil onto the ice below. And the burning illuminates the ice floes, which take on an appearance, from a distance, of candles moving strangely southward in some mass religious vigil.

To be geographically correct, this overlook does not look over the Missouri River. This overlook is located within the general area where the name of the body of water changes from the Missouri River to the Oahe Reservoir. The water is held back by the Oahe Dam, which is located way south of this overlook and well into South Dakota.

The Oahe Dam produces a huge reservoir that is more than a hundred miles long and, in certain places, fifteen miles wide. Once the ice floes get to the reservoir, they essentially stop moving because the current essentially vanishes. The water, blocked by the dam, is not running downhill anymore. And because the water surface is not moving, the ice on the reservoir is packed differently and freezes quicker than the ice moving on the river—the chunks are smashed close together and have no room to independently maneuver. The burning candles stop moving, and the masses of burning oil coalesce.

That act of coalescence makes it easier for the several helicopters, flitting about like scavenging petrels, to fly over the burning flows and monitor them to make sure that as much of the oil as possible is, indeed, burning. That's necessary because burning the oil is the most efficient means of cleaning up the spill. Every once in a while, a flash of flame from a helicopter-mounted flamethrower zips onto a floe and ignites another patch of dead, unburnt oil. It's a spectacular ceremony to watch.

It's below zero tonight, and after a few more days of this freeze, the ice will set firm. No more oil will be able to dribble off a floe and slide down into the water. Any oil that slips under the ice is going to stay buried until spring. The kind and degree of environmental damage is mostly unknown, but any damage can be lessened by burning as much oil as possible while it's still puddled on the surface of the ice.

Observers watching from the shore cannot see—and so certainly cannot appreciate—all the intricate dancing with the helicopters and the lights. Few folks notice one helicopter, a mile out, has lowered itself almost to the surface of one particular ice floe. This large floe is of interest because the helicopter's lights have illuminated the burnt carcass of an oil tank car—or at least a twisted piece of one—that was blown off the bridge. Among the remaining chunks of this tank car is a six-foot tubular piece of the tank. This tubular piece is still attached to its truck—that set of four wheels supporting one end of the car. The copter's searchlight illuminates several white painted numbers—ELP44356—printed on the black piece of tank tube directly above where the truck's wheels are attached to it.

Two workmen, Brad and Tony, are lowered to the surface of the floe with enough cabling to form the necessary slings to allow the copter to pull up this piece of car ELP44356, carry it to a staging yard, and set up on the shore for a recovery procedure. The retrieved tank car pieces will give the sleuths something to investigate in the days and months to come.

Brad and Tony remain tethered to their safety ropes, which dangle from the copter and prevent them from slipping through a crack and into the water. As this partial carcass of tank car ELP44356 is lifted off the ice, additional globs of black, grimy stuff are revealed beneath it.

Tony radios his supervisor up in the copter and says, "Ya want us to torch that oil before we leave?" Before he even receives an answer, as he shines his powerful light on a certain portion of the oily mess, he yells, "Holy shit, Brad. Look at this!" He reads the one small white word his torch illuminates amid all the black gunk. "Thing says 'Puma.' There's only one thing I know says 'Puma' like that."

Brad hurries over and pokes at the glob with a steel prod. "Good God, Tony. That's a human foot."

Tony screams into the mouthpiece on his helmet: "Damn, we just found a body down here, hidden under that tank car section you just brought up. Send down an air-rescue sled."

*   *   *

Four hours later, at 11:49 p.m., Governor Rolfes, receives a second call from FBI Special Agent Harrison Brock.

"Good evening, Governor. You wanted me to call—no matter the time—so I'm calling. Nothing's final here yet. Final ain't gonna happen for hours, maybe days. But I'm on speaker here with Dr. John McGee, the chief medical inspector at the State Crime Lab. He'll tell you the result of his preliminary autopsy."

"Thank you, Agent Brock," says Leon. "I wouldn't be able to sleep with this hanging unresolved."

"Me neither, Governor," says Dr. McGee. "I can report that the victim we pulled off that floe is a male. A small, thin black man, and he looks to be at least sixty years old. And the strange part, Governor, I autopsied those Williston kids a couple weeks ago, and I'm gonna say—better than that, I'd be willing to bet my medical license—that this guy's also a Somalian. Isn't that weird?"

"Yes. This shatters the notion I held earlier today, which was that the train explosion was connected to the pipeline standoff. I must now connect this thing to the Williston explosion. Is that right, Agent Brock?"

"I would agree, Governor. We now have found dead Somali men at each explosion venue. That is powerful evidence of a connection."

"Also, Governor," says Dr. McGee, "I'm confident he did not die in the oil car explosion this morning. He's been dead for several days. And likely a lot longer. I'm nowhere close to certifying the time of death. His body's saturated with oil. If I'm allowed a guess, I'd say this guy was riding inside the tank car with the oil. He's a small guy and thin enough for someone to stuff his dead body through the fill hatch and into the car. Then, when the car exploded, the tank ruptured, and he was flung onto the ice with the oil. This is about the weirdest thing I've seen as ME, Governor."

"What are the odds that with only a couple dozen of the 152 cars actually exploding, that one of the exploding ones held this body?"

"About zero, governor," says Brock. "This car was deliberately chosen to explode. You must keep Dr. McGee's report confidential. I'm not going to release this story till I know where it's going."

Leon shuts his phone. "Mom, I'm gonna change my mind again. Seems this train explosion is connected to the Williston explosions."

"Why? What happened?"

"According to the ME, the man found with the oil in Mandan had been stuffed into the oil tank—already dead—and he couldn't have been shoved into the car unless it was not moving. The last time that oil train was not moving for any length time before it exploded on that bridge was at the staging yards in Williston where they loaded the cars. That means the poor man was killed in Williston, same as those other guys, and that means I gotta rethink this whole messy incident. And that's gonna keep me awake all night."

"I'll get you some warm milk, honey. Drink that, and it will make it easier for you to get to sleep."

"No thanks, Mom. I'll be okay, but thanks for the thought."

"You go on upstairs, son. I'll close down things in here. Good night."

"No, it's not, Mom. It's not a good night. It's not a good night at all."

CHAPTER 46

COUNTING DEAD SOMALIS: ONE, TWO, THREE

MONDAY, NOVEMBER 28, 2016

AT NINE O'CLOCK ON MONDAY morning, Special Agent Harrison Brock enters the *Bismarck Plainsman's* small fourth-floor conference room.

Before Steffie can hang Brock's coat and scarf, the breakfasts arrive from Kathy's Kitchen—the first-floor cafe with a sixty-year catering association with the newspaper. This meeting is Brock's idea. He scheduled it after Agent Carol Parker from Minneapolis told him on Saturday night that three Minneapolis Somali men are missing. Then, last night, in Mandan, the fourth dead Somali was plopped onto the Missouri's ice.

"I need your help here, Ms. Cobb. I'm having difficulty making any order of this mess."

And that is a problem because Special Agent Harrison Brock, is, if nothing else, a well-ordered man—a sharply dressed black man with an attention to detail confirmed by his extremely thin, extremely horizontal, extremely black mustache. Brock's a smooth man, perhaps a different species, and he speaks in very precise, uncomplicated sentences as if English were his fourth or fifth language. He attacks his toast and egg like a surgeon might, with utensils held in the English manner. He seems out of place in the muddy, sooty, oily mess that he's stepped into in North Dakota.

"Ms. Cobb, we've got two dead Somali men in Williston, yet your compatriot, Hasani, has found that three Somali men from Minneapolis are now missing. How do you explain this?"

"I have no answer," says Steffie. "But two of those three have been visually confirmed as the two casualties found in Williston."

"And you have no idea where the third one is?"

"He apparently hasn't shown up yet, Agent Brock. If he has, Sheriff Faber is keeping me in the dark. However, Hasani and I do know who he is." She hands him a copy of N. R.'s student ID, which Hasani had emailed her on Saturday.

Special Agent Brock studies the photo. "This picture certainly is not the oil-drenched elderly man Dr. McGee and I examined last night, is it?" His phone buzzes. "Special Agent Brock here." He listens silently for thirty seconds and then says, "Thank you for returning my call, Agent Burroughs. I have just been given information that blows up the theories we discussed last night."

Brock readjusts N. R.'s student ID photo on the table in front of him. "Miss Cobb's associate in Minneapolis sent me a third photo ... of a third Somali youth gone missing in Minneapolis. He is an acquaintance of the two other dead Somali boys. The sixty-year-old found last night does not match this third youth. That can only mean we now have four dead Somali men."

"What?" Steffie spills a splash of coffee. "But I thought—"

His phone buzzes. "Yes, this is Agent Brock." He listens for another thirty seconds. "Yes, Agent Parker, I will." Another pause. "Yes, ma'am. I will. Thank you." He stows his phone in his pocket.

"Ms. Cobb, my associate tells me I'm to congratulate you and Hasani for a superb bit of detective work. If you two ever want a career in law enforcement—"

"Thank you, Agent Brock. Hasani's the one who found the trail. I'm not nearly patient enough to do that."

"I have been cleared to tell you a piece of information we have been keeping secret."

"I knew it!" Steffie pounds the table. "You have found the third boy's body, right?"

"Yes, it was found in the ashes of the Drilling Platform. My boss wanted to keep that off the record until we learned about all the casualties."

Steffie points to the TV on the wall. "Excuse me, Agent Brock. I believe we should listen to this. Mr. Basehardt's giving another news conference … or a rally … or something."

Will Basehardt is addressing a gathering. Behind him, oil tank cars on the Mandan Bridge are pumping fire and black smoke into the blue sky, making clear, blatant, visual associations with ISIS situations in Syria and Iraq.

Steffie grabs the remote, increases the volume, and sets her phone to record the sound and images from the screen. "Nobody told me about this news conference? How'd Channel 5 get this—and I didn't? Heads are going to roll!" She realizes then what's being broadcast is not a news conference; it is a political rally. And it is not live. "This piece of political theater was taped yesterday afternoon. See, Agent Brock? It's late afternoon, and there's a clear blue sky. She points out the window. "It's overcast this morning. This is a rebroadcast." She relaxes a degree or two.

"Here they come, folks!" Basehardt says. "The terrorists who blew up this oil train are being issued a free pass to enter our country by the imbeciles now running Washington. And this is what we get." He points to the smoke and flames. "Look, folks! This is what we get. Ugly black smoke staining our beautiful blue sky. Makes me sick. Makes you sick too, right? Am I right?" He waits for his supporters to quiet down. "These are radical Islamic terrorists, people. They blow things up. They blow our trains up. Believe me, we're going to stop this. Sure it'll take serious measures, but we gotta do it."

"Can't you stop him, Agent Brock?" Steffie places her hands over her ears and starts pacing. "Just stick a plug in his maw?"

"Starting on January 20, things will be different, folks. America's going to get serious about foreign terrorists flooding our country and preventing us from producing and marketing our own oil. It's obvious! Folks, ISIS wants to cripple our homegrown oil industry—so we're forced to buy their crude. We've already let four ISIS terrorists infiltrate North Dakota. They haven't killed any Americans yet, but what about next time? Fortunately those four have been killed, but what about the next wave? And we all know about waves—they naturally come in bunches. How many more ISIS terrorists are we gonna allow to sneak into this country to blow things up? How much more destruction are we gonna take before we strike back?"

A wave of applause and jeering rushes over the small crowd.

"I'm so mad at him, Agent Brock. If you don't take him off the street, I just might go shoot him myself."

"When our new administration enters Washington, you'll see these terrorist attacks stop. Pronto! Believe me! No more political correctness, right? Am I right? We're gonna make foreign Islamic bullies afraid of us again. I guarantee you these constant terrorist attacks will stop. We're gonna make North Dakota safe again."

His dozens of supporters yell and cheer. He suggests he'll persuade the president to come out to North Dakota, personally throw retardant on the fire, wave a sword, and run ISIS back to wherever.

"I can't watch it anymore, Agent Brock. I'm not sure he's keeping terrorists out or inviting them in. He knows damn well that those Williston explosions were not detonated by ISIS terrorists. He's talking more terrorism than any of those Islamic guys ever did."

"I do wish he would tone it down," says Brock. "The more he rants and raves, the more work I must do."

CHAPTER 47

COUNTING DEAD OIL RIGS: THREE, FOUR

THE MORE STEFFIE DISCOVERS ABOUT the nature of the oil business in the Bakken Field, the less she knows—and the more confused she gets. After the meeting with Agent Brock, she drives the two hours out to Williston to look under a few more rocks. She leaves the highway and takes county roads toward the site of the first explosions.

In the middle of nowhere, she's blasted by a strange image. As an investigative reporter, she knows it's her duty to investigate strange images. She stops on the side of the gravel road, which intersects a gravel drive. A couple hundred yards west, at the end of the drive, she sees a forest of oil drilling rigs in a fenced compound, huddled together in obvious storage mode. She turns onto the drive and advances toward the yard slowly. She approaches the imprisoned rigs, and dead-ends at a tall security fence with a locked gate. On the other side of this fence, there are rows and rows of dirty oil drilling rigs. She counts twenty-seven towers. Then, behind those rigs, thirty-two equipment trailers are set in several rows. Rows of oil field equipment are sorted and stacked. She counts and photographs everything inside the fence.

She then records a short essay: "Let's say I'm a nefarious dude wanting to blow up some oil rigs in Williston for the insurance money. Why would I choose an active site with the potential of supervisors and engineers lurking around when I have twenty-seven rigs and thirty-two trailers—I'm guessing fifty-million-bucks' worth of equipment—compressed into a tight formation. A couple bombs would nicely tangle them, and I could place my explosive devices out here in the middle of nowhere with little chance of anyone stopping by to question what I'm doing." She looks around and sees no evidence of any human activity. "Twenty-seven drilling rigs? Twenty-seven. Hmm. A couple weeks back, a news story noted the total number of active drilling rigs in all of North Dakota, as of September 1, had fallen all the way to twenty-seven.

"Recheck that number, Miss Reporter Lady. That would make an eerie comparison. Two years ago, if I remember correctly, more than two hundred drilling rigs were operating up here. Check that number too. Twenty-seven drilling rigs compared to more than two hundred must mean the Bakken oil industry is plunging toward certain death, right?"

After gaining as much information as possible from the twenty-seven drilling rigs, she continues her drive south and then east to the BX&F site. Two Sundays ago, several active rigs were blown up there. She stops at the half-open gate because she needs to know more about this site. Why was it still active when most others are shut down? Is this site still a moneymaker? Is it a big money pit? She plays by the rules, for the time being, and honks her horn to announce her arrival.

A man in dirty coveralls runs toward her. He is flailing his arms like a Canada goose. "No, lady. Stop! No, lady. Stop! You can't come in here!"

Steffie leans demurely against her car and recognizes Cletus. She's talked with him before.

"No, lady. Stay in car. Please!"

"Hi." She pushes off the car and stands up. "Remember me, Cletus? I'm Steffie. We talked before, and I'd like to you ask a few more questions."

"I am sure you're a nice lady, Miss Steffie, but I've got orders. No one comes in here. It's dirty—and dangerous."

"I think it'll be all right. I'm a reporter with *Dakota Fracking Magazine,* and I'm used to dirt and danger. I don't need to go inside. I want to ask you a few general questions, and then I'll leave you to do your work."

"Lady, my boss will fire me if I talk to you. So, even if I'd like to, I can't."

"Can you tell me why these wells are still pumping oil when so many others are being dismantled? I just saw dozens of dead drilling rigs in a storage yard several miles that way." She points northeast. "What you got inside this fence that other wells don't? Is that the reason for the fence? Are these special rigs?"

He points vaguely up into the air. "You wouldn't want me to get fired, would you?"

Steffie looks up to where he pointed, but she can see no cameras on any of the poles. She smiles and waves to any possible cameras. "Okay, so we won't talk here. Take my card. Call me tonight when you're alone in your room. We'll talk, off the record, and I'll never bring your name into my story. No one will ever know I talked with you—cross my heart and hope to die."

"I can't do it, Miss Steffie." He refuses her business card. "I'll lose my job." He looks sad, but his disposition suddenly changes. He gestures violently and stomps his foot. "Sorry, lady. You must leave now." He throws up his hands dramatically and walks back toward the beige trailer with the BX&F sign. Every couple steps, he turns around and says, "Go away."

That's odd, thinks Steffie. She takes a quick peek over her shoulder and recognizes the problem. A pickup is coming up County Road 342, trailing a rooster-tail of dust. "Uh-oh. Here comes trouble."

In a few minutes, a white GMC pickup skids to a stop by her car. Dust swirls about, and little stones sprinkle her legs and shoes. The driver's side window slips into the door, and the man inside the truck says, "Are you lost, miss? Williston's back that way."

"I figured that out by myself, sir." Steffie leans against her car again. "You've got some really nifty equipment in there, haven't you? Ya know, most people don't have the foggiest idea what marvelous things you're doing with pipe out here. Just imagine, going down nine or ten miles and then—"

"These wells only go down about five miles, miss. The nine-mile-deep ones are farther east of here."

"Oh!" Steffie says with a pout. "Those deep wells are what my readers want to know about. I thought that smart-looking security fence meant this must be one of those state-of-the-art super-deep wells. Where are those nine-mile-deep ones located? Do they look any different? How can I tell?" Though her phone is still in her pocket, she pulls a notebook and felt-tip pen from her purse. Like a teenage cheerleader talking to the star tailback, she says, "Could you answer some questions about those deep wells for me—even though you don't have any here?" She points into the compound.

"Afraid I can't do that, ma'am. I'm very busy, and I've got to talk to my engineer, Cletus."

"Well, thank you for taking with me, Mr. uh …"

"L. D., ma'am."

"Mr. L. D., my readers really want to know things. How about I buy you a beer after work? I'll be at Hurley's Irish Pub after six. Thank you very much, sir." Steffie thrusts her card at him. "If that isn't convenient, just call me. We can chat." She wheels around, opens the door, and slides into her Subaru Forester.

L. D. looks at her glossy black business card. *Dakota Fracking Magazine* in orange letters takes up the top half of the card. "Steffie Cobb, Chief Reporter" is printed in small white letters across the bottom. "I am not going to call you, Miss Cobb, or meet you in any bar. I, unlike you, have real work to do."

"I'm working too, you slimy SOB," she whispers into her shirt. She wiggles her fingers at L. D. as she passes him. She's half a mile away before she reaches inside her shirt pocket and removes her phone. "Well, that didn't go so well, Steffie, did it? At least I have his license plate number to check." She shuts off the voice recorder and assesses the odds of L. D. showing up for a beer to be absolute zero. "Hell. Might as well go back to Bismarck. I'll get nothing more done here."

CHAPTER 48

DISSING SEVERAL PRAIRIE SPIRITS

Tuesday, November 29, 2016

CARL TWO DEER IS DRIVING up to Bismarck to talk with the governor. It's a short drive, normally half an hour, but the swirling snow slows traffic to thirty miles per hour. Even at the reduced rate, several cars have spun off the road. Sanding trucks are keeping the roadway fairly passable, but the driving is tricky. Carl respects nature. He started half an hour early, and he is confident he'll be on time for his appointment. Leon will understand the precautions Carl has taken to arrive on time and—as payment for his punctuality—take it easy on him.

After only a few minutes, Carl realizes the conversation's gone sour, and he finds himself on the defensive.

His friend, Leon, jumps all over him. "Just get over it, Carl. You keep talking about the sacred prairie—about land given directly to indigenous people by some Great Spirit. This is the twenty-first century; we two must get past all that."

"How can you say that? I've known you for thirty years, and not once in all that time have you said such hurtful things."

"I'm sorry, Carl. I'm in a foul mood, and I let that get between us. I apologize. I am your friend, so I should not be saying hurtful things to you. However, I admit I meant to say uncomfortable things, and by so doing, I am attempting to shock you. This conversation is uncomfortable for me also, but I believe once you see where I'm going here, you'll also see the value of looking at our situation from a different perspective. You must understand your standard argument—that Standing Rock people can do whatever they want because their Great Spirit gave them their land—is insulting to me. In effect, you're claiming your Great Spirit cares only about the Standing Rock people and discards other people—my people, for example."

"Hey, Leon, for God's sake, ease up—"

"Essentially, that means lower animals—guys like me, or my great-grandfather who first moved the family out here—have no rights to, or interest in, the stewardship of that land."

"I'm not even close to saying such things, Leon. Where did those words come from?"

"What I'm saying is this discussion about who has the responsibility for making decisions about pipeline installations must be between actual people. It should not be between your Great Spirit and my Great Spirit. You and I must protect the interests of the people who've chosen us specifically so we can discuss topics such as the one we're now discussing. You and I must find common answers to common problems facing our constituents."

"Those words sound quite innocent, Leon, and they may even be true. However, they seem, just below the surface, to be very disrespectful to our heritage, to my forefathers who lived on this land since it became land. This is, you certainly understand, the land our Spirit Father gave to us, and you cannot tell me otherwise."

"Let's say that I agree with you. Your Spirit Father gave the Standing Rock people a specific place in North Dakota on which to settle. It should also seem reasonable, then, that I can argue that some other Spirit Father, as equally credentialed as yours, has given my people the same rights to the same land as your Spirit Father gave to your ancestors. Tell me why your Spirit Father can give you this land, but my Spirit Father cannot give that same land to me."

"Leon! Our Spirit Father was here first."

"Oh, so it's like the two kids in a sandbox? Huh? One says, 'My Great Spirit says this sand belongs to me.' The second one says, 'No, my Great Spirit says the sand belongs to me.' What about the Spirit Father who owned this sand before either of our forefathers came over here, say around fifteen thousand years ago?"

"There were no people here for us to displace. This was an unpeopled continent!"

"Are you suggesting that the buffalo and the wolves had no Great Spirit looking out for them?"

"What?"

"What gave your Great Spirit the audacity to think he could just walk over here and disrespect the territory of the buffalo's Great Spirit."

"Leon, you're talking loony. Buffalo have no separate Great Spirit."

"How do you know? I'm sorry, but I find I must say strange, and maybe inflammatory, things in an attempt to provoke you into understanding that your argument—that your Great Spirit gave you exclusive rights over a piece of the earth's surface to use only as you desire—is not a persuasive reason that I should act against the construction of an oil pipeline. It's not persuasive, and perhaps it's even counter-persuasive, specifically because it's an argument of the 'my God is more powerful than your God' kind. And, frankly, neither of us can think that argument is rational because neither of us can accept the other's argument. You don't think my Great Spirit is more powerful or more righteous, and I don't think your Great Spirit is as good as mine. Right?"

"You're talking nonsense, Leon. I didn't drive up here through the snow to talk religion. I thought I was coming up here to talk about the damn pipeline."

"My point exactly, Carl."

"What?"

"You tell me, Carl: Why do you think the pipeline's a bad idea?"

"There are many reasons. First is the great potential for environmental disaster. And it seems to me that the developers, PFUMP, have not shown much concern for that potential disaster. Second is the weak argument for its economic viability. Basically, the thing seems to be a hedge for big oil money, such that we might very well have an unused turkey on our hands for years. Third is the idea of encouraging the development of expensive— and in the Canadians' case, highly toxic, hard-to-extract oil in this time of cheap oil. That's just stupid and a waste of good money. Fourth is the whole carbon emission—"

"Exactly, Carl! Solid, scientifically viable reasons not to build the damn thing and reasons having nothing to do with spirits, great or otherwise." Leon grabs a paper from his desktop, studies it for a few seconds, turns it around, and plops it on the desk in front of Carl. "I had Margie type up this joint position paper for us. It's a draft, but it states exactly what you just said—and damn near verbatim. You didn't know Margie can read your mind? Huh? I think she's Irish or Scottish or something, but she certainly is not Standing Rock."

"You went through that whole dance just so I'd agree to focus on the science of the thing? You are one devious bastard, Leon."

"I'm a realist, Carl. I only work with facts. If I don't respect the facts, our state will suffer. And if our state suffers, then your people suffer just like my people. So, right now, we two, thinking of the welfare of our two peoples, must talk about physical stuff. I'll allow no metaphysical stuff to come creeping into this conversation. You and I have to issue a joint communique arguing that the PFUMP pipeline is not viable for the long term. I'll read this to you, and then you tell me what you think of it."

1) Standing: The PFUMP pipeline does not go over/ under the Standing Rock people's land, though it does go over/under land controlled by the state of North Dakota and the US government.

2) Human artifacts: North Dakota, in association with both state and Native American organizations, has regulations and protocols in place for protecting historical artifacts unearthed during construction, and this pipeline has already been subjected to additional scrutiny—higher than any of the thousands of other casual construction projects in the state.

3) Drinking Water: The pipeline segment under Lake Oahe does have a potential of contaminating drinking water for the Standing Rock people, but they are but a very small percentage of the people downstream, from Bismarck south to New Orleans, who also pull its water. Drinking water safety is a much wider-area concern—millions of people.

4) Pipeline Leaks: The new pipeline will actually improve environmental safety. It'll be much safer than the current mishmash of aged, rusting, and badly maintained pipelines, trucks, and oil tank cars—like the ones that got blown into the river the other day.

5) Oil Quantity: No more or no less oil is going to be shipped east from the Bakken fields than is being shipped now. PFUMP's pipeline will but replace existing transfer facilities. Therefore, no increased threat to the global climate change will occur, solely because of its construction or use.

6) Tax Hedge: Because our oil is so much more expensive to extract, the potential exists that in the near future, our fields will close and no oil will be exported through this pipeline from North Dakota or Alberta, except periodically as a hedge, applied against a tax levy.

7) Job Creation: The pipeline is already 95 percent built. Most construction jobs went to Texas and Louisiana, and manufacturing jobs went to China and Korea. The new Texas-owned pipe will replace locally owned trucks, rail lines, and pipelines. North Dakota actually loses local jobs.

"There's no way that list exited Margie's machine, Leon. Those are your snarky words, and as usual, they're in need of Margie's editing. However, they do make good sense. Though it's all true, much of it seems absurd, doesn't it? And strangely realistic, huh? You make it seem almost noncontroversial."

"Exactly, Carl. It is my proposal that you and I take our land back from the Texas oil goons. I want you standing right there next to me when, in a couple weeks, the Subsurface Materials Ownership Act gets signed. It protects both our people—all our people—jointly."

"I'll be there, Leon. I wouldn't miss it for the world."

"One other thing before you go. Just before you arrived, I received a message from Mr. Bowstringer. He told me that five hundred military vets arrived at the site this morning to support the Standing Rock people as they fight through this harsh winter. Five hundred US soldiers are now voluntarily supporting the Standing Rock community—even though actual pipeline work is now closed down at the protest site. Isn't that a beautiful irony? It's a beautiful idea? Everybody's joining together, Carl. Shouldn't we all be proud of that?

CHAPTER 49

OLD OIL TYCOONS BASHING YOUNG OIL TYCOONS

WEDNESDAY, NOVEMBER 30, 2016

SINCE WILLISTON EXPLODED THREE WEEKS ago, Leon's internal pressure has been building. Migraines, heartburn, muscle spasms, and melancholy take turns smashing him. He only sleeps intermittently. He's been throwing things horizontally at vertical surfaces. His friend Larry tied him up, strapped him into his pickup, and whisked him out of the city to his cattle ranch in Bottineau County, up near the Canadian border, for a couple days of pressure-free R&R.

This morning, the two of them were up before dawn, playing cowboy in the cold—riding fence lines, clearing brush from drainage swales, and inspecting cold weather systems. They returned to the house, changed their clothes, and are back warming themselves before the fire in the big room. Larry's grandfather clock announces eleven o'clock and begins bonging the hours.

"Nicely planned, Larry. It's Vikings time."

"Not quite yet, old buddy. We've got one piece of business we gotta do first." Larry crosses the room to his grandfather's liquor cabinet, which is next to the still-bonging clock. He returns and deposits two glasses of bourbon on the pine-plank table in front of Leon. "It's now noon here and in Minneapolis on this fourth of December. My clock has just now stopped bonging. That means it's Vikings kickoff time, and also it means the Army

202

Corps of Engineers' cease order just kicked in. Our Standing Rock standoff problem is, for the time being, past tense. And so now, theoretically, I'm out of a job." He picks up his glass, waits for Leon to grab his, salutes him, and takes a gulp.

"Thank you, Larry, for your work at that pipeline. It took a load off me. At least we've made sure no one's going to freeze to death—not for a couple months anyway."

"So, after we've gotten our rest, gotten our exercise, and recharged our batteries, we must turn our attention toward pushing that next boulder off your highway. We gotta get your Subsurface Materials Ownership Act into the books quickly."

"That boulder's already being pushed, Larry. I've briefed the leaders of both bodies that I'm calling a special session a week from Thursday, that's the fifteenth, to deal only with that initiative."

"I understand that, Leon, but it's my job as your advisor to energize you, propel you to lead our team to overpower the opposition, and focus on winning the state championship."

"No, no, no, Larry. That's not part of me taking a couple days off. I've gotta relax here and watch the Vikings game now. Your morality play must wait!"

"No, I'm afraid not. You've got to make one big decision first. Do we lie to our people and let the Texans kick us in the teeth, suck up our oil, and watch the rest of the world fall apart with a death toll of billions—or do we tell the truth, recognize the danger looming, and start taking measures to protect us from those looming dangers? Either way, Leon, the truth is that we won't be here in forty years, and we won't have to worry about the damage done by our decision."

"What? You're telling me that the governor of North Dakota must now, single-handedly, solve the problem of global warming before I can watch my Vikings lose?"

"Yup, and you've got till January 20 to do it. However, the big decision must be made right now."

"What big decision?"

"You must decide the answer to the one big question: Am I going to gamble the future of my state and my country on the lurid dream of climate-change deniers and pipeline builders?"

203

"That question has nothing to do with football. Can't we watch the Vikings game first?"

"No, we cannot."

"Why not?"

"Because the passage of your Subsurface Materials Ownership Act requires that you make this decision first. If the Subsurface Materials Ownership Act is not enacted, those Texas oil guys are going to bankrupt North Dakota by using our oil mostly as hedging against their absurd Texas profits. On the other hand, if your act is enacted, then Dakota oil will become unavailable for Texas guys to hedge. Texas guys will be forced to find hedges elsewhere."

"I need another brandy, Larry."

"Not now, Leon. What you need is proof. Let me show you something." Larry removes his laptop from the desk and brings it over to Leon. "I've got my spies. A friend of mine recorded this two days ago—on Friday night. It's your buddy, Basehardt. He's down in Houston, talking to Texas oil guys. He's looking for money. Seems that's most all he does is chase money. He's telling oil guys how to propagate the big lie."

"We're in a race, guys, and the finish line's drawn somewhere around 2057. He who pirouettes nimbly and sprints forward is rewarded, and he who looks back and stumbleth will be toast. We sprinters have got forty years to make ourselves a super bundle of cash. Forty years of pumping oil. By that time, I'll be ninety-five.

"That means everyone like me—guys over about fifty as of today— don't need to plan for what happens after carbon. We don't care. But you younger suckers? You're the ones with the problem. You're the ones who could be cruising Houston's streets in gondolas in 2057. You're the guys who better start building windmills now." Basehardt laughs.

"But guess what? You kids can't do that because we old farts have cornered all the money and all the oil, and we won't let you have any of it. The next war's going to be between the young guys and us old codgers. And since we've got a codger in the White House now, we're gonna get all the money now. We got Big Mo on our side. 'Eat my dirt, sonny,' that's what I tell those MBAs just now walking out of HBS and Wharton. Eat my dirt. Or, rather, drink my oil. Drink, baby, drink. Lots of luck, you young suckers."

"Basehardt makes a great argument there, Leon. He's all in as a climate change denier—but not because it may or may not be true. He's only looking out for himself. He's gonna come in first, and the hell with everyone else. You, as governor, have to look out for all the rest of us North Dakotans, especially the North Dakotans of the future."

"Thanks, Larry. You've just ruined my appetite for football."

"And it gets worse. As all this international intrigue in Russia, Brazil, and West Texas overpowers poor North Dakota, it's obvious that we little guys in ND will get affected the hardest. Even now, our local, low-level entrepreneurs and scavengers are getting burned, families are moving or splitting up, bankruptcies are common, and fights, broken windows, and sabotaged equipment are forcing law enforcement into overtime. Right here is where the human suffering is happening. It's not happening in the Houston boardrooms of the pipeline speculators. The story is here, Leon. The 'oil versus renewable' story is a local story."

"And there's one other thing to think about before I turn on the TV. You just saw Basehardt's rant?"

"Yeah, so?"

"So, here's a question. Do you personally know any Houston oil tycoons or master partners who fit into Basehardt's under-fifty category? Youngish tycoons who gotta worry about the danger of global warming?"

"Oh my God, Larry! My private headache? My Kathleen?"

"Yeah! And we know Basehardt also knows that, huh? And what's he gonna do with her?"

"I don't even want to think about that, Larry. She's gonna find herself running against the herd, huh? And you're thinking I should show her that video, show her who her enemy is, get her on my side, and then persuade her to lobby for my Subsurface Materials Ownership Act?"

"Something to think about, huh, Leon?" Larry pushes a button, and the super-screen comes alive. It's halfway through the first quarter, and the Vikings are already up fourteen-zip.

"Wow, Larry. Things are lookin' up, huh?"

CHAPTER 50

PRELIMINARY WORK ON THE SPECIAL SESSION

MONDAY, DECEMBER 5, 2016

"THIS THING'S ONLY FOUR PAGES, Margie? You'd expect it should be at least forty or fifty. After all, we're changing the entire landscape of the entire state of North Dakota."

"Remember, Governor, big things come in little packages."

"Yeah, I've heard that said, but I don't believe it. Maybe I should print it on stone tablets or something. Give it some heft."

"Your job is to go into your office, sit on your couch, and proofread the thing. You go over every word with a fine-toothed comb. Make sure every i is dotted, every semicolon is removed, and every snarky bit is excised."

In North Dakota, the governor alone has the power to call special sessions of the legislature for certain emergency issues, of which this "oil rights" bill certainly qualifies. This measure became an emergency because of the results of last month's election. And so, one week from tomorrow, at this special session, the governor will present only one item, this four-page Subsurface Materials Ownership Act to both bodies of the legislature. This SMOA mandates the state to assume the subsurface material rights for all materials found deeper than eight feet below grade.

Leon's bill is structured to honor the natural condition that, as the Standing Rock people claim, no individual is able to own the rights to the underground resources that, some Great Spirit promised, we all have in common and have been given to all people living in the state. Therefore, Leon is but confirming a natural law that no person, individual, or ethereal Texas partnership, is able to own the rights to harvest those deep materials. Such resources belong to all the people living on the top surface of the land—all citizens of the state—because they all are living "in common" with respect to the buried resource. And that means the governor, by exercising his duty as representative of the people, must act to preserve all people's rights by having the state, and only the state, be the only entity to control the extraction and sale of any buried commodity. And no one can disagree that a pool of oil five-miles deep is, indeed, a buried commodity.

The law being argued will void all existing private ownership documents with respect to "claimed rights" to extract materials. As far as the state is concerned, there's no value whatsoever to be placed on any "commodity" located beneath the surface of North Dakota. The existing rights were never sold to the present owners of the materials—they were only "claimed." That means that, legally, no Texan owns any of that deep oil they are currently pumping. They have but "claimed the right" to harvest it. And since, technically, they now own nothing, this legislation will be taking nothing from them. Leon is aware his is a fairly technical argument, but it's a very good, and very simple, technical argument. It mandates the state to act as overseer of all subsurface materials for the good of all people of the state.

Leon has tried hard to find a typo or misprint. He has gone through two bottles of orange juice. Eventually, he accepts the truth. He walks out to Margie's desk and puts the four sheets on it. "I tried hard to find something wrong, Margie, but it ain't in there. First thing tomorrow, push whatever buttons you gotta push to send it out."

"I'll do it tonight. It'll only take a few minutes. You look beat, Leon. Go home—and get some sleep."

"I'm with you there, Margie. I am beat." He slowly dons his boots and coat. "See you tomorrow, Margie."

*   *   *

Two years back, when Leon Rolfes won the North Dakota governor's race, he defeated the Republican candidate, a well-connected Bismarck attorney named Arthur Conlin. Conlin, after his defeat, signed on as chairman of the state Republican Party. Conlin is giddy regarding last month's election, and he believes such a landslide allows, and perhaps requires, the new federal government to station transition agents in the North Dakota statehouse who might act to prevent the current rogue governor from completing any power grab he might be considering before the new era comes sweeping over the prairie like an afternoon thunderstorm. Mr. Conlin quickly assumed that liaison position for himself. Thus credentialed, he is stalking the capitol's hallways for remnants of the old regime.

*   *   *

Leon has a lot on his mind, and he is anxious to get home. He chugs out of the elevator on the first floor and barges into the central rotunda, paying little attention to his surroundings. Arthur Conlin, like a cartoon character might do, jumps in front of him with his overcoat swooshing and his briefcase swinging.

Leon despises Arthur Conlin, considers him no smarter than dirt, and hasn't talked to him in ages. Initially, he is confused by the sudden apparition. "Is that you, Conlin? You've gone right off the edge, huh? Get out of my way."

"Leon, I've been waiting for you."

"Show some respect, you fool. I'm your governor."

"Senator Basehardt and I declare your fake Dakota First Party illegitimate, Leon. Your votes won't count any more. We're gonna win every vote 40 percent to 18 percent. You should give up now."

"Earth to Conlin, you gotta stop listening to that blowhard from Texas. You've gained a few seats, but essentially things haven't changed. You guys will control about 40 percent in each house. That certainly beats the Democrats with 18 percent, but my Dakota First Party owns the remaining 42 percent. And with us and the Democrats voting against all your nonsense, you're always gonna lose 60 percent of every vote."

"Just you wait, Rolfes. We're gonna challenge every vote."

"Show me some respect. It's Governor Rolfes to you, sir, and I suggest you hire a smarter consultant—some math whiz who can add and subtract." Leon pushes him out of the way and is out the front door in a flash. He's halfway to his car before he realizes the walk's icy—and he should be paying more attention to careful foot placement.

* * *

After dinner, Leon is watching his mother clean up. He's attempting to explain his earlier encounter with Conlin.

"Lucky you didn't slip and break a leg or something," she says. "I'm sure your mother told you about ice."

"It's nothing to do with my mother, Mom. Conlin is either certifiably nuts or criminally naive. He's basing his euphoria on Basehardt's fantasy that, since he doesn't accept my Dakota First Party as a legal entity, it doesn't exist. And since it doesn't exist, it can't have any votes. He thinks Republicans will win everything by 40 percent to 18 percent. Where's he been for the past two years? Can he possibly be that stupid?"

"Perhaps he skipped third grade? That's when he should have learned fractions and percentages."

"Could be. It might also be the kind of math they use in Texas. Both Conlin and Brian Bass have heavy connections to Houston oil money. The incoming secretary of energy is a guy named Bing Cherry, a previous Texas governor and an oil interest's lapdog. Conlin's hoping I'll back away from what he calls my 'Socialist Proposal.' He said Cherry might march his new Energy Department soldiers into my office and try to force more Texas math on me. Wouldn't that make nifty theater?"

"Let him try a stunt like that. I guarantee it'll backfire."

"I think you're right."

"Can you imagine the ruckus? A hundred fancy-dressed Energy Department troops being laughed at by thousands of North Dakotans! Maybe you could sell popcorn to the crowd, like at a circus."

"Don't get your hopes up, Mom. Those clowns will never get their own Energy Department army. They have laws against that kind of nonsense, don't they?"

"Could be. But it's a great visual."

"More to the point, Mom, I cannot wait until the new year. As we speak, Margie is filing the paperwork for a special Session for the fifteenth and sixteenth, next Thursday and Friday. I've gotta push this through quickly—before national oil interests get themselves organized."

"I agree, son. You want this over and done with before the holiday pandemonium hits."

"That's my plan."

"Though you risk that Texas oil army calling you a 'commie pinko.' You ready for that?"

"I've already talked with the Republican governor of Alaska and the conservative governor of Alberta. Both states have statutes similar to my proposal, and neither place has dived into a communist state yet. They'll help me make the conservative argument to counter the knee-jerk blithering by Bast and Basehardt. I'll frame it as North Dakota's 'enlightened citizens' versus Texas' 'oil goons,' rather than Commie Leon versus godly Republicans. I don't see many problems. I've enlisted some heavy hitters—normal Republican guys like Larry, Charlie, and Russell—to push my side. I think we're gonna do fine."

CHAPTER 51

CONSIDERING WHAT'S UNDERGROUND

THURSDAY, DECEMBER 8, 2016

LEON KNOWS HIS MOM IS correct. He must deal with his goddaughter. Kathleen is the primary Texas-based oil carnivore operating in North Dakota. He knows he can deal with her because he, as overseer of her father's trust accounts, holds the rope that controls the glob of concrete hanging over her head. He's reasonably sure they can structure a win here if they both operate in a rational range. However, before he can talk with her, he must wade through the several layers of protective fuzz she has inserted in between his phone and hers. After fifteen minutes of getting switched and held, he finally hears her beguiling voice.

"Well, well, Uncle Leon," Kathleen says. "I'm not sure how you found your way through my minefield. Damn government spies are everywhere. Can't get no privacy up here."

"Cool it, Kathleen. I'm the governor. Don't tell me your whole body doesn't quake at the thought of all that power I can marshal to reach you if I need to do so! Also, I'm the executor of your dad's will and his trusts. You gotta listen to me—whether you want to or not."

"So, what are you doing with my piddling inheritance now?"

"This call isn't about your inheritance concerns. It's about my governing concerns."

"Your concerns? Why should that concern me?"

"I'm offering a heads-up. It's to your benefit to know what I'm thinking, and doing, because my thinking and doing will affect your bottom line. And, as your godfather and your financial counselor, I have a unique interest in your bottom line."

"Already this doesn't sound good, Uncle Leon. What can you possibly know about my bottom line? Should my lawyers jump in here?"

"You don't have to comment—just listen. I'm going to tell you a story about things that are going to happen, and if you listen carefully with an open mind, you might find that you're better off than if you didn't listen."

"Sound pretty spooky, but, lucky for you, I understand spooky."

"We both know eventually your North Dakota oil business is going into the toilet, Kathleen."

"Not so fast, Uncle Leon. Did you hear who just got elected president? I'm going to start mining hard to reach deeply buried Dakota coal and fracking ten-mile-deep North Dakota oil. It's like heaven just splotted out of the clouds and fluttered down on my assets."

"Splotted? Whatever that means, I don't think so. There's not enough coal in Dakota to drool over. Second, even at fifty bucks a barrel, you lose money fracking crude. What's gonna happen when it hits ninety bucks? Third, heaven's never gonna be anywhere close to you."

"Uncle Leon, you can't say that. You're my godfather."

"You know, as well as anyone, Williston's oil business is collapsing."

"That's one scenario, but a few enlightened folks think otherwise."

"And we both know you'll profit big-time from this crash. I want to make sure your profiting, crashing, and burning does not leave huge craters smoldering in North Dakota for me to clean up. Something like the crater the governor of West Virginia is trying to clean up."

"Though I don't think one can 'clean up a crater' as your mangled metaphor suggests, I do follow your argument."

"Good! I'm hoping we can find some mutually acceptable method of providing you with a reasonable exit strategy and me with a minuscule cleanup bill. But you and I are going to have sit down and work out this deal—and we have got to do it quickly. Quick, quick, quick, Kathleen. It's gotta happen before ISIS blows up something else—or it ain't gonna happen at all. If this meeting doesn't happen, you're gonna be the one going down in flames. I won't be able to help you even though you're my goddaughter."

"Okay, okay. Enough, Leon. I get it. You want me to support your Subsurface Materials Ownership Act. Is that it?"

"Well, yes, Kathleen, that's the first step. And that's the easy step. But before we even discuss that, we need to settle a few other things. Primarily, I believe quite strongly that we won't have any additional ISIS attacks within the borders of my state. Am I correct?"

"I think you might be, Leon. Though you realize that I, myself, had nothing to do with those explosive events. I was technically, even physically, out of the country. Nevertheless, I'm confident I can predict, even promise you, that no more ISIS fighters will be blowing up any more oil stuff."

"Good! And thank you for that, Kathleen."

"You realize the problem here, Uncle Leon, I'm the only Texas oil guy who is not a Texas native. I'm a North Dakota gal, remember? And I still have a soft spot in my heart for the dear old sod."

"Bull pucky, Kathleen! It's well known you don't have a heart, but I also know you don't have the need to blow things up for insurance. I assume you've already hedged your future Dakota losses, right? And hedges, as we all know, come in many packages—tax credits set against business losses, leveraged buyouts, legal stuff like that. Some folks we both know, though, are old school and still rely on what you in the oil business call Louisiana lightning. That's the kind of hedge stuff's been striking Williston lately."

"You're right, Leon. Things seem to be crossing into the spooky range. Do I need to grab some legal armor?"

"This is serious, Kathleen. Here's the deal. I, acting as both your governor and your godfather—and I think you should also keep in mind I'm the executor of your trust—am in a position to structure the loss of your North Dakota oil empire, which we both know is now worth about as much as dirt, so that you can write it off as an unforeseen business loss. Wouldn't that be nice for you? And with no messy things like cratered oil fields, burning ice floes, Williston being a smoldering rubble heap, or a trail of dead Somali youth?"

"I resent your making the rather disgusting connection between—"

"Stuff it, Kathleen. I need you to focus here. I need your guidance. It's that damned pipeline. Not too much about it on either side is making much sense to me, though both sides think the cosmos is going to stop spinning if I close it down or if I don't. I need to find out the truth from you since you're the expert. Is there any value to that stupid pipeline other than as a hedge?"

"Hmm. That's an interesting question for my governor to ask me. Of course, the first answer is no, the cosmos does not spin. Jeez, Uncle Leon, you should know that. And, you are, of course, correct about the pipeline. Mainly, it's a hedge. In the short term, I'm hoping it might go gangbusters. Long term? Nobody knows if it will be carrying anything five years from now. I'm betting probably not, but I've made my bundle from it already as a PFUMP master partner. I must admit—you got that part right."

"Thank you, Kathleen, but you realize my North Dakota is hemorrhaging while you guys play your hedge games. I must find some way to stop that hemorrhaging."

"It's my state too, Leon. Of course, I'm making oodles of money building my pipeline, but look at the jobs I've created—and the money I've spent in North Dakota. Soon, under our new president, you and I will be completely independent of foreign oil. And that's all thanks to me playing hedge fund games in North Dakota."

"Bullfeathers! I've got my spies out, and I'm fairly certain that you are, as we speak, actually in the process of drilling that tunnel under the Missouri to which my friends, the Standing Rock people, object, and which the Army Corps of Engineers have told you to stop drilling. But you're drilling it anyway, but at some humongous depth such that you don't think I can detect it, and also so it will be of no environmental risk to the reservoir. I thank you for that, Kathleen, but I will get you for that, especially now, since you've told me the only reason to drill that pipeline is so you and your buddies can make money by not pumping oil through it. This nonsense makes me irritable, Kathleen, and we've got to come to an understanding here so I can sleep at night."

"Okay, Leon. Here are a couple things to ease your mind. One, for your information, you are technically wrong. I can assure you that I am, at this time, not installing any pipeline in the entire state of North Dakota. And two, we both know why you are proposing your Subsurface Materials Ownership Act. It is because you realize you now have no control whatsoever over what happens to the vast unknown areas beneath your precious state. You do not know, for instance, who owns the rights to dig tunnels deep under your prairie top, am I right, Uncle Leon?"

"I hate to even think about that. You and I have got to talk this out, Kathleen. At a neutral site. How about Donatello's in Dickinson? Is Monday okay? Let's say six? I'm buying. You can write it off as talking with your trust fund advisor."

"Okay, I can do that. Before you hang up, Uncle Leon," she turns on that seductive voice that's been known to melt a phone's copper landline, "I've a little gift for you."

"A gift, huh? It's nothing explosive, is it, Kathleen?"

"Behave yourself. I'm on your side here. As a token of my good intentions, I'm offering you the following tidbit of information—to use as you see fit. Last Sunday, after that railroad explosion, I got an email from a politician looking for a gift. That's not unusual. Lots of politicians want my money. However, this particular politician insinuated that if I didn't give him money, there would be additional explosions, like the one ISIS gave us last Sunday in Mandan. He also said that without my money, he couldn't guarantee he'd be able to stop your 'subsurface land grab'—his words Leon, not mine. 'Stop your subsurface land grab.' He tried to threaten me. Made me wonder which dog he has in this fight. Do you follow me?"

"I know a politician, or maybe two of them, who might have the brass to send that email. I appreciate the heads-up. Thank you, partner."

"You're right about that, Leon. He is a partner, and I think his threat puts you and me on the same side in this fight. We've got ourselves a common enemy. That's a first, huh? See you Monday, Uncle Leon."

"Goodbye, Kathleen."

CHAPTER 52

CONSIDERING WHAT'S UNDERINSURED

N<small>O ONE, NOT EVEN THE</small> governor, can assume Kathleen will obey the usual regulations and conventions regarding time and space. Physically, she's located at the time and place she needs to be. At this moment, she is high above Oklahoma in her jet, returning from Houston.

"That was one spooky phone call, Trevor. Uncle Leon wants me to be his friend—or his partner—or maybe he just wants me to acknowledge we have common enemies."

"I'm not sure I follow that. What's he up to?"

"He's referring to your crazy friends in Williston, those guys who've been using religious firebombers in their demolition work."

"Although they are crazy, Kathleen, they are not anywhere near religious, and most certainly, they are not my friends."

"I'm assuming that whoever they are, we're not expecting any more fire and brimstone to pour down on Williston or Bismarck, are we? Is there any way I can make certain that's not gonna happen?"

"Certain is an all-or-nothing word, Kathleen, and nothing about Texans is certain. However, I do know BX&F's insurance plan has been grossly underfunded and badly needs cash. Some observers are suggesting they're having food chain and insurance problems only another act of God can solve."

"What can we do to make sure their food chain problem doesn't start infecting the whole refrigerator?"

"Same as always, Kathleen. The rotten food gets excised before it explodes and ruins the good fruit."

"You believe any rotten fruit can be thrown away quickly, so it explodes somewhere other than Williston?"

"The refrigerator purging is already in process, Kathleen, and I've been told the squishy veggies are being composted rather than simply tossed down the disposal."

CHAPTER 53

CONSIDERING WHO'S UNDERGROUND— AND WHO'S NOT

Friday, December 9, 2016

It's three thirty on Sunday afternoon, and the game is over. The Vikings lost again. Leon's brain is hemorrhaging, his heartburn is screaming, and he can't stand the pressure any longer. Both his head and his stomach require heavy medicine. On Thursday, immediately after his phone call with Kathleen, he'd put her question to him to both Steffie and Larry. "I need to know who owns the rights to dig tunnels deep under my prairie? And who controls what happens in the vast unknown areas beneath North Dakota?"

Pushed by his indigestion, he calls them both and tells them he can't wait till Monday. They can have meat loaf this evening if they come over now and report what they've found.

* * *

"My legal eagles tell me there's little precedent here," says Steffie. "We're pretty much operating in virgin legal territory. We do know owners of North Dakota surface land have no claim on the mineral or liquid rights to goodies buried beneath that land. It's also well established that the right to extract any mineral or liquid from below that land cannot be purchased; it can only be claimed. Some case law suggests that because underground substances cannot be purchased, they cannot therefore be owned. So, technically, it may be true that Kathleen doesn't own any of the oil she's extracting, but since she's claimed it, she has the right to take it and sell it … though the technical definition of 'sell' gets itself a bit mangled—"

"But," Larry says, "the state also might reasonably argue, that since Kathleen doesn't own the oil, she has no standing to sell it either. No one's had the audacity to test that bit of theory in court."

"The situation seems either very stupid or quite reasonable," says Steffie.

"So, you're telling me that I, the governor of this state, have no control over what happens down there?"

"And it might be even worse than that."

"God, Larry, what could be worse than that?"

"Remember that Keystone pipeline? Last season's big pipeline kerfuffle? Down in Nebraska? It was scheduled to cross over a portion of that huge Oglala Aquifer, remember?"

"I don't like where you're going here."

"Though the application was withdrawn, and the matter is now in legal limbo, there's a bit of extraneous legal fluff left unresolved. The proponents of that pipeline and their opponents agreed on one thing having nothing whatsoever to do with the pipeline—a kind of collateral point. Neither believed the state of Nebraska has any legal ownership control over the water stored in the Oglala Aquifer. Therefore, the state has no legal right to prevent some third party from simply claiming all that water and then draining the whole thing if they wanted to. I can only imagine the bundle of lawsuits spawned by that idea. I know for a fact that Texas cattlemen have filed several of them, and Nebraska lawyers are having fits."

"Apparently, there's also a legal precedent for cutting the Great Father Spirit out of consideration, such that He is unable to actually use any of His own resources."

"I have no idea what those words mean, Steffie, but it's hard to imagine any Great Father Spirit putting up with nonsense like that."

"Seems one of the legal wizards at my paper, a guy named Terry, has a sister who lives in Colorado along the Arkansas River. She cannot collect rainwater, put in a duck pond, or even remove snow from her property. Do you want to know why?"

"Sure, I'll bite, Steffie. Why?"

"Because farmers way down in Arkansas have a historical claim on the rights to every drop of water or snow that leaves the clouds over the Arkansas River watershed in far-off Colorado. Notice, Leon, I did not mention the word 'buy.' I said 'claim,' as in 'they did not pay any money for it.' Nevertheless, it's illegal, except for several clear exemptions, for anyone in Colorado to prevent any water that would naturally drain into the Arkansas River from not doing so. And the body of law developed from this is now taken to legally mean that Terry's sister cannot even minutely increase the evaporation surface area in Colorado by building a duck pond or swimming pool on her property. If the Great Father Spirit can't control the ownership of His liquid falling as rain over Colorado, it's hard to see where that Spirit can have any legal right to liquid buried five miles under the Standing Rock people's land either."

"So, you guys are suggesting that if Kathleen wants to bury pipe under the Oahe Reservoir, all she has to do is claim the right to remove the dirt from any subsurface area and then just insert a pipe in the void she's created? She can do any damn thing she wants to do down there—and without her plans having to even go past my desk for any approval first?"

"Pretty much, yeah. There are a few glitches, but my legal team thinks she can make a strong legal argument for that."

"Where does that leave me, the most powerful man in North Dakota?"

"Well, lucky for you, Leon, you've already found the solution."

"I have? I think that's news to me."

"For two years now, you've been trying to convince the more enlightened citizens of our state and members of our legislature that they should take the step of having North Dakota seize control of all subsurface oil rights in the state. So far, you've been concentrating on oil, but, technically, I think your subsurface initiative could be worded so as to include state ownership of all subsurface materials, valuable or otherwise, located from, say, about ten feet below the surface down to the center of the earth. That gives the state legal authority to regulate the drilling, mining, pumping, or—let's say sometime in the next century—the building of a high-speed underground rail service from Bismarck to Minneapolis and Denver without the need to spend big bucks on any expensive right-of-way battles."

"Wow! Where the hell did you get an idea like that?"

"Well, frankly, I think your goddaughter is the deviant mind you can thank. She's apparently the one who initiated this concept."

"Are you saying if I were an astute business guy or a sneaky politician, I might claim the rights to the underground usage of all of Minnesota's and Colorado's subsurface volume while I'm at it? Then, when that high-speed underground line is proposed, we North Dakotans would have a clear shot—with no approval or right-of-way interference from our dear neighbors—to tunnel from Bismarck to downtown Minneapolis? Wow, what a deal, huh?"

"And it might even be worse than that."

"Like I said before, Steffie, what could be worse than that?"

"Just because investigating stuff is the kind of thing investigative reporters do, I went down to the Crow County courthouse on Friday and checked the register of claimed mineral rights for properties in the pipeline's path."

"Oh, no! Please, tell me this is not true, Steffie. Or, if it is, just lie to me and—" Leon holds his hands over his ears and starts humming.

"She did it, Leon—fifteen months ago before anybody even knew the word *pipeline* or the initials PFUMP. Unlike out in the west around Williston, there is no oil in that area of the state. Therefore, no one in the history of the state has ever bothered to actually claim any subsurface rights in Crow County. Kathleen has absolutely no competition. She now owns the subsurface rights to every piece of land in the path of the pipeline through Crow County. I did not have the heart to check any other counties, but my instincts—"

"Yeah, yeah. We both know what you will find in the other counties if you check. And damn! If I had been paying attention ..."

"What?"

"I think Kathleen told me that. She said I was 'technically wrong' to assume she was drilling under Lake Oahe. I think I remember her exact words: 'At this time, I am absolutely not drilling anything in the entire state of North Dakota.' That's a fairly aggressive use of the present tense, isn't it? Damn! I'm certain she intended to say, 'Not this current minute, buddy, but yesterday I did, and tomorrow I will.' I had this little ping in the back of my head when she said it, but I wasn't paying attention. Damn, I'll bet she's already drilled that pipeline tunnel under the reservoir. What do ya think?"

"I have absolutely no idea, Leon, but like with those dead Somali boys, you know I'm gonna find out."

"Before you start on something new, Steffie, I'd best tell you about your Somali boys. This is top secret, but since dead Somalis was your idea, I'd better tell you."

"Dead Somali boys was not our idea, Leon. We're the ones who found it out."

"That's what I meant. The FBI's found one specific and very alarming link between those fake ISIS explosions in Williston and the tank cars blowing up on the bridge."

"Wow, you're right. I gotta know that."

Leon hesitates, trying to find the specific words.

"Come on, Leon. Let me have it. Come on."

"Yeah, I just have to be very careful. This is really spooky, and the FBI's controlling stuff."

"So tell me!"

"There was a human casualty associated with those oil car explosions."

"Someone died out there? Who?"

"That's the problem, Steffie. No one knows. He's a nameless old man, but what makes the Williston connection clear is that the FBI is positive he is an old Somali man."

"Wow, is that weird? And it's good you told me. It means I'm now allowed to bring you up to date regarding another semi-unknown Somali guy."

"Semi-unknown? What's going on here, Steffie?"

"You remember my friend Hasani? From Minneapolis? She looked into the possibility that the two Somali youths found in Williston had disappeared from Minneapolis. And she, being the expert sleuth she is, found that there are actually three Somali boys missing. And she found all three of their names."

"No! Really?"

"Yep, and then I talked with Special FBI Agent Harrison Brock. It was the Monday after the oil cars exploded, and I was with him when he was informed of your secret, third, oil car death—the nameless Somali—and since Hasani told me, I could then tell him the name of that third guy. Isn't that a coincidence?"

"I'm blown away, Steffie."

"But that didn't work out. My secret Somali guy could not be the same as your secret guy because my guy is a college sophomore, and you said your guy is an old man. Why didn't you tell me?"

"Same reason you didn't tell me your secret. The FBI told me not to. They wanted it kept secret. So we both knew there was a third Somali guy, but we each thought he was a different guy. That's truly bizarre."

"You and Hasani found the names of three dead Somalis? And Agent Brock found a fourth dead Somali!"

Steffie jumps to her feet. "Four dead Somali terrorists! Damn, I think he actually said, 'Four dead terrorists.' Four of them. Jeez!" She slaps the tabletop. "I'm such a dolt."

"What the hell are you talking about?"

She grabs her bag, removes her computer, opens it, and aggressively pounds the keyboard. "Okay, the voice here is Will Basehardt's. He's speaking on Sunday afternoon, the day the train exploded. I recorded this rebroadcast off the TV in the *Plainsman*'s conference room the next morning, Monday. It was just after Agent Brock got the call from his boss and told me about the third Somali found dead in the oil train explosion. I assumed they were talking about my missing third boy, but he was talking about your unknown old man. Damn! Just a sec. Let me find the right place." She listens to little bits and dribbles of words here and there. "Here it is, Leon. Remember, the train exploded on November 27. I taped this the next day. No one except you and the FBI knew about the fourth body in the tank car. That fourth Somali did not officially exist yet, and even the third boy was only known to about four people."

She turns the volume up, and Will Basehardt's voice sounds clear and distinct: "Folks, ISIS wants to cripple our homegrown oil industry—so we're forced to buy their crude. We've already let four ISIS terrorists infiltrate North Dakota. They haven't killed any Americans yet, but what about next time? Fortunately those four have been killed, but what about the next wave? And we all know about waves—they naturally come in bunches." Steffie stops the video. "He's saying this on Sunday afternoon … saying there were *four* dead Somalis."

"I was at his rally," says Larry. "Two Deer and I were working for Leon, and we stood right there and listened to Basehardt spew his garbage. I recorded it too … if you need verification. Steffie's right, Leon. It was still daylight."

"Basehardt said four—and, Leon, that was before either you or I knew that. So … how could he have known that?"

"He could've just been blowin' smoke off the top of his head. Making stuff up 'cause it sounds good. He does that all the time."

"But how could he have known there were four? At the time Basehardt spoke, the sheriff only knew of two. I was aware of three missing—but only two dead. And Agent Brock, at that time, was aware of two in Williston but none yet at Mandan."

"I suppose the Mandan fire chief could have told him," Leon says.

"No," says Larry. The body in Mandan didn't even turn up till ten o'clock on Sunday night … several hours after Basehardt's bloviating."

"So Basehardt couldn't know that 'four' number on Sunday afternoon?" says Leon.

"Right, Leon. Unless he knew about it firsthand. He knew about two more dead Somali guys than he was supposed to."

"Damn, Steffie, you've done it again. Put me in a pickle. I must send you over to the FBI and have them copy that piece of Basehardt speaking from your computer. And you too, Larry. Your audio recording of his rant corroborates Steffie's story. My god. Talk about explosive."

"I'll do that, Leon. And I've got another thought. I'm hoping your buddy Nathan Goodbrother, bless his soul, is up there listening to our conversation. He's the master choreographer. He would've loved all these interesting twists and turns."

"Yeah, Steffie. You're right. And his daughter is also into urban theater. Don't forget that."

Leon walks to the mantel, removes the championship game basketball, dribbles it a bit, and looks at Steffie. "Damn you, Nathan," he says. "I could use you here. I need your creative brain working here. Get your ass down here right now, Nathan. Just like old times, Larry and I need you right here."

CHAPTER 54

SPAGHETTI: A METAPHOR FOR MASTER PARTNERSHIPS

MONDAY, DECEMBER 12, 2016

LEON CAN NO LONGER TALK with his friend Nathan, but the next best thing may be talking with his goddaughter, Kathleen. So, this evening, Leon's carefully placed himself in Donatello's Italian Restaurant, a neutral turf near the eastern I-94 interchange in Dickinson. It's about an hour-and-a-half drive for both of them. Leon's been here before, during his run for governor, but he doubts the staff remembers him. Nevertheless, he dresses casually in Levi's and his Stetson, and he drives his red pickup. He blends in fairly well. He doesn't know what to expect from Kathleen. She's able to change her appearance dramatically in a few minutes with the equipment she normally carries in her truck.

Donatello's is typical for a third-generation Italian restaurant with hundreds of photos on the walls and red and green napkins and wallpaper. Two grade-school girls buzz about the entry podium and talk with their mom or aunt as she monitors the book.

After a couple swigs of orange juice, Leon recognizes Kathleen. She follows a reception girl across the room to the table. She's playing Urban Cowgirl tonight—designer denim stuff, a nifty Stetson, and glossy red high-rise boots.

Leon rises as she approaches the table. "Ah, Kathleen. I see you also rode your horse this evening."

"Lucky for me, they've got a heated barn for Trigger—and some Parmesan hay to munch on. Good to see you, Uncle Leon."

Once they get past the initial irreverent remarks, they both sit down. She orders a glass of Merlot. Leon's fixed, for the time being, with his orange juice.

"I've a couple pieces of information for you, Uncle Leon. I know you well, so I'd be surprised if you don't already know this stuff. First, I'm on your side with respect to your Subsurface Materials Ownership Act. I understand what you're doing and believe that if it passes, we both will emerge winners. But we both know that statement will not leave this table, right? I'll certainly deny I told you anything. It's our little secret."

"Sounds reasonable. I don't want to blow your cover as the bad-ass villain."

"Thanks, Uncle. Secondly, I want to emphasize that I own North Dakota. That means, as I prosper, then you, as my governor, also prosper. However, if my investments fail, Dakota fails. You already know that, huh? I'm telling you so you'll understand, exactly, the financial power I have over you and this puny little state of ours."

"Your fellow traveler, Will Basehardt, is on a similar power trip. Which one of you should I believe?"

"Basehardt's a complete moron. He's a thug with no morals. He's been lucky so far, but luck is not a continuous function. I want to establish my bona fides with you, so I'm giving you a gift, Uncle Leon. I'm taking your nemesis, Will Basehardt, down. His crashing and burning will be my gift to you."

"Am I supposed to thank you?"

"Damn right, Uncle Leon."

The waitress stops by, takes their order, and tops up their water glasses.

"I need to know stuff, Kathleen, about who I'm working against. First, who is PFUMP, the firm building this pipeline? It seems like a fairly shadowy entity for such an aggressive project. I can't find out where to mail my bribe requests."

"Calm down. Just listen hard, cause I'm gonna talk technical. PFUMP operates as a convoluted business form designed specifically for oil companies. It's called a class-2 master limited partnership. The great thing about these MLPs is that partners don't pay income taxes. Instead, they pay taxes only on received quarterly cash distributions. But, since high executive salaries, excessive construction costs, and new corporate acquisitions soak up most all the income, there are no distributions because earnings go straight into investment. That gives MLPs a lower cost of capital for acquisitions and construction projects, and that means the MLP must grow, as any carnivore does, by acquiring its competitors."

"Is that actually legal?"

"Yup, and there's another obfuscation layer. There exists a second higher-level entity, called an equity master partnership, which holds a reasonable equity position—plus, of course several incentives like distribution rights and other claims on the cash flow—in the lower-level class-2 MLPs. Just so you understand my world, Leon, my ghostlike shadow EMPs make all operation decisions for all my MLPs. Last year, my EMPs paid me $504 million just to oversee the MLPs that own my real-world oil service companies."

"Are you trying to tell me that you own the PFUMP pipeline?"

"That's an interesting, but obviously unanswerable question. Another of the good things about MLPs and EMPs is that it's almost impossible to find the names of the actual partners or the stakes they might have in any partnership. In an act of disclosure, I must confess that I could be one of those master or equity partners in the PFUMP-MLP. Many of them are, I would guess, like me, executives affiliated with Houston's major oil players."

"Are you telling me it's your personal money—and not your firm's development arm money—that's actually financing PFUMP's pipeline?"

"You're one quick learner, Uncle Leon. Who wants to put their firm's assets at risk, for God's sake? I knew you knew all this stuff already. It's a bit of a circular moneymaking machine for us oil company executives. This is really cool. I'll show you how it works. First: Each of my several dozen oil field operation LLCs pays me, its founder and CEO, an exorbitant salary. That salary is counted as a pretax expense by each of my companies, so the larger my salary, the greater the expense, and the less the tax on earnings. The whole idea is to make sure those LLCs either show no profit or lose money.

"Second, my exorbitant salaries are deposited into personal accounts, some physical and electronic distance from the oil fields of North Dakota, where they'll be safe from the explosions you seem to be having a lot of around here."

"Easy, Kathleen. Keep this civil."

"Third, those accounts invest my personal money into closely held class-2 LMP's, in this case PFUMP, which uses my money to perform a specific task—to plan and construct a pipeline.

"Fourth, PFUMP then contracts with my construction firm to construct their pipeline."

"Fifth, once the pipeline is built, PFUMP contracts with another one of my companies to pipe my oil—actually, as you yourself just noted, it is, indeed, your oil—which my drilling firm is extracting, from beneath your western Dakota—out to Illinois. Since my pipeline is now a monopoly, it is charging quite outrageous prices. However, since it's pumping it much more efficiently than my old pipeline company could do it, it's probably worth that elevated fee.

"Sixth, as CEO of my old—now abandoned—pipeline company, I mourn the loss of its income because of my new pipeline, but I can still make money pumping oil in the new line. I can structure that loss of income from the old pipeline to offset some of the massive income I'm making by building and using that new pipeline for PFUMP, of which I am a partner, and ultimately for some EMP, which—"

"Stop it, Kathleen. Stop it. I'm impressed, okay?"

The soup is delivered: cream of broccoli for Kathleen and clam chowder for Leon.

Kathleen drains her merlot and then installs a smug, satisfied moue.

"So, Kathleen, here's the deal. The word on the street is that some folks in Williston were kind of expecting some act of God would strike. Such a work would allow a rationale that supports some folks' belief that they could collect insurance to compensate for their losses for their now worthless oil and real estate assets. I was just wondering—"

"There is not one bit of evidence—"

"Stuff it, Kathleen. Let's agree that, for the purposes of this evening's discussion, what's past is past. I'm gonna be talking about the future. Let's say I'm aware of a certain plan that arranges stuff so even though an investor loses most of his assets, that loss would be able to be classified as a 'work of God' and thus be covered by some sort of insurance."

"You're not talking about those explosions and fires that happened a couple weeks ago, are you? For the record, Leon, I had nothing to do with them. Also, as you can imagine, God would never have done that for me. We're not on speaking terms."

"Oh, I don't doubt that, but I'm living in the future and not the past. I wasn't thinking of any historical God as you might normally think of as a god—"

"Oh, stop it, Uncle Leon. Just stop it. Okay?"

"But perhaps of a god like, yours truly, a kind of legislative god. Let's say that kind of god seized all underground solids and liquids rights from under your state. Boom, you immediately lose all your subsurface assets—and with absolutely no fault from you. It's just like what happened in Venezuela twenty years ago. Yesterday, you owned rights to harvest billions of gallons of oil. Tomorrow, poof, you still own those rights, but only in common with every other resident of the state. You might expect compensation for that, right? We both know that after that Venezuelan thing, every oil insurance contract that's been negotiated, at least in the Western Hemisphere, contains some Venezuelan language regarding works of—"

"I get your point, Uncle Leon, but I would guess a certain non-Texas, Dakota-based oil field management firm might have the ability to negotiate with that local god for a contract to extract his state's oil and then to pump it to Illinois for his state?"

"That might be something that could be discussed between the local god, or the Department of Natural Resources, and that North Dakota-based conglomerate that suffered the loss and might be operating a brand-new pipeline. I'm thinking that any arrangement will have to be a short-term contract because we both know that the Bakken oil fields are gonna get shut down sooner or later, don't we?"

Their spaghetti Parmesan arrives, and the waitress sprinkles little shreds of cheese, to their specifications, on the top of the pasta piles. "Enjoy" she says and then twirls away.

"And that is the beauty of what you're proposing Leon, isn't it? I can start moving my money out of oil and into renewables and not have to worry about my firms because some god is going to compensate them for all that lost oil revenue, huh?"

"I think that's a reasonable assumption, Kathleen. You want to know how it's all going to work?"

"I'm thinking that if I take one more step here, Leon, I'm going to be in the minefield, right? I'd better pay close attention to the directions."

"Right you are, and just so we understand each other, there's one tail-wagging-the-dog issue that must be settled first, in order for all this wonderful negotiation about God and compensation to be finalized." He stuffs a forkful of spaghetti into his mouth to allow the seriousness of this next sentence to be amplified. "I need another orange juice. How about you, Kathleen? Do you want more wine—or maybe an orange juice?"

"Jeez, you're a piece of work, Uncle Leon. Okay, I'll have some more wine."

Leon signals to the waitress, points to both empty glasses, holds up two fingers, and wiggles them back and forth to indicate they both want refills. "Good! Kathleen, you've heard of the term *quid pro quo*, right?"

"Uh-oh! Is now a good time for me to go out to the barn and check on Silver?"

"You've got your rides confused, Kathleen. You said before you'd left Trigger out there. Anyway, I'm thinking about those ISIS boys that found themselves dead up in Williston. That episode kind of jump-started this whole insurance story, huh?"

"Oh, no you don't, Leon. I told you I had nothing to do with that. I do admit ISIS and I have discussed doing oil field work, but back in Iraq. I would never agree—"

"I don't doubt that, Kathleen, but I also know very little up in the Bakken happens without your knowledge. I'm hopeful you can make a few inquiries on my behalf. I need to understand how those Somali guys died on that Sunday morning. I want you to think about this a bit and maybe find some way to help solve a little problem for me. Maybe, in a week or two, you remember a conversation you overheard. Maybe my friend, Mayor Allison, gets an envelope filed with coupons for help in rebuilding his downtown. Maybe I hear where some Good Samaritan left a basket of fruit, or something more substantial, on the doorstep what might ease the discomfort of those women who lost their boys. Know what I mean?"

"Leon, I swear I had nothing to do with any of those explosions."

"I understand the folks working on the Missouri oil spill cleanup need equipment for cleaning oil from ice floes. I talked to Chief Two Deer—"

"Will you stop it, Leon? This deal you're proposing is preposterous. I'm the victim here. I've done nothing wrong."

"Oh, we both realize that, Kathleen. But a certain Texas oil person operating in this state very likely did massive bits of wrongdoing. That kind of oil person would understand about the blaming of unreliable, unscrupulous subcontractors, the much-used corporate deniability ploy, the unlinked chain-of-responsibility ruse, and all that. And the thought just occurred to me that those slithery mounds of type-2 MLPs and EMPs are kind of like this plate of spaghetti here."

"I see absolutely no connection, Leon. You'd better lay off the orange juice. You're hallucinating again. Please come back to the real world."

"Do you realize, Kathleen, that it's nearly impossible, I should think, to trace a single spaghetti strand as it winds through all the meat sauce and sticky Parmesan?" Leon pokes around with his fork and knife trying to find the end of a particular piece of spaghetti to support his rather ridiculous metaphor. "It's like trying to trace a kill order from the mouth of the guy giving the order to the forehead of the guy getting the bullet." He looks up from his spaghetti plate and smiles at her.

"Stop it, Leon. That's an insulting thing to say to me, especially since I think I am on your side in this."

Leon looks up at her. "You are on my side? I don't understand that, Kathleen."

"I'm an expert businesswoman, Leon. I've done my economic homework and leveraged my gains with some quite substantial losses. I run a pure Harvard Business School-approved operation. Everything I do is done exactly by the legal book. It's all technically perfect. It's a beautiful legal machine, or group of machines, maybe a whole armada of—"

"Let's not be hyperventilating on me, Kathleen."

Kathleen finishes her wine. "An armada of perfectly legal machines, Leon. Isn't that a great vision?" She looks up to the wood-beamed ceiling. "Even I think so. However, there are other guys out there not as legally astute, smart, or lucky as I am, and they're really hurting. Those guys are gonna need big insurance payouts—and they need that money fast if they want to shift their operations to Texas in a heartbeat like I'm already in the process of doing. As you might possibly imagine, Uncle Leon, I'm way out ahead of the curve on this. I'm pretty much covered. Others ain't so smart or lucky. They're the ones needing the acts of God."

"So how can I—a non-Texan, legislator type—theoretically figure out who is the bad guy here?"

Her fork—containing a piece of meatball exquisitely wrapped by several strands of spaghetti—points first to Leon and then back at her mouth. She maintains the suspense for a few chews.

Leon gives up the feigned interest and studies his plate for the next target.

"Leon, we both know who the bad guy is. He's the one with no roots in Dakota like I have, but he still thinks he's lord of the prairie. Bull-feathers, Leon. He's from West Texas. They don't have prairie there. It's continuous scrub desert. However, you must realize that all us oil guys are tied together by partnerships. If one of us fails, there's the chance we all go down together. That's the hedge that being a partner gives an oil guy. But the particular Texas oil guy about whom we're talking is stupid, and he takes big chances, and since gambling on oil is a zero-sum game, he, sooner or later, will flame out. You can bank on it. Sooner or later, that meatball's going down. I must just make sure the 'play by the rules' guys end up winners, and those other pigs can be the losers. Sooner or later, Leon, he's gonna be one dead meatball."

"So, you're saying, when I get to the end of this spaghetti," he tugs on it a bit, but the damn thing is still stuck in the pile, "I'm gonna find no meatball hooked to the end of it?"

"It's been an interesting discussion, Uncle Leon, but it's become way too theoretical. I can't stand it any longer. I'm going out in the cold to saddle up Silver. You know how to reach me if you need to. Tonto and I are gonna ride out there and take care of the bad guys, Leon."

"Tonto?" Leon stops playing with his spaghetti. "Who's Tonto?"

Kathleen abruptly stands up, smiles at him, and walks toward the bar, making sure every eye in the restaurant follows her as she maneuvers between the tables.

Leon pokes a bit more in his Parmesan sauce, still excavating for the end of the spaghetti string, and then he gives up and whacks it off with his knife. "Tonto? That's why I prefer lasagna,"

The waitress arrives to see if she can take Kathleen's plate back to keep it warm.

"No," he says. "She had to go see some man about her horse. I'll stay here and finish mine. It's very good spaghetti. Can you bring me a take-home box? I'll take her dinner home with me. Oh, and I'll need another orange juice please."

CHAPTER 55

THE GOVERNOR AND HIS MOM PREP FOR THE SPECIAL SESSION

TUESDAY, DECEMBER 13

THE WINTER SOLSTICE APPROACHES, AND the sun won't peek above the prairie horizon until almost ten minutes after eight. This means much important work of the North Dakota government will be done in the dark—without the normal blessing from the sun.

An hour before the sun arrives, Russell Cordoba and Larry Oosterhaus step through the kitchen door for a breakfast strategy session at Leon's mom's house. This morning, her pancakes do the heavy lifting, augmented with deer meat sausage made using a friend's traditional Norwegian recipe.

"You boys need more coffee before I sit down? It's your last chance. Once I'm seated, you're on your own."

"We know the house rules, Mom. Please sit down so we can start."

It doesn't take long, maybe three or four mouthfuls, before Leon's mom can't stand the silence any longer. "Did any of you lugs by chance take the precaution of handcuffing that Basehardt boy to a fence post, maybe up in Bottineau County, so he doesn't cause any trouble today."

"He can't do anything, Mom. He's not a legislator yet, not till next month, thank goodness. We won't let him onto the senate floor."

"Yeah," says Russell, "but he can sit in the visitors' gallery and pout. If he, or his army, starts making noise up there, then we've got a problem."

"Mom has a point, guys. Somebody should keep an eye on him and make sure he doesn't embarrass himself."

"Yeah," says Larry. "But who's going to do that?"

The other three all look at Larry, and Leon points his forkful of pancake at him.

"Oh, no you don't!"

"It's you and Russell. You're the guys gonna be in the gallery watching my beautiful choreography play out on the floor. All you gotta do is watch one more thing. Multitask, guys."

"I'll take care of him for you," says Leon's mom. "If he's in the balcony, I'll sit behind him with my cane. First time he opens his mouth with something uncouth, I'll whack him."

"Thanks, Mom. I knew I could count on you."

CHAPTER 56

BEGINNING THE GOVERNOR'S SPECIAL SESSION

L EON AND HIS POINT MEN, Larry and Russell, are milling about in the great lobby of the capitol doing their final bits of, well, lobbying. Since this space, unlike the house and senate meeting chambers, is open to the public, there are paid lobbyists and other non-legislator political guys running about, holding court, and lobbying mostly for a "no" vote.

Leon Rolfes, the governor, is not allowed into the legislative chambers, of course, but he is working the crowd in an attempt to ease fears of a communist takeover and spread the good news of removing Texans from bankrupting the state's economy. Leon hears his name called, turns, and is surprised to see his old nemesis, Brian Bast, walking toward him across the marble floor. He's towing another man who Leon thinks he should know. The man's face looks familiar, but Leon can't quite match it with a name.

For the eight years prior to Leon's election as governor, Brian Bast almost ran the state as the office manager for two Republican governors who were both completely inexperienced in elected politics. Leon recalls quite a few knock-down, drag-out battles with that sniveling little creep. Bast also is the slime bag who ran the campaign for his gubernatorial opponent, and then, after his guy lost, hightailed it to Washington, DC, where, for all he knows, he's still slinging the stuff from a much larger manure pile. He does look fairly spiffy today. Nice suit, good haircut. It appears life in Washington has cleaned him up a bit.

"Well, hello, Leon." Bast puts out his hand, preparing for a shake. "Long time, no see, huh?"

"Did you remove your boots before you entered our pristine governmental center?" Leon looks down to determine if the answer is obvious.

"Easy, Leon," Bast says. "I'd like to keep this civil."

"Well, then, start by being respectful, Mr. Bast. You're supposed to address me as Governor Rolfes."

Bast wasn't expecting that, and it takes a while to sink in. "Uh, all right, Governor. I'd like you to meet someone who you'll be dealing with for the next four years. Since he's going to be our new secretary of energy, I think you should listen to what he's selling."

Leon remembers who the guy is now, that former Texas governor and wannabe energy secretary, Clifton Cherry.

"You're from Texas, right?" Leon makes the first jab.

"Yes, sir! A fellow governor, Cliff Cherry, from Houston."

"No offense, sir, but I don't usually talk with folks from Texas." Leon points to his ear. "Can't understand 'em. Not a word. You should've known that, Mr. Bass." Leon pivots away and starts moving swiftly across the hall.

"What the hell?" Cherry asks his slippery-looking sidekick. "Thought you said you two were old buddies."

"Never said he was an old buddy, Bing. Said we worked in this building together when he was senate leader and I worked for the governor. Leon often comes across as haughty, thinks of himself as a moralist."

"Moralist? What the flaming hell's a moralist? This here's oil we're talking about, Bast. No room for moralists in oil, is there?"

Leon's so distracted running from Bast that he almost runs into the back of Will Basehardt.

"Leon, how fortunate that you ran into me. I gotta talk to you."

"You remember the rules, Will?"

Will looks at Leon like he just spoke to him in Latin. "Rules, Leon? What rules?"

"House rules. If you want to talk to me, we do it out by the elm tree." Leon points out the expansive glass wall at the several giant elms across the drive. "Remember?"

"Oh, for Christ's sake. Can't you ever be serious? I get the joke. Ha, ha. We've got to talk about oil. Leon, you can't—"

"I can do any damned thing I want to, Will, especially since you continue to not address me properly as 'Governor.' However, I am the governor, and right now, you're officially a nobody. I don't want to talk to you."

"Leon ..."

"It's Governor Rolfes to you, sir. And you have no reason to be poking your nose in the official business here today because you're not yet a member of this fraternity. I don't have to officially talk to you. If you've got something important for me, I'll be glad to meet with you after the current elected officials go back into chambers. We can meet in my Southern Office if you want. You know where that is."

Leon watches the steam spraying out of Basehardt's ears.

Basehardt turns, takes two steps, and runs smack into Larry Oosterhaus. He then swings away, muttering expletives and stomping his feet.

"Hi, Leon," says Larry. "What the hell was that about?"

"Basehardt thought he could drive right through me for the lay-up. He's not agile enough, Larry. He got called for charging. I think I need an orange juice."

*   *   *

Since it's almost zero outside, Basehardt opts for the grand foyer of the capitol to hold a small conference. The real lawmakers have withdrawn to their chambers for deliberation, and maybe twenty lobbyists and hacks have nothing now to do but listen to him rant. "The incoming administration will have the power, and the absolute will to, by executive order, overturn whatever silly or stupid last-minute laws the puny North Dakota lawmakers pass in their closed room, especially since this particular law is obviously designed to do nothing but embarrass the incoming administration."

*   *   *

Behind those closed doors, inside the senate chamber, one member, an accomplice of Mr. Basehardt, actually has the gall to introduce a motion seeking to invite Basehardt to address the chamber for the purpose of speaking against the proposal. A second motion is quickly introduced, this one authorizing a special committee to be selected by the senate president to shoot Basehardt if he walks through the door. That leads to a fifteen-minute discussion, under the rules-of-order provisions, as to whether it would be legal to order a state-senator-to-be to be shot inside the senate chambers.

CHAPTER 57

ENDING THE GOVERNOR'S
SPECIAL SESSION

FRIDAY, DECEMBER 16, 2016

L EON'S SPECIAL SESSION DID NOT need two full days to consider and pass
his Subsurface Materials Ownership Act. Arguments for and against
have, during the past two years, been exhausted. The only thing unknown
is how many Republicans will vote nay under pressure from the president-
elect's surrogate, Will Basehardt? Not many, as it turns out. Only six voted
against the measure in the house and two in the senate. By three o'clock in
the afternoon, the gavel sounds—and the circus concludes.

At 4:03 p.m., Leon approaches the podium erected in the grand
lobby of the state capitol for the express purpose of enabling bill-signing
ceremonies to be witnessed by citizens. A dozen or so legislators crowd into
a tight group behind him to fit nicely into the formal photograph of the
signing, and at 4:09, Leon starts the ceremony.

Article 15 of the Subsurface Materials Ownership Act specifies that the
act will not be finalized unless and until the governor and a representative
of the Standing Rock people, acting also for the various conclaves of
indigenous non-Sioux peoples, both sign a statement of understanding,
the wording of which is included in the act itself. Article 15, paragraphs
b and c, state that any native peoples' claims to the subsurface materials
are now, and will under this statute, be no different and no more or no
less impressed on them than they are on non-native people. The act states

that all natural material underlying the surface area of the state is sacred material, and sacred in a secular sense, meaning that any use or harvesting of those materials must acknowledge the sacredness (defined in article 2, paragraphs 1–3) of that material, and that any use and/or harvesting of such materials must be done only using legal measures as described in the statute.

After the official photographs are taken, Carl Two Deer walks, with suitable restraint, over to the podium and shakes hands with Leon. Both men sign the statement of understanding and pose for the required photographs.

Article 5 of the Subsurface Materials Ownership Act states that no governmental, corporate, or individual entity has the standing to own any material located deeper than eight feet below the surface of the ground.

Article 6 of the Subsurface Materials Ownership Act states that the state of North Dakota has the sole right to oversee and control any unnatural removal or use of the subsurface materials (as described in the act) located in any soils beneath the state. Much traditional legislation includes those little crevasses through which unscrupulous operators think they can drive big yellow bulldozers, trucks of fracking sand, and shiny stainless steel pipelines. There are no such crevasses hidden in this bill. The simple language is unambiguous, and definitions are very restricted.

Leon's office staff noted that immediately before he signed the document, Leon—and the rest of the civilized world—received a tweet from Will Basehardt, the incoming Republican state senator, calling the vote to approve the governor's provision: "Shameful, and something from Fidel Castro's Bag of Communist Tricks."

Margie tells Leon that even though she knows Leon will never read any Twitter coming into his machine, he should probably be aware of the fact that the governor is the subject of a nasty tweet directly from the flexible fingers of the president-elect himself; the tweet strongly indicates that the new administration in Washington will pay no attention to such an obvious unconstitutional maneuver as the North Dakota legislature just performed.

When asked about this, Leon replies, "Back in the olden days, they had a saying that went: 'Sticks and stones may break my bones, but words can never hurt me.' I think the phrase should be updated to: 'Tweets and texts may break my necks, but they cannot replace the truth.'" Leon isn't yet happy with several specific word choices in that statement, but it made his point—and he's not going to spend a horrific number of hours assessing his own word choices.

Will Basehardt, however, does intend to spend a horrific number of hours blasting the governor's words. He has inveigled a few dozen supporters and anti-communists he either found in North Dakota or imported from Texas to assemble in the ankle-deep snow under the American elms across the driveway from the entry to the statehouse steps. A couple TV cameras, here to record the grand signing ceremony just concluded inside the rotunda, bring their equipment into the snow to record Basehardt's certain bombast. Every Basehardt rant is wonderful, entertaining theater, and they draw cameras like honey draws flies.

"I know folks outside the Williston area don't much know me yet," Will Basehardt starts off this press conference—or it could be a rally or a sales event. "That's only because I have not yet been sworn in as state senator. But, believe me, I'm going to run for and be elected leader of this senate, and then you'll know who I am. I'm a close confidant of the president-elect, so by this time next month—I'm telling you the truth— we're gonna turn this state around. We'll throw out the baggage, throw out the idiots running this place, and like my friend in Washington says, 'pull the weeds.' Right? Pull the damn weeds—and let the wheat grow up! And the first weed we're pulling up is that piece of garbage your current governor just rammed through your legislature while that bunch of yellow-bellied weasels in the state senate sat on their thumbs. Boy, are things going to change around here."

The small gathering yells and screams for the cameras.

"I have to tell you a little story, let you know how out of touch our governor is. He has said that this area under these elms is his Southern Office. Ya know, folks, these are majestic American elms." He gestures dramatically for the cameras. "He tells me I'm not welcome in the statehouse, that I will drag mud and snow onto the marble floors, and that if I want to talk to him, I must do it out here. Well, I'll tell you what. Listen up, Governor, I'm taking over in your office here right now, and soon I'll kick you out of your other office up there." As the small crowd cheers, he points to the upper floors of the towering statehouse where

Governor Rolfes's primary office is located. First thing I'm gonna do as senate leader is to impeach that commie." He puts a serious look on his mug. "Absolutely! First thing! I was talking to a historian who knows everything about history. Everything! He tells me that what that Commie Rolfes did is exactly what Fidel Castro did back in Cuba. You people want to live in a Cuba-like Communist state?" He waits for the crowd to calm down. "I didn't think so."

After a long harangue about the evils of 1960s international-style Communism, Basehardt gets around to his speech's focus.

"Remember that historian I told you about? He also warns that by tending toward a socialistic state, we're actually inviting radical Islamic terrorists to attack. And I'm very much afraid that we're gonna continue to have ISIS attacking our oil fields until we start getting tough with those guys. We're gonna make our Bakken Oilfield a safe place to work again. I mean it, folks. I really do. I mean it! We're not gonna allow commie ISIS terrorists into our oil fields. Period!"

The crowd is growing because the capitol is emptying, and the normal office workers are heading home.

"Right now, under this governor and this legislature, Williston's unprotected from another attack. That, in itself, is a crime. As soon as we move into the statehouse, we will change all that. We're going to repeal the socialist legislation those idiots have just put into place and make North Dakota safe again. I've already scheduled another special session to repeal Rolfes's overreach. It's happening the first day after I take office."

"Hold on a minute, Mr. Basehardt," a reporter yells. "You can't call a special session. Only the governor can do that."

Someone yells a follow-up comment: "You're nuts, Basehardt. The legislature automatically reconvenes the day after inauguration—no special session is needed."

Many in the informal crowd laugh at him, turn away, and head for their cars.

Two black SUVs ignite their soft sirens and slowly push through the exiting crowd, stopping just opposite Leon's Southern Office. FBI Special Agent Harrison Brock and three other agents quickly exit their SUVs and approach Basehardt. "Mr. Basehardt, I am requesting you come with us. We have questions we need you to answer."

"I'm afraid this isn't a convenient time, sir."

"We need to ask you several questions, sir. Will you please come with us?"

He looks at his watch and looks across to his supporters. "I'm expected at a meeting downtown in a few minutes."

"You were supposed to have been at that meeting half an hour ago," says Brock. "You stood us up, Mr. Basehardt. You've lost any sympathy I once had for your schedule. Now, please come with us."

Agent J. opens the rear door to his GMC van, suggesting to Basehardt that he should enter.

"Do you know who I am, young man?"

"Would you please enter the car, sir?"

"I do not think I want to do that. If you have a question for me, ask it right here."

"Enter the car, sir!" A pair of plastic cuffs somehow materializes in agent Brock's hands. "Must I use these?"

"How dare you threaten me!"

"I'm not threatening you. I'm asking you, quite politely, to get into the van. If you'd like, my friend here," he nods to Agent J. who is holding the door open, "will drive your car downtown for you. Then, if everything goes smoothly in our interview, you can drive it home from there."

Agent J. holds out her hand for Basehardt's keys. It takes several seconds before Basehardt recognizes he's not in control. Eventually, he acquiesces.

CHAPTER 58

FINDING A COMPANION FOR SIMBA

KATHLEEN DRIVES ACROSS THE SNOW-COVERED scrub and gravel in front of her house, cruises past Simba snoozing on the wall, slips her pickup into the garage, stomps her boots, and enters her house. She sees Trevor in the kitchen. "I don't know about you, Trevor, but I'm about mad enough to fly over to Bismarck and firebomb something myself."

"What ya gonna blow up today?"

She angrily bangs her bag on the table. "Driving up here, I was listening to Basehardt on the radio. So help me God, I'm gonna kill that bastard."

Trevor's heard this before. He's busy chopping veggies, but he doesn't miss a beat. "What's that fool done now?"

"He's suggesting more terrorist attacks might happen in the Bakken. He's completely loony. There's not a single person in the entire Bakken who thinks ISIS terrorists have ever been near North Dakota. It's all a stage play. He's waving his fake ISIS flag in front of the president-elect. He wants his new leader to throw him federal subsidies to prop up his Dakota oil business."

"He sounds confident another attack's gonna happen."

"If he thinks another attack is beneficial to him—and I think he does—then he'll get his fake ISIS to attack again."

"The FBI's on him like a parka. He wouldn't explode something with them watching, would he?"

"Dakota's a big state, Trevor. The FBI can't cover it all."

"Why would he firebomb more stuff? His operation's low on cash, and his hedges are poorly constructed. He's running in the past. The big downturn really slapped him. Hell, it slapped us all."

"But most smart folks were ready for it, and they had their hedges in place. It seems, from what I can tell, he got caught in between. He's stupid—stupid as a brick. He's acting desperate, and desperate men are inherently dangerous."

"I've been watching him, Kathleen, to make sure we don't have more Louisiana lightning or ISIS bombings. I'll stay on him—and make sure he behaves himself."

"That would be a reasonable precaution. However, I'm thinking we must do something unreasonable ... perhaps something that would be more constructive."

"I'm thinking the most constructive thing would be to shoot him."

"No, no. No killing. I want him put on a chain and have him share the front porch with Simba. That might mellow him. Maybe deflate that ego?"

"It might give him the idea that when one, like him, is old and worn out, one might want to eschew public office and spent his last days stretched out on a rock, soaking in the sun.

CHAPTER 59

WATCHING SOME OTHER GOD PLANT EXPLOSIVES

Saturday, December 17, 2016

Trevor's on L. D.'s tail. He's installed a quarter-sized sending unit on L. D.'s GMC pickup, which constantly streams its GPS coordinates. He's continuously watching and documenting where L. D.'s going, who he's talking to, and what he's doing. He's arranged the logs and videos by date and topic and stored them on thumb drives. Trevor has recorded meetings and noted purchases, and he's alerted Kathleen to the fact that it seems like another event is in preparation. Trevor's seen no evidence of L. D. recruiting additional fake ISIS gunmen or scouting out additional targets. Trevor is coming to believe that either someone else is doing the preliminary work or the target site is so well known that no scouting's necessary.

Tonight, at 11:31 p.m., as the industrial-sized garage door at Roseborough Drilling's warehouse roll open, Trevor powers up his infrared camera. L. D. opens the garage door and carries four cardboard boxes to his truck. Nothing else happens for several minutes. The GMC is on because Trevor sees the white exhaust puffing out and hears the sound.

L. D. opens the cab door and climbs in. He's got his phone to his ear the entire time.

"This looks interesting," Trevor says to his voice-activated recorder. "At 11:41, L. D.'s GMC exits the shop, turns north on Third." Trevor tracks

247

him from a couple miles back as he drives north, then east, and then north again on County Road 44.

At 12:12 a.m., L. D. turns west onto a private dead-end drive. Trevor cuts his normal lights, ignites his infrared array, and drives a quarter of mile past the access road. "Looks like an access drive to an equipment storage yard." He stops, pulls off the road, and parks behind a horizontal LP tank connected to an irrigation system pumping station.

Roseborough opens the metal gate and drives into the storage yard. Several signs attached to the equipment confirm the yard holds dead BX&F equipment.

Trevor, through his high-powered, infrared videocam, watches L. D. attach several bundles—Trevor expects they are explosives—to various pieces of equipment in the yard. L. D., who is definitely not dressed in ISIS gear, seems to be preparing to blow up these mothballed rigs.

Trevor instinctively rotates his infrared device around a full three-sixty, but he sees no evidence of another breathing human for miles. He and L. D. are alone out here, and he is certain that L. D., not trained by special forces in night surveillance, is not sweeping the area for human heat sources as a trained operator would do. Trevor despises such incompetence.

L. D. works intently and finishes in about fifteen minutes. He returns to his truck, leaves the yard, locks the gate, and heads back toward Williston. After L. D.'s taillights vanish over the slight rise a mile ahead, Travis pulls out after him.

As he closes in on Williston, Trevor closes the distance to a quarter of a mile. L. D. eventually turns South onto Second Street, the main highway through town, and enters a Shell station on the right.

Trevor pulls into a vacant motel parking lot, cuts through a driveway, and stops in the shadows, fifty feet from L. D.'s truck.

L. D. nonchalantly leans against his truck and pumps diesel fuel. The time stamp in the lower left corner on the videocam indicates it is 1:09 a.m. on December 18, 2016. No other customer is using the pumps, but two other cars are parked in front of the store. A man exits the store with a small plastic bag, walks over to L. D., talks with him for maybe thirty seconds, gives him the bag, and then walks to a white Lexus, one of the cars parked at the front. The Lexus leaves the station and heads south into town. Trevor records the entire encounter, including the rear license plate of the Lexus.

He watches L. D. check the oil and tire pressure. *Seems he's wasting time playing Joe Casual. Could be preparing for a trip.* After this ritual, L. D. leaves the station and heads south into Williston, following the same route the Lexus took. Trevor repacks the scope and the camera in their respective cases, exits the parking lot, turns north, and heads back to the fenced-in storage yard.

Trevor's not concerned if Basehardt blows up his own stuff. He just wants to record his involvement in it. Back at the yard, he installs three infrared cameras. They're attached to motion detectors and will run through several weeks without recharging. If any equipment in the yard blows up during that time, he'll be able to document the mayhem. Even if the button is pushed, or the phone call made, and the equipment goes boom, Trevor knows for dead certain that L. D. will not be the guy who will be pushing those buttons.

CHAPTER 60

GRILLING SENATOR-
ELECT BASEHARDT

Sunday, December 18, 2016

IT'S BEEN ONE WEEK SINCE Will Basehardt was initially questioned by Agent Brock. Brock has been unable to secure enough evidence for an indictment due in large extent to their inability to find any corroborating witnesses. The guys Brock needs to talk with are subcontractor L. D. Roseborough and his subcontractor, Gary Gralapp. Both men have vanished, and Brock is left with no spaghetti connecting the money and the meatball.

At 3:13 p.m., Agent Brock, exasperated and with a puny physical case, gives up for the weekend. "All right, Mr. Basehardt. This is your lucky day. We cannot at this time generate the evidence needed to hold you. You are free to go home for the Christmas holiday, but the FBI will be working through the holiday—and we will stay on you."

"You better watch your step, Agent Brock. I am this close to suing the bejesus out of your FBI." Basehardt gestures with a thumb and forefinger. "I've got pull with the new administration. You're coming nowhere near me. My friends in Washington will back me 100 percent. One more word from you, and I'm going straight to DC."

"We are watching you, sir. If you try to leave North Dakota, you'll be detained. And I dare you to test me and try it. I'm not given to boasting, Mr. Basehardt, but I'm a dedicated and aggressive FBI agent. And you had better understand that. I know you are responsible for those Somali boys' deaths, I know you're responsible for setting set those fires, and I know your operatives killed those two employees in the bar. I cannot yet prove it solid, but I'm on you like a glove.

Basehardt rises and gets his coat from the rack.

"Again, Mr. Basehardt we will not let you leave North Dakota. You'd better be careful. Keep one eye in your rearview mirror because we'll be watching you. One little misstep, email, or substantiated link, and you'll be back in that chair!"

CHAPTER 61

THE FIRST DEAD MAN MESSAGE

Hasani Indaak sits on the second chair from the north end of the coffee bar at the Kafe Korol. It's where she normally sits because the low sun, now hidden by the office block across Riverside Street, cannot spray light through the windows and onto her computer screen.

A young waitress Hasani's not seen here before puts the mug of jasmine-spice tea in front of her and then adjusts it so the handle faces her. A fluffy puff of steam swirls off the top and jumps into the cool December air.

"Thank you," she says. "My name's Hasani." The young barista, also Somali, smiles nervously, adjusts the strap on her apron, nods slightly, and silently turns to other tasks.

The phone Hasani's placed on the polished wood countertop, carefully aligned with the top corner of her Mac, softly buzzes. Hasani glances at the screen: "Caller ID Blocked." *This might mean something very good or very bad,* she thinks. But she takes the chance. *What the hell? It's Christmas Eve—maybe it is Santa with a merry message.* "Hello, this is Hasani."

"Jusef Abi Sadi? He's dead." The voice is a young—maybe even preteen—Somali voice speaking English, but not speaking it well. The voice vibrates, suggesting the speaker's terrified or at least under stress.

Her automatic defense mechanism, sarcasm, kicks in. "Lots of people die," she answers. "Why should I care?"

The tentative voice repeats, "Jusef Abdi Sadi. Really, he's dead."

"Who is this Jusef? Do I know him?"

"Jusef Abi Sadi! He's dead!"

"Who gave you my number?"

"Jusef Abi Sadi. He's dead."

"Someone is with you. I hear his breathing. Let me speak with him."

"Please!" Hasani senses the boy's fright morphing into anger. "Jusef Abi Sadi. He's dead!"

This boy is in danger, she thinks. *I must change my attitude.* "Okay! I believe you. Jusef Abi Sadi is dead. Why do you tell me this?"

No more words jump from her phone.

"Hello!" Hasani slaps the countertop. "Hello!"

She's not heard that name, Jusef Abi Sadi, before. And, being a good reporter, she remembers every name and every phone number from every story. So she's confident that she's not heard that name before. Nevertheless, someone wants her to know this Jusef is dead—and to know his death is something she must care about.

The light from her phone fades.

Hasani's mind quickly jumps to the three dead Somali boys. *I know the names of three dead Somali men,* she thinks. *Might this be the name of the fourth one Steffie's told me about—the older one? I must tell Special Agent Carol that Jusef Abi Sadi is dead, but I need to call Steffie first.*

CHAPTER 62

THE SECOND DEAD MAN MESSAGE

O N CHRISTMAS EVE, STEFFIE IS not thinking about exploding trains and dead Somalis. She is thinking about enjoying the holidays with her family. Her parents have flown up from Phoenix, her boys are home from college, and her husband's relaxed because the farmwork is in the slow season. Anxieties and conflicts are mellowed out or have been put on hold for the holidays.

As a surprise for her parents' visit, her husband, Ross, has taken an extra effort with Christmas decorations this season in an attempt to present himself as a soft and caring human being, especially since this turbulent political atmosphere has been pushing them in opposite directions.

Steffie's entire family, including her parents and her two college boys, Jake and David, are watching the Hallmark Channel's sappy Christmas romance marathon in the big room. They're eating popcorn and watching the snow outside. Tension and apprehension in the Cobb household have slowed to a crawl. Just like in the Hallmark movie, there's a fire in the woodstove.

Steffie's cell phone buzzes and skitters on the end table. She picks it up and looks at it, but she doesn't recognize the local number. "Hi! This is Steffie Cobb."

"L. D. Roseborough, he's dead." It's an awkward, disguised, and probably Latino-accented voice speaking deliberate words.

Anger jumps into her voice. "Who the hell is this?"

"L. D. Roseborough, he's dead."

It sounds the same, like it could be a recording. "Who is this?"

The line goes dead. Her husband and sons watch her morph into a dragon.

"You bastard. Who are you?" She holds the phone in front of her and stares at it.

She dares it to ring again, but it doesn't. She pushes "recent" and taps the last number, noted "unknown caller," at the top of the queue.

The call goes straight to a curt message: "The number you've dialed is not active. Please make sure you've dialed correctly."

Steffie holds the instrument and stares blankly at it. While she's concentrating on it, it rings. That startles her. She recoils, looks, and recognizes the number.

"Hasani, you all right? I just received this strange call—"

"Me too, Steffie. I also received a strange call ... from perhaps a child. Told me a someone, a name not familiar to me, is dead!"

"That's exactly like my call, Hasani. But I recognize the name on my call: 'L. D. Roseborough.' That's a real Williston guy. I've talked with him."

"That's not the name my caller used," Hasani says. "My caller said: 'Jusef Abi Sadi, he's dead.' What's happening here, Steffie?"

"Is that a Somali name?"

"I don't know. They were just sounds spoken by a terrified child. I don't know how it's spelled. I assume it's a Somali name. It could be, although I'm unfamiliar with it."

"Run the name past Agent Parker," says Steffie. "See if anything pops up on her screen."

"Be careful, Steffie. Someone's killing men so easily. He'll have no problem killing a reporter lady."

"I hear you, Hasani. I'll be careful. I'll let you know what I find out."

Steffie stows her phone and looks at her parents, her husband, and her boys. It's obvious they're terrified. Steffie, however, isn't frightened. She is angry because this jerk's upset her beautiful holiday. She is angry because Somali people are still being killed. She's angry all over, and when she's this angry, her first thought is to call Leon. "Sorry, Mom and Dad. I've got to report this." She smiles. "It's okay, Mom. I'm a reporter. This is what we do. We report stuff."

Jake throws a piece of popcorn at her.

Steffie walks into the kitchen and calls Leon.

"Hi, Steffie. Merry Christmas!"

"There's nothing merry about this call, Leon. Someone's turned my world upside down. I'm angry as hell—so I call you!"

"Like I said, Steffie, merry Christmas—and happy holidays too."

"You're not getting off that easily, Buster," she says. "Right now, I'm gonna make you a small wager. I think—or rather, my friend Hasani and I together think—we may be closer to solving the killer of the Somali boys than all those secret police guys running around out in Williston. We're going to find the connections and solve the murders before they do."

"Wow. That's something," he says. "Can I have your autograph?"

"Your sarcasm's not easing my anger, Leon. I am livid!"

"I can tell that. What's going on?"

"You got a pencil? Some stranger called both Hasani and me and told us that two guys, L. D. Roseborough and Joe Abisadi, are dead. Why are those people calling us on Christmas Eve, Leon? Why call both Hasani and I with different death notices? What the hell's wrong with calling 9-1-1? Why are they calling us?"

"Please ease up on me, Steffie. It's not my fault. You want to talk to my mom?"

"No, I want to talk to you. I want you to make this whole fake ISIS thing just go away. Again, the dead guy's names are L. D. Roseborough and Joe Abisadi. I am out of it now. I'm not involved anymore! Call your secret police. Have them solve it. Leave me out of it."

"There are no secret police, Steffie."

"I am going back to watching my sappy Christmas story on TV. And I'm turning off my phone. I'll return to the real world after Christmas. Goodbye."

"I have no secret pol—" Leon looks over at his mom. "She hung up on me."

"What was that all about?"

"Terrorists are picking on Steffie, Mom—so Steffie's picking on me. What did I do to deserve that?"

"It's Christmas Eve, sweetheart. Terrorists can't be so irreverent as to work on Christmas Eve, right?"

"Yeah, well then, maybe it's the Texas oil guys. We all know Texas oil guys would do that."

CHAPTER 63

SANTA'S PACKAGES GET DELIVERED

A S CHRISTMAS EVE SILENTLY SLIPS west into Montana, much of Williston—especially the commercial area burnt out last month near First and Second Street—lies numb, incapacitated, disused, and lifeless. The requisite Christmas cheer is not available, even for the rest of the city. Along the Second Street main drag, no wreaths are hanging from light poles, half the streetlights remain off-grid, and few stores even attempt security lighting. Folks are afraid of another bombing, and no one dares wander through the charred remains. All through traffic has been rerouted. There is no place for happy holidays here, and everyone knows Santa won't risk slipping his sled into this neighborhood tonight.

But one life form is slipping through the deep shadows. As this night before Christmas slips away into the past, a curious non-elf is delivering an unconventionally wrapped package into the neighborhood.

Trevor backs his dark blue Ford pickup to the steel mesh gate in the steel mesh fence, on the back side of the devastation area, off South Third Street. That fence has been installed to secure the ruined shells of several buildings. Trevor steps down, walks to the back, lowers the tailgate, opens the tonneau covering the pickup box, quickly pulls out a plastic-wrapped bundle, and lets it tumble, rather unceremoniously, in front of the locked chain-link security gate. Then he closes the tonneau and the tailgate, reenters his truck, and, like every Santa has done countless times, quickly removes himself from the scene.

Then, unlike a normal Santa, he grabs his cell phone, pushes one button, and makes a report. When the phone is answered, he says, "The first Christmas package is delivered."

That's all Santa needs to say.

CHAPTER 64

AGENT BROCK OPENS HIS CHRISTMAS PRESENTS

SUNDAY, DECEMBER 25, 2016

A T 8:06 ON CHRISTMAS MORNING, the first package is found by a security patrolman on a routine drive-by check of the perimeter of the arson sites. The charred areas are surrounded with chain-link fencing, and several gates have been inserted at entry points. In front of gate 2, a half-asleep patrolman finds a black body bag. It contains something that seems consistent with a body's shape. Therefore, the patrolman does not even think about unzipping it to confirm his hunch. He knows the routine and immediately calls his supervisor.

Five minutes later, four other vehicles pull up. The responders quickly do their work and photograph the location with both still shots and video recordings. Except for the lumpy black bag, nothing of interest is found at the site. Once that bag is loaded into the medical examiner's van, there's nothing left to do.

Once everyone leaves, the area reverts to its vacant status. The light snow continues, slowly to infill the outline of the body bag which, until about ten minutes ago, prevented one from viewing the exposed gravel in this irregular area of smooth un-snowed-upon driveway.

* * *

A second discovery is made several hours later by Cletus Landreau. Oil field work is continuous and does not consider holidays or weekends. Pumps pump continuously. Cletus, operating in accordance with the schedule posted last week on his company's website, stopped by for a routine inspection of this currently blown to bits and with the exception of one of the eight pumps, nonoperating drilling compound a dozen miles east of Williston. Although Mr. Landreau has never actually seen an occupied body bag, he quickly recognizes the nature of the lustrous body-sized thing resting in front of his gate.

Cletus is faced with two unpleasant options: call his boss, L. D. Roseborough, or the police. Given the fact that another dead body was found by the police at this very site last month, he thinks the police would be extremely interested in another dead body found at the same site. Mr. Landreau opts for the police, and he calls 9-1-1.

Many of the vehicles that answered the first call respond to the second one. The procedure at this site is almost identical to the first one, and the site is soon cleared. Cletus opens the gate and starts to do his site inspection. He believes now is the time to disturb his boss on Christmas morning and report the excitement. So, as usual, he calls the number, talks to Mary C.'s machine, and immediately erases the entire incident. It has nothing to do with him and the work he's scheduled and required to do.

The FBI and sheriff's teams quickly determine the contents of one of the two body bags. That first bag holds the body of L. D. Roseborough. He's been a known commodity in Williston for several years. He's known by dozens of people with interest in the workings of the oil fields. Although he hauled mostly equipment, dirt, and sand for BX&F, he also contracted with other Texas-based firms, like Bakken Oil Partners and Kendell & Figg, for overflow and emergency work.

The police know him because his name has appeared in their records rather frequently over the past years. He was an aggressive drinker who, several times after skirmishes in local drinking holes, required restraint, detention, or an escort home. He was also a known quantity in the Williston District Courthouse because he'd often been sued for not acting in the way some contract he'd signed seemed to imply that he should've acted. Several people told police they thought he was from Louisiana, but Louisiana's a big place. Since it's mostly shut down on Christmas, Sheriff

Faber isn't expecting an immediate response to his inquiries regarding L. D. Roseborough to come floating up quickly from Baton Rouge.

Although JD's body carries no keys, wallet, papers, watch, or phone, the police make a positive identification from personal experience with him. L. D.'s body does, however, present the searchers with one strange clue. Investigators find, stuck deep in his buttoned shirt pocket, a single unmarked business card for a reporter from an oil industry magazine, unknown to anyone in the office. The name on that business card is "Steffie Cobb," and that name is well known by the Sheriff Faber's office.

Although it is Christmas morning, Sheriff Faber calls the number on Steffie's card and asks her why this dead man might be carrying her obviously fake business card. That's when Faber learns that Steffie received the Christmas Eve call announcing that "L. D. Roseborough is dead."

The picture the police are painting of L. D. changes after they talk to several subcontractors who give the impression that L.D only fronted the business, despite his name on Roseborough Drilling's letterhead, his warehouse, his fleet of Peterbilts, and his many pieces of oil field equipment. Apparently, he worked for an LLC that supplied the firm's money and held its profits. The L. D. Roseborough these men knew was not the guy to make quick business decisions by himself—at least without a good deal of pain, anguish, and beer. Someone else must have been making the decisions while L. D. did little but drive his GMC pickup around and observe other guys working.

*   *   *

FBI Special Agent Brock and his crew have no such luck with the contents of the second body bag. Cletus hadn't paid much attention to it, but the medical examiner knows, even from several feet away, that this bag contains no body. When he unzips it, it is stuffed with straw. However, he does find, concealed inside, a piece of cardboard that he handed to Agent Brock.

A business card belonging to Hasani Indaak has been taped to that square.

Brock calls the number on Ms. Indaak's card and asks her why this dead man's effigy in western Dakota might be carrying her card. He learns about the call she received yesterday claiming Jusef Abi Sadi should also be considered dead.

Brock assumes, given this strange ritualistic double presentation, that the straw in the second bag is meant to represent the body of Hasani Indaak's mysterious and assumed dead man, perhaps known as Jusef Abi Sadi. However, unlike with L. D. Roseborough, Jusef Abi Sadi has no history with local police or the FBI.

Ms. Hasani explains that she has no idea how the name is spelled because she has only heard it pronounced by a frightened child, mumbling English words he may have hardly known, over a fairly scratchy phone line.

After Special Agent Brock interviews Ms. Cobb and Ms. Indaak about these bizarre circumstances, he is certain that the straw must represent the man whose name Hasani received last night. Each man was mentioned, each to a different reporter, as being dead, in phone calls received by the two reporters on Christmas Eve.

Everyone involved in this mess now realizes the truth these bodies present for them. The fake ISIS fighters found dead in the explosions announced the beginning of this drama, and this duo of body bag murders, most likely now indicate, and quite powerfully, that this drama has ended. Steffie, however, considers the puzzle as nothing close to ended.

These found body bags convince Agent Brock that, after today, he'll be uncovering no more evidence regarding this strange opera. He immediately accepts that he will not uncover any clue leading to suggest what, exactly, happened in the time between finding that first Somali body and this last straw-man non-body. And these bags suggest to Brock that some Lone Ranger has meted out justice here, delivered the body bags as confirmation of that meted out justice, and then probably rode out of Williston on a white horse. Brock sees, in his mind, the Lone Ranger pause to let Trigger prance on his hind feet. Brock sees this Lone Ranger galloping into the frozen, pristine, snow-covered hills west of Williston. "Hi, ho, Silver. Away!"

CHAPTER 65

GOVERNOR ROLFES OPENS HIS CHRISTMAS PHEASANT

THE CANDLES ARE LIT, THE wine is poured, and the side dishes are positioned in their predetermined locations.

Larry enters the dining room with the four-generation-old, hard maple cutting board—on which rests the pheasant. The only required thing not yet settled in its required place at table in Mrs. Rolfes's dining room is her son, Leon.

"Leon, put that phone down now. Time for Christmas pheasant." It's been a longstanding tradition in the Rolfes family to, if the good Lord so provides, serve the results of the fall hunting season for Christmas dinner. The pheasant in question was taken by Leon—his first in approximately a dozen years—from Larry's farm up near Rugby, on the very last day of the recent pheasant season.

"I'm sorry, Agent Brock. Mom says the turkey's ready. I'm needed at the table. She insists I've gotta hang up. Thanks for keeping me in the loop. Have a nice remainder of your Christmas. We'll talk this out tomorrow. Merry Christmas." Leon puts his phone on an end table and walks into the dining room.

"It's about time, Leon," says Margie. "That pheasant is calling to me something fierce."

"How's Steffie doin', Leon?" asks his mom. "She okay?"

"I was actually talking with Agent Brock. He's over at Steffie's place. It's a long, strange story that we all agreed not to even think about until tomorrow. Steffie has convinced Brock, who apparently is from Milwaukee and all alone out here on the prairie, to stay for Christmas dinner with them, but on the condition that no talk is allowed about FBI stuff till tomorrow." Leon points to his mom. "And that includes you."

"What's the FBI doing at Steffie's house on Christmas morning?"

"Margie! Didn't I just say we're not going to talk about that?"

"What?" says Larry. "Brock is over there? On Christmas?"

"No one talks FBI talk at this table," his mom says. "Or they forfeit their mincemeat pie. We must concentrate on the pheasant."

Leon picks up his wineglass. "Merry Christmas to everyone!"

"Merry Christmas," says Margie. "And thanks to Leon for shooting our bird—and to Mom for fixin' it up."

CHAPTER 66

HOW DOES A SOMALI SAY SNAKE?

MONDAY, DECEMBER 26, 2016

FIRST THING ON MONDAY MORNING, Steffie goes into the office and electrically plods through about five tons of records generated in last spring's investigation of the sex trafficking ring in Williston. She's hoping she can find mention of anyone named Jusef, or even Joe, linked to any aspect of that case. But when her search is complete, she's found nothing. She calls Hasani to commiserate. "I found nothing, Hasani. Not a single Joe or Joseph. However, I did find two references to unknown men. One of the girls interviewed called some guy 'the sick bastard.' And one witness made mention of a guy with a street name of 'the snake.' Do either of those words, when translated to Somali, sound like your dead guy, Abi Sadi?"

"No I don't think so. Although Jusef Abi Sadi could refer to an unknown or unnamed man, similar to 'John Doe' or 'Joe Blow' in English or a generic 'Joe' referring to a generalized man. It might be a tribal derogatory term, or maybe it's only gibberish. Later this morning, I'm gonna talk with a friend who is an expert on Somali tribal dialects. I'll let you know what I find out."

*   *   *

After talking with her friend for only a few minutes, Hasani believes she has her answer. She calls back to North Dakota with the news.

"I think I've got an answer for that strange name, Steffie. My expert says it's possible the words I heard the boy say, Abi Sadi, could be the pronunciation of the Somali word *abeesadii*." Hasani spells the word out for Steffie. "That word is not normally translated as 'snake.' However, it can be translated, as like an Old Testament-based word, referring to a sly or treacherous man, perhaps a 'serpent.' That definition might fit in, right?"

"That's great news, Hasani." Steffie lets her computer sift back through her notes. "Here, I got it. The guy called 'the snake' appeared during the FBI's questioning of the man who ran the brothel in that Williston motel. Apparently, this snake character was one of the missing links in the chain to supply Minnesota girls to the operator of the Williston brothel. His 'snake' name came up a couple times, but no one knew him, saw him, or even talked with him. The FBI arrested people on both the Williston and Minneapolis ends of the gang, but this connecting figure, this 'snake' guy, stayed someplace in the middle and slithered away."

"So, you suppose this dead Jusef Abi Sadi or maybe Abeesadii—this Joe, the snake guy with no body but a bundle of straw stuffed into a body bag—is actually the final nail in the coffin of last year's sex traffic case. Would that be the strangest thing ever?"

"And here's even a stranger thing, Hasani. We now have a dead Somali with a name but no body. And Leon told me that my friend, FBI Agent Brock, has a dead Somali with a body but no name in his freezer in Bismarck. I'd best give him a call and make his day."

CHAPTER 67

AFTER THE SUBSURFACE
MATERIALS OWNERSHIP ACT

TUESDAY, DECEMBER 27, 2016

I T IS 7:30 A.M. IN Bismarck, and the governor is convening a powwow
to analyze the myriad programs the state might undertake to react to
the almost certain, almost immediate, death of its oil economy. Larry
Oosterhaus and Russell Cordoba are at the table with Leon's secretary
of energy, Wilson Dikta, Bernie Ramble, the state development director,
Susan Detloff, a professor of oil economics at NDSU, Charlie Neubauer
from Agribus, Steffie Cobb, Carl Two Deer, and a few others.

This meeting is being held in perhaps the most spectacular conference
venue in all of North Dakota—the Mandan Room—which occupies the
top floor of the fifteen-story statehouse. The huge circular conference
table is surrounded by twenty-five floor-to-ceiling windows that give each
conferee a different long-range view of the snowy North Dakota landscape.
The scenery is most striking at sunset or sunrise when the long view west
is remarkably different from the long view east. On this morning, the
view is not at all striking because it is, at this particular time, nonexistent.
The heavy drapery is still in place, preventing any view of any potential
striking sunrise, which may, or may not, be happening to the exterior of
that drapery.

"Welcome to you all," says Leon. "Thank you for coming over here to
talk about our energy future. I intend for this to be an extremely serious

discussion. It is the first necessary act that we, as a state, must undertake to fully understand how to effectively use our state's new authority and responsibilities as established by the recently approved Subsurface Materials Ownership Act. My first act here is to open the curtain to the future of our state, which opening then requires you to open your eyes, and minds, and tell me what you see out there."

"You're pushing this theater stuff a bit too heavily, Leon," Larry Oosterhaus says. "Don't you think?"

"It's only begun, Larry. Watch this." Leon pushes a button on a remote control, and the lights dim to almost complete darkness. Leon pushes another button, and the drapery slowly reveals the predawn glow exploding on the eastern horizon. Everyone in the room is mesmerized by the beauty of color and of life gradually exploding outside the windows.

After a minute or so of letting the visual pyrotechnics blast them, Leon says, "You are watching the dawning of a new day. More than that, it's the dawning of a new era in the history of the great state of North Dakota. Pretend with me for a minute that we can suspend this grand illumination and stop the action of the cosmos for a few seconds. Please bear with me. Close your eyes. Okay! Now, in your personal darkness, you each have the freedom to simply rearrange a few things, just a few, perhaps only one thing for each of you—based on your education and life experience—that you think is not perfect and would like to change. Keep your eyes closed, please, for just a short while longer.

"All right, thank you. Open your eyes and look through those windows again. You tell me. Is the view of the future of the state of North Dakota brighter now than when you closed your eyes? And if the answer is yes—and of course the answer must be yes because of the physics of the thing—then can you somehow believe that the interest, dedication, creativity, and hard work of the people in this room—as representatives of the population of this state—is, or certainly could be, responsible for that difference?"

Larry Oosterhaus—Leon's friend, teammate, and sandbox playmate—says, "Good grief, Leon. What the hell did your mom slip into your cereal this morning?"

"It is my duty to get your attention—and generate a mood of creative fervor. You folks have probably been seated around similar tables, talking about similar things before, but this is the most serious project you have ever been associated with. Such a serious subject must only be discussed without the burden of that seriousness weighing down on you. We all must remain lofty and agile and keep our heads in the clouds in order to do our best creative work.

"And I've got one more surprise, designed to shake up your thinking regimens and thought processes. You all know each other to some degree. But, except for Larry, I don't think any of you has met this woman seated here next to me—even though she knows more about the role oil will play in the future of North Dakota than any other person at this table, or this state or perhaps in the entire country. I asked her to be here because the things she knows are things you do not now know, but that you must know in order to make decisions for our state. I would like to introduce Kathleen Carter. She is, among other things, my goddaughter, the daughter of my best friend, Nathan Goodbrother, who you all certainly did know. Kathleen is, most importantly, the owner, in one way or another, of half of the businesses doing things with oil in the Bakken. It is necessary that you understand what she is offering to us. Respect what she says because she is the voice of the real world of Big Oil. She has promised me, her own godfather, that she will be brutally candid with you this morning."

Margie enters the room with a fistful of papers and distributes them.

Leon says, "I'm gonna have Kathleen read you this outline. I feel a turning point must be anchored around here somewhere, and before we reach that point, we'll have to know exactly what's happening with respect to the oil industry in our state, how we must react to its potential collapse, and how we can tweak the levers we have control over it to protect our state from total economic destruction. Kathleen's outline is meant to get your juices flowing. Also, everybody speak up clearly. I'm recording this meeting, and I don't miss any pithy comments or nifty dialogue floating around the room. Okay, Kathleen, go to it."

"Thank you, Uncle Leon." She starts in all business. She eschews social niceties, no cute little story, no listing of her various degrees or criminal entanglements. Leon noticed she's got her severe Harvard Business School professor outfit on today, and she's not wearing the sidearm, either real or metaphoric, she normally straps to her hip.

"To start us off, I am going to make a set of statements about both probable and outrageous events we might run across on our road to North

Dakota's future, and your job here is to analyze the information in your skulls and react to these statements. You each will have a different view, and my hope is my uncle can use those comments to provide the state with a pathway to Valhalla where we all end up rich and happy in the magic year of 2057. I certainly intend to be one of those rich and happy people.

"First is global climate change. We must today, immediately, choose between two evils. Either GCC's the greatest single destabilizing issue the world has faced since that great meteor slammed into the planet several billion years ago, or GCC's a giant bunch of fluff being strewn about by unknown flaky forces for some unknown diabolic reason. In forty years—the Paris Accords sets the target date as 2057—we'll know which answer is true. By then, Houston's streets will either remind folks of Venice, or they won't. So, do we start now to ween ourselves off carbon so Houston's streets stay above water, or do we start pouring concrete every few years to raise Houston's streets—and everything else now that we're thinking about it—so in forty years, the city will still be above water—or do we do nothing, take our chances, and buy stock futures for both golf cart and kayak firms.

Second, if you are an old oil guy, over fifty-five, your surest path to billionaire status is to assume GCC is a hoax. You go all-out pumping oil and trying to make the most money you can in the few years left before the spigot's turned off. If you're younger than fifty, which I am, my surest path is to invest in alternative fuels. Then, in 2057, when the world outlaws oil, I'll make my fortune with the next greatest energy-producing moneymaker.

Third, assume, in forty years, oil is outlawed. The Saudis have two advantages over everyone else. They have a 120-year supply they can harvest at a few dollars a barrel. Why wouldn't they sell all their oil before the deadline? They'll pump for forty years at prices that bankrupt the rest of the world. Do Texas and Dakota go broke trying to sell their seventy-dollar oil for twenty dollars and forty years of losses? I don't think so either.

"Fourth, Texas also has more oil than they can possibly sell in a hundred years, but they must sell it for around seventy dollars to make a profit. How much money you think they make selling seventy-dollar dollar oil at twenty dollars just to keep the Saudis honest? They'll bankrupt Houston in ten years.

"Fifth, after the recent Texas discoveries, can you think of any reason, except for generating hedge losses, any oil guy should still be excavating oil in Dakota or Alberta? Uncle Leon could make more money by turning the whole region into a historical theme park.

"Sixth, given the above to chew on, you folks have got to find North Dakota's path to peace and prosperity. You must know exactly what will be happening when you see that same beautiful, powerful sun," she shields her eyes with one hand and points out the window with the other, directly at that fireball, now fully risen and dancing gaily along the horizon, "rises on January 1, 2057, will we be better off on our dogsleds than our Houston friends in their gondolas?"

Leon rises. "Thank you, Kathleen. And now for the fun. Russell, you've spent many years in Silicon Valley where they pray to the future and curse the past. How about you jump in first? What does North Dakota's future look like to you?"

CHAPTER 68

FINALLY GARY'S INSURANCE—
OR SOMETHING—KICKS IN

WEDNESDAY, DECEMBER 28, 2016

THE TEMPERATURE'S STUCK ON NINETY, and the sky's so blue it hurts. The water is crystal green, and the beach is, for some reason, almost devoid of sunbathers. Gary Gralapp's body is casually plopped into his beach chair, which is casually plopped into the sand a few feet from the gently lapping Atlantic. He allows several schizoid beach birds to entertain him, chasing their shadows or their lunches around his chair. Gralapp's mind, however, is located nowhere near this beach. At one moment, it's wondering about fire insurance on his now-vacant house overlooking the Missouri in North Dakota, and in the next moment, he's thinking about today being the first day of the New Year. He's thinking New Year's Day is a good time to start a new life, maybe across the water to where his eyes are focused, at the horizon line of the Atlantic. He pictures that Rand McNally in his head. "Hmmm?" He points toward the horizon and addresses a comment to the sandpiper, pecking at bugs a few feet in front of him. "What ya think, bird? Out there, over that horizon? Ya think that's Morocco out there? Or maybe Portugal?"

"I believe it's Portugal, Gary."

Gary's absolutely startled to hear that almost familiar, deep American voice speaking his own name, and with some almost military authority. His body spasms. He splashes his piña colada over his newly dried swimsuit. He jerks around to see who's invaded his paradise.

He doesn't recognize the speaker. Hell, he can hardly even see him. What does capture his attention is his North Dakota partner, Paul Burtress. He's standing, pale as a sheet, needing help to keep from keeling over. He's being kept upright by this NFL linebacker guy, the one with the smart mouth. Gary throws the almost empty piña colada glass into the sand, jumps up, and embraces Paul like his friend's just been released from Guantanamo.

"My God, Gary," says Paul. "Man, is it good to see you."

Paul, however, doesn't look like he's good to see him, or really anyone. Paul looks white as a sheet and scared as shit. Eventually, Paul relaxes a bit, takes a step back, puts his hands to his face, and begins to cry.

Gary hasn't the foggiest idea what's happening. "What the hell you doin' down here?" He glances to the muscular bodyguard supporting Paul. "And … and who … who the hell are you?"

Paul takes a step aside and wiggles out of the guard's grasp. "Der Ord is dead, Gary. Damn, I'm sorry I have to tell you that. Did it with his Colt .45. I'm sorry, Gary. They found him in his Jeep in his garage on the day after Christmas. I've been having nightmares ever since. Been trying to get ahold of ya. You're not answering your phone, Gary. Why you doing that?"

"Gary," the bodyguard says, "I think it's best Paul stay with you for a while. He's a complete wreak. His nerves are smashed. You both need time to heal."

None of this makes sense to Gary. He tries the question again. "And who the hell are you?"

"What's the matter, Gary?" says a voice from the opposite end of the scale—and from somewhere behind him. "You don't remember us? We're your insurance company!"

Gary spins. He sees this goddess a flowery bikini with long black hair wet-plastered to her head. She is deeply tanned like a native down here would be. She emerges from the surf like she is in a James Bond movie, water dripping and sunlight glistening.

Gary crumbles to his knees, and his vision clouds. He can't remember yesterday! Hell, not even this morning. "I can't remember—"

"Sure you do, Gary. Remember, we talked in your office? We're here to help. To save you."

"Help? Save me?"

"We're going to keep you two bags of jelly alive. We're gonna find you clean, bullet-free air to breathe."

"Who … who are you people?"

"I'm Trevor," the muscle guy says. "It's a common name down here. I'm a common man."

"Excuse me if I say I don't believe you're a common man. Just looking at you gives me goddamn goose bumps."

"You need to know nothing other than I'm your Insurance Goddess, and this is Trevor. And you gentlemen are, strangely enough, our insurance policy—and that means we must keep you alive. And we intend to do that."

"Everything will work out okay," says Trevor. "I think first I'll get you some fresh piña coladas."

"And, Gary," the bikini goddess says, "while Trevor's gone, I'll tell you what's happened in the real world since you left it for this beach."

Trevor spins around and heads toward the wooden shack that serves as the beach's drink dispenser.

Gary climbs halfway back onto the reality raft. "I can't believe der Ord's dead? Suicide?"

"It absolutely blew me away, Gary. He kept playing with that stupid gun. Playing at being a macho man. I never in a million years thought he'd actually do it."

"What are you doin' here?"

"I was all alone, man. Hank died. You vanished! Hell, I thought you were dead too, snuffed out by some guy higher up the food chain. That's when Trevor shows up and tells me my insurance is kickin' in?"

"I was frightened stiff," Gary says. "That's certainly true. Things were blowin' up, things were collapsing all around, and Jenny left. The walls kept closin' in. I couldn't frickin' breathe. I panicked. I'm sorry."

"We're all sorry, Gary. The whole sorry world's sorry. The question is, what the hell we gonna do now?"

"What you are going to do, gentlemen," the linebacker says as he returns, "is take these piña coladas, and then we'll have a reasonable discussion about your future."

"A reasonable discussion?" Gary yells. "A reasonable discussion?"

"You either take these drinks now—or I'll dump them over your head, Gary. Let's all take a deep breath, a gulp or two, and then we'll talk like rational folks. That's the plan."

Though Kathleen and Trevor understand the rational aspects of the plan they've put together to save these two, neither Gary nor Paul seem to be located in the correct universe to appreciate the plan's logic.

Kathleen says, "Your problem, Gary, is that if I can trace you down here, then others can trace you down to here, and that means your life's not worth diddly-squat. You two must disappear. That means permanently relocate, and do it quickly."

Trevor takes two envelopes from the case slung over his shoulder and hands them to Kathleen. She looks at them and gives one to Gary and the other to Paul. "In your packets are everything you'll need to live a safe life. Gary, you're going to deed your property here in Nevis to a shell firm neither of you is aware of. Then, for a few days, you'll stay in your house here, which I will rent from that shell company for you. The lease is in the envelope. Also in your packet is everything you two will need to transfer your banked assets to me, and then I, in turn, will put the money into the accounts referenced in the envelope. There are airline tickets in the packet to access your new life. The tickets are for Thursday, January 6. That gives you guys five days to access reality. You then take the ferry over to Saint Kitts and then a taxi to the airport. Then you fly away." She dances around flapping her arms, pretending to be a jet airliner or, perhaps, a Canada goose.

"What the hell is this?" says Gary. "What the hell is this?"

"Just think of it as your insurance policy." Kathleen puts out an arm and helps Gary to his feet. "Your insurance coverage just kicked in."

Gary looks bewildered. "Jeez. I'd completely forgotten about insurance. Never in a million years did I expect insurance!"

"So, guys, have a nice rest of your lives."

"What about Williston? My folks? Jenny? My new house on the Missouri?"

"Those things are past tense, Gary," Kathleen says. "At least till

Basehardt dies and my need for insurance vanishes. And if that happens, we'll let you know."

Trevor and Kathleen turn their backs and walk down the beach south, right into the sun.

Gary will recollect later that they both seemed to pop into the air, sink into the sand, or be swallowed by the water. At any rate, they vanish somewhere before the sand ends and the real world begins. It's how he might imagine any meaningful insurance goddess would be expected to vanish.

Gary and Paul stand rigid in the sand. Their minds, however, are already drifting out over the water—maybe to Portugal or Morocco. They stumble about aimlessly, unsure if they still have legs. Neither can yet build up enough courage to look at the boarding pass to see where they'll be flying to. The only thing they do have is "the next five days" and the realization that they're gonna need every last second of those five days to learn how to walk again.

CHAPTER 69

WILL BASEHARDT'S INSURANCE—OR SOMETHING—KICKS HIM

ONCE AGAIN, WILL BASEHARDT MUST walk all the way across the legislators' parking lot to the visitors' lot. He must park his Lexus sedan way out on the far side of the government center complex. He does this under protest, but his protest does not seem to carry much weight around here. The Capitol Police won't let him park in the legislators' parking lot even though it's almost empty since it's not in session. He's argued with them and given them the story about being the duly elected state senator from Williston. They've towed his car twice, though they did treat him fairly well and moved it, not into the normal impound lot, but into the visitors' parking area across the street. Even so, Basehardt does not think he's being handled fairly. He's the most powerful new member of the legislature. He'd made quite a stink about it. Since it generated much less drama to park where they told him to park, he's been doing that without much incident for the past couple months.

He can't wait. In a few more weeks, when the magic day arrives, and he's a member of that state senate, he'll be assigned a space in the legislators' lot. It'll be a much shorter walk. Damn, it's cold. He's already started the engine remotely, so his Lexus will be warm when he gets there. He approaches the car and can tell the engine's running because he sees steam puffs easing from the dual exhausts. The cabin will be warm, thank the Lord. There are times he thinks he should've stayed in Houston. He clicks the device to unlock the door, slips inside, and slams the door shut. A couple inches of fluffy snow cover the car, and he activates the wipers. He's surprised to find a white envelope fixed under the driver's side wiper. It is stuck to the window and doesn't move back and forth with the blade.

This is a bit strange, but perhaps it's the papers for the move to the legislators' lot. He exits the car, reaches over, and notes the envelope is taped to the glass. He grabs the edge and pulls it off. He gets back in his car, opens the envelope, and pulls out the single sheet of white paper.

Dear partner:

On the reverse side of this paper, you will find a photocopy of one page of Gary Gralapp's notebook on which, as you can see, he notes L. D. Roseborough purchased three items from a certain entity named "Joe the Snake" for certain illegal purposes. Please notice the date of the purchase: October 4 of this year. You must consider this notebook to be my insurance policy. Be aware: the remaining pages of this notebook are also in my possession, as well as several incriminating photographs and videos of both you and Mr. Roseborough involved in criminal acts. I have two live witnesses with firsthand knowledge of your connection to the so-called ISIS terrorists who were found dead in Williston.

I am afraid Mr. Roseborough's purchase for you will turn out to be quite expensive for you—perhaps as expensive as it was for him. I am giving you another exit strategy. I have established an endowment that will be wholly funded by you, and the purpose of which is to repair some of the damage you have caused to the people of North Dakota and to compensate the families of the men whose lives you've stolen. You must make the first installment funding that endowment by 12:00 noon on January 12, 2017, in the amount of $100,000,000. The administrator of this endowment is Dr. Elaine Provosa, of Council to Olson, Ingraham, Larpenter, EMP, in Houston, and she will be in touch with you soon to set up the necessary fund transfer documents. Your participation with this endowment is not negotiable. Your cooperation is absolutely required. Please understand that the remainder of your life starts at this moment, and it continues only as long as you honor this commitment to alleviate the damage you have caused.

I anticipate your cooperation. Happy New Year, partner.

Dr. Elaine Provosa

Will Basehardt checks his dashboard clock. It's 3:47. He stares straight out the windshield of his Lexus. The snowing has stopped. He sees several hundred naked American elm trees in the foreground, and beyond, the wide white expanse of the Grand Mall of North Dakota. And there's a white sky. A single white car moves right to left across the landscape several hundred feet away. He should check in with his Washington friend Brian Bass and find out how that assistant secretary for energy thing is going. If that job comes through, then that hundred million dollars will be just piddle change and no big deal. Better yet, if he structures this correctly, he may be able to claim that payment as a charitable deduction—or maybe a work of God for the insurance rebate. That makes him feel better. He'll talk with his money guys. They'll figure it all out. It's only a hundred million.

He puts the car in gear, carefully guides it through the two inches of new snow in the lot, exits onto the driveway, and halts at the stop sign at the exit from the capitol grounds. "It's only a hundred million!" he shouts. The sound reverberates around the car. Chump change for a partner.

His phone buzzes with an incoming text. The timing seems odd. He looks at the message displayed on his dashboard monitor: "Eleven minutes and thirty-five seconds from the time you open the door until your wheels turned. Is that time enough to consider the import of my message?"

Will looks around frantically, thinking he's gonna see some guy with a stopwatch and a machine gun. He sees no moving thing—not even a slight wind. Absolutely nothing! He doesn't remember time passing. He blinks once, twice, and then realizes nothing he sees out there is white anymore. The sky, the snow—it's all turned gray. And it is going to black quickly. This could be a dream. He slaps the side of his face.

The phone buzzes again, and another message appears: "Do you understand your soft life is over? You are now a reconstituted man, or maybe only a half-man, perhaps a slave. You will spend the rest of your life working for me to better the lives of the good people of North Dakota."

It is getting darker—much too rapidly. A sensor somewhere in his Lexus reacts to the darkening and automatically ignites his headlamps. *This is not normal.* He slaps his face again, hard. *Did I fall asleep? Maybe it's a dream.* He then flicks his headlights to high beam. Some of his dark dream jumps back to glittering white again. *Yeah! That's it. It's probably a dream.* His phone beeps again, and a new message jumps onto the screen on the dashboard:

Memo from the Office of Dr. Elaine Provosa:

Please note: An appointment has been set up for 11:00 a.m. this Thursday, January 13, 2017, with Dr. Provosa, at her office in Houston. Attendance is mandatory. Please be prompt. Directions and required items will be sent to you later via email.

CHAPTER 70

OLSON, INGRAHAM, LARPENTER, EMP V. WILL BASEHARDT

WILL BASEHARDT FINDS THE STAINLESS steel door. He notices the letters O.I.L.-EMP etched at his eye level and the numbers one through nine etched in little squares below. He punches in the code he'd been texted—1-8-3-6—and steps back, unsure of what pyrotechnics are going to accost him.

The stainless steel door opens inward quite deliberately and slowly, and Will, costumed like a Texas oil partner in his dark blue suit, red tie, Stetson, and hand-tooled boots, assertively strides into the room. Pneumatics hiss softly as the door closes behind him. Except for him, the room is empty. There are no doors or windows, and stainless steel panels cover all four walls. They are the same exact size as the doorway. It's like he's stepped into a science experiment. He scans the room, and each of the four walls has ten of the three-foot by nine-foot stainless panels. The room is lit somehow, but Basehardt sees no light fixtures. A slight hissing sound comes and then fades away. *Perhaps that's the air-conditioning—or the poison gas.* The floor is grass, or a grasslike product, like the field at the Houston Oilers stadium.

"Good afternoon, Mr. Basehardt." A voice speaks while swirling, disembodied, around the room.

Will jerks his head around, looking for the sound's source, and he sees a gray face projected onto one of the panels. The face says, "Welcome to the offices of O.I.L. EMP. I am Dr. Provosa."

A square of grass tilts itself up, and a small square stool and table rise from the floor as the grassy area flops back down. "Please, make yourself uncomfortable. I assume you've brought the requested items with you. Please place them on the table and then sit on the stool."

Printed in the United States
by Baker & Taylor Publisher Services